TEASE AND DARE
ANGIE & ELLA'S SUMMER OF DELIRIUM

Also by Robert Scott Leyse

Novels

Attraction and Repulsion
Self-Murder

Collections

Adoration and Affliction: Novellas and Short Stories
Playgrounds and Battlegrounds: Four Novellas

Novellas from the above collections are
available separately as eBooks:

Penelope Prim
The Urban Primeval
Excitation and Oblivion, or Kaleidoscopic San Juan
Playgrounds and Battlegrounds
Idleness and Unrest
Nighttime Euphoria and the Field of Reeds,
or One Can Get Away with What One Dares

TEASE AND DARE
ANGIE & ELLA'S SUMMER OF DELIRIUM

Robert Scott Leyse

The second edition of *Liaisons for Laughs:*
Angie & Ella's Summer of Delirium

ShatterColors Press
New York, New York

Cover illustration: Mark Edward Leyse
Book design and layout: Robert Scott Leyse

The first edition of this book was published under the title *Liaisons for Laughs: Angie & Ella's Summer of Delirium*

Paperback ISBN 979-8-9985093-1-5
eBook ISBN 978-0-9821710-9-7

Library of Congress Control Number: 2025909346

Testimonials

"Fun, steamy, and intelligent."—*LA Weekly*

"Licentious. Salacious. Those rich, naughty, mannered words from another era are given a cunning and contemporary twist in Leyse's reinvigoration of a classic literary form—the epistolary. At a time when so many 'real life' intimacies are overlooked because we're too tired to be seduced or to instigate some imaginative new direction in our mortgage anxious relationships, it's refreshing to be reminded of the pleasures, prurient and also just plain human and often very funny, of overhearing other people's intimacies. Fun and eroticism don't go together nearly often enough. They do in Leyse tit for tat. This is clever, humane, word-sensual writing."—Kris Saknussemm, author of *Zanesville* and *Private Midnight*

"Some friendships are bonds that can't be broken. *Tease and Dare: Angie & Ella's Summer of Delirium* tells the story of two best friends in a frank and entertaining method. A hilarious and endlessly entertaining collection of stories about the little things of life, *Tease and Dare* never stops its assault on the funny bone. A fine and entertaining novel, *Tease and Dare* is a choice pick for fiction readers."—*Midwest Book Review*

"You can feel the humidity in your own backyard as Angie and Ella soak up the summer in New York with various paramours with their super sexy, sex-positive attitudes. This is one of those books that, finally, puts sluts in their rightful places. They aren't shameful or shamed. They're proud of it, and having the time of their lives, and the reader will, too."—Susan DiPlacido, author of *24/7* and *House Money*

"Re-enlivens a venerable literary tradition, the epistolary novel, but now in an arousingly contemporary form. The erotic e-mails of these two libidinous heroines recount their escapades with wicked charm and droll humor. Their tales memorialize the lusty landscape of the New York corporate world, and the bratty sophistication of their narrative voices makes their sensual adventures all the more appealing. Angie and Ella are trollops for our time, and Robert Scott Leyse is a Trollope for our time."—William T. Hathaway, author of A *World of Hurt* and *Summer Snow*

*For all the bright beautiful BratCats
in this world. Were it not for you,
Angie & Ella would never have been born.*

Contents

Author's Note

When *Liaisons for Laughs: Angie & Ella's Summer of Delirium* was published in 2009, the title *Tease and Dare* was being held in reserve for another book. Shortly after publication of *Liaisons for Laughs* I realized *Tease and Dare* better suited Angie & Ella's adventures, and so never published *Liaisons for Laughs* as an eBook, intending to change the title at some point and publish in all formats. A full time job intruded and free time was devoted to traveling, learning to surf, falling in love with Puerto Rico. Compensating for the first five-days-a-week job in my life was highly enjoyable, in a twisted sort of way—confinement inspires rebellion—unauthorized recreation on company time builds morale and intensifies joy.

As I'm finally free of employment responsibilities, Angie & Ella have been retitled, revised, rereleased. Revisions primarily consist of tightening the narrative/accelerating events. Word count has been reduced.

Eternal gratitude to the playful BratCats who inspired Angie & Ella.

Our Heroines

Angie and Ella are Ivy League law school graduates employed as second year associates in the corporate department of a prestigious midtown Manhattan law firm. They are fast friends and fond of reliving their escapades, as well as concocting new ones, via email. Angie is 5' 7" and has wavy chestnut hair. Her brown eyes easily flare with emotion, and she has a reputation for being excitable. Ella is 5' 5" and has raven black hair. Her blue eyes readily flood with silver light, and she has a reputation for being adventurous. Both, on account of their comeliness of visage and shapeliness of figure and playfulness of disposition, routinely attract lingering glances—inspire desire.

I. Summer's Delirium

I.1
Ella to Angie
Saturday, June 21, 2003 (First Day of Summer) 9:47 AM

Hey there, Snoozikins! Time to shake the slumber from your bones—summer's arrived. Not that we haven't already tasted summer sensations aplenty, it's just that it hasn't officially happened in summer and, as you know, I'm a stickler (slightly superstitious) concerning dates. The first day of summer might only be a date on the calendar, but for yours truly... OK, accuse me of being in thrall to delusion—insist I'm enslaved to an imagination-fabrication—but I'm convinced it's necessary for us to play in the park today if our summer-to-be's to be chock full of the sort of escapades that keep our complexions fresh. So indulge me, Dearest: flog your lethargic carcass to life.

What a bust the first day of spring (seemingly thousands of years ago) was: 'twas still frigid, not a flower or bud in sight. We celebrated, sure (thereby—ha ha!—ensuring ourselves of a memorable spring), but were draped in furs, shivering. At the time it didn't seem like winter would end anytime soon. So, considering the first day of spring's unseasonable chill, today's the day for us to finally celebrate sprouting-of-leaves-and-blossoms time, giddy unity with lush new growth. It couldn't be more perfect: the first day of summer's unfolding on a sunny Saturday.

In honor of our summer-inauguration frolic-to-be (Because you *will* shake yourself awake, or I'll come do it myself!), I'm putting on a pinafore I've been reserving for the occasion. "What? Have you kissed your fashion sense bye-bye, become a fuddy-duddy frump?" you'll doubtless cry in amazement. Sure, a pinafore's essentially an apron, something I wouldn't be caught dead in (So domestic, reeking of puttering about indoors.), but my pinafore's of the finest pink silk, with a hem of scarlet ruffles. I'll wear lacy black half-cups and a G-string underneath, nothing else. And it's sleeveless, meaning the boys will have views of my half-cupped breasts from the sides. When I sit on the lawn, knees raised to chin, I'll allow the scarlet hem to slide halfway down my thighs, come maddeningly near to fully revealing the goodies concealed. There'll be exhibitionist games galore, oodles of hungry man glances feeling me up and making me wet. The pink silk absolutely glimmers, catches and reflects the light something fierce. Pinafore? Ha! It better resembles a skimpy nightie, and I'll be brighter than a neon sign. Nor to forget the parasol: white as the driven snow, with scarlet edges and white fluff balls dangling on curly pink ribbons from its ribs. Pinafore and parasol in a pink, scarlet, and white color scheme: I feel the hint of prissiness serves to heighten the sex impact. I fully plan on upstaging the other cuties, outdoing them in flipping the boy's heads about, via an apron and umbrella—being the vampishest tramp.

So cast aside your grogginess and get girly for me in that backless white polka-dotted aquamarine number you scored at Saks last week, then hightail it over so's we can celebrate on this made-to-order day.

Your,

SummerElectricElla

PS: Or wear anything else that screams: flirty frolicsome floozy! I've flung down the gauntlet with my pinafore and parasol: you've got to keep pace, be an eye-snatching pussycat I'll be proud to prance with.

1.2
Angie to Ella
Saturday, June 21, 2003 10:49 AM

What the hell, wench? You call on my secret cell (Only you and my parents have the number.) as if it's an emergency (Because, allow me to refresh your memory: that phone's for emergencies only!), chide me for being in bed? You phone like a reproachful mommy when I have a very good reason for still being in bed, as in that Stevie and I were up late wiping the kitchen floor spic and span with my twitchy behind?

Stevie's fascinated by my kitchen floor. Says he likes the way the tiles blaze bright white in the overhead light; says he likes the way my ivory skin seems to lose itself in, unite with, the luminescence; says: "What a fine figure of an alabaster girl floating like a butterfly in swirling light!"; says the blinding light symbolizes purity and he'll purify me. Also says a naughty trollop like me needs to be kneaded against the tiles whilst he's plowing me, lest I forget the path to Paradise is strewn with thorns. Sometimes reads from Genesis, where it states (I'm looking it up.): "And the Lord God said unto the woman, What is this that thou hast done? And the woman said, The serpent beguiled me, and I did eat."—at which point he solemnly declares: "Woman, thou shalt be disciplined for effecting the fall from Paradise with thine wicked inclinations! This unpadded floor shalt remind thou of thy shamefully weak-willed acquiescence to temptation! Penance is required of thou, and penance thou shalt serve!" Well, thanks be to Stevie's Sunday school teachers, without whom he might lack the education needed to add titillating religious atonement dimensions to funtime with tramps like us.

Stevie didn't depart until sunup—yours truly was on the kitchen floor getting fulfillingly sore for at least two hours, plus participated in plenty of other divertissements, as pleasing as they were plunderish. And you have the nerve to phone me on my secret emergency line and: cry wolf! Wishing to romp in the park does *not* qualify as an emergency.

Ella, to hell with your first day of summer ritualistic rubbish! It's a sunny Saturday like many another—always divine, but hardly worthy of "flogging my carcass" awake and hopping to and dressing lickety-split like a soldier in boot camp prepping for a drill. So, if you'll excuse me, I'm going to languorously twist myself back into SnoozyLand under fluffy comforters. Yup, the AC's on high and I'm going to revisit dreaming below mounds of down! I'm going to live in my blankets *all* day and, thank you very much, do not wish to be pestered again!

Your,

SnoozyFloozy

1.3
Ella to Angie
Saturday, June 21, 2003 11:21 AM

Angie, I'm baffled—stunned—by your refusal to galvanize yourself alive! Since when do you balk at springing to action the second frolic's proposed? Since when do you allow a night's recreation to get the better of you, whine that it's tuckered you out, as if you're some wheezing half dead thing who doesn't take care of herself?—as if you aren't in the prime of girlhood, bursting with health, fit and feisty as a tomcat primed to send a rival packing? Since when do you embrace sloth?

Maybe I ought to cast about for a new girlfriend. Maybe I'm depending on you to fly to my side to assist me in scratching crazy itches, feeling disgracefully neglected. Maybe I'll find a girl who doesn't turn pusillanimous when I need her to be strong, and thrives on the fact I need lots of lustful attention. Hell! You're so far gone into prissiness you probably wouldn't care if I found someone else. Maybe you're so far from being the girl I thought you were you'd breathe a sigh of relief.

Living in your bed? What kind of pathetic sticking-of-your-head-in-the-sand avoidance of life is that? Who lives in bed other than an invalid? It beggars belief, Angie! Under your blankets when the sun's beating at your windows, calling, "Come outside and play!"? What sort of girl avoids a beautiful day? Are you a wilted flower on the sidewalk, waiting to be swept into the gutter and washed down the drain?

Angie, either flog your sluggish carcass out of bed and join me in doing honor to summer's first day or I'm coming over to flog you myself!

Your,
ShamefullyNeglectedNubile

1.4
Angie to Ella
Saturday, June 21, 2003 12:27 PM

Guess what summertime strumpet? Your call prodded me alive as much as you could wish—I was jus' prankin' wi' cha, you gullible goose of a goofy girl! My emergency's line's 100% open to you for anything whatsoever at all times, and frolic's a most scrumptious cause.

A night of sex thrills, far from flooring me, primes me for more action: the more this nubile gets, the more she needs. First day of summer? Count on sentimental calendar-watcher you to be aware of such things. Charming, but I don't need an excuse for funtime in the park.

I'd surely wilt without Central Park's reassuring presence—I'm constantly aware of its blood-quickening emanations throughout the upper east and west sides, swirling about me as I stroll the streets, seeping under the door and through the windows of my apartment, whispering of pleasure and abandon. Central Park's a force of nature beckoning with lush lawns, colorful gardens, mini forests and plashing streams; it's the booming croak of bullfrogs at dawn, soaring songs of cicadas during daylight, fireflies flickering at dusk—scent of wildflowers and freshwater shorelines; it's Cleopatra's Needle and Belvedere Castle and Cedar Hill and the Mall's breeze-rustled elms; it's The Lake mirroring golden sunsets, children yelling for joy at Alice in Wonderland playground, a red-tailed hawk devouring a pigeon on the Great Lawn; it's the hidden nooks of rock outcroppings, streambeds, shrub-smothered hills; it's a stare straight up into a cloudless sky as seagulls and swallows wheel on invisible rivers of wind; it's serenity and balance and freedom, an irresistible urge to become uncontrollable with my urges. Central Park's a delirium-inducing aphrodisiac.

Oh, yeah! I hopped to when you phoned, Honey, like a conscript caught goofing off by her DI! Instantly dolled myself up real trollopsome in a snug-as-a-glove white one-piece with a hemline that flirts with the lower boundaries of my cheeky-cheeks, and naturally with black lace brassiere and panties underneath—not too different than going out in underwear, considering the semi-transparency of the dress. My footsies are snug in purple pumps—my hair's ponytailed with a candy-cane ribbon sluttishly dangling down my back—my head's topped with a purple floppy-brimmed hat with white feathers sprouting every which where. My parasol's pink and purple: I chose the shoes, hat, and ribbon to match it.

So there, arrogant gauntlet-flinging Ella, I do believe I'll be stylishly floozy enough, a hussy you can proudly prance with. Which begs the question: will you be enough of an eye-magnet to be worthy of me? I need to see your pinafore getup before I'll believe it's not utterly silly. Like, really? An apron? But go ahead and slip into your pinky pinafore, risk me laughing myself dizzy. At any rate, I's a comin' ovah NOW!

Your,

PrimedForPrancingPrincess

I.5
Ella to Angie
Sunday, June 22, 2003 2:04 PM

Salutations, Summer Playmate!

Where to begin? How do yesterday justice? Only thing's to plunge in:

When we entered the park at 84th I was so itching to do summer's first day proud I was as good as drunk. The sun was shimmering on the slanted glass of the Met's Egyptian wing—dizzy silver undulating light. So reeling, deliciously topsy-turvy, with excess energy was I the lawn and trees were swaying, dancing—flooding my field of vision with emerald mist. It was as if I was floating over the grass instead of walking—as if a breeze was bouncing me along.

The Egyptian wing's ivy smothered wall, right of the gleaming windows, beckoned—I don't even recall strolling to it, might as well have been wafted there on the scents and colors and energy in the air. 'Twas out-of-my-skin delight when we were pressing our backs into the ivy, gazing skywards up the wall of writhing green. Breeze-fluttered ivy tickled my legs and arms and neck and cheeks, enfolded me; I was seemingly falling into the wall, drowning in foliage; the leaves' tickles meshed with the beat of my blood as my sight swam in the sky's vastness, blurred. For how long were we lulled from consciousness of being puny humans cut off from nature by civilization? Ha! 'Twas merely the onset of our wrapped-in-Mommy-Nature's-arms day.

Angie, the finickiest girl ever born would be tickled-pink-proud to be parading side by side with you—off the charts svelte in your white silk flimsy ineffectively veiling lacy-racy black lingerie. Twirling our parasols in unison, dipping and rising them, as breeze tousled our hair and hemlines—I was too entranced to be aware of, or care about, attracting the sort of lustful stares that generally excite me—was excited above where mere stares would transport me. Cleo's Needle swirled on by, then we took a turn at the top of Cedar Hill—so uplifting the sight of rock outcroppings set against lawn's emerald, with stately evergreens—and thence south past The Boathouse and through Bethesda Terrace's tunnel, fertility Goddess representations gleaming on its walls among shadows. Then the Mall's elms were towering above us in an eyeblink, as if we'd been magic-wanded there. Again, I have little recollection of our *physical* wending of our way to the Mall. Our stroll over there was seemingly waves of tingling warmth and a sunblasted sky, birdsongs and flowers in bloom and butterflies flitting and The Lake shimmering.

There was a birdwatching group in the Mall. We...

##########

So that's where I was when you called to inform me a thunderstorm's brewing—thank you, Sweetest! May you be as uplifted, spared vanity and ego via communion with the elements, as I'm hoping I'll be.

Your,
TitillatinglyTinglingTrollop

I.6
Angie to Ella
Sunday, June 22, 2003 2:19 PM

We've just finished speaking: I'm a giggling little girl, like as not to leap out of my skin for joy, and why not? A thunderstorm's darkening the sky—a hint of night's invading daylight—sheer swoonsville!

Hear the rumbling, Ella? Are your windows as wide open as my terrace door so's you can invite elemental unpredictability indoors, relish the rising wind?—atmospheric charge, plummeting temperature? 'Twas a sunblasted day in the low nineties, a clear sky; now dense clouds are swooping in—the curtains violently rustle, swift breeze engulfs and semi-chills me; energy crackles in the air, invades my curls: it's as if soft electric fur's swishing against my curves—as if an invisible ghost of a lover's hugging me close, beaming sparkles under my skin. I'll be on my back on my terrace right after I send this to you, naked but for a big beach towel atop me, deliciously drenched whilst lightning flashes, thunder cracks—intermingling my moans with the storm's power.

Will read your email later, Ella—storm's arriving in full force soon, both within and outside me, and I don't want to miss a moment.

Enjoy thyself!

Your,
StormStimulatedStrumpet

I.7
Ella to Angie
Sunday, June 22, 2003 5:21 PM

Oodles of gratitude for phoning to inform of the storm, Angie! Though it's with shame I confess it, confess I must: I was oblivious of the wonders of nature coming alive outside. My windows were shut, curtains drawn, and music (Campra's Idomenee) playing loud; I was so immersed in savoring recollections of our first day of summer romp I was blind to the priceless opportunity for more wildness in the here and now. Thanks to you, I'm able to assert I stimulated and enjoyed myself in a manner that'll bring a smile to your face and make you proud.

You call up, announce (in a voice *so* charmingly heated, oozing wantonness) that the wind's rising, clouds blotting out the sun; that it'll be orgasming outside soon and you'll be channeling lightning. Soon as you confirm I comprehend what's happening you hang up. I wrap up my last email, go to the windows and part the curtains: WOW!

I open the windows high as they'll go and fling myself on the couch below them, shed my nightie, prepare for reception of the sacred thunderstorm electricity: so chilly-thrilling-invigorating's the wind's caress upon my nakedness. I'm gazing into the dark disturbed sky while twisting against the cushions in response to the wind blowing across my legs, dancing upon my tummy and breasts and throat and fluffing my hair: what a wild lover is the vacillating wind of a storm—now furious, now subdued. With each surge of the wind I gasp deeper—tense deeper—churn deeper; with each lull of the wind I seem to spill outside my body's confines, float over the floor. I'm sinking into cushions while seeming to soar into the clashing gray of the clouds; I'm being pulled outside the windows, scattered like mist, as rain begins falling. Surely I'm ceasing to inhabit my body, becoming an elemental spirit no physical boundary can contain; and, yet, I've never been more vividly aware of my body—sensory fireworks sparkling in every sinew. Shsssss! Rain's striking the screen, splattering me! Crisssh! Thunder's pounding my ears, vibrating my bones! Flicker-flisssh! Lightning's saturating eyesight, shimmering my spine! Ah! Now I'm writhing-gasping to the tune of an inserted finger: as finger strokes and wiggles, I tremble to the storm's roar—shudder to thunder's shout! I'm the expansive convulsive sky outside my windows, electric charge of the atmosphere; I'm the earth pummeled by driving rain! Ooooo! I'm inhaling deep draughts of storm-freshened air, holding them hard inside me—pitching, shaking: the storm's whipping through me! I'm assuredly the sky as I die brightly—for a few illuminated moments! Then I'm sighing, quivering, gloriously limp on the cushions: it's as if their softness is pulling me down inside it, closing over me like a sea, rain still splashing me.

Sweetie, now that I'm pristine-serene with a thunderstorm dousing, romping inside with post-coitus reverberations, it's tough to resume recollecting our first day of summer romp. So it's up to you to take up the thread, weave it into faithful documentation, should you choose: there's not enough detachment in my head. Had you not told of the storm I'd still be reliving yesterday, but the storm's made me far too energy-elevated to focus. And of course I wouldn't have it any other way—thank you again, from the depths of my juice-oozing womb.

Your,
Storm Tossed Tartlet

I.8
Angie to Ella
Sunday, June 22, 2003 7:50 PM

And thank *you*, Dearest, for coming under the influence of celebration mania and dragging me to the park, uniting me with summer's elemental exuberance. Yesterday was truly Paradise Regained.

Central Park (nearest approximation of natural wilds any town could hope to have) tosses me off-balance in the best way, teeters me towards greater impulsiveness and daring, and yesterday the effect was heightened. I was vividly—almost unbearably—aware of every flying, scampering, noisy sustenance-craving creature; my blood was ahum with the struggle each living thing shares—the never quiet urge to prolong its stay on earth and propagate. Do I exaggerate? I'm telling you the buzz of insects about the flowers, blur of squirrels racing up and down the tree trunks, twittering of birds in the canopy was beating in my ears, throbbing in my temples, sizzling in my nerves: all of it was heat-accumulation in my skin, exchange of thought for compulsion. A small part of our adventures I'll attempt to tell—my Boathouse stunt:

We're seated at a deck table, dangling our feet over The Lake's sun-silvered surface; we're sippity-sipping Champagne and nibbly-nibbling strawberries whilst twirling our parasols, being the sweetest lil' well-behaved darlings. Well, I'm not in the mood to be well-behaved—I'm squirmy and impatient, thirsting to introduce disorder into this peaceful place. Ha! Want some communion with nature cause and effect? Want some "Summer caused it!" stuff? How's this: the sun's movement on the water's thrusting at my eyes, dizzying me; the midday heat's making my skin itchy, discontented, clamorous; the fact we're here instead of off alone under a patch of trees is making me doubly intolerant of the polite behavior imposed upon us simply because we happen to be dining at a restaurant. Yeah, it's the whispering of trees in the distance—promise of frolic in some hidden nook of a rock outcropping under a towering oak—that's causing my thoughts to dance dervishly, needle me. It's the proximity of The Lake that's flinging pictures of upwelling springs, swift mountain streams, silver waterfalls and fountains into my head. Then comes the clarity: a plan of action materializes, fairly glimmers, amidst the churning mix of my discontent, and I quiver in response. 'Tis with blitheness in my voice and joyous expansion of heart that I bid the waitress bring us two large bottles of carbonated water.

The water's poured into tall glasses: bubbles are rising in the glasses, bursting at the surface, sparkling and hissing—mirroring the state of my nerves. In a flash I'm lifting the bottle of remaining water high, pouring it down my neck, onto my chest and into my lap: I'm simply, quite innocently really, chasing after a chance at calm. And when the water sloshes over me—ooooo! Icy fizzies! I'm sheer electrification in a second, surging skywards! A fizzy frigid water bath on a hot summer's day does wonders for unease! The emotion-claustrophobia engendered by overmuch proper behavior goes poof! like a bad dream does soon as one opens one's eyes. Whirlies wildly dance within me at touch of the water's sparkling cold, whisk oppressive sensations away.

Too brief is the shiver-surge of relief; almost instantly, I'm aware of our fidgeting neighbors. The starts in their stares, discomfited hushes in their manner (as if some are presuming to be embarrassed on my behalf), nor to omit the snippety mutterings of others, rapid whippings about of their heads at me, are an assault in a way—killjoyishly intrusive.

I glance at myself: nearly the whole of the front of my bright white dress has changed from semi-transparent to seriously transparent due to the drenching; viewed from the front, I'm not wearing much more than my skimpy lacy black underwear.

Then you upsy-daisy your glass onto yourself, and the upper portion of your pinafore clings like a second skin, reveals your half cups aren't covering your nips. I'm giggling, and our neighbors don't like my having the nerve to giggle one bit, plus there's the fact you've brazenly chosen to copy me, as if it's all a game to us (which, of course, it is). A number of the looks they're giving us are quite unkind (which, of course, I must needs counter by languorously stretching, ensuring my dressy clings tighter, displays my curvature more accurately).

Yet seated at the deck's far end are four sunbathers in bikinis: although they're much nearer to being naked than us, no eyebrows are raised at them. But the drenching of our dresses has transformed us into shameless hussies. If we were wearing bikinis, we'd be inoffensive sunbathers—completely socially acceptable—and the manager wouldn't be directing glances of apprehension at us. Girl presentation's relative. Bikinis are A-OK; drenched dresses are not. Even though we're more covered up than bikini-clad girls we're Hester Prynnes with Scarlet Letters sewn on. It's nothing short of astonishing that many of the social conventions governing our lives are utterly silly and arbitrary.

Naturally I'm squishing my slick wet thighs together under the table so's to tickle flowerpuss, come closer to thoroughly feeling at one with The Lake's shimmering water at my feet. As we well know and constantly lovingly confirm, exhibitionistic concealment, getting away with secret self-stimulation in the face of rude stares, is even more fulfilling than exhibitionistic showboating, which is saying something.

Ella, we're *obliged* to further explore the nuances of public dousings, radiant kaleidoscopic expansiveness swooping in on us. We won't abandon the game prematurely, as yesterday, since we couldn't wait to fling ourselves back into the verdancy, get wild in the Ramble. We'll shiver-quiver, flip each other inside out to our heart's content, completely live up to our motto (One of many!): "Unfettered joy despite disapproval!" We'll greet accusatory glances with seeming obliviousness of doing anything wrong ("Act like you belong," my Dad would say.), simply giggle like innocent lil' girls! Hahaha!

On that note of future exploration, Sweetest, I'll lay recollections of yesterday to rest. After all, I've tickled twatsie to the tune of a thunderstorm's fury—been elements-blasted today—as well. Cresting whilst storm-doused is insanely euphoric and our summer's off to an incandescent start—luscious auspices for us. May we both be spun from one deliriously surging day to another all summer and beyond.

Nightie-night, Celebrational Sweetheart!

Your,

DamselOfTheDousings

I.9
Ella to Angie
Sunday, June 22, 2003 9:04 PM

Yesterday was Paradise Regained, and that's why I'm always eager to mark something as a special occasion. Summer's first day, anniversary of our first frolic, whatever. Being a "calendar watcher" has its rewards. Special occasions demand special exertion and, as such, liberate us from the mundane, and we've never failed to exceed expectation—we're *insanely* lucky. A special occasion's a rebirth—an inundation of anticipation, yearning, and daring that obliterates the day-to-day world, erases preoccupation with work and care. I'm a little girl again, unafraid of anything, naïve enough to feel I can get away with everything. And being with you, frolicsome strumpet, is icing on the crumpet.

Final bit, concerning our stroll home: as we head east on 79th I'm gloriously ablur, in a state of seemingly no separation between myself and every sight and scent and sound, sensuality engagingly disembodied. A simple glance towards the upper stories of buildings, and I'm suddenly there—drifting amidst the hanging gardens of the balconies, touching and smelling the flowers, drinking in eyefuls of colors tingling me to the roots of my nerves. It's as if the breeze is blowing through me, my body unbounded. Illusory? Who cares? Elevation triumphs.

Central Park's as near to unaltered Mommy Nature as we'll get without leaving town—our approximation of untamed wilderness. I was a maenad wending my way home—head-to-toe electrified, excitation lingering in my veins. Was a snake or two entwined in my hair?

Delirium smashes through self-dividedness, the gap between ourselves and nature—does away with civilization's debilitating mirrors.

That's all, Darlingest!

Your,

Summer'sDeliriumDarling

II. Trailer Trollop Romp & Martin's Comeuppance

II.1
Angie to Ella
Monday, June 30, 2003 10:03 AM

Ella, why on earth would you not report for duty? I thought we had the maul-Martin's-peace-of-mind project set to go. I was thirsting to hike up my skirt and get him salivating without you but, of course, that would preclude having the added dimension of yourself posing as sympathetic confidant and providing advice as to how he's to court my favor. But I want to punish him in the worst way! Want him languishing in the toils of knifing desire he's unable to sate! Want him thirsting for me while showing him unabated disdain! And you know this! So why would you call in saying you needed to take a Personal Day (Oh, yes, I already know: Sylvia told me.) and deprive me of my revenge?

I expect an answer, Ella, and need to know if you'll be here tomorrow, or flake off again. That creep has got to blaze in his very own hell of an inflamed body he's unable to escape from. What he did to Linda's inexcusable, and he's going to suffer.

Let me know, Miss Unreliable!

Your,

AnnoyedAngie

II.2
Ella to Angie
Monday, June 30, 2003 11:46 PM

Darling, I apologize profusely! And don't you worry, we'll have arrogant thoughtless Martin incurably melancholic by the end of the week. I'm definitely coming in tomorrow, as much to assist you in your project as justify Sturmheld's confidence in me. (I've been busy pacifying him for the past couple hours for today's absence by scanning/emailing comments on the [_____] IPO.)

Why was I absent? Simple: I had another Stevie adventure. They've been coming rather thick and fast of late, taking up all my spare time and intruding on time I don't necessarily have to spare, but why shouldn't they? Stevie's a bottomless well of imagination-stimulation and there's no sense in letting such abundance go to waste, because if my imagination's stimulated then my svelte lil' body's stimulated and *la petite mort* truly becomes a fountain of life. Stevie's always willing and I'm always willing: I'll never say nay to another fantasy-becomes-flesh adventure. Stevie makes me feel sultry and seductive, as if a dying man would spring to health at the sight of me: such sensations are irresistible to a vain lil' fashion plate plaything like me. I apologized for missing work today, but I'm actually not sorry in the least. And before you get miffed at that lil' confession, let me tell of today's fantasy fun: maybe then you'll understand why the mess-up-Martin's-manhood project, worthy though it be, had to be placed on hold. I'm sure you'll understand, since you're a funloving—fantasy-mongering—floozy too.

My fun as follows:

I finally fulfilled one of my most treasured fantasies: indulgence in a trailer trollop fling. Dressing for the fling was delight-unto-itself: I had a fine doll-myself-up time of it at my vanity, blaring dance music, an organic health bar and plate of mixed berries for nibbles, fizzy spring water with lime juice infusion for quaffing. (Ha, ever notice how annoyed some people get at our finicky health food diet?—accusing us of being food snobs because we have the good sense not to cram our gullets with hydrogenated oil saturated garbage?—because we refuse to undermine our energy with empty-calorie trash? We eat right to play right, right? There's nothing more essential to having fine sex adventures than a clean bill of health, and if one makes oneself *ridiculously* healthy... Oh, ho ho! I eat right to lust right! Good nutrition fans the slut fires! Good nutrition brings about that itching-to-rut bouncing-off-the-walls feeling of empowerment I adore!) I spent nearly two hours doing trail-and-error mirror star stuff. After all, why bother to get ready for a date if I can't play like a little girl who dreams of growing up gorgeous, having the boys fawn at her feet?

As for what I wore: 1) a polyester leopard print skirt, slits sloppily cut up each side with scissors; 2) a pink pullover, sleeveless and of faded cotton with bleach splotches; 3) a God-awful wig, dirty mousy brown, piled high in a circa 1950s do; 4) the cheapest brassiere I could find at the drugstore, with the tan straps exposed (A discomfort I was willing to endure for the sake of trailer trollop authenticity.); 5) plastic gold bedroom slippers with the toes cut off (Not the easiest things to saunter down the sidewalk in; but, again, for the sake of being a highly noticeable trailer trollop.); and 6) pink stockings with lots of runs. Then there was the makeup, layered on like I've never done in my life: I was something of a hybrid of clown and witch, fit for a carnival or Halloween. There was enough makeup on me to make me feel like my cheeks were being yanked down my face. I didn't merely look like a trailer trollop, I was a caricature of what a city girl thinks a trailer trollop looks like. By the time I was done, make up was spilled all over the vanity and floor—nail polish splattered, sparkles scattered, a compact shattered, 'Twas a labor of Hercules, and I was like as not to orgasm sheerly from the delight of making that kind of mess.

OK, I'm ready and it's nearly eleven. Stevie's taken a room at the Essex House, a brilliant ad lib of setting (He called at about nine-thirty to tell me.) that lends more of a myself-as-a-trampy-out-of-towner feel to this grand event—worth it for what happened in the lobby alone.

The deskman's reaction is priceless. First, there's a drop-jawed gaping-eyed look of utter disbelief—"His eyes opened up to swallow the sky," as they say, then there's a huffy gathering of his dignity, a look like he's about to shoo me away, a frown verging on a sneer. So I speak up and, in my very sophisticated (if I say so myself) attorney voice, say:

"Mr. Bergendahl is expecting me in room 1544. Please inform him the girl from Arkansas is here to discuss the legal matter."

The deskman's face contorts every which way; the shoo-away impulse makes an embarrassed retreat, confusion reasserts itself. "Yes, Ma'am," he finally manages while continuing to look me up and down, "I'll let Mr. Bergendahl know." He makes the call while exchanging a sort of "She seems to really know someone who's staying here, so I guess I have to do this." look with a fiftyish woman he appears to be sharing desk duty with. She's looking at me as if I'm some sort of riddle to solve—undecided as to whether I'm a hooker, lunatic, bona fide hick, or bright girl playing games: no real way for her to know.

During the deskman's call Stevie distinguishes himself in the pranking department, asking (as I soon discern) the man to describe me.

"Uuuhh...what?" the deskman manages to articulate. His eyes skitter about, as if seeking to locate someone to pass the phone to; it's clear he doesn't dare bother the woman, doubtless a superior. There's no one else: he's stuck with the unpleasant situation. (And I *do* enjoy being an unpleasant situation a rude pompous dolt must deal with.)

Stevie obviously reiterates his request more emphatically, because the deskman answers: "Sir, I realize it's a simple question. I wasn't sure I heard you right. No, Sir, I'm not trying to be difficult. I don't doubt you, I..." He trails off, treating me to a glance of alarm. You'd think he's being asked to provide intimate details of his sex life, or lack thereof. But a look of relief comes into the deskman's face. He tells Stevie, "I'll pass her the phone." and extends it towards me in a manner I find insulting, since there's an implied command to take it from his hand.

"Oh, no!" I respond, stepping back in horror. "Public phones are contaminated—unsanitary, covered with germs. I just got over a bad cold, and I know a public phone caused it. I'm *never* touching a public phone again." Ha, as if I'd allow a conceited clown to wriggle out of a ticklish situation. As if I'm the sort of girl who's going to do violence to her dignity by blindly obeying the laughably fake firmness of manner with which he holds the phone to me while giving me one of those pseudo meaningful looks. I'm thinking: "The moon will fall into the Atlantic Ocean before I'll take that phone from you, buster."

Then I add in an evil-polite, laced-with-poison, tone: "Sir, I'm very surprised that a man in a professional situation would thrust a phone at a visitor as you have done. In the first place it is very rude and disrespectful; in the second place it is not your place to ask me to do your job for you; in the third place I have no idea where that phone's been or whose lips it's touched. *(Here I give him a particularly derisive look.)* Sir, it is a health hazard and I am truly astonished."

Now our deskman stammers: "Ma'am, I meant no disrespect. The gentleman asked me to describe you. All due respect to him, he's put me in an embarrassing circumstance. I thought it might be indiscreet...wanted to cause no offense, Ma'am!"

"Well, just please do your job and describe me, as requested—I won't be offended. Mr. Bergendahl's an important man who must guard against unsolicited visitors—he's being careful. Tell him what I look like."

Angie, I had to turn away and pretend to cough to conceal the grin that flashed onto my face. And I know what you're thinking: a shameful lack of self-discipline, failure to maintain my playacting front. But you had to be there. An icy-mien hanging judge would've laughed at the deskman's twitching cheeks. Plus Stevie starts speaking on the phone so loud I can almost make out the words and, in his haste to bring the receiver back to his ear, the deskman butterfingers it, drops it on the desk.

Then the deskman's saying: "Sir, there's no problem here. I dropped the phone, I apologize. No, Sir! There's not a robbery going on—no commotion. Yes, of course. She's wearing a leopard dress and a pink shirt. Yes, Sir, I think her hair's a wig. *What?*"

I sense Stevie might be going too far. It wouldn't do to give the game away.

"Her stockings, Sir?" Here the deskman turns to the fiftyish woman, says: "I think something's funny. He wants to know what kind of stockings she's wearing."

"Uh, begging your pardon, Ma'am," he adds, turning to me. "I can't be responsible for what Mr. Bergendahl's asking me to tell him."

Then, turning back to the woman: "Will you please take the phone, Claudia? I'm not going to do this."

Before Claudia can take the phone I say: "Sir, here's my company ID. Tell Mr. Bergendahl, then this will be over." I already had my ID ready so's to hit the deskman with contradiction, the reality-contrasting-with-appearances thing. Now I'm forced to present it prematurely.

With a gesture of impatience—because he's beginning to wonder if he's being toyed with, thanks to Stevie's pushing the envelope (Doesn't he *always*?)—the deskman brings the phone back to his mouth and says: "Mr. Bergendahl, she's handed me her company ID. It says that she's an attorney at [_____]. Sir, it's her picture. Her name's Ella Washington. I wasn't stalling, Sir. I would've checked her ID first thing had you requested it. We're not in the habit of asking for the IDs of visitors of our guests at the Essex House, Sir. Yes, Sir, she'll be coming up."

The deskman stares at my ID for a few moments longer, then at me, clearly perplexed by the contrast between my present appearance and that of myself in the ID, where I'm immaculately corporate in a Bergdorf suit. Choosing to be annoyed at the man's presumptuous look, I state with calm coldness: "Sir, I do not feel it behooves you, as an employee of a world class hotel, to concern yourself with matters that are none of your business. I will not tolerate being stared at in that way."

"Uuhhh..." is all he can manage, looking for all the world like he'd dearly love to sink into the floor.

"That's hardly an answer that does you credit, Sir, and now I believe I'm through with you, if you'll kindly return my ID instead of reading all the information on it," I say. Ha! He's completely forgotten to wonder if he's being toyed with, is only wishing our encounter to end, and that's what he gets for being nasty from the get-go—treating me to shoo-away impulses, thrusting phones at me, seeking to not speak to me. Now he's aware he has no idea what the parameters are; now he's unable to compute the contrasting evidence concerning yours truly; now he isn't going to venture to so much as blink, lest I get *really* riled and spring who knows what additional surprises on him. For all he knows, the mysterious Mr. Bergendahl could make an appearance.

What a nice aphrodisiacal way to kick off the festivities—pranking reliably wets my pinkling. Being the center of attention in the lobby of the Essex simply because of my clothes? And behaving the opposite of my appearance? Being Miss Corporate in intonation, vocabulary, mannerisms, and carriage while decked out in polyester trash? It's pure scrumptious prepping-of-flowerpuss-for-pollination fun.

I'm on my way to the elevator bank when it occurs to lil' Miss MoodShift me that my dealings with the deskman have been too one-dimensional: it won't do to *only* be the girl who's annoyed at the treatment she's received. So I do an about-face, stroll back to him smiling, place ten dollars on the desk, say quite sweetly, "Notwithstanding your shortcomings, this is for your trouble, Sir. I trust you'll work on your manners a bit and endeavor not to hurt people's feelings going forward? Have a nice day."

Oh, Angie! The apprehension on the deskman's face as I approached; the flinching backwards impulse that semi-seized his body when I extended my hand; the wind-gone-out-of-him expression of utter bafflement and relief when my gentle intonation was heard and the ten dollars materialized... 'Twas money well spent.

OK, let's get me upstairs:

When Stevie opens the door he bursts out laughing at sight of me, and I say: "Hey, it's not like you to break character. I'm trailer trollop and you're trailer slob. A trailer slob would never laugh at a trailer trollop: they're of one and the same world, cut from the same cloth." Although I'm doing a wee bit o' giggling on account of his acid wash jeans (The *worst*, right? He purchased them for our trailer romp and they were tossed in the trash immediately afterwards.) and torn tank top.

"Right, chide me for something then turn around and do it yourself!" he announces in response to my amusement. "That's girl logic in all its self-contradictory glory!" Isn't Stevie the *sweetest*? He's lobbed me a pitch, straight over the middle of the plate, and is waiting for the home run.

"But, Stevie dear, you're overlooking the fact it's logical for us girls to be illogical, because it keeps men off-balance, forever guessing what we mean, never knowing what to expect. We say one thing and do the opposite, then we say another thing and stick by it religiously—for a while anyway, 'til we decide to do something else after all. There's no predictable pattern and that's how we want it. It's our way of seeking to keep men spinning their thought-wheels in efforts to decipher our reasoning. It's our way of countering the male impulse to sit us down and explain what's what. If we decline to comprehend what's what, choosing instead to go off on an illogical rendering of how we view the matter, then what can men do other than fling their arms up in resignation and allow us to remain fickle, flighty, finicky, whimsical, mood-driven creatures? Logical illogicalness is maintenance of our freedom and independence. We wind up getting our way precisely because we refuse to accord reason enough reality to control us."

"Very impressive," Stevie says sarcastically. "I wholeheartedly agree we poor reason-hobbled males are like monkeys in a pitch black room full of marbles—always falling on our asses, getting nowhere—when we come up against the eternal question: "Is it possible to understand women?" But you've overlooked something, Miss Vain: the smarter males deal with that question by simply ignoring it and giving you what you most want and will never admit you want, which is firm *discipline*. You silly females get so lost in your vanity that imagination and reality blur and you can no longer distinguish the difference, and therefore you're in need of a dose of firm grounding in physical actuality to disentangle fantasy from actuality, return them to their proper places, and as long as we males routinely take the time to give you such you'll be our devoted slaves. So get in here *(He seizes me by the nape of my neck, pulls me into the room.)* and receive the discipline you crave."

"So you admit you mentally insufficient males, incapable of comprehending women, must resort to brute force to subdue us? That's a pretty shoddy solution, reeking of inferiority-fueled compensation." I spout this while Stevie holds me against the entryway's wall.

"I always tell women I'm baffled by women: it flatters them and inclines them to being compliant. Not that you have much choice at the moment," he laughs, continuing to press me to the wall, cupping my nether cheeks in his palms, squeezing with gusto.

"Actually, it's a typical male avoidance of responsibility ploy. If a man informs us it's impossible to understand women, the implication is he isn't going to make much of an effort to do so, and he'll use it as an excuse whenever lapses of communication occur." I feign an escape attempt, squirm vigorously, to encourage him to seize me more firmly.

There's more preliminary banter, but I'll skip the remainder (plus allow myself to have the last word) in the interest of moving this along.

Soon enough Stevie's seated on the couch with his pants off—swilling a beer, putting on an uncouth leer, availing himself of assorted crude comments: faithfully acting the part of trailer slob. Per my request, he commands me to 1) pour myself a glass of Scotch, 2) light a cigarette and dangle it, and 3) pace about smoking and drinking while doing an inept striptease. OK, I know what you're thinking: what's a fit toned aerobics and yoga princess doing with a cigarette? But, hey, I'm willing to sacrifice for the sake of playing a role to the hilt, and it's liberating to go in opposite directions from my normal. What sort of trailer trollop would I be without liquor and a smoke? (Besides, I wasn't inhaling.) The atmospheric effect of these props, plus the all-around cheapness of my get-up and ridiculously clumsy dancing, such that I'm wobbling hither-thither, sometimes bracing myself against the wall... Girl, it's as if Scotch is being poured into my pinkling, so blazing hot and bothered, aflush of face, am I becoming. One often feels like what one wears, right? (Wild how it's a way to manipulate emotion.) I was wearing trashy clothes and two bad habits, and thus feeling fabulously like an uneducated vice-ridden teen with no care for the future, only mindful of indulging self-destructive tendencies in the moment. Such a refreshing vacation from being a health conscious career girl! You definitely need to try traveling to the opposite-of-good-sense place—you'll *adore* it.

So I swig from the glass and drag from the smoke and put the smoke back in my mouth while setting the glass down, then pull my top over my head, kick off my shoes, start slipping out of my skirt. I can't begin to describe the delight of feeling my ass-cheeks pop into view as I trip over the skirt, reach for the wall to steady myself. I am, indeed, an unprincipled tramp performing for a slob in a trailer in a rundown country town, rusting appliances in the front yard; I am, indeed, a high school dropout thumbing my nose at life below the poverty line, compensating via display of the only assets I possess—economic disadvantage vanishes when I'm naked and desired.

Then my skirt's on the floor—I'm wearing torn thigh-highs, gobs of makeup, a wig.

What follows? This is important—I'd told Stevie it was important, and he held true. The moment my skirt's on the floor and I'm hot and squishy and tingly and still tugging on the cigarette, he springs from the couch, picks up one of my shoes, shouts, "Shameless hussy! You're gussied up like a whore and drunk and smoking like a whore and, by God, will be punished like a whore!" He seizes the nape of my neck with one hand, my left ass-cheek with the other, rather roughly forces me to circle to the back of the couch, bend over it. "Give me that!" he says, taking the cigarette from my mouth, crushing it out. Then he announces, "If you're going to behave like a hayloft harlot in heat, you'll be brought to heel like one—I'll give you religion you won't forget, Godless strumpet! No modesty, no morals, no decency—you're a fine piece of work! Puffed up with pride, flaunting yourself, so pleased with the lust you inspire! Laughing at men you lead astray! But that's over! You'll wish you went to Sunday school and attended church, learned how to behave with decorum, once I'm through with you! You're not going to paint your face until it screams 'Whore!' anymore! You're not going to swill liquor again! I'm going to make a right proper decorous lady out of you, whatever's required!" Having finished this fine speech, Stevie commences swatting my behind with the shoe while shoving my head into the cushions, continuing to grip the back of my neck.

Ooooo, baby! A flurry of blows tanning my behind as I'm regaled with insults that are actually complimentary, flattery in disguise, if that makes any sense (although I know you understand). How describe the stimulation streaming through my veins, throbbing me? I'm whipping-inside-out dizzy—doubt I've ever wanted to be plowed more desperately. (OK, as you've sagely pointed out: most times I have sex I'm saying stuff like: "I was mind-alteringly heated to a degree previously unimagined!," "Never gushed so intensely!," "He elevated me heavenwards as none before!," and the like. But what can I say? I exist in the sex-present; new escapades erase previous escapades. If I'm silly with tendencies to exaggerate, so be it—indeed, I embrace it. Anytime I roll in the hay I want it to be as if I've glimpsed God, don't feel it's outrageous to expect that—life's too temporary.)

Stevie's our priceless treasure—we're insanely fortunate, no judgment of us ever—no insecurity-caused impulses to control us, only fun stacked atop fun. Discarding all pretense of being morality-motivated, he openly—proudly—succumbs to my charms, shouts: "Lusciously twitchy-assed hot-twatted wench, I see you're lubricated for me! Wide open wet warm bright pink passageway, hungering for a hammering! No need for saliva or butter or oil!" He's shoving his shaft deep, pummeling backend of pinkling something fierce. Oh, right: mindless brute force isn't usually the way to get me to flood—slug-fests often irritate rather than stimulate—rubbed raw isn't generally my idea of a fulfilling time, I've wanted to kill for such. I'm clawing and biting couch cushions, hissing. Maybe I ought to go full-out wildcat, retaliate with scratches, bites? Maybe I'm riled enough to draw blood for real instead of only imagining the possibility? Silver's bursting in my head.

Of course Stevie becomes *lusciously* tender—gentle-firm lingering thrusts tickle-soothing pinkling's walls—he's vibrant with savoring of me. I'm on my back on the bed, gripping his girth, undulating not only there but seemingly all over—his gaze going to the childlike happy blissed place, eyes pulsating with kindness and my cheeks trembling. Then he's uncouth, pummeling me clumsily, again—mumbles incoherently, burbles. Am I enraptured or irritated? 'Tis tough to tell! (And, hey, I *adore* being blurred, so long as I know and trust the man delivering.) Then respectful relishing of me again, reverberating me way up inside tummy-tums. Angie, the most scrumptious *la petite mortie-mort* seizes me, Stevie and I simultaneous! I'm flooded with hot milk while melting moaning—sucker-biting-licking one of his arms or his neck or a cheek. (And how did I get to the bed, atop silky sheets, from the couch, anyway? I don't recollect the change—sheer yumsters.)

Oodles more fun follows (Essex House is hardly going to be used for only one flutter-gush of my pleasure-treasure.), but I'm breaking this off, 1) 'cause po' lil' trailer trollop me's jus' plumb tuckered out, and 2) I'm conscientiously going beddie-bye so's I can be at the firm refreshed, eager to be of use to you in execution of your worthy project.

Don't cha worry 'bout a thing, Hon' Doll: we'll show nasty Martin what girl vengeance is. We'll ignite him with yearning for you then slam the door shut, see to it he thrashes in flames he's unable to quench. We'll cram his head full of tantalizing needling maddening images of you, then deprive him of the means of dissipating them. He's going to be drowning in unrequited desire, suffer mightily and want to die.

'Til the morn', Sweets—nighty-night!

Your,

TitillatedTuckeredOutTrailerTrollop

II.3
Angie to Ella
Tuesday, July 1, 2003 11:27 AM

Infinite thanks, Darlingest! The way you sidled up to Martin in the hall with an expression dripping sympathy after I flung him into tumult was divine, and the way he visibly entrusted you more so. Plus the restraint you tactfully imposed with body language, to prevent him entertaining the notion—in his desperation—of overstepping acquaintanceship's boundaries. I observed from around the corner before you entered his office, where I *know* you kept handling him such that he was under no illusion about you being a rebound girl. Our girl-vigilante project's unfolding pricelessly—I can't wait to hear what happened in there.

But here's what happened in Martin's office when it was he and me. He's at his desk and I'm seated within a yard, as we're perusing Rikert's revisions to the [_____] offering. I permit my hemline to ride up my thighs: the forward-scoot-in-a-chair while forgetting—tee hee!—to hold onto one's hem works wonders: a swift slide up, lots of stocking-sheathed leg exposed as if accidently. Then as I cross my legs I raise the knee of the upper leg quite high, such that poor Martin has a panty shot (black lace, semi-see-through) staring him in the face—ha ha! 'Twas precious comical to die for, his struggling-to-not-look embarrassment. Pages must be flipped to continue reviewing the document and this allows me to reach across said document, over his outstretched arm, to turn a page and—lo!—when I bring my hand back again I as-if-accidently swish my fingers across his wrist, impart some mischievous sparks. His hand twitches in response; an inner wave of discomposure engulfs him and he can't help but turn to me with a questioning look—a look I play at being oblivious of. Nor do I relent: a slow uncross of my legs yields the rasping-of-stockings sound (electric sandpaper) that drives men nuts (I feel him start) and also causes my right leg to lightly brush against him, again as if unintentionally. I'm also reaching behind my head, fiddling with my hair while thrusting out my chest: it seems the top two buttons of my blouse have come undone and there are two breasts in scarlet half-cups barely over a yard from his face. Martin's looking uncomfortable, pleased, and perplexed: he doesn't seem certain his good fortune's for real (I've always been unwaveringly professional, never overtly familiar), but he's doubtless beginning to dare hope it is. He doesn't seem able to trust the evidence of his senses, but I'm sure he wants the evidence to continue to mount. And the evidence definitely continues to mount—especially, my Dear, when I contrive to drop my pen on the floor, then must exit my seat and bend to retrieve it.

Put me in a room with a man and allow me to maneuver him onto the floor with me, and he'll be whatever I want him to be. So I bend to pick up my pen and—oh, my!—quite forget to guard against my dress riding up in back, such that a bit of behind's kissing the open air: I feel his stare fasten onto my cheeky-cheeks. Then I kneel, rump on heels, with my hemline halfway up my thighs in front. I look into his discomfited eyes all innocent and say in a sweet voice, "Martin, why don't we work on the floor—I'm tired and it's easier on me." I lean forward as if abstractly, causing my blouse to dip at the top and my breasts to spill into view again. Hahaha! Martin appears to be in a trance—a troubled trance. "Uh, OK...if you want," he sputters, clumsily gathering the papers and coming to where I am, struggling to avert his eyes but not entirely succeeding in doing so. After all, I'm sitting bolt upright again and my hemline's been nudged higher, nearer to my stocking tops.

Martin's uncomfortable with sitting too close but, as we both need to see the document, can't sit too far away: such a dilemma for the poor man. Then, Ella, the unexpected occurs: I find myself experiencing a pang of sympathy on his behalf. Why? Because he, contrary to expectation, hasn't been acting like a pompous self-assured clown. It's cute, the way hesitation, bewilderment, and shyness are hovering about him, causing his hands—as he arranges papers on the carpet—to ever so slightly tremble. And, along with my pang of sympathy, there's an inner shimmer—a delicate upwelling flush. And, damn! What is it with us females? Why does sympathy often pave the way for desire?

OK, it was shamefully remiss of yours truly to commence to get caught up in, allow myself to be affected by, my own weavings of seduction. On the other hand, it worked out well, because I quickly punished Martin for it. "Kill it off!" I commanded myself. "Remember his ghastly treatment of Linda, stick to the plan! No mercy! Time to strike!"

Full disclosure: had Linda's horror tale of being unceremoniously dumped by Martin in such a nasty haughty fashion, despite her copious tears and pleading for an explanation and protestations of love for him, not been in the forefront of my thoughts I *may* have allowed Mommy Nature to take her course, gazed upon Martin sweetly and clasped his hands, indicated he should pull me close, kiss me. As it was, I suddenly envisioned myself being duped into trusting him—being subsequently mistreated, disrespected—and therefore became doubly ruthless, close to angry in a personal way, as if it had already happened. Ignoring the manner in which he was wrestling with discomfort—informing myself his vulnerability was nothing but a cold calculating act—I kicked sympathy to the curb, proceeded to inflict the distress I came to inflict.

"So you think you leer at me, with the most presumptuous creepy smirk on your face, simply because my clothes are momentarily out of order," I state in an icy tone; then, upon rising to my feet and slapping my dress down, raising my voice, "This is a professional situation and you behave like a pig and I'm not going to stand for that behavior." Panic convulses Martin's face; not allowing myself to be swayed by it, I abruptly wheel about and—without glancing back—exit his office.

Ella, the reverberations from my display of anger were trembling me from my ankles to the top of my head, and I wanted to hyperventilate—I wasn't close to being the emotionally impervious girl I'd set out to be. Fortunately, you were waiting, your presence the warmest of blankets. Martin follows me into the hall to doubtless plead I've misread the situation, sees me whispering in your ear. After you glance at him with pity I stomp around the corner. I, so to speak, transfer him to you. Then I backtrack to observe: you're playacting empathy to perfection.

But what went on in his office? I'm burning to hear.

Your,

ConnivingWitchBitch (or should I say: ConnivingWitchBitch-*Wannabe*, since I was inexcusably trembling at the end?)

II.4
Ella to Angie
Tuesday, July 1, 2003 1:54 PM

Angie, I'll state it outright: Martin absolutely did *not* deserve the panic you plunged him into. You traumatized the wrong man! Linda's view of the circumstances of their breakup—sincere and guileless though it probably is—doesn't accord with the facts.

Here's the story:

When I presented myself to Martin as a sympathetic observer I was of course ignorant of the particulars of what transpired in his office—had no idea you'd become so extreme—but the degree of his disturbance spoke volumes: his eyes were bleeding worry. What began as playacted sympathy rapidly became authentic sympathy. No man as upset as Martin was could possibly be the pompous unfeeling manipulative schemer of Linda's interpretation of the truth. I found myself sincerely endeavoring to ascertain the truth about Linda, instead of doing so as part of an act, or assuming I knew the truth, since I was beginning to believe I had no clue. I told Martin you were prone to rashness and sometimes didn't read situations as they may have unfolded, and he was clinging to me with his eyes. He needed to discuss the matter, not as one ready to lie and make excuses, but as an authentically baffled person.

We enter his office and he circles to the opposite side of his desk, unsure how to begin. Finally, while gripping the desk-edge, he says he may have looked at you more than he should have in a way he shouldn't have, then stalls, hesitant to reveal how much of yourself you were revealing. So I help him along: I say you're prone to exhibitionistic display and sometimes become annoyed at the responses your displays inspire, then ask him if you were showing off. He looks at me, barely nods, glances away. I believe him—that is, believe his confusion's authentic. Then he says, "Why these misunderstandings with women? I adore and respect women, could never mean any harm. I'm a nice guy."

And Martin *is* a nice guy. I'll skip the halting words, uncomfortable pauses, that led up to him speaking of Linda—my efforts to make him comfortable with speaking of her. What he finally brought forth is he felt he loved Linda, and still does, but she's made it impossible for him to be with her, because he happens to have some self-respect, and life's too brief to be perpetually embroiled in conflict. Hints are dropped as to Linda being extremely disturbed below her cute amiable exterior—as to her rages having a quality of helplessness, as if there's no means of mitigation, try as he might. As near as he can make out, relationships are a means by which Linda, even if unintentionally, externalizes inner conflict; her inner war evolves into warring with the man in her life. He hastens to add there's no willed malice: becoming close to a man triggers excess, occasionally violent, over which her will exerts no sway. She often imagines affronts where there are none, becomes suspicious without cause; there's a tone of innocence, childlike naïveté, to her accusations and resulting storming. He said he didn't mind hints of friction in relationships—wasn't above being somewhat difficult now and then—but that Linda seemed guided by a blind impulse to plunge relationships into sanity-straining strife, and he couldn't endure being with her any longer. He feels he gave their relationship more than a fair chance and hopes she finds happiness with someone. I believe him.

Angie, please don't get annoyed, you had to be there—all's well, believe me. I confessed to Martin your behavior was revenge motivated. (Angie, *please* don't be screaming as you read this!) I informed him you put on your provocative display so you'd have an excuse to reprimand him (on Linda's behalf). I took equal share of the blame, apologized for unwarranted and inexcusable rush to judgment, solicited forgiveness.

Gratitude was Martin's overwhelming response—his relief was palpable. He's authentically good-hearted and decent. We wound up speaking at length, friendly and laughing. When I suggested you ought to make amends, apologize, he waved that away, said such was for you to decide. Mostly, he reiterated gratitude for my coming clean.

Hey girl, he likes you—admires how you were focused on righting a perceived wrong done another woman; said that, if he was a woman, he hoped he'd be prepared to do the same. Also, Martin's neither stupid nor a coward. You do recall Linda's details of some of their escapades? Martin, I can assure you, is a man who appreciates a spirited girl and knows how to treat her, Linda may have some nasty demons tucked away in her hidden places (I reaffirm, I believe Martin), but who denies she's the cutest—nay, the most beautiful—dishling on the premises, even edging us from the top position (and we know that's no mean feat)? In short, Martin's as discerning as daring, and non-intimidated by beauties. Should we allow him to go to waste? I think not!

So I expect you, WitchBitch, to march to Martin's office and be sweet and remorseful and apologize, make amends and hint at the possibility of frolic. I assure you he'll be an exemplary gentleman and employ an amount of tact that will surprise you, considering your former perception of him. I'd almost bet my life he won't allow you to feel guilty.

Do it *now*! Get your tush to Martin's office, be the apologetic charmer! And I'm pretty sure you'll be properly pleasured by him pretty soon, and that you'll be indebted to yours truly. Tally ho, Sweets!

Your,

MollifyingMatchmakingMiss

III. Office Rescue & The Nightie Shred and Tie-Up Game

III.1
Angie to Ella
Tuesday, July 1, 2003 6:46 PM

Sure, I've spilled the scrumptious details by phone but wish to savor the lingering tingles of sweet surrender in Martin's office, plus document the bliss. Again, profuse thanks, Miss Matchmaker, for paving the way: you talked me up to Martin so effectively, painted me in such appealing colors, I doubt I would've needed to say a word. All I would've had to do was appear at the door of his office with an apologetic and demure expression, and Mommy Nature would've seen to the rest. I quickly discovered the pang of sympathy I'd felt on Martin's behalf earlier hadn't been misplaced. He's a prince, and shame on me for believing Linda's lies and seeking to make a good man miserable. Thankfully I'm once more a cheerful bouncy pleasure-addicted mischief-minx.

The moment I stepped within Martin's office the air turned dense and crackly with desire's undercurrents. Sheer thrillsville when a man's so tense with yearning one feels sparkles race up one's legs, spread over one's back and up one's neck, and when one becomes tense, blood humming, in response. Martin spoke first, saying, "Ella tells me I've offended you, and that you're seeking satisfaction." His eyes were fastened onto mine, quivering a bit as if he was doubtful about being able to hold them there, but there was also a glint of challenge.

Well, I did a 'lil blush thing, fluttered my eyes towards the floor: it's immensely flattering to a man when a girl gets flustered in his honor, plus it provides him with any encouragement he may need, nudges him along. I answered, "I was a silly girl who believed another girl's slander. I deeply apologize and hope you'll accept my apology." Then I slowly raised my eyes—gave him a dose of the hopeful hesitation look—while continuing to look shamefaced. Martin, bless him, said you'd explained everything and an apology wasn't necessary, but that it was very kind of me to offer. To put it another way: he accepted my apology in the delightfulest of ways, as I've described to you over the phone.

But I still can't leave off describing here—reflecting here—having fun here. There's nothing like a lil' frolic at the firm for ridding oneself of the twitchy-bitchies—a sweet lil' fling-thing does wonders for revitalization, eliminates accumulated thought-din, facilitates focus. Far from winding one, frolic enables one to resume one's work responsibilities with a second wind of dedication. And the pleasing pictures of playtime that linger in one's mind's eye, dispense comfort and consolation! As, for instance, when I'm sucking at Martin's succulent neck-skin, soft-pinching, leaving my mark. Sheer shimmers when I, Miss Sucker-Bite Specialist, am plying my craft—I take pride in my skill at painlessly causing purple blotches to appear on unblemished skin. (I call them sucker-bites instead of hickeys because I first heard them referred to as such in middle school, a happy recollection.) I'm a lithe skin-sucking vampire beast who thrills to the gentle wounding of flesh with my mouth. I admire my art afterwards—enjoy tracing the wounds with my fingertips, causing nearby skin to twitch. It's immensely delicious for pictures of sucker-bite-creation to accompany me as I add comments to the [_____] shareholder's agreement. (Still a new matter, but trust Rikert to ensure it's soon billable.)

One of the most memorable pictures is of our clothes scattered all over the carpet after we're done—not to mention the stuff that used to be on his desk (our make-do bed) in a heap against the wall, and we're drenched with sweat. How rash, and deliriously fulfilling, to engage in full nudity frolic at the firm. The door was locked, sure, and, had anyone knocked, Martin would've yelled he was on a personal call—and done it with stress in his voice, so they went away. But we were both pretty astonished and slightly uneasy. We were surveying the scene and exchanging glances and our eyes were saying something along the lines of: "What a spell we were under! Are we insane?"

It was nearly four when I phoned and I can't thank you enough, Darling, for dashing down with my emergency kit lickety-split. Martin had his gym bag with a big towel in it and we used that to dry off, but it wasn't close to sufficing for a girl. My hair was near-soaked in places, in utter disarray, and I don't know what I would've done without my brush and blow dryer. And I always worry about the sweet smell of sex giving the game away, so thanks for the perfume. I was in Martin's office for almost half an hour recreating my pre-frolic appearance. My makeup was so smudge city I had to baby oil everything off, start over.

So imagine it's bye-bye 'til morning, assuming I've sent this soon enough for you to read it now. I trust our Stevie's treating you well (Boy, are you two *ever* on a frolic-tear.) and can't wait for you to tell.

Your,

OfficeFrolicFloozy

III.2
Ella to Angie
Tuesday, July 1, 2003 8:17 PM

Stevie's been delayed. Seems the seamstress was fighting with her boyfriend on the phone and wailing and throwing stuff (Stevie knows this because her cousin gleefully spilled it.) and neglected her work. She's presently finalizing the costume, plus she's down on Delancey, so he probably won't be here until nine at the earliest.

You should've heard yourself when you phoned from Martin's office, your voice edgy with apprehension while lilting with elation—easy to ascertain your dizzy blurred frame of mind. What a happily fulfilled floozy! Oh, and get this: you say I brought your emergency kit lickety-split? Well, not nearly as lickety as I'd have liked! Because when I reached Martin's floor, guess who was gabbing in the hall, two doors down from his office? Why our favorites, of course! The two sloppiest autocratic schoolmarm partners: DeRhight and Blumklin!

The former darts me an unfriendly glance and the latter copies so, Honey, I keep walking. I was going to call from around the corner to let you know when I saw them waddling down the hall: took them forever to reach the elevator bank. The second they passed through the glass doors, I strolled down to make sure they were leaving. (Can't be too careful with those two.) When they entered an elevator and its door closed I raced back with your kit. So how do you feel, knowing the witches were so close?

When you opened Martin's office door after I did our knock twice, pause, knock three times... What a cute, ruffled, wet pussycat you were! Hair matted and tangled, eyes joyfully glazed, lipstick smeared! Hey, I'm very surprised and worried! You were so far gone you forgot to blot? I'm sure most of your lipstick was on Martin. Caution, girlfriend, is the ticket to continued frolic at the firm: you're my elder (So what if only by two months?) and I'm counting on you to lead by example.

Well, you *do* lead by example: I want to be just as taken by surprise, inundated with invigorating fearlessness. I envied you (brief glimpse though I got) when I saw you *so* sweaty, mussed, roused—and not even half dressed. It's something prudes will never experience: transcendence of self and tedious caution via a fine plowing at the firm. Prudes will never understand the whole wide restorative world of Slutdom.

Speaking of Slutdom, yours truly's in a pink-hinting-at-scarlet nightie—semi-transparent, feathered trim—awaiting tonight's adventure. I'm eager, tense, aroused already—becoming wet, nips tingly. OK, I don't want to blather about what hasn't happened, would rather relish anticipation privately—prance before the mirror, preen some more.

Signing off for tonight, Dearest: sleep healthful and wealthful once you've finished catching up with your neglected work, on account of frolicking with Martin. All kidding aside, though: I'm *so* glad it worked out scrumptious, am pleased as punch I facilitated.

Your,

RavenousForRaptureHarlot

III.3
Angie to Ella
Wednesday, July 2, 2003 11:34 AM

How come I haven't heard from you, neglectful girl? A Stevie night's a thrill-ride so I'm ablaze with curiosity, plus need uplifting reading to offset this due diligence index confirmation rubbish the incompetence of fools has thrust upon me. Confirming every document's account-ed for, double-checking the paralegals, lifts boredom to dispiriting heights. Rikert's having me do it because he wants it done right, once and for all, to stop the client raising a ruckus about time billed. Seems that worst of paralegals (What's her name: Sabine? Sappy? Sloppy? She should've stayed in litigation instead of infesting corporate.) got into the act and mislabeled stuff galore. Rikert's DNUed her from further involvement on his projects, but that's no consolation as I clean up her mess. Where's the accountability? Why isn't she fired? And right after my lauded role in the [_____] closing that ought to have earned me some respite.

Again, it would be appreciated if you could toss uplifting enter-tainment my way: I need a window on life's joyful aspect. I'm implor-ing, Sweetie! Please soothe with an engrossing adventure! Hurry and feed your poor due diligence flogged Angie an absorbing narrative.

Your,

VicariousThrillThirstyVamp

III.4
Ella to Angie
Wednesday, July 2, 2003 12:41 PM

Patience, please! On it but not nearly done. It was impossible to get a jumpstart on recapitulation at home, since Stevie stayed until we left for work. We showered and then he lingered in the bathroom, watched me do makeup, nails, hair—the whole girl dress-up shebang that en-tertains him so, from panties and stockings and perfume to earrings and bangles and barrette. He says he wants to see how a mystery's put together, have a front row seat on the girl-arsenal of cosmetics, underthings, clingy fabric, fluffed hair. Says he needs a refresher course in hook-and-eye clasps, mascara wands, base application. Says it's up to me—because he showed me a good time, and I owe him—to rectify shortcomings of his childhood education. Says he missed Mass last Sunday and watching me dress will be a stand-in religious experience. Says his imagination's drained of stirring images and he needs it filled up. Says watching a girl primp is enlightening, therapeutic, salvational, dispenses emotional fortitude. (Ha, is anything our Stevie says to be taken at face value? And we *adore* that, right?) Meanwhile, he starts licking-nibbling my thighs up to where they curl into my tush—seizes the latter, squeezes—ooooo! flips me inside out! And now I'm nearly in that sensation again.

But you've called me neglectful, made a bad assumption, Unjust Miss, when the fact is I've been conscientiously busy with recapitulation since setting foot in my office—made possible by the other side taking forever to get back to us with counter-comments on the [____] S-1. A fair amount's done but you don't get a word of it until later. Yeah, good show, behaving like a pestering client—the more you pester the longer it'll take, and I won't compromise quality to slice off time. Sometimes we have leeway to make pestering clients wait a good while after we're done with a task, so I believe I'll be doing such with you! Hahaha!

Your,

PleasedToTeaseElla

III.5
Angie to Ella
Wednesday, July 2, 2003 1:04 PM

I make a crack in jest and you get miffed? I can't tongue-in-cheek chide you without running the risk of you using it as an excuse to dredge up flustered dignity, get high and mighty on me, seek to guilt me? Oh, and comparing me to a pestering client? Threatening to do to me what we do to pestering clients, make them wait sometimes *much* longer because the parameters of an assignment make it possible? Like, when we very conscientiously apply ourselves to completing an assignment as quickly as possible without compromising accuracy, then gleefully *sit on it* because some twit is behaving unprofessionally? And you're planning on doing that to your best girl, who'd kill for you? Shame on you!

Your,

Mistreated'N'MisusedMiss

III.6
Ella to Angie
Wednesday, July 2, 2003 10:27 PM

(Quick note, necessitated by your interruptions earlier: missive commences without reference to said interruptions, since was commenced well before you started being a pest. Additionally took longer because, as expected, some [_____] S-1 action happened.)

Sweetheart! Again our Stevie promised and again he delivered, we're truly blessed he's in our lives. First, he arrives from Delancey Street annoyed, hardly glances at me, yells along the lines of: "Goddamn lovelorn lunatic seamstress, simpering masochist! Couldn't stop blubbering about her boyfriend while making final adjustments! She's so tearful on account of affection rejected she lets her finger wander under the needle and gets stabbed, plus messes up part of the hem and has to do it over! I'm there having to put on a face of sympathy and assure her the guy's childish and shortsighted!—taking care to strike a balance, not overdo the negative, because she loves him and he must therefore be a prince who's worthy of such love! I loathe having to listen to crybaby relationship crap, a comparative stranger forcing it on me in a professional situation—emotionally blackmailing me because I needed this costume done! Hope you appreciate the costume!"

"You *know* I appreciate it, Stevie! Thank you, thank you!" I gush, hastening to wrap my arms around his neck, soothe with a kiss.

But he nudges me away, resumes speaking vehemently, still uncharacteristically hardly glancing at me (usually he eye-rapes me dizzy): "It's demoralizing when some ninny decides she's been trampled on by a man, subjects me to recitation of how ghastly it makes her feel! Same with whiny guys! Male or female, same difference! When they're of a mind to wallow in self-pity on account of love gone sour, they're the most insufferable idiots! The seamstress detailed her ills, cursed one Tyler, sought to draw me in! I'm only there to pick up the costume she was supposed to have ready by seven, right? Despite the bother of waiting I'm in an elevated mood, since I've worlds of bliss to look forward to with you! Seamstress resents my good cheer, gives me a clinging borderline parasitical look, bewails her situation with multiplied fervor, as if I'm expected to do something about it! Her demeanor's saying: 'You've no right to be happy when I'm miserable—no right to look forward to a blissful night when my man's been mean and I'm in hell—no right to believe in joy in another's arms when all I've gotten from it is living death.' That's what the seamstress is saying between the lines and, try as I might, I can't stop it threatening to negatively affect me! The moment she finished the costume, I fled as if from the maw of hell! Her clinging eyes are still in my head! Self-pitying killjoy! What a menace! It was like she was going all out to put a curse on our night!"

"I'd say it's safe to say we're immune from curses, Stevie!" I laugh, again seeking to slip my tongue between his lips, wrap a leg about his legs and wiggle, kickstart our fun, ignite a blaze. I want him to forget the simpering seamstress, honor my hot lil' tramp's body that's gift-wrapped in a fur-fringed pink nightie. I know he likes the wrapping and likes what's inside the wrapping and I won't be nudged aside again. Unbelievably, he attempts it. I seize the offending nudge-me-aside hand, squeeze tight, then reach up his arm, kiss his cheeks, tickle his ears, coo sweetness. Oh, he likes it—adores ear-tickles—gets scrunchy delighted, like he can't help it. If only he'd clasp me close, kiss me,

But Stevie twists his head away, seizes my wrists, says: "Stop trying to draw me into cuddling and cast a veil over the image that troubles me! The resentful eyes of the seamstress are still ablaze in my mind's eye, poisoning these moments! Regardless of whether I want to be, I'm haunted by the thought of love's casualties! We're going to need to do an awful lot tonight to kick the unhealthy idea of love's emotional wreckage out of my head! I'm going to need help to defeat negativity, step back into the light of love's bliss! Sweet Ella, do you understand?"

"Perfectly," I answer, delight inundating my veins. Is my moment nigh? Will I soon be sighing to the tune of Stevie's lips upon mine? Will his hands soon be seizing and squeezing, conducting explorations of, my caress-craving curves? Damn! He's still gripping my wrists, holding me away—still being difficult. Why won't he pull me close, open the sluice of the dam behind which desire churns, have his way with me?

"The seamstress is a disgrace!" I declare, eager to court Stevie's favor—get him to grant the wish I know he's reading in my eyes—by echoing his ravings. "It's tacky to trot out one's misery, with no thought as to whether it'll infect and depress others. Life's already far too fraught with stress, wrong turns, sour emotions, unfulfill-ment—everyone gets their share—so the hell with people who go about advertising their troubles, scattering their gloom, infecting the well-being of others. Clinging leeches is what they are—eager to hob-ble spontaneous joy. Nothing's more unhealthy than someone who's begging for pity, because anyone who's begging for pity is annoyed that I'm not. Just keep people like that away from me. They're poisonous; they're dangerous; they'd rather I dropped dead than experience a happy moment in front of them."

Before I can finish this fine speech, Stevie shoves me a bit, says: "So you're making a show of sympathy, seeking to soften me with playacted heat of conviction? It's interesting that you're seeking to ingratiate yourself by chiming in with my annoyance at the seamstress, considering you're the one responsible for my having to listen to her wailings on account of the costume I had to get for you. It's... "

"But the costume was your idea—a good idea," I interrupt.

"Who instructed you to speak when I'm speaking?" he inquires with an evil grin—an immensely pleasing grin, since I know such a grin always precedes something as interesting as amusing—in a word: *action*. "I thought you were a well-bred sophisticated city girl, perfectly primped and poised, with immaculate manners. But if your mommy neglected to adequately instruct regarding manners. If she failed to instill... Oh, hell! Just get on the couch, ill-mannered Miss! Gyrate and strip!"

A girl never knows how a Stevie night will flow, and that's no small part of a Stevie night's appeal. I kick off my slippers, stand on the couch (adore the sensation of my bare tootsies sinking into silky cushions), start winking and licking my lips while doing itsy-bitsy flick-ups of nightie's hem—a sort of decoy move, this latter bit, since I'm meanwhile peeling it off from above, slipping the shoulder straps down my arms, allowing my breasts to spill from neckline's fur trim. When my clothes fall off and my nakedness hits the open air as an adored man's eye-raping me I feel invisible hands upon my curves, immediately feel head to toe scrumptious squishy, become gushy wet.

Seems I've misunderstood Stevie's command. He says: "Silly girl, not a simple slip off the nightie routine! What's more typical? Take it off, yes, but when I say *Strip!* I mean shred that nightie, snip it into strips! Here you go. *(He hands me a pair of scissors. I've no idea where he obtained them.)* OK, slice up your pretty nightie! Cut it into ribbons, then hand them over!" I kneel on the couch, commence snipping.

"No!" he yells. "Not on knees, scrunched up in a ball and hiding half yourself! I can neither see the length of your legs nor your twitchy wenchalacious ass! Here, hand them back! *(He takes the scissors, tosses them on the floor.)* Into my lap you go! Righto, your skin's liquid silk—what a lissome plaything!" He's sucking—nipping—my neck; seizing—caressing stimulatingly soft—my breasts. But suddenly he shouts, "Christ Almighty!" and stops. "Lithe scrumptious svelte slut of immaculate musculature," he continues, "it isn't easy to keep my hands and tongue off, and then my blood rushes and I stiffen! I'll bet you're very pleased about that—preening yourself before your ego's mirror because I'm under your spell! We'll see who's the most under the other's spell—dictating the terms of this engagement, laying down the law! Discipline's in order! Hell! Have I left something out?"

So cute! Stevie's slightly glaze-eyed—seems to be seeking to figure out what sort of storyline to frame our frolicking in. (He's clearly discarded pretending to be haunted by the seamstress' complaints, the love's wreckage stuff.) Finally, he flops me onto my tummy, across his knees, reaches down for the scissors, his tummy briefly pressed to my back. "Want a job done right, got to do it myself!" he yells, cutting about three inches into my nightie's hem all around, making it fringed. "Bet this flimsy thing's ridiculously expensive! Am I right? What sucker did you con into laying out for this silky number? Oh, very high class!" he snarls. "And I'm ripping it into strips! Did you believe my hemline-cuts were decorative? They're preparation!" He tosses the scissors aside, begins tearing my nightie into ribbons. "Stay still, no use squirming! You won't be salvaging this souvenir from an ex-lover! What a conniving—gold-digging—ass-auctioning—strumpet you are!"

I adore being complimented while rough-handled by a capable man—Stevie absolutely knows what soars me. Allusions to petite moi getting males to shower me with pricey trinkets, plus assertions my assets are a shapely behind, cute face, beguiling personality. I'll play any game a man wants me to play if he leads me to believe he thinks I'm no different than a well-paid kitty of fine pedigree in a kittyhouse! I don't know why this is the case and I don't care why! It simply IS!

"I see you're resisting, seem to believe escape's possible," Stevie observes. "Time to lay that misinformed belief to rest!" Suiting action to words, he ties a ribbon of my shredded nightie about my ankles. "Anything to say, gold-digger? Any smartassed remarks?" he taunts. "Whatever you wish to say, you won't be saying it!" he continues, wadding up another ribbon, stuffing it in my mouth. Then he binds my wrists—not only together but also to a belt of additional ribbon he ties around my waist, thereby immobilizing my arms—I can neither raise them nor move them left or right; and, damn girl, the effect of being thoroughly tied up and rendered helpless is I'm like as not to leap out of my skin for joy! It's gratifying to be extensively attended to, a man taking so much trouble on my behalf! Because I'm not making it easy! I'm wildly writhing, flexing my knees—my ankles might be bound together but I can still kick! Oh, my thoughts are blurring! I'm losing awareness of everything besides my hot hungering flower-puss—tingling breasts, earlobes—tightening tummy, flushing cheeks.

"Have you gained weight?" Stevie suddenly asks, and I freeze with terror in every sinew. He's pushing just about my worst button in the cause of fun and play—being contrary, knifing me mentally, so's to scramble my emotions, transform my body into a mood oscillation machine. But the question (that I've *never* been asked) is so unexpected, mocking and shocking, I lose the ability to place it in game-context: it's as if I've been doused with frigid water, tossed in a snowbank. From happy radiant slut I whirl into paralysis of desire. How could he be *that* nasty, sadistic? Sure, I'm well aware of how much I weigh—I monitor my weight as conscientiously as a nurse monitors a heart patient's pulse—and my weight's precisely where I want it, but such is immaterial: the fact I've been asked such a debasing, unconscionably cruel, question is so outrageous I hardly know what to say! I take exceptional care of myself, am slender, fit, firm! So how dare he? From shock I flip to fury! Alas, I'm tied up and muffled: what can I do?

"Yeah, that got your attention," Stevie laughs. "Bound like a pig as you are, it seems you've become heavy as a pig on my lap, so onto the floor with you." He turns me onto my back (I've been on my tummy the while), lifts me and thence lowers me to the carpet, adding with an infuriating grin: "Maybe you ought to consider dieting."

"Aaaahhh!" I scream through the ribbon crammed in my mouth, glaring at Stevie like I want him dead. "Aaaahhh! Aaaahhh! Aaaahhh!" I'm screaming loud as I can (I'm not sure how well *Aaaahhh!* approximates screaming but so be it and, thankfully, the ribbon's muffling me: it wouldn't do to alarm my neighbors.), relishing every moment. Supremely uplifting to reach way down inside myself, shriek for all I'm worth as I yank at the ribbons binding me, strain to escape. Stevie, bless him, is treating me to an extremely liberating experience.

"Come now, my sweet," he suddenly says in the gentlest tone, with precisely the gaze of affection every girl lives to see in a man she admires. "You know I'm kidding! I'll let you in on a fiendish male secret," he continues, bending to softly caress—caresses I spurn with grimaces of disgust and hisses, and by rolling away. But he straddles me to halt the rolling; ignoring my continued glares and hisses, he continues: "It's not something we men need to be taught—just basic survival instinct, infallible means of puncturing a girl's vanity should she become insufferable. The question 'Have you gained weight?' deflates and enrages the female ego like no other; it haunts a female like nothing else could do, when she's examining herself in the mirror afterwards and wondering if it's *really* true! Hahaha!"

If only I could rip the ribbons away, leap free, claw him! He's not only admitted to toying with me but is pleased as punch concerning the nefarious method employed, mocking women in general. He definitely deserves a clawing. Hahaha! It's delicious to play at rage, Angie! It's, as Kafka says (admittedly in reference to something totally different), an ax with which I'm breaking apart the ice of my frozen inner sea. Plus the more I slip into the role of being infuriated, the more our Stevie will make nice with rejuvenating looks, and oodles of other delights.

"Come now, Ella, ease off with the dagger-glare," he says softly, gentle-firmly grasping the sides of my head to stop me twisting my face away as he kisses me forehead to throat. "I apologize for subjecting you to the rile-a-girl question. I acted disgracefully, and without cause."

I make a show of wincing with annoyance, indicating I'm nowhere near willing to forgive, so's to be treated to additional comforting words and caresses and kisses. Stevie's kind gaze is tingling me dizzy.

"Do you have any idea how rejuvenating you are?" he asks, continuing to make nice. "Allow me to describe yourself to you: there's slender symmetry, with just the right amount of curviness, the likes of which would suit Aphrodite. Your skin's mouth-wateringly soft and smooth, healthy, glowing—your complexion's revelation. Waves of vitality ebb and flow among, lend stirring radiance to, the heavenly contours of your visage. And the silver flashing in your sapphire eyes, hinting at emotional depths that will never be plumbed. Ella, you're an invitation to overcome annoyances, annihilate tedium, visit an oasis of the extraordinary, and I'd like to take you up on that invitation. I want to gaze upon and caress you, turn electric, until I forget my name."

So Stevie's altered the framework again. I'm no longer a shamelessly gold-digging hussy deserving of discipline, nor am I overweight (as if that's within the realm of possibility). Now I'm what I truly want to be and what our Stevie always makes me feel I am: a beauty deserving of adoring ministration. I soften my eyes, gaze kindly upon him; I indicate via a couple drawn out "Uhmmmm!"s—a sound the ribbon in my mouth permits me to make—how pleased I am. He's momentarily lost in thought, mulling options—shortly thereafter crosses the room, grabs my plant-mister—returns and mists me, says: "Delectable flower dusted by morning dew as the sun rises, spills golden scarlet over her irresistible musculature. Observe how droplets trace the flawless lines of the flower's curves, find the valleys and flow through them. Ella, you're a pristine stream and I'm perishing of thirst. I'm a wayfarer in a vast desert, with a throat so parched it's swelling, near to choking me, and I need to drink of you to remain alive." Then he twists off the plant-mister's top, slowly pours water from my throat to my thighs while holding it higher than his head. What a scrumptiously tickling tap-tap trickle—silver streamlets shattering into droplets over me.

Then Stevie's lapping the water off me—his tongue darting from throat to breasts to tummy to calves—rising to midriff, forearms, biceps, forehead, then back down. Licks, kisses, nibbles, caresses, squeezes simultaneously surround me—he's touching me so silk-softly it's like his fingers are ten more tongues. Nor to forget I'm firmly bound: sensation accumulates, outright throbs, as a consequence of being immobilized. Freedom of movement would more evenly distribute stimulation, scatter it from my extra sensitive spots: accumulation of delicious crazy tickles in my special places is so forceful it's as if I've been Tantric, hoarding hunger, for days. Stevie's quivering against me, our legs intertwined, when he shouts: "I want to be the water shaping itself to your contours, hug you as close as it's able to do, mirror your skin with mine—want to blur the boundaries of our bodies, so I can't tell where your skin ends and mine begins—want to sparkle in your nerves, flow through your veins, unite with your heartbeat! Christ! Why did I tie your ankles here?" He's referring to the fact he's unable to spread my legs far enough to facilitate frontwards entry: he's bound my ankles nearly at mid-shin. "Fine, turn over!" (He rolls me onto my tummy, assists me to my knees.) "Good, raise your rear, forehead to floor—I'll be your doggie-woggie! Are you OK? I don't want to strain your neck."

The new problem is that, after binding my wrists, he tied them to the ribbon-belt at my waist: in a raised-rear position I'm unable to support myself in front with my elbows, can only use my head, and the rocking motion induced by his plowing of me may stress my neck. Bless him, Stevie's always hyper-vigilant concerning a girl's safety. He's shouting: "Disgraceful lack of foresight, failure to account for anatomical limitations! Sit upright, please, so I can remove these ribbons. (Utilizing the scissors that aren't far away on the floor, he cuts the ribbons at my waist and wrists.) Good, we're set!" But he's soon yelling again: "Doggie's for dogs! I want to gaze into your eyes! Can't fully unite with a girl without her eyes guiding me! Back on your back and off with these! (He cuts the ribbons at my ankles.) And let's give you the gift of speech!" He removes the ribbon that's stuffed in my mouth.

I'm giggling—Stevie's saying: "You're right to laugh! You trusted me to treat you a swept-out-of-your-senses experience, and what happens? I stall matters by overlooking simple logistical details, as in a girl with tied up legs isn't able to spread them very far."

"But being tied up was sweeping me out of my senses," I smile, fluttering my eyelids. "Why did you unbind me, undo all your good work, sabotage freedom-via-restraint?" I poke him in the ribs.

"Because when I do this (He thrusts himself inside me; I go "Oooommm!," make a lil' pleasure wince.) I want to gaze into the crystals of your eyes and fall inside them until I'm at least under the illusion I'm meshing with your life-surge. I want to read the ebb and flow and swells of sensation inside you, thrill to fluctuations in dilation of your pupils—want to absorb your vitality while inundating you with mine. I want our personalities obliterated in the interest of uniting in procreation—want to reach temporary oblivion, go to the rebirth-via-blackout-of-myself place. (He's steadily thrusting, alternating deep plunges with near withdrawals: he teasingly retreats so's to stun me with a fresh advance.) The eyes mirror the soul, and what energy flares in your blue crystals—shimmering silvery surges! Why can't we exchange places? Why can't I gaze into my eyes from yours? I come maddeningly near to believing I'm diving into your eyes, living there, then realize I'm still only gazing at them from the outside. Abundance of teasing intimations but the distance can't be crossed."

He does a zipping-mouth-shut gesture across his lips with thumb and forefinger, indicating he isn't going to speak anymore—seizes my wrists in one hand and holds them over my head to the carpet; wraps his other arm about a thigh, compelling me to lift my knee; presses his chest to my breast, kisses me gentle-insistent—lo! I'm firmly pinned, immobile again! Vibrant shivers—hints of spasms—surge into my tummy, spread throughout me; waves are swelling, seeking to roll into breakers, foam. I tighten myself downstairs, get extra taut, seek to make it tougher for Stevie to pierce me; then when he thrusts through my resistance the slick wet friction's caressing ticklish sparkling claws. I strain to yank my arms free—test his strength outside of me as well as inside. He fights me off, keeps me firmly pinned, and it's such density of sensation I'm tumbling into blurred brightness, seeing everything swimming.

I've attempted oodles to accurately convey orgasm—always come up short and, truth to tell, wouldn't want it otherwise. Orgasm's miraculous, elusive—I love an unsolvable mystery. Time warps, condenses, concentrates—seconds are worth days and weeks. Lust-accumulation's constantly stalking me, deviling me, and then I'm as if passing through a needle's eye, wildly expansive afterwards—the changeover's insanely swift. I'm rigid, contracting, convulsive—bursting in my tummy, aflail in a multitude of blurred whirling kaleidoscopic images. My calves occasionally cramp, shoulders grindingly ache, pre-orgasm, so tight do I become! Then serenity hits me like I'm occupying the sky.

(The French are dead-on accurate: calling orgasm la petite mort is genius. Orgasm's communion with the cycle of life and participation in birth implies association with death; renewal's only possible when something constraining's cast off, as when a snake sheds its skin. Orgasm flushes away irritation as it allows joy to surge; therefore, a part of oneself—never mind one wishes it gone—always dies. And you and I, Angie, are dying a lot more often than the average girl! We're orgasm-addicted dishlings who can't go an hour without getting the urge!)

So I've beaten Stevie to the flood—am in expansive, sighing, influx of serenity mode when his hot splash washes my womb, and all I'm saying with regard to that is it often seems to me my body's a toy to play with, an electric dancing-of-the-senses machine. Then we're alongside one another tummy to tummy on the carpet, laughing and bantering. A priceless part of a Stevie night's the postplay banter, right?

Would be a labor of Hercules to faithfully transcribe our banter. Lively conversation's a living entity with a will of its own, unpredictably twists and turns, loath to be controlled by puny humans; tangents galore occur seemingly of their own accord; unexpected topics seize one's attention, suggest new ones. Does anyone have a clue what they'll wind up speaking about? And another reason it's impossible to do conversations justice in transcription is that facial expressions and nuances of voice (as well as tickles, pokes, caresses, kisses) are an invaluable component. So I'll attempt to approximate a couple examples of our postplay banter, near as I'm able to recollect and mainly because it's fun.

First Example:

"What's with licking me until I'm soaked, mad-tongued saliva-fetish wench?" Stevie asks. "My face is drenched! (He runs a finger over his cheeks where I've licked him, then wipes the wetness on mine.) Ha, subliminal makeup! Ever thought of mixing saliva with rouge?—mixing flowerpuss nectar with face-base, infusing eyeshadow with procreative juice? No telling how powerfully it would affect males, subliminally enchant them, change them into happy slaves. I'm sure it's occurred to a flirt like you! You're constantly secreting honey—a permanently wet-pantied bunny, so why not use it? Liquid gold shouldn't go to waste."

"Pretty transparent pretense of ignorance," I respond, leaning in to lick one of his cheeks. "You know full well I adore messy drippy kissies during love, getting slippery-faced together—I'm a slippery-slide girl, our cheeks seeming to melt because soaked. I just like to like it, OK? And you can pin me to the floor and imprison my arms all you want: you'll never stop me from licking, making you wet. (I trace a wide circle around his mouth.) Right, I was pinned but you couldn't stop me! You made yourself vulnerable, those times when you left off with kissing to treat me to an I've-turned-into-a-wondering-child gaze. Even the most scrumptiousliest eye-communion won't stop me lovingly anointing you! (I lick his other cheek; he retaliates by turning me onto my tummy, love tapping my behind; between giggle-attacks I continue speaking.) As for mixing love juice with makeup, trust a mixed-up male to suppose we girls do that! There isn't a chance I'll be diluting the formula of my makeup—I pay a pretty penny for my makeup, won't be tampering with it. Nor will I do damage to my self-esteem by supposing I need to resort to silly subliminal tricks (of dubious effectiveness) to have boys salivating like starving dogs. There are plenty of attributes of this wench that reliably get the boys gape-eyed, not the least of which is the ass that's presently fascinating and tempting you, as always."

Second Example:

"Damn hair-trigger trollop!" Stevie exclaims with feigned exasperation. "A few tickles of your inner thigh and some tummy-sucking and you gush again. You're so permanently lust-wound I'll bet the simple sensation of wearing tight-fitting frilly panties stimulates your passionflower enough for you to cream, and if you're not wearing panties I'm sure breeze blowing up your skirt will do! I'll bet..."

"Sure thing," I interrupt, pouncing on this engaging subject. "I'm sex-disturbed from the moment I open my eyes of a morning, unable to climb out of bed and brave the new day without scampering my fingers to Miss Muffy. I tweak my love-nubble at morning tea, fondle my flowerpetals in the shower, probe myself with one hand while wielding a mascara wand with the other. Such is merely teasing and priming, though—prepping of pinkling for the cab ride to work. If I'm not oozing by the time I arrive at the firm, I consider it a bad omen concerning the rest of the day. That is, I'm sure I'd need to consider it a bad omen: to date, my nectar's never failed to flow during morning commute—I know I can rely on pleasure-puss to bless me with favorable auspices. Fact is, all I need do is cross my legs and jiggle! Am I telling the truth, Stevie? Or putting you on for the purpose of stoking male fantasies? Well, a girl's got to have her secrets, so I'm not telling if I've made it up or not—secrets are an aphrodisiac in their own right. Secrets..."

"Secrets, shmeecrets!" Stevie counter-interrupts. "Secrets only have value if the person one's keeping them from actually gives a dead horse's ass. Have all the secrets you want, I'm not going to be dying to pry them from you. Ha, that's girl vanity in all its delusional glory! You think we men are upset that we owe our existence to the female vagina, as if there isn't some male seed involved. You think we're pathetic creatures who stumble through life utterly baffled by the fact we spent the first nine months of our existence cradled inside something you possess that we don't. You think we're immensely intimidated by our mommies because they're a former place of habitation and, by extension, intimidated and frightened of all females, consciously or not. Supposedly we're prone to assign all manner of mystery to females and feel inferior as a consequence. Supposedly we're so hung up about feminine mystery we extend this to every girl-secret, no matter how trite and insipid. Supposedly we have nothing better to do than sit around wondering what you chat about in the girls' room. Yeah, supposedly! Because, darling Ella pie, it's really just your ridiculously inflated female egos dreaming up far-fetched reasons to feel superior to men."

#########

It's been a long day, Angie—many interruptions, not the least of which was when you semi-traumatized me by falsely accusing me of being neglectful, when I'd already pounced in this missive. So I'm done, despite the fact the second banter-example's incomplete. My reply follows—I tease Stevie, say what he said's a confession, then there's his reply, then much tickle-tussling, but not for you. If you're going to call me a neglectful girl then I'm going to turn around and *be* one.

Yeah, plenty more delight was had, the rushing dip and sway of a Stevie night—mood-shifts he flings me through, breaking apart of my mind-set. As for the costume Stevie went to so much trouble to get and that sent me stratospheric once I put it on, I'm not telling what kind it was.

Your,

CycleOfLifeAndDeathDarling (ByAngieAbused)

III.7
Angie to Ella
Wednesday, July 2, 2003 11:09 PM

Sweetie, you've written a great deal, amused me mightily, and you know I appreciate it and love you so stop being a baby, sulking like a spoiled priss. Ridiculous that playful joking's gotten twisted and turned into a full-fledged insult! Time to grow up and let it go.

You're the one behaving badly, Ella—you're misusing *me*. After all the fanfare about the costume—what Stevie was willing to put up with to obtain it, how special it is—I would think you'd have the decency to disclose what kind of costume it is. Stop teasing and tormenting your best friend! I want to know what kind of costume it is NOW!

Your,

NotToBeToyedWithTrollop

III.8
Ella to Angie
Wednesday, July 2, 2003 11:18 PM

But, Sweetest, I'm authentically distressed by your classification of me as "neglectful." The manner in which you jumped the gun, thoughtlessly falsely accused me, is communication breakdown verging on traumatic. I'm trembling as I key these words, will have difficulty sleeping.

Nor am I seeking tease you: perish the thought. It's just a silly costume, right? So who cares? And me tease you? How is such possible? You're the eldest, more experienced. I unhesitatingly acknowledge you as the Mistress of Tease, and wouldn't dream of messing with the Mistress.

Your,

DissedAndDisturbedDamsel

III.9
Angie to Ella
Wednesday, July 2, 2003 11:25 PM

But, Sweeeeetest! Don't you know that if you continue trying my patience with this fake victim act, childish withholding of information, I'll be retrieving Miss Whippie from her hiding place in the closet and flaying your sweeeeetest lil' behind raw? Don't you know Miss Whippie will wound the silk-soft ultra-sensitive skin on the insides of your sweeeeetest thighs? Huh, Sweeeeetest? Don't you know your chastisement will be swift and merciless; that I won't lift a finger to intervene as Miss Whippie makes you writhe and squeal? But 'tis easily avoided, Sweeeeetest! Simply stop wailing about nonexistent persecution and provide me with the information I covet, and all will be forgiven. Tell me what kind of costume it is THIS INSTANT!

Your,

WickedWhippieWieldingWench

III.10
Ella to Angie
Wednesday, July 2, 2003 11:36 PM

Sweetest, when have you known me to turn down a date with Miss Whippie? A date with Miss Whippie's most edifying, and necessary for a spoiled BratCat like me. How else am I to be restored to balance and perspective, shown that being a pampered princess doesn't entitle me to feel secure at all times? How else am I to taste of physical and emotional distress and thereby gain a greater appreciation of the feelings of wellbeing I generally enjoy? How else am I to experience some psyche-balancing humility? You know as well as I do that Miss Whippie's an essential component of our relationship. If I'm misbehaving at the moment, trying to tease you, then I'm doubtless overdue for a session.

Sweetest, I'm absolutely NOT telling you what kind of costume it is, much less what enlightening activities Stevie and I pursued after I put it on. Miss Whippie needs to beat everything out of me.

Your,

CravingEdificationElla

III.11
Angie to Ella
Wednesday, July 2, 2003 11:58 PM

Yummy, Sweetest—it's a Miss Whippie date, we'll make the time. Why does part of me occasionally need to discipline others, in a vividly physical way? It's not like I'm a meek girl and need to dabble in aggression to compensate. I suppose it comes down to how I go about disciplining. Of course I'm without mercy as far as ensuring authentic discomfort's applied, but—OK, Ella, I know you understand, as you do all else connected with me. I mete out discipline with such love in my heart, care upwelling from within: so much tenderness I have for you when cracking the leather across your immaculate behind. It's like the compassion inside me's welling too strong for me to continue breathing—sometimes—when I'm leaning in hard with the strokes, causing you to twist and moan. It's like I'm near to fainting when grimaces assault your radiant face; when your legs, feet, hands convulsively jerk; when you cry out, or plaintively whisper-warble. I sometimes need that weak-kneed sensation to weaken me—need your discomfort to inundate me with wildly ungovernable love.

Sweetest, I'm pausing to flex my wrists, make whip-wielding movements—so delightful's the anticipation. I know you speak true when you assert you want Miss Whippie to sting you; likewise, I speak true when I say I want to become erratic in my breathing, teeter on the edge of a swoon for love of you, while administering discipline.

Your,

PleasedToBeProddedToPunishPussycat

IV. Circumstances of Spying

IV.1
Angie to Ella
Thursday, July 3, 2003 10:57 AM

E lla, it seems a girl isn't safe from spying eyes anywhere, even when she's in a locked office. You heroically brought me my lifesaving clean up kit lickety-split on Tuesday after Martin and I made each other mussed and sweaty; you avoided the notice of DeRhight and Blumklin, lingering not far from his door—you asked me (sorta smiling) how I felt about those rule-enforcing witches (with the power to enforce rules) being so close. I unfortunately answer: there's more than those witches to worry about in this minefield-littered world. By the time you arrived with my kit the windows of Martin's office had already betrayed us.

Gist of it: some pathetic meddling busybody at the firm across the street witnessed our desktop delirium, apparently couldn't rest easy until phoning the firm, ratting us out—called HR yesterday. Easy for the spy to pinpoint our location—counted eleven windows from our building's east side, forty-one from its base—HR informed me of such.

As for how it was discovered I was the girl, your guess is as good as mine. Did a HR stooge investigate? If so, said stooge could've been waiting to see who emerged from Martin's office, even seen you bring my washy up stuff. Would like to think the firm's above such things but HR people can be a different animal, something like secret police. Can't take anything for granted with HR, assume concessions will be granted—that a sterling work-record, glowing annual reviews, will carry weight. Some just don't care, are solely focused on enforcement.

Poor Martin! He's at the tail end of his first year, hasn't had as many opportunities to prove himself as us, and now an indiscretion. And I'm the cause! Would you believe it? He phoned to apologize for getting me in trouble, when I'm the more responsible party by far. If I hadn't been suckered by Linda's mangling of the truth, teased him, baited him, tormented him! And how could I have failed to note the danger of leaving the shades up, not anticipated chance of a witness? Swarms of windows opposite, only a cross-street's width away. I told Martin to stop worrying on my account—was touched to my bones, explained I was the bad one, apologized profusely. To be neglectful when I'm the sole person who may suffer consequences is bad enough; to be neglectful when a very decent man's at risk is an absolute disgrace.

Here's the situation: Rikert, as my billing partner, has been informed of my alleged indiscretion; Laerfield, as Martin's billing partner, has been informed of his alleged indiscretion. A meeting of partners has been called to review the matter, decide what disciplinary action should be taken. I know this from Lenny in Secretarial who, as we know, always knows everything. (How he does I'll never know, but that's one of the mysteries of the gossip pipeline, which is mystery and miracles itself. How news does travel, and what a pipedream "Private and Confidential" is in this place. Want a secret to remain secret? Then keep it to yourself or only tell a TRUSTED confidant (You're my one and only within these walls.); otherwise, the whole place will know about it insanely fast. I'd lay a bet the contents of many HR files have wound up in the gossip pipeline, been discussed at length. "Private and Confidential" is an absolute joke. Like, for instance, those links to surveys the central office sends us and they inform us the link is unique to ourselves but also confidential. Hahaha! Is *anyone* naïve enough to buy it?)

So that's the story—I'll be informed of the meeting's outcome today. Hopefully, I'll have good news and we'll be laughing. But I'm by no means counting my laughs in advance. Unwise to tempt fate.

Your,

TreacherouslyTattledUponTartlet

IV.2
Ella to Angie
Thursday, July 3, 2003 11:09 AM

Angie, are you kidding me? Neither you nor Martin thought to draw the shades? I'm aghast! Too mesmerized with one another, were you? So cute!—actually, NOT a bit cute! For shame—you know better!

Alright, I'm going to plunge into the hallways and secretarial clusters, pick up on the prevailing mood, see where the wind's blowing.

Hang on—calling Martin now.

Martin? He was laughing, joking—too proud to acknowledge the worry I detected in his voice. Such pride's the sign of a strong man.

Damn that informant to hell's innermost circle!

Getting back to you soon as I know!

Your,

PrivateInvestigatorPussycat

IV.3
Ella to Angie
Thursday, July 3, 2003 11:43 AM

A quick note, Honey. It's my feeling that, aside from unwanted attention that may get in the way of some future frolic opportunities, you have little to worry about. The prevailing view is this incident will blow over quickly, because it involves two hardworking attorneys who are involved in important transactions. Turns out Martin's had enough time to prove himself—the firm wouldn't want to lose him. And definitely decidedly emphatically the firm wouldn't want to lose *you*.

More to follow.

Your,

InordinatelyElatedElla

P.S. Calling Martin to tell him the good news.

IV.4
Angie to Ella
Thursday, July 3, 2003 1:14 PM

Thank you, Dearest, for selflessly gathering info where I dare not go! Martin and I are lying low and remaining inside our offices until the verdict's pronounced, plus my deal's likely to become active again later today and I'm awaiting instructions from Rikert—instructions that'll hopefully contain no reference to the Martin matter.

The "Martin matter"! Why not phrase it correctly, as in: the delightfulest doings of Martin and I in his office—my apology that transformed into supreme titillation, the room swaying and dipping and spinning, dimensionality a blur. I was gasp-panting in Rutsville, purring and meowling like the SexCat I am, so fast. Martin's shoving everything off his desk to make room—papers fluttering to the floor. I'm spreadeagled on the desk—my skin partly sticking to its hardwood surface, uncomfortably stretched when he undulates me about. (Could've used some oil.) But do I care? Ha, it's no wonder I neglect to notice the shades haven't been drawn! I'm too wildly galloping in my tummy whilst sucking Martin's neck to recall my name! And, hey, I'm getting lost in HappyRecollectionLand! If I was truly quaking in my boots, I wouldn't have the leeway to flit about in scrumptious memories.

Hey, I'm getting a kick out of sharing top-billing in today's number one gossip feature. My pillar-of-virtue personality (Ha!) has succumbed to carnal yearnings—I've uncharacteristically cast modesty aside in the cause of lust—and all are telling of it, investing me with an aura of notoriety. (Is notoriety a bad thing? Nay! It's free firm-wide publicity. All will know my name, plus it'll give me an opportunity to counter any bad feelings towards me by being ultra-sweet—an opportunity to win people over, make new friends. Nice people like to forgive.)

On the other hand, this is me warning myself not to be an imbecile: "Stop gloating, Angie! You know better than to make light of an event that could erode the high standing you and Martin have heretofore enjoyed at the firm. You know better than to take your pardons for granted, assume there'll be no distressing consequences. Especially, you know better than to allow yourself to tickled by a potentially disastrous situation, when there's another person involved and you're mainly responsible. And while it's true many people love to be given reasons to dispense benediction, others relish being judge and executioner. Think the informant across the street has any goodwill? There are others who have less! Wake up, Angie! Stop being an overconfident ninny!"

Still there's satisfaction (guilty-pleasure pride) in being talked about firm-wide for having frolicked in an office. And that there's apprehension mixed in, tension due to the meeting taking place, readying myself for the outcome: it makes for a swirl of purrishly pleasant inner friction, despite my attempts to caution myself against enjoying it. Right, the engrossing wait for the verdict! The reasonably strong sense all will end happily, coupled with the understanding that—in theory, at least—Martin and I could be shown the gate.

I can handle notoriety, but for God's sake let the Martin matter come to a sensible conclusion—I'll be such a good attorney for them. I mean, I already am—competitive me can't be anything else; but if they handle this nicely I'll be *wildly* grateful—I'll be such a stepping-up-to-the-plate girl when it comes to putting in extra time, going that extra mile, bringing smiles to our clients' faces. I *adore* my job.

I called Martin—he said: "There are worse things to be fired for, like incompetence or no social skills or a bad attitude. If I'm fired for having a good time, while otherwise focused on getting deals done and getting along with people, I'll survive. Plenty of other guys are dying of envy, because I kissed the prettiest girl in New York." You're right: he is worried below the banter but at least able to indulge in banter, keep worry at bay. This shoddy business has to turn out well.

Eagerly awaiting your follow-up.

Your,

Stimulatingly(DespiteMyself)StressedStrumpet

IV.5
Ella to Angie
Thursday, July 3, 2003 1:15 PM

I reiterate that the prevailing opinion—and I've spoken to lots of people—is you and Martin are too valuable not to be forgiven: you'll probably be given a rote warning, for appearance's sake. Mostly, people are having a high ol' time with your adventure and laughing with you, not at you. An engaging anecdote's surfaced: a partner was spied doing the identical thing in the identical manner (also tattled upon by a meddler across the way) when an associate. None other than Linda Vrauler, special envoy to the Supreme Court. People are making flattering jokes, as in maybe it's a sign you'll be fast-tracked as well. A favorable omen! (It's clear you'll make partner, but now there's a bona fide omen to expedite matters—fate's favoring you.) I inquired if said partner was disciplined. Seems she and her consort were merely advised not to do it again. As for her consort, he resigned after failing to make partner, then went on to start up a multi-million-dollar Internet commerce venture. So Martin's stars are also aligned.

Other blasts from the past are surfacing: Michael Trough was caught having fun with a paralegal in the records room; Ekaterina Vivarina (love her name) advanced her career (she's special counsel at Goldman) by sleeping with some partner who isn't here anymore; the previous second shift secretarial supervisor—described to me as a "voluptuous Venus, earthy and sensual, looked like she ought to be working in a bar"—rarely said no to any man, whether he was a partner or associate or in the mailroom or with maintenance. You've dredged all that up with your Martin escapade: the whole place is sexcapade recollection mania—amusing recollections and rumors flying thick and fast. People are grateful to you and Martin for having the decency to get caught.

To return to what's paramount: it's almost a foregone conclusion you and Martin will remain in the firm's good graces, the powers that be brushing your doings under the carpet. At any rate, I'm eagerly awaiting the official version, even if I'm sure it won't differ much from mine.

Your,

Gossip(PrevailingOpinion)GatheringGirly

IV.6
Ella to Angie
Thursday, July 3, 2003 1:24 PM

Honey, we Xed emails and so I'm wondering if my assessment that you and Martin are all but home free has deprived you of invigorating apprehension. Should I have withheld my assessment so you could thrill to your state of blood-stirring uncertainty longer? Are you annoyed?

OK, now I'm getting into the act: it's not appropriate for me to make light. It's alright for you and Martin to jest (It's psychic defense, alleviation of distress.), but I need to be sensible, vigilant, cautious, firmly grounded. Bad me—*bad*! (More Miss Whippie fuel, right?)

Your,

FauxPasFloozy

P.S. Absolutely awaiting the meeting's outcome with baited breath, on tenterhooks—fairly digging my nails into my palms.

IV.7
Angie to Ella
Thursday, July 3, 2003 2:11 PM

Cute, Ella—your mockery's not unnoticed. If I declare uncertainty regarding my fate's stimulating and I'm relishing the tension, nerves stirringly jangled, it's a simple case of your emotionally resourceful Angie making do with what's available to jumpstart tingles. If I was incarcerated in a filthy cell that had a window I'd manage to gush at the view, but that doesn't mean I'd enjoy being there. I'm an optimist of the emotions: surround me with gloom and I'll find a flicker of light to smile at. Plunge me into this distressing situation of having been informed upon and I'll invigoratingly quiver to the tune of the suspense.

Worried, even if in jest, of undermining the apprehension that's set my blood racing? Cast *that* worry aside, Dearest. Don't cha worry, loads of *better* apprehension's on the horizon. What about our next on-firm-premises frolic, assuming I'm not kicked out? Because of course there will be *many*—we won't back down. Considering I've been outed, acquired notoriety, I'll be under suspicion going forward. Even if I abstain from workplace shenanigans, the rumor mill will have me in the thick of them. Even if I'm chaste as a devout nun, it will be supposed I'm indulging in sexcapades galore. Every time I enter a male attorney's office and the door shuts, winks will be exchanged and tall tales will be told. So when we *do* get around to our next within-the-firm frolic I'll taste of more blood-quickening alertness than before, and so will you, Sweetiepie—guilt by association. Refraining from office frolic would mean the miserable loser informant has won, which is unthinkable.

But check me out! I'm doing what I've advised myself to avoid, taking happy outcome of a threatening situation for granted. Your thorough investigation notwithstanding, the outcome of my indiscretion won't be decided by the firm's prevailing mood. For better or worse, public opinion often has little to do with actions of the powers that be. Circumstances are never above taking an unexpected turn for the worse. The partners could decide to make an example of us. They could be reasoning: "Sure, Angie Chantal's work record is spotless; sure, she pounces on new deals like a hawk diving for prey, knocks herself out to bring them to fruition, loves her job; sure, she's popular among coworkers, an asset when it comes to client relations; but, still, she's not above necessity of enforcing policy, maintaining order. So we could and should make use of her to send a message. The firm is not a bordello and anyone who treats it as such will be terminated." They might very well be reasoning along those lines, so I'll prepare myself for the worst.

Ella, you won't hear from me until the verdict's been handed down.

Your,

JadeAwaitingJudgment

IV.8
Ella to Angie
Thursday, July 3, 2003 2:15 PM

Holding your hand, Sweetie! Praying for happiest of endings!

Your,

DearlyDevotedElla

IV.9
Angie to Ella
Thursday, July 3, 2003 4:01 PM

Ella, your investigative skills are unparalleled and your assessment concerning my fate spot on. The meeting at which the fates of Martin and I were weighed in the balance, examined relative to our exertions on behalf of our glorious legal profession? It was mostly a laugh fest!

You know Elizabeth Reyes, director of corporate ethics and compliance, who oversees professional conduct issues, greenlights HR in internal disciplinary matters? Yeah, you know her. She's the delightful gossip-mad woman who (bless her) can't keep anything to herself, is as mirthful as anyone could be. (It's her shapely twitchy behind that keeps her cheerful: the behind hordes of people ogle with their eyes.) She was at the meeting, charged with reciting the violation to the partners, and guess what she does once the meeting's adjourned? She comes flying down the hall laughing. The look on her face, according to my never-to-be-praised-enough secretary, Sylvia, is that of someone who can't wait to spill amusing news—tickled pink. She approaches Sylvia and, looking at her meaningfully (Because she knows Sylvia will pass it along to me.), says that, when she detailed the doings of Martin and myself to the partners, they were in hysterics. Elizabeth's words: "They couldn't stop laughing!" And what amused them most of all was the manner in which Martin and I were caught. "Someone at [_____] saw them through the window?" "Someone over there squealed?" They were asking variations of those questions over and over, laughing harder each time. At the end of the meeting they're saying: "OK, just tell Angie and Martin not to do it again." "Tell them we don't care what they do outside the office but they should know better than to do it here." Accompanying these proclamations are further cracks, such as: "They should have the sense not to do it here because the morality-watchdogs at [_____] will report it to us!" Then some official firm policy, pertaining to possible disciplinary action, is trotted out as a matter of form—something touching upon suspension without pay. Rikert (My supreme father figure of a mentor, I'm *so* lucky to have landed on his deals.) says something like: "You can mention it's an option, but say we've declined it based on their work records, lack of absenteeism, proven dedication. Just get it done." He impatiently waves an arm dismissively, resumes joking.

Infinite blessings to Elizabeth for telling all to Sylvia, knowing it would come back to me verbatim. I'm giving that woman a nice Christmas present. (Maybe anonymously, so it doesn't look like a payoff.) And of course to Sylvia as well, as always. (I'm as fortunate in the secretary assigned to me as I am in the partner I'm assigned to.) Wild how I knew about that mirth-fest of a meeting before my official call came, as Sylvia told me before Elizabeth called. Elizabeth handled it as becomes the class act she is: recited firm policy in a professional tone; touched upon the excellent work records of Martin and I; stressed it's none of the firm's business what we do outside work, but that outside activities must remain outside activities; stated the situation had been deliberated upon at length and it was decided an off-the-record warning, in lieu of a recorded warning or suspension, was in store; was careful to add this was an isolated incident that had been dealt with by itself which would have no bearing upon the firm's future dealings with us, as in reviews and bonuses; cautioned the incident could not be repeated and that, should there be a repeat violation, an official warning would be issued and period of suspension imposed, and termination possible. Then you know what she says? She says, "You should've pulled the shades down!" and hangs up. I can hardly believe my good fortune.

By the end of Elizabeth's call I'm gazing out the window at the park's soothing greenery (No nefarious tattletale's able to stare my office windows in the face, thank God.), upwelling with gratitude.

Your,

AccusedAndExcusedAngie(DelightDazzledDamsel)

IV.10
Ella to Angie
Thursday, July 3, 2003 4:23 PM

Supremely relieved, Dearest—joyously bouncing off the walls! But let me get this straight: you've been tattled upon for being naked spreadeagled on a desk at the office and the outcome's an impatient wave-away amidst guffaws? You've been caught proffering the pink within the hallowed halls, and the outcome's an off-the-record warning, assurances your performance review won't be influenced? That's the gist of it, right? That, this time, it's not an official warning? That you're allowed an office plowing before actual disciplinary measures are undertaken? And I'm not being sarcastic! I'm sincerely appreciative, in awe—will never be able to respect the firm enough. The firm truly values performance over mediocre mindless toeing-of-the-line.

Angie, I'm so giddy-happy-leaping-out-of-my-skin I could come there and love-tussle you to the floor! (Not that I'd ever need a special occasion, mind you.) But I suppose such would be pushing matters, fall under the category of "flagrantly foolish and hubristic tempting of fate."

Your,

TinglingTickledPinkPussycat

IV.11
Angie to Ella
Thursday, July 3, 2003 7:17 PM

Sorry for delayed reply, but it's been serious rush-rush since my pardon! Rikert had a good reason to instruct: "just get it done." Think he cares if I got banged on Martin's desk when there's massive stir-up on the

[____] deal? The sane man was looking out for his own interests and you'd better believe I'm going to kill myself to justify his faith in me.

Hail my mentor Rikert! Does he, by the least twitch upon his face or flicker of a glance, indicate he's aware of my misdeed? Nay! I'm lost in admiration for the man. He's consistent within his world-view, couldn't care less what shenanigans I've been up to so long as I'm primed to pounce on a deal, effectively counter the other side. He once said to me: "You really like this, don't you?" with laughter and appreciation—identification. He said it during a stressful pre-filing session at the printers when the house of cards of a hostile acquisition was threatening to fall to shambles, decimate two months' work. He knows I love the hunt—the pinning down of the other side, atmosphere of conquest. Merely love it? I'm insanely head-over-heels crazy for it! Yeah, *conquest*! I'm sure I'll be reborn as a man in the next life.

The amateurish opposition attempted to pull a fast one, as if Rikert doesn't have a half dozen of us pouring over the financials after every new draft to make sure they haven't slipped funny figures in. Unbelievable how naïve and self-defeating they are. Where do they think they are? Who do they think they're dealing with? They're in NYC, dealing with New Yorkers, and we can see their pathetic suburbanite machinations coming well in advance, and they've no idea, are wasting time, running up the bill. They'll be regretting their attempt to hoodwink us, up all night bathed in icy sweat when they see the agreement we've struck with the underwriters. Total ORGASM!

Got to run, Hon!

Your,

ConquestCravingCaesarina

IV.12
Ella to Angie
Thursday, July 3, 2003 8:21 PM

The powers that be are very wise! They pardoned you and you're in seventh heaven performing for them, as they surely anticipated.

My deal fizzled—early rumblings came to naught. The client instructed, "Let's wait and see what they do." and that was it. I prepared in anticipation of a flurry of activity, but now it looks like Monday at the earliest. Apparently they will be celebrating the 4th, as is appropriate.

You're in the thick of the action and I'm on the sidelines—spectating, idling about. I envy that you're Miss Caesarina today! You get to review the enemy's ineffectual strategy, hit with countermeasures—get to anticipate further attempts by the enemy to defeat you, beef up defenses, make secret alliances, take the field confident of victory—get to wake the enemy up, smack 'em down! Welcome to NYC, suburbanites!

As I'm otherwise unoccupied, will misbehave a bit—tee hee!—to be more deserving of Miss Whippie's stings. I'll cease envying you and about face, say: "Downtrodden law slave, you're stuck at the firm and I'm not! You're in for an all-nighter and I'll be soaking in a soothing bubble bath, babying my complexion with coconut oil, indulging in eucalyptus and myrrh aromatherapy! I have it easy, am in clover, and you're being flogged! My night belongs to me, your night belongs to the firm! I'm freedom blessed, you're bound fast! I'll stroll home through the park, delight in the rejuvenating colors and scents and sounds of summer, while you're cooped up in a conference room, and it might as well be the dead of winter for all the good summertime will do you! Mostly, I'm getting paid the same as you are today for lots less exertion! I'm a snooty spoiled princess prima donna, pleased as punch! I believe life's obliged to unendingly shelter me from stress! I believe it's my right to effortlessly float across the surface of existence, never needing to comprehend what discomfort consists of! I'm so removed from the everyday ordinary world I haven't been obliged to recoil from a loud noise or crude gesture, any form of aggression, for *years*!"

How's that, Sweetheart? Am I spoiled and smug enough to be worthy of severe disciplinary measures? Have I taunted fate, taken comfort and security for granted, enough to deserve a Miss Whippie thrashing?

Dearest, as you doubtless don't have time to read a lengthy missive, I'll sign off. Have fun as a law slave! You may rest assured I look forward to some serious Miss Whippie playsy-daisy once time permits.

Your,

FateFlauntingRipeForFloggingFloozy

IV.13
Steven to Angie
cc: Ella
Thursday, July 3, 2003 8:28 PM

Angie, my mouth was agape with astonishment, fists clenched with rage, when you told me of that spy! It's beyond belief there are pathetic snitching rat losers in this world, with nothing better to do than make gratuitous trouble for complete strangers. I'd love to get ahold of that worthy's name, apply prankster justice, be your vigilante.

But beauty and brains and social tact and verve and, especially, The Bottom Line readily stomp on meddling trash—justice prevails. It's always been a given you're a valuable asset: now you have added proof. Sure, it's advisable to lie low for a spell, but don't allow that worthless killjoy (probably has a social life that takes place in front of a TV) to triumph. It's important not to allow jabbermouth creeps to steal spontaneity from you, afflict you with terminal second-guessing, predatory self-consciousness. Your proud spirit must continue indulging in the fun that feeds it. You must frolic on firm premises again many times. But, yeah, yank the shades shut going forward. Check for vulnerabilities—never forget bloodless meddlers are around.

Kisses and ass-grabs, my gloriously vindicated princess!

Love,

Steven

P.S. Ella, wasn't it fun when you were a nun Tuesday? Want to do it again next Tuesday? We two have a high ol' time on Twos-day! Two slinky nighties are waiting for you, to replace the mauled ones! Maybe I'll maul the new ones too, on Woos-day! When you slip out of the habit and are in a flimsy nightie the contrast floods me so intensely I feel like I'm being grabbed all over by dozens of girl-hands! YeeHaw!

IV.14
Angie to Steven
cc: Ella
Thursday, July 3, 2003 9:49 PM

Stevie, since you've mentioned divertissements: I've assembled the essentials for our Marie Antoinette game. Took me nearly a fortnight to track everything down (Mainly, find the best costume shop for eighteenth century French fashion, come near as possible to matching paintings of Marie in her glory.) and am athirst to do it right this time, instead of in amateurish fashion with modern things that only vaguely approximated what Marie wore. Now I have a priceless 18e Siecle style wig—fluffed way up, a multi-tiered edifice; and a pearlish silver-sheened blue hat with white feathers sprouting something like two feet from the top like fountain spray; and a billowing blue-silver dress—huge enough for you to hide under; and matching bodice (which, incidentally, Marie hated wearing) so's you can roughly lace me up real tight, yank me around, whilst chiding me for being an uppity fashion plate brat.

Ah, yes... Darling delicate Marie, who couldn't flee the revolution without being decked out in the height of finery—who, by placing large orders for such finery, inadvertently betrayed the flight and caused her family to be seized on the road. Sweet Marie, who'd rather place herself in peril than dress in yesterday's clothes—very literally a fashion victim! I adore projecting myself into the role of the brattiest of all brats, whose own mother said she dressed like an attention-craving actress instead of a Queen; who drained the royal treasury on account of never feeling she had enough diamonds and dresses; who caused many women to emulate her and plunge their husbands into debt as well. Don't cha jus' *love* it?

I fully realize irresponsible brats must be disciplined, am *so* ready! I know you'll dream up novel ways of taking Royal Miss me down a peg or two, making me eat cake again. But don't forget: delicate, frivolous, fashion-addicted Marie went to the guillotine bravely, without fear. The petite wisp of a spoiled brat had an inner core of solid steel, exemplified aristocratic aplomb to a T. Likewise, I'll greet your punishment with an even temper, won't recoil; and if you wish to truly involve me—truly smash through my veneer of royal detachment—you'll need to get wildly creative, work wonders. What a wonderful contest it'll be.

I might be (temporarily) hobbled at the firm frolic-wise, but such has nothing to do with the rest of the world, thank goodness. And now, having allowed myself this mini-vacation of an email (energized myself with sweetest anticipation), I've got to get back to work.

Your,
AngieAntoinette

V. Miss Whippie

Heavenly Ella! Due to yesterday's shoddy state of affairs, your girlfriend shamefully reported for having enjoyed herself in an office, plus the finish-line frenzy of the [_____] deal, an all-nighter lasting to noon, our Miss Whippie date's been delayed. (But what fun the deal-concluding session was, especially the conference call when the opposition was crawling. Rikert grinning and pumping his fists like a teenager—very appreciative of his team, especially his treacherously-informed-upon second year who did, indeed, kill herself going over the financials again and again; so appreciative of yours truly that he told me: "We couldn't have done this without you."; plus mentioned my "high level of performance and gutsiness and resourcefulness." Sweet vindication.)

Experiencing so many sharp emotional contrasts in a brief interval and emerging smiling's what living's about—I'll never be able to do the mood-swirl justice, even if I've had nearly seven hours sleep. OK, then! Circumstances outside our control have delayed Miss Whippie, but anticipation's intensified. I'm something like vaporizing in the air, Ella—driving myself nuts picturing when your immaculate posterior's presented to me and I'm expected to punish you for being insultingly vainglorious. I'm fresh from a shower—skin glistening, pink and violet towel wrapped about my head—sipping spring water, nibbling raspberries—feeling pristine, giddy out of my skin. I'll soon retrieve Miss

Whippie from her carmine box in the closet, uncoil her, anoint her with oil—uncoil and oil her with a smile on my lips and love in my heart while naked on the fluffy white carpet of my pale blue and white bedroom. Then I'll place Miss Whippie on my bed and dress for you.

What to wear? Neck to toe leather with abundant steel studs? Lots of rubber? Some sort of mask? Yeah, right! Like you'd believe *this* girl would stoop to wearing clownish nonsense when she's going to reintroduce you to the flip side of a life of ease and luxury, invade your sheltered existence with a dose of vividly physical stress. And, hell, why not rant a bit? It's healthy for a girl to rant now and then, and does a girl know when impulses to rant will seize her? This girl never does.

So, to be rantish:

What is it with women who wear tacky comic book dominatrix crap? What's with the ass-high boots, breath-hindering masks (that smear makeup something awful), and chains? I mean, chains? Please! Think I'm going to wind chains around my waist and over my shoulders and clink clank about as if loaded down with carpentry tools? Want to feel stiff and cramped, then step into a leather or rubber bodysuit! The truly masochistic person in a dominatrix dungeon is the dominatrix herself—she's less graceful than a robot, imprisoned in ungainly armor. How can dominatrices look in the mirror without feeling they've been played? Cheap costumery doesn't confer force of will. So-called dominatrices are slaves who've allowed men to sucker them into looking like fools.

Dominatrices have zilch idea how to get the upper hand, maintain dignity. The only acceptable Miss Whippie clothing's girly stuff that floats on my body soft as breeze. When I'm facing off with my dearest Ella or anyone else I'm in frilly nighties or silky summer dresses or diaphanous scarves. I'm dolled up as an innocent dolly, blushing little girl. Fluffy on the outside, steely on the inside. I believe the contrast between my sweet appearance and merciless execution makes for more consternation on the part of my—ha ha!—victims. (As when I was crawling on hands and knees towards prostrate Clarence, clenching Miss Whippie between my teeth, glaring at him like I wanted him dead. He was glancing nervously about, darting his eyes at the door, contemplating flight while too afraid to infuriate me further by attempting it. And I daresay there isn't a single cliché-dominatrix-outfit wearing female alive who'd be able to make a man as scared as I made Clarence. And I was, mind you, merely in a flimsy nightie and furry slippers. And should some dominatrix twit decide to get annoyed at my mockery of her laughable costumes, let her try something! I'll rip her eyes out with my immaculately manicured nails, leap on her back, sink my teeth into her neck until she's passed out and bleeding out!)

Dominatrix losers dress *faux* intimidatingly because they're wimps below the bluster, need to compensate. They need pathetic "Cruel Mistress" props to conceal that they're pusillanimous prisses. They mimic an icy manner, ape sternness, to conceal how *ordinary* they are. Anyone can put on fake scowls, let's see them deliver real fear! Clumsy theatrics have zilch to do with bringing anyone to heel, exerting will.

Dearest, you'll never catch your Angie indulging in low self-esteem compensation by donning a sorry dominatrix outfit. For tonight's Miss Whippie session I'll be sunny-Sunday-picnic-in-the-park. First, matching lace-trimmed brassiere and panties—color's the chaste white of whipped cream, driven snow, lily petals, dove wings. And also white stockings, and all's of butter-soft silk. After all, the goal's to lash your delectable globes purple, I'm not about to blemish myself. What else? Oh, right: the white polka-dotted aquamarine skirt—knee high, pleated—from Sak's which delectably swishes when I walk. And my locks curled, partially ponytailed with a blue ribbon. And open-toed aquamarine pumps. Clear nail and toe polish. Pale pink lipstick. An outfit to attend Mass in; or meet a boyfriend's uptight parents in; or gain admittance to a strict co-op in; or speak at a Daughters of the American Revolution ("Are you Mayflower, Madge?") fundraiser in. A sweet lil' conservative-girl costume that makes me appear naïve and nice.

My blood races, tingles my temples, at anticipation of your arrival, Ella! Myself dolled up fluffy as I open my door, gigglingly bid you enter, then escort you to the bedroom while inquiring if you've had a nice day and offering you mango, kiwi, and papaya slices. Then I'll grab Miss Whippie and grasp you firmly and twist you 'round and push you down 'til you're face down on the mattress—rip your dress off, lash you raw.

But I don't want to live our encounter in advance, only want to anticipate. Who knows what'll transpire? That's the beauty of our sessions—I never know. When you pitch and cry such love for you surges within and threatens to choke me, fling me listless to the floor.

OK, Honeypie Dollface—Love of my Life! I need to dress—prepare for holy communion. I said I'll be dressed in clothes befitting a good girl at Mass? It's Mass we'll experience—mysteries of prayer and love.

See you soon in my silky white and aquamarine cutiepie best!

Your,

FeistyFloggerInFluffStuff

V.2
Ella to Angie
Saturday, July 5, 2003 8:27 PM

Angie, whether it was the yearning that was nearly choking me—expectation urgent enough to throb my veins, scramble my senses; or psychological projection, my needs expressing themselves visually; or actual distortion of the light: the second you opened your door the entryway's brightness surrounded and clung to and altered you. Your aquamarine dress was shimmering, alchemizing into silver, and your chestnut hair—well, your hair was aglow, a halo! You were an Angel, resplendent in Holy light! Beneficence was pouring from your inspired eyes into the depths of me, dizzying me with joy! I kid you not, Angie, at first glimpse of you, I lost my breath and was wobbly! I didn't fall to my knees—I was knocked to them! I began crawling towards you.

"Stop, Ella!" you react. "It's not for you to presume to approach me at will—it's for me alone to approach at will, if and when I deign to do so." You deftly dart (You're a deft dart of a tart—flaming arrow that darts straight to the center of my heart, flares there.) behind me, seize me by the nape of my neck and squeeze, and—*presto!* I'm your limp doll to do with as you please. I'll leap to my feet and stand at attention should you wish; I'll prostrate myself in prayer on the floor should you wish; I'll march about reciting lines from Byron while worrying my breasts with my nails should you wish; I'll lie on my back and gaze up your skirt and praise your symmetry to high heaven and bite your shoe and declare I'd dearly love to be gagged and swatted dizzy should you wish.

(You said you'd start off as sweet little girl—greet me with giggles and feed me fruit and guide me to your bedroom, then pounce? Things started faster, my being overdue for a Miss Whippie session saw to it. Who says you're the only one who directs our Miss Whippie sessions? I have a say in the matter too. But of course I know you know that.)

Where was I, Angel? You seize my neck, compel me to stand—I gasp to catch my breath as euphoria tears through me. (Which is how I always feel when you commence to show how much you care.) Then you announce: "You're a disgustingly spoiled comfort-befuddled creature desperately in need of primality, an ample dose of raw-survival sensations! You're in need of rebirth via strife and fear, without which you'll inwardly rot! Fear is what'll churn and purify your psyche, flush out the stagnation that's set in! There isn't one aspect of your life that's rooted in emotional authenticity: directness of emotion's been eliminated, and you're wilting! What of our mist-shrouded past, when our ancestors were obliged to crouch close to fires to escape being devoured by vicious predators, including saber toothed cats? What of the way the Greeks had of remaining in touch with mystery and danger, their Bacchic rites? What of faith in the Middle Ages, when hell's gaping maw loomed near and inspired trepidation that led to beatitude? You're infinitely removed from rejuvenating realities like those, emasculated by luxury! So I'll be reeducating you, precious! I'll make you writhe as if a wild animal's sinking its fangs in your ass!"

(Angie, you may look like a girly girl in white and aquamarine, curls dancing about your face in front, ponytailed at the back, but you're strutting and half-shouting and speechifying like a man. You're right, it's sharp contrast, but the difference between your appearance and behavior doesn't cause consternation in *me*: I adore it when cutiepie you sets about expertly breaking me down like a drill sergeant.)

Then you crush me face-first to the wall, announce: "Believe it, PrissMiss, I *am* a wild animal and *will* sink my fangs in your ass, see you squirm! As for your ass, let's have a look! Off with those panties! Lift your skirt! Oh, yes, here it is! The precious ass! A pampered ass, a namby-pamby ass! An ass that's only known bubble baths, herbal rinses, aromatic oils!—that's only known the touch of panties, night-ies, slips, stockings, skirts!—that's only known the hesitant caresses of weaklings who, like yourself, have been swindled by civilization into thinking comfort's the true path to inner glory when, in fact, comfort's what undermines and destroys inner glory, replacing it with lazy self-satisfaction, a pathetic sense of entitlement! Do you really believe you can go through life with an ass that pampered and taste one-hundredth of the range of emotions you need to be tasting in order to be an authentic girl, instead of a pseudo girl—a fabricated girl—a victimized-by-society girl? My oh my, is Angie ever going to show your ass a thing or two tonight and lift you into the light of what it's possible for a girl like you to feel! Have no illusions! Civilization doesn't exist here: it won't intercede on your behalf, stay my hand, rob you of an education!"

Here, Angel, is when you bestow the first kiss of the night upon unworthy me. You say, "civilization doesn't exist here," and squiggle your tongue twixt my lips, scrape my behind with your nails: the com-bination of snarling assertion with kiss with scratches (nor to forget you're still grinding me on the wall) has me wondrous vertiginous, as if it's the first time you've done it to me and I'm surprised. Such is the miracle: how are you able to continue to surprise me? How is it the rituals and kisses (Oh, the kisses!) are always as vivid as the first time? How is it you're able to make me tremble and quake as if we've just met, and I'm uncertain with whom I'm dealing, how far you'll go? Luscious suspension of familiarity! You place me in a magical love-inundation state in which anything's possible and all wildness surges forth. (All wildness! Should that be our motto for Miss Whippie nights going forward? "All Wildness"?—or maybe "Mystery Surge" or "Lashings of Life" or "Punishment Pristine"?)

My legs have lost the ability to support me (it's you and the wall holding me upright) when you hiss: "To the floor, precious! Know your place!" and yank me down by my hair while pulling my skirt over my head. "Face on the carpet!" you continue. "Ass in the air! And would you look at this?" you intone with venom, rustling my dress in your hand. "A name that isn't yours is stitched inside this skirt's neckline! It says: 'Property of Colette Covington'! Fancy that! I'll bet it's a castaway you filched from a Salvation Army bin! Is that what you did? Did you take advantage of Mrs. Covington's generosity, raid a Salvation Army bin, steal from the needy to clothe your penny pinching ass? Answer me, you thoughtless—selfish—thieving—disgraceful excuse for a girl!"

"Yes," I whimper while biting the carpet, bracing myself for the hail of blows I pray will follow—that I'm hungering for with every itching pore of my flushed bothered skin, frayed edges of my inflamed nerves.

"What, you outright admit the theft?" you fairly scream. "You don't trouble to lie, attempt to mollify me? Do you think creampuff stuff's awaiting you as retribution? Do you feel justice at my hands is a joke? Is that why you don't try to lie? Answer me, misinformed fool of a girl!"

"I despair of concealing the truth!" I gasp. "I'm guilty—filthy guilty—and there's no hiding it! My guilt reeks to high heaven and I can't mask the smell! I fully deserve to be prosecuted to the fullest extent of the law!" I'm grinding my teeth when I resume biting the carpet: you're cruelly holding Miss Whippie in check. I'm thinking, "Why don't you thrash me, Angie? Why don't you raise the welts I deserve, Angie? Why don't you rescue me from agonizing unease, for Christ's sake?"

"Oh, you're a real player, aren't you princess?" you sneer. "You're buttering me up so much I'm about to slide away on it! You 'despair of concealing the truth' from me? That's your pathetically transparent way of seeking to wriggle off the hook with flattery! Your flattery only fuels my ire! Here, Miss Primrose Path! This is the skirt you stole from those less advantaged than you, and guess what? You're going to *eat* it!"

Angie, I love you for (among a trillion other things) knowing me from the inside out, being as familiar with my preferences as if they're your own. I adore biting soft things (skirts, pillows, nighties, stockings, fur, sheets) when Miss Whippie cuts me and you're aware of it, plus it's a signal, way of alerting me to, preparing me for, her attack. You stuff my skirt into my mouth and I bite for all I'm worth, hands clenched.

I hear Miss Whippie slicing the air, hissing—it's a small eternity of waiting, in split seconds, for her kiss; in that small eternity my body braces itself, twitches; in that small eternity I feel as if I'm abandoned and alone; in that small eternity anticipation of pain's greater than the pain itself. Then compression of perception, sensation shoving thought aside, when Miss Whippie's first cut lands. Liquid stings surging up my back, down my thighs, even somehow setting the back of my hands afire—electric heat pulsating at my cheeks, tingling my ears and the top of my head. A flurry of light flicks from ankles to waist, each a tap of fire, follows. Hey, fire ants once streamed across my feet on Sanibel, nonstop stinging, the sky spinning upside down near ocean's roar—wildest expansion, myself transported outside the ordinary! I'm screaming into the softness I'm biting, bliss upwelling—vanishing from in front of myself—liberated from the burden of being me.

Miss Whippie's slash and gash is life on overdrive. She slaps scalding oil onto and within me, awakens me from the limited realm I inhabit. Sometimes it seems I could swoon for all eternity, die happy with the knowledge I've tasted of Paradise in this life. Angie, you're the most gracious and understanding girlfriend imaginable—no one else has whipped religion into me. What's religion, if not propulsion into states of being hinting at realms further reaching than the one we're stuck in?—gloriously uncivilized places, uncompromised by society?

It's the first round of cuts and I'm a blazing lake, spiraling into my watery depths. Pleasure? Pain? What's the difference? I'm somewhere outside pleasure and pain. Pain alternates with pleasure too quick for either to wholly identify itself. I'm still biting the fabric, writhing; I'm seeming to endlessly fall without hitting bottom. Then you're kneeling beside me, caressing with the mink glove, accentuating the waking dream—I'm a babe in Mommy's arms, cuddled and comforted.

Angie, I feel I'm becoming incomprehensible—may not be stringing thoughts together logically. On the other hand, when has Miss Whippie operated logically? Is physical violence expected to yield abiding inner serenity? How is it the welts you raise on my behind dispense so much that's good? How is it that when I trace my fingers over them now, I flood inside with pride and joy and the knowledge I'm truly loved? Answer me please, Honey. I'm feeling too illogical to continue.

Your,

AdoringPenitentPrincess

V.3
Angie to Ella
Saturday, July 5, 2003 11:49 PM

Sweetest, you ask questions your devoted Angie would never presume to answer directly: she cannot wholly be you and feel what you feel. But what your Angie *can* do is tell of the sensations/emotions that overcome her as she's administering chastisement—administering love.

Know then that when I turn domineering and shout commands, I'm trembling head to toe. Trembling as when (already seems like dozens of personality alterations ago) I spread my legs to bid maidenhood bye-bye. Strange, right? But it's so. My final moments of virginity came swirling back last night—suspense preceding maidenhead's loss churned my tummy. When I first brought Miss Whippie down on your quivering behind, watched welts accumulate on your unblemished skin, I was trembling like that young virgin version of me in Paris at—I remember the address—31 Rue Campagne Première, 14th arrondissement, in the upstairs room on the bed by the window that spilled the glories of Paris before me. Barely twilight it was, sunlight's diffused amber flooding, but did I appreciate the beauty of the scene? (After all, such a setting for virginity's loss is the stuff misty-eyed romances are made of.) Nay! I was quivering with apprehension, as if near to fainting with fear. At that age I had zilch inkling of my sexual aptitude-to-come, or even of what sexual aptitude is. I was a shy freckled little thing! Did I consent to my deflowerment? I honestly don't know! He was Scandinavian, tall, pretty skinny—had such a way with his hands. It's his hands that undid me! My facial expressions and gestures and perhaps even words may very well have been saying "No!"; but my melting sensations when he touched and caressed me were assuredly saying "Yes!"—drowning out the "No!" enough to incline me towards compliant. He had long tapering fingers—they beamed a type of electricity into me I'd never felt before. So I got naked for him, was lying there paralyzed and mesmerized and, as I said, so fearful, and the Parisian scenery didn't mean a thing.

Whoa! Didn't mean to veer off to Paris! (But that's one of the wonders of our email world, right? We sometimes get yanked in unforeseen directions, turn topsy-turvy timeframe-wise, play about in our past.) I was seeking to say that when I get violent with you, I'm that frightened virgin again. When Miss Whippie strikes you it's as if another person's guiding her, administering cuts. I'm watching you writhe and cringe and strain and turn rippled, tight and hard, in your musculature, and then suddenly it's as if I'm leaving my body, entering yours. It's all I can do to continue whipping you when I'm standing there stunned as if those cuts are landing on me, and the upwelling of love for you that grips me! When I cast Miss Whippie aside—or, more accurately, allow her to drop from my limp hand—and put on the mink glove and crouch beside you, commence caressing, it's almost as if I'm caressing myself. You speak of Miss Whippie dispensing serenity?—tracing your fingers over her welts, flooding with love? That's my love for you, Ella! That's me hovering on the edge of a swoon, our Miss Whippie bond.

I recall whispering while caressing with Minky: "These marks bear witness to my undying love for you. Later on when you touch them—wince at them, twinge—you'll feel my love anew. Darling, I hope you know that, for each welt I placed upon you, I died a thousand deaths."

We speak of restoring balance—endlessly kid around, say spoiled prissy flighty princess you must be brought down to earth, placed in touch with the capricious vicissitudes of fortune, shown life isn't always rosesy-posey and stress can erupt at any time, and there's something to that (Not that you're a priss, but that each of us, as members of society, are falsely shielded from nature.), but what Miss Whippie's really about is affirmation of our love. Doesn't civilization seek to weaken and stifle love, discourage heart-overwhelming emotion? Isn't dizzying sensation forbidden fruit, from a maintenance-of-societal-order perspective? So we're subverting civilization, prioritizing Mommy Nature. Miss Whippie facilitates communion, enables depths of feeling, the daily grind suppresses. We're lovebirds relishing the vividness of being alive.

Love isn't rose-tinted slop. Love's serious responsibility, people committed to guarding each other's spiritual well-being. And spiritual well-being's a tricky beast: in the same way that our bodies thrive on exercise and deteriorate without it, our spirit needs doses of stress to stay strong—a taste of outright panic and confusion isn't all that bad. Storms endured and lassitude earned. Miss Whippie's a means of trembling and being disoriented together, recovering our bearings and rescuing one another together, strengthening our miraculous bond together.

Looks like I've veered from last night's action again, will resume: when I was soothing your wounds with Minky what you didn't see were my upwelling tears as I bent to kiss the nape of your neck. The sight of your delicate wounded body, Ella!—I was quaking to the marrow of my bones. Your slender trembling arms—way your fingers were spasmodically closing and unclosing—way your curls spilled about as you continued biting the dress I'd crammed in your mouth. Sweetheart, the vulnerable aura of you reached into the pit of my stomach, churned my nerves—raked me from my center of gravity, had me gasping and listless. I collapsed onto you, trembled in unison with your stunned body—was pulled into your undertows, brought to a state of abject surrender. I'm supposedly the dominant one? Why? Because I issue commands, seize you roughly, direct Miss Whippie's cuts? Such has nothing whatsoever to do with who's the dominant one. Neither of us is the dominant one. The dominant one's the emotional motion, submergence in each other's hidden places. Love's the dominant one.

(Right, it's not easy to be wholly comprehensible—logical, if you will—when detailing our Miss Whippie enabled energy-exchange: the influx of uncivilized things that seem to break us at first, until they uplift us.)

I fell onto you utterly limp, seemingly only sensible of your breath swelling your lungs. I'm unsure how long my limpness lasted before tingles commenced fluttering throughout me like soft breeze: it was as if I was mist caressed by warm air. Then I raised myself to elbows and the act of moving, in and of itself, surged delight up my spine. I rolled onto my back laughing, was staring at the ceiling: so forceful was the joy. It's as if I was a shattered thing being reassembled from the inside out.

Alas, all too soon the onrush of bliss was dwindling in intensity, and an impulse seized me that could be translated as: "I can't let these moments escape—must chase after them, get rapture to crest again, for strength later on when I'm back in the workaday world. It's why Ella and I are here: to overwhelm ourselves, cleanse ourselves—wash away as much of the psychic residue of stilting flimflam behavior as possible. Society requires us to adopt false personalities, play parts—Ella and I are here to rid ourselves of self-dividedness, shake off civilization's yoke. Another round of violence will bring about another upwelling of joy."

As indicated, it was an impulse I've put it into words in retrospect. In practice next to no thinking was involved when I seized Miss Whippie again—sprang to my feet, caught you by your curls, yelled: "What are you doing on the floor, lazy slouch of a useless girl? Get up! Shake the sloth from your unworthy bones and rise! Stand at rigid attention, become a statue—don't you so much as dare twitch a finger!"

Then I'm tapping the small of your back with my fingernails, snapping Miss Whippie at your ankles, driving you ahead of me into the bedroom, saying: "On your back on the bed! No more face down on the floor, facing away from me, afraid to look into my eyes! No more lounging like a limp doll, taking it easy like a drugged sleazy, lacking the will to so much as lift your head! I want a plucky victim, rebellious slave, spirited captive! I want some resistance, and I want it now!" So captivatingly rigid you are, the nightstand lamp's pink light undulating on you. A rigid sapling of a slut on my bed—chest heaving, hoarsely breathing, eyes ignited. You actually make an effort to rise, escape.

"What an unbelievably stupid, vainglorious, gullible girl!" I cry, pushing you back onto your back. "You really fell for my ruse, believed I'd grant your undeserving carcass liberty? Prissy, you've as good as spat on me, slapped my cheeks, by assuming I'd be willing to relinquish the upper hand, turn you loose! It's not about to be tolerated! It's you who gets spat at, slapped! You're not worthy to grovel at my feet, lick my ankles!" I shove at your breastbone, press you into the mattress, spit on your breasts, smack your shoulders. "Oh, ho ho! You weren't expecting that, were you?" I sneer. "Guess you aren't expecting this either!" I straddle your tummy with my back to your face, commence thwacking your ankles, steadily moving stings up your shins.

I'm gripping your midriff with my thighs, sensible of your deliciously bothered body's twitches and pitches, undulating waves. Miss Whippie's approaching the tender insides of your thighs and, the nearer she gets, the more you writhe, gasp, hiss, and I show zilch mercy, redouble Miss Whippie's thwacks at those most sensitive spots; and—wowee! your squirming tummy's stimulating my flowerpuss something fierce. The more incandescently dizzy I get, the more I sting you, apply the leather where you're reddening the most—I keep gripping your bucking body with my thighs: you're a wild mustang of a girl seeking to throw me. Sweetie, your motion's as good as a soft sword rammed way up within me—I can't continue, collapse sideways onto the bed, scramble to embrace you hard. Miss Whippie falls from my hand as I flood.

I'd sooner die than fail you, Ella. I know my place, ever at your service. I flutter my fingers over your pinkling's swollen lips, and you moan. I slip my fingers within, softly massage, and you flood in instants. Our united flooding, your pulsating tummy and surging heat and undulations as I dissolve, always haunts me later in the best of ways—both of us upwelling bliss—happiness continuously teases, beckons.

At some point, as if in a dream, I'm daubing ointment on your wounds, the nightstand lamp's rose water light flowing over your lusciousness—bedroom seeming to float, gently spin. My final rec-ollection, before dozing, is of ineffable sweetness brimming in your half-lidded eyes.

Your,

LostInLove'sSwellLassie

V.4
Ella to Angie
Sunday, July 6, 2003 2:02 AM

But of course, Angie, I'm stunningly aware of the tenderness that overwhelms you, tears welling in your eyes—it's your tenderness that wields the greatest power and tumbles me under. Without your ten-derness—trembling gripping you head to toe, trace of an as-if-horri-fied-at-yourself aura—Miss Whippie would be a charade and joke.

I'd hardly consent to a flogging if you weren't scared while admin-istering it. Proud priss miss me wouldn't agree to be so much as flicked by your pinky, much less lashed nearly 'til bleeding, if you weren't quaking along with me, shuddering with concern for my welfare—if you weren't as storm tossed as me, cast into like tumult.

(But I know you know I'm well aware of the state into which you're propelled when flogging me. So why, then, are we asking each other questions to which we know the answers? Why are we describing our respective responses as if the other needs to be enlightened? Well, it's tough enough to descend into the depths of our love via Miss Whippie, break one another into rising towards bliss, and to describe it afterwards sometimes seems nigh impossible. But we're analytical attorney girls who know plenty about logic, right?—as in when it's to be cast aside because it falls short of the task. We pretend ignorance, then exert ourselves to enlighten one another! Such, I believe, is the most reliable way to flush out our Miss Whippie nights—set ourselves to quivering again, come as near as we're going to get to duplicating—reliving—the Miss Whippie experience during the telling. But why am I dawdling, indulging in delay tactics, like this? I'm a silly girl! Enough!)

OK! When I was on my back on your bed and you commanded me to resist, I didn't wish to escape any more than you were about to allow me to—only wished for you to pounce like the fierce feline you are. We're synchronized dance partners! Whether we're putting people on in public, scampering to conceal an indiscretion, teasing a man to maddening distraction, or emotionally orienting ourselves for a Miss Whippie eruption, it's all the same. You inform me to get plucky when you're on the point of wielding Miss Whippie? Translation: "Give me an excuse to become riled and wrestle you into submission, attack." Would I dream of hesitating to hasten matters? Nay! So damn right I lunged for the edge of the bed, sought to flee! I would've been sad had you not shoved me onto my back, straddled me, tap danced Miss Whippie at my ankles.

So you're gripping me tight with deliciously vibrating thighs as the nightstand lamp's pink flows over the fluffy down comforter I'm sinking into as it rises and falls—I'm losing myself in downy ocean-motion when Miss Whippie commences flicking. Then she erupts in earnest, bites and claws! I've no idea how long it takes for her to travel from my ankles to calves, time's advance blurs—awareness is solely Miss Whippie's tiny leather-bites alternating with full-out slashes, crisscrossing stings. I'm aware she's attacking the insides of my calves, forcing my legs wider—aware that if I fail to spread my legs as she wishes she'll continue striking until I can no longer withstand, hasten to comply. The comforter's waves are losing solidity, transforming into pink mist—your curls are tumbling down your back, swishing and hissing. Or is it your curls? Nay! It's Miss Whippie's swish I hear, but as if from faraway, as if she's wind whispering outside the windows. How explain that I often lapse into intervals of dreamy vagueness while Miss Whippie's subjecting me to the sharpest of sensations? I believe I'm making jerky snow-angel movements with my arms, not wholly sure—seems to me I could be sinking further into the comforter.

Angie, you do, indeed, love me as fiercely as I need. When Miss Whippie climbs higher, commences cracking my inner thighs in twatsie's neighborhood, the sting's such that I'm hyperventilating, eyesight blurred. Only my spiritual double could gaze upon the wounds appearing there and grit her teeth and continue striking, steel herself to do what needs to be done. A lashed inner thigh's something of mind-altering pain, and Miss Whippie's repeatedly lashing. I'm gasping a near-steady wail, such that the neighbors might hear were it not for the pillowcase you've stuffed in my mouth. (You left out that detail.) I'm yelling into the pillowcase and seeking to get up and out of there, no acting! Believe me, I'd leap up and run if I could! But your thighs grip my torso tighter; your rear rocks harder into my chest; your free hand presses on my tummy as Miss Whippie continues tapping where I agonize the most. Agonize? Oh, at first, without a doubt, but then there's the miraculous transformation: the act of seeking to escape with all my strength, and being prevented, yields wildest buildup of energy. I'm, with every sinew and spark of will, seeking to escape but am firmly held in place, and so my exertion's deflected back upon me, inundates me, sends me towards out-of-my-body sensations I can only compare to mystical entrancement. What vivid pictures whip through my head, swift as a flashflood! I can hardly feel you atop me or feel Miss Whippie flicking, discern the room's dimensions—all's inner radiance for a spell. At some point I become aware Miss Whippie's ceased stinging and that you're alongside me, pulling me close, slipping your fingers within kittikins, stroking. Your gaze alone's tingling me to shivers.

Honey, that's all for Miss Whippie—I'm spent. Detailing fun at the firm or park, or pranking in public, or Stevie nights is a cinch: my fingers can barely keep pace with the words popping into my head. But I can only do so much Miss Whippie recollection, never feel I've come close to doing her justice. Besides, Miss Whippie's sacred: not only does she make her secrets tough to tell, I'm not sure she wants them told. So no more telling of our religious rites, digging on sacred ground, tonight.

Love is the greatest responsibility, beside which others pale. If I'm hurt, you're hurt, and when we're both hurt we join forces to heal one another—return to the world pristine fresh, strong. That's what Miss Whippie's about! She prepares us for, enables us to deal with, the unkind turns life can take. She's us watching one another's back.

You know I would die for you, Dearest!

Your,

MatedWithAMiracle(That'sYouAngie)Ella

V.5
Angie to Ella
Sunday, July 6, 2003 3:23 AM

So be it, Honey—we'll lay Miss Whippie to rest for tonight. And yes, Miss Whippie's exhausting, whether we're playing with her or recounting our play. Is being in love exhausting as well? Love's exhausting in the way that flinging oneself into a swift river and enjoying the rip of the current as it sweeps one along's exhausting. Love transforms mundane existence into an engaging waking dream; love invests the tedium of civilized society with magic and mystery; love's the fire Prometheus stole from the Gods. Sure, love's exhausting—occasionally suggests a state of seizure—but it's also an inexhaustible well of adrenaline, the desire to live for two thousand years. Mostly, love's the image of my radiant Ella permanently alive in my mind's eye and on the screen of my dreams, dispensing goodness and joy. Miss Whippie heightens my awareness of how blissfully bonded we are, in love and friendship and work and play and stress and conflict.

Speaking of conflict: what of my having been informed upon? Are we going to allow that ad agency snitch to poison funtime at the firm—deny us the kicks we crave, are entitled to, on company time? We are NOT!

Miss Whippie places matters in perspective. The heights she swirls us towards and depths she plunges us into enable us to see through clinging ordinary things, deprive them of the power to oppress us. And I must say the timing of our Miss Whippie session couldn't have been better. She's restored me to full courage and clarity with regard to our situation at work. Ha! Of course we'll continue frolicking on company time! Why? Because we're (Why be modest?) two of the firm's brightest stars, valued as much for our intelligence as our commitment; and because we're possessed of social tact and quickness of wit to burn. We keep clients happy (willing to pony up upon receiving our billing) with our legal expertise, and also spread good cheer with our infectious personalities, and therefore will always benefit from the wonderful things known as "extenuating circumstances" and "positive intangibles."

But we (omitting my stupidity regarding the window shades) actually don't indulge in risky behavior: if a man's involved, then it's never anywhere but in an office, door securely locked, and we're never fully naked, thanks to dresses. Dresses were invented, I'm convinced of it, to allow easy access to a woman, permit her to be pleasured without stripping, and afford her an easy means of reverting to the state modesty requires: a simple flinging down of the hem and—presto!—all's right and proper. (OK, so I was also fully naked in Martin's office, but it was the first time and it's easy to slip on a dress quick. And, yeah, I'm owning up to having been an idiot! Escaping detection's absolutely essential.) As for our girl games, how could we be caught? Again, it's the beauty of dresses, and also the beauty of panties so skimpy we needn't take them off, as they're readily held aside; that is, assuming we're wearing any. Whether it be tweaking our twatsies in the ladies', taking turns slurping each other in the records' room (I adore being pressed against a row of musty files as you tongue-flick me. The contrast between the freshness of flooding and dank atmosphere—my pristine sensations amidst moldering residue of thousands of transactions—is life triumphing over death, like frolic in a cemetery. Ella, we're overdue for more records room fun!), or anywhere else, we don't need to yank up our dresses, so how's anyone going to know, for an irrefutable fact, what's going on? Even if someone were to catch you with your head within my dress (which is of course utterly farfetched, purely hypothetical), it would be explained away as "She's assisting me with a woman problem, it happened without warning, I'm scared."

In short, we need to reaffirm that the firm's one of our favorite playgrounds—reclaim our *right* to frolic ourselves dizzy on company time—soon as our workload allows. Screw lying low for a spell!

I realize next week's tricky. Sure, an ass grab here, kissy session there—there's always affection-on-the-fly, but it doesn't appear we'll be free to indulge ourselves full out. But once we *are* free we need to sex-kicks ourselves silly on the premises. It's as essential as continuing to upstage and annoy smug Rhodora with my greatly superior fashion sense.

Are you game, Girlfriend?

Your,

RandinessReclamationRompCat

V.6
Ella to Angie
Sunday, July 6, 2003 5:01 AM

What, Angie? You actually deign to upstage Rhodora—the cheap-knock-off-wearing pretender? Surely you're putting me on, but I'll pretend you're not so's to enjoy thrashing her. Rhodora's smug enough to think people are fooled by designer duplicates, fake labels prominently protruding from the collars. Even her perfume's garbage, the poor-approximation-of-the-original slop sidewalk vendors sell. She's the equivalent of a bald guy with a toupee, never suspecting all are aware and laughing. Oh, not because he's bald, mind you (Many delicious men are bald in varying degrees.), but because he's put fake hair on his head and isn't fooling anyone except himself—his vanity's the joke. Rhodora? Who cares if she's annoyed or not, or anything else? She's upstaged simply by being her tacky, classless, ignorant, always-jabbering-for-attention self. She's upstaged simply by being a penny-pinching rich twat who has zilch clue how to be anything but shoddy, affected, pompous, lecturing, boring. Any clever girl on a budget can present herself a hundred times better than Rhodora, using purchases from drug stores and thrift shops. And the jumpsuit thing she had on last week! Fluorescent emerald, with silver trim looking like aluminum foil! "It was shown in Milano!" she says (Note how she says "Milano" instead of "Milan": to her mind, this indicates she's "international."), flinging her head back with a comically snooty look. Meanwhile, everyone's in disbelief at how ugly and misshapen the thing is. Every other woman in town dresses with better taste than grasping wannabe Rhodora, so I *know* you were joking about troubling with her!

Speaking of bloodless people (I'm on a lil' rant-tear), what of that pasty-faced-unwashed-smelly creep, Daniel L? Always boasting about his travels, by way of denigrating every place he visits: "Buenos Ares was extremely archaic, like Europe." What does he do on trips besides mindlessly gawk at scenery, stew in hotels? His trips are boring because he's boring. Try as he might to escape himself by switching geographical locations, he winds up stuck with his petty, backbiting, snitching personality no healthy person wants anything to do with.

What of that self-important media-raped zombie, Osbore? Evidently does nothing outside work but watch TV. Comes to work blathering about some program as if, by the very act of wasting time watching it, he's immediately been indoctrinated into an august secret society. Jabbers about a new sitcom as if he's become privy to a fabulous and extremely meaningful cultural experience. Gazes upon us with condescension and pity because we've failed to realize watching garbage on TV is the present day equivalent of reading a novel or going to the theater. Says reading became obsolete when filmmaking was invented, and then makes a move on me, trotting out worthless pop culture trash inspired platitudes: that he's "a cutting edge guy," and do I want to be a part of it? Says brain-raped-loony stuff like he "lives for celluloid," and requires a "movie star quality girl," then admits he stole that line from a movie, as if that will seal the deal and really make me want to tolerate him for longer than I have to. Yuck! Nonsense like that gives me the creeps! It's depressing to know there are people so desperate for a personality they're willing to construct one from slop spouted in movies. He was, if you recall, assigned to the [_____] deal with me last April. Thankfully Sturmheld tossed him off it two days later. Had he not done so, who knows what I would've done? I nearly kicked the twit at the printer's one morning. He'd been patronizingly explaining to me that I'm ignorant, because I was refusing to understand a worthless Russian independent film was superior to anything Dostoevsky wrote.

OK! Enough of shredding imbeciles and onto the subject at hand, as in no girl could be more athirst to fling herself into frolic at the firm again than me. When that creep reported you, I was punched in the stomach! What hurts you, hurts me; and when we're hurt we rise to transform hurt into healing. That's what Miss Whippie teaches us and I'm an attentive student, eager to apply her teachings. Silly Angie, asking if I'm game! I'll play any game anywhere you propose, no matter how perilous. I'm your obedient game playing girly, with a welted rearend to prove it.

Sweetheart, you know I share your rage at the shoddy attempt to restrict your—that is, OUR—freedom, and wish to reclaim that freedom right now. If we were at work I'd make a beeline for your office and fling your hemline over your head and pounce on your flowerpuss, tongue you delirious, like a starved kitty. Added danger, real or perceived: who cares? When an attempt's made to fit tramps like us with chastity belts we pick the locks and get wilder than Marines with a weekend pass.

A confession: I'm agitated because I've stayed up too late. How can I have stayed up too late when it's a Saturday? It's because the [_____] IPO's filing this week, meaning I'm on call and have no reliable days off. I received notice an hour ago, informing me I'll be needed at two. So I'm antsy, starting to worry my post Miss Whippie excitement will keep me

awake, cause me to turn up too frazzled for comfort. I need to break this off, see if I can settle down enough to sleep and dream.

Nightie-night, Love of my Life!

Your,

SlutChasingSlumber

V.7
Angie to Ella
Sunday, July 6, 2003 5:12 AM

By all means sleep, Honey!

Remember: we're adept at setting inner proddings and love-rapture aside, snuggling into our pillows and drifting off, when duty calls.

Your,

LassieSingingLullabiesForYou

V.8
Angie to Ella
Sunday, July 6, 2003 5:54 AM

Something for when you awaken, Darling. I'm not envious of your situation, but remember being called upon to exercise our legal expertise is partially what we live for. Worse could've happened, as in no one asking you to help. They've requested you not only because you're capable, dedicated, and smart but because you light up the room.

Although our work sometimes seems obstructive we adore it, right? Aside from making a living, we need a restraining influence to keep us from getting lost in emotional excess with no front or back to it, losing the ability to appreciate it. We're contradictory creatures who require order in our lives, a solid foundation from which to launch into unbridled escapading. We need the framework of steady employment in a demanding occupation like a rocket needs its launching pad. It's impossible for us to soar to heights of delirium without firm grounding in—dare I say it?—regimentation. A wise man (his name escapes me) wrote: "The secret to happiness is performing at least one unpleasant task every day." (Not an exact quote, but near enough.) I think what the wise man means is that the unpleasant task provides necessary counterpoint, or simply that happiness needs something to react against if it's to truly blossom. Not that our work's unpleasant, but it is discipline, necessity of setting our hunger for frolic aside, which allows hunger to regather for future expression, and when resume expressing ourselves frolicsomely I know we're all the more uninhibited.

Ella, I'm positive this missive will find you fully prepared for today's exertions—I've no doubt you're humming on mind-sharpening adrenaline that'll breeze you through your IPO reviews.

Here's blessing your assured triumph!

Your,

DisciplineAdoringDamsel

V.9
Ella to Angie
Sunday, July 6, 2003 11:55 AM

Am wide awake, Angie, and thank you for your lullabies—I *know* they wafted through the atmosphere and arrived here and calmed me. I'm well-rested and crazy energized, had soothing dreams.

Wish my Sunday could be with you but, yes, it's an honor to be a part of this huge IPO and I'll be making the most of it—even relishing it.

Time to shower and get fluffy! Infinite kisses!

Your,

EnergizedIPOElla

V.10
Angie to Ella
Sunday, July 6, 2003 12:17 PM

Happy to hear you're electric and on the path to glory, Ella!

As for me, I'm decked out in a goody-two-shoes ensemble, will be attending Mass at St. Vincent Ferrer, acquiring solemnity. Afterwards I'll mosey over to The Boathouse and be very proper, exemplarily behaved, so's to contrast with last visit's exhibitionistic dousing. I'll be *excessively* religious, reading the Bible, while puff pastry flouncy.

Show 'em how it's done, Sweetness! Infinite blessings and kisses!
Your,
MissingYouInsanelyAngie

V.II
Angie to Ella
Sunday, July 6, 2003 8:59 PM

Imagine you're effortlessly conjuring forth legal brilliance, Darling, skimming along like windblown leaves on a lake's silvery sheen of a summer's afternoon, as I was pleased to see at The Boathouse.

Recently returned from The Boathouse I am, without having ruffled one feather—a fact that pleases me to no end precisely because we ruffled many feathers on summer's first day. A couple glances of apprehension from the staff greeted me upon arrival (nice to be memorable) and I accepted them as my due, all the while being a soft-spoken downcast-eyed girl following Mass, the program deliberately displayed in my hand. I do relish being opposites: two weeks ago a troublemaker, today an immaculately mannered young lady; two weeks ago shamelessly exposed in a drenched white skirt and black lingerie, today 100% decent in a gray dress with mid-shin hemline; two weeks ago my hair wet wildness spilling all over, today my hair wound tight in a bun.

The hostess in particular indicated she recalled our antics of summer's first day, greeting me with a penetrating look of warning that said: "Think twice before drenching yourself again!" I responded with flawless composure, a serene gaze that said: "I'm a good Mass-attending girl who wouldn't dream of misbehaving." Silent and instantaneous and civilized was our understanding of one another. She smiled and led me to a table on the deck, not far from where we'd drenched ourselves. When the waitress appeared I ordered a flute of bubbly and fruit plate.

I was there to quietly contemplate, not stir people up—was facing The Lake, gazing upon the ever shifting patterns of shimmering sunlight on the water, conferring with myself along the lines of: "Nothing's more fleeting than the fragile existence we've been given; whoever—whatever—gave us this gift of life did so with strings attached galore. I'm still a youngster, relatively speaking, but know it won't last long. Childhood's already gone (Strange how it seems like only yesterday, even though it seemingly lasted for decades.) and ten years hence will arrive in the blink of an eye. I'm in my prime—a beauty all the boys stare at lingeringly lustfully—but I'd be an idiot to fail to realize I'll be thirty, forty, fifty, sixty, seventy, eighty (with the grace of God) and looking back at this period of my life in no time. That's what my grandparents say—that the distance traveled from their twenties to their sixties seems shorter than the distance traveled from childhood to their twenties. Time's as precious as one's health and nothing's more unhealthy and self-defeating than being loathe to indulge the hunger of my slut's body while I still have a slut's body—no chance am I going to tolerate being reined in, denied my natural aptitude for lust kicks, by pathetic self-appointed guardians of 'decency.' When I'm old and gray, looking back on my life, do I want to be able to say with pride, 'I ignored cause-infatuated bores in the interest of my happiness, and had an uncountable amount of rejuvenating experiences'; or do I want to have to admit with shame, 'I heeded the preachings of judgmental killjoys at the expense of living a full life'? When I'm old I plan on being tickled pink at the choices I've made, how I've lived.

"And what's with this twisted notion of 'decency,' as in using the word to dissuade from sensory indulgence? Near as I can tell it's a con perpetrated by depressed, sickly, envious, backbiting failures who've relegated themselves to the sidelines of life. Near as I can tell it's the attempt by bloodless, coldhearted, mean-spirited haters of nature to subjugate those who thrill to the tingle of their blood. Near as I can tell it's the living dead seeking to drain away blood from the living.

"I'm still in wild young womanhood, privileged to hunger for frolic just about every waking moment and no one's going to get in the way of that or take it from me, because nothing's healthier—more productive of happiness and inner balance—out-and-out delightful—than frolic. It's beyond belief there are people who are dead set against me chasing sex-kicks when, far from harming anyone, I'm making myself and others cheerful—beyond belief sniveling killjoys are perverting the word 'decency,' using it to serve selfish, base, ignorant, anti-life ends.

"Mass was wonderful, something else I couldn't live without, and there's another variety of narrow-minded meddlesome self-serving twit, equally as contemptible as the 'decency' people, and it's those who attack religion; who preach (The people who hate religion always preach.) that the only worthwhile activity is devoting oneself to political causes, being an 'activist'; who cite assorted instances of religion being subverted to oppress others and then oh-so-conveniently conclude the world would be a better place without it. Well, what do these smug political-cause-infatuated dolts know about the nature of faith and prayer, that places them in a position to judge it? Fact is, religion's the *healthiest* subversion: it teaches us there's far more to existence than the civilization mankind's dreamed up; teaches us awareness of the transience of life and the necessity of living well and free, unhindered by the debilitating distractions of materialism; teaches us to shun the shallow pop culture trash that's displaced authentic emotion and communication, suckered weak-willed lazy fools into mistaking falsified existence for the real thing. Religion places the mysteries of existence—world previous to our birth and the world that will follow our death—before us and gives us the courage to question the doctrines of a society that neglects to take these mysteries into account and only seeks to imprison us in a finite dead-end world of arbitrary rules and obligations.

"Mass, like Miss Whippie, highlights matters of import. The readings from scripture, singing, recitations, hushed solemnity combine to create an atmosphere that empties my head of temporal distraction. I forget about my occupation and apartment and attendant responsibilities; forget about my wardrobe, newest pair of shoes; forget about my family and friends and neighbors and enemies; forget about my beloved Manhattan and my best male frolic mate Stevie and even my dearest Ella; forget my very name, when I was born; and, in place of these things, is an inner world that opens up and draws me within it. In short, I *pray*.

"Prayer is like gazing at the nighttime sky and understanding what a small part of the universe this world is at the same time one's opening oneself up to the starry distances, allowing them to wash the preoccupations of this world away. Prayer is the act of gazing upon the vastness within oneself and realizing waking consciousness is but an infinitesimal fraction of it. How deep can one delve before thought dissolves, surrenders to the unknowability of what makes us tick?—why we're on this earth, what the grand scheme is? Prayer is freedom via self-examination, act of communing with the wellsprings of life responsible for our breath. Prayer's another form of orgasm, turning inside out, surrendering to life's healing flow, being reborn.

"I emerge from Mass feeling pristine: assorted annoyances—differences with others, tedious practical tasks and errands—are rendered easy to deal with, deprived of the ability to irritate me. And why not? What are these things when placed alongside the inescapable precariousness of our existence? Our steady march towards the great unknown—a march that can be altered without our consent at any moment, as swiftly as shimmers shift on the surface of this lake in front of me?"

Ella, I've done my best to transcribe a hint of my contemplation-whirl—a futile endeavor, as one will never achieve more than an extremely insufficient approximation when one only has words to work with. Contemplation-whirl isn't linear: thoughts occur simultaneously, and are supplemented—sometimes entirely shoved aside—by emotions and images. Images and emotions, transcendent of thought and words, appear and vanish quicker than lightning slashes the skies. Watching sunlight flicker and shift and flare on The Lake, allowing rhythms of light and water to lull me into cycles of contemplation, was a beautiful way to spend a Sunday by my alonesome following Mass.

So it's early to bed, early to rise; then probably a week of being a lust-on-hold legal slave. But we'll emerge from enforced nundom soon enough, won't we? I anticipate that, by next week's end, we'll have reclaimed our territorial rights via a memorable frolic on firm premises.

Your,

ContemplationWhirlCutie

VI. Territorial Rights Regained & Fantasy Recollection Dress-Up

VI.1
Angie to Ella
Monday, July 14, 2003 10:30 AM

Ella, it shreds comprehension: how could you fail to report to work today, after we'd made plans upon which—need I say it?—our emotional and spiritual well-being depends? Our reclamation of the territory the ad agency snitch sought to snatch from us, remember? The girls' room stimulation fling that was to be reassertion of our right to please ourselves on firm premises whenever our workload permits. Did you forget, irresponsible girl? Today—following last week's please-our-clients frenzy that kept us hyper busy—was finally going to be chock full of feline funtime cheer. I arrive in one of my favorite dresses, with nothing on underneath, am afire for our projected adventure, and what happens? You don't show—doom me to unrequited desire, searing knots of frustration. In order that you may measure the extent of my desperation, I was compelled to insufficiently approximate our plans by tickling twatsie by my lonesome in one of the girls' room stalls—a stall we should've been sharing. And then Battleaxe DeRhight (partially identifiable by her plodding gait, beyond a doubt identifiable by her rancid throat-inflaming perfume) enters and takes the adjacent stall as I'm finger-flicking myself silly. Damn you, Ella! It would've been the quintessential reclamation of territory experience if you were with me, immediate restoration of our rightful frolic foundations. Not to mention I missed your tongue and heat. And, now? Alone, unfulfilled, and hating you in my office, glancing over this player's list without seeing the words—unsated lust blurring my attention span. I was so salivating for our girls' room rendezvous, and you're an extra bad evil girl.

It's the second time in two weeks you've let me down on a Monday, and what I want to know is: what's your excuse this time?

Your,

DisappointedDamsel; BetrayedBeauty; MessedWithMinx; VictimizedVixen; AngryAngie

VI.2
Ella to Angie
Monday, July 14, 2003 1:41 PM

Angie, I apologize profusely—humbly beg your indulgence. I wish I could say Stevie treated me to a surprise visit and swept me into another all-night fantasy excursion that necessitated a "sick" day due to sleep-deprivation, but I can't. Fact is, I got caught up in a fantasy remembrance thing last night, utterly lost track of time, and didn't climb into bed until five or something. I tried to go beddy-bye shortly after midnight, but accumulated heat in my body wouldn't allow it—was clearly Mommy Nature's chiding of me for not frolicking over the weekend. A randy girl like yours truly has got to keep her hot lil' butter-box well-churned if she expects to turn in at a reasonable hour.

Although failing to frolic over the weekend was hardly my fault, since I was catching up on work. I very conscientiously (I mean it: I was motivated by the best of intentions, with a mind to being free to bring our plans to glorious fruition this morning.) stayed indoors and shepherded five full versions of the [____] Agreement and Plan of Merger through, using my trusty scanner and the firm's never-to-be-praised-enough secretarial department. Alas, I was too conscientious: my neglect of girl needs caught up with me, derailed our plans.

I climbed into bed desirous of courting slumber and awakening refreshed and arriving at work hot for our adventure, but my skin was shimmering all over underneath itself and I couldn't close my eyes. Then my trailer trollop adventure of two weeks ago (Coincidentally, my first failing to report on a Monday violation.) comes swirling back in memory and sets me further ablaze; not content with that, memory further devils me with vivid pictures of my last nun-escaped-from-a-nunnery escapade. I had two choices: 1) lie awake blazing all night and get no sleep, or 2) get up and play in front of the mirror for a spell, seek to achieve some measure of calm, enable myself to sleep. Being a sensible girl, I chose the latter. You would've done the same.

What a curse it is to be a girl! And what a blessing it is to be a girl! No man will be prevented from sleeping by compulsion to play dress-up for half the night; by the same token, no man will know what it's like to melt with squirmalacious bliss while prancing before a mirror in stimulating costumes. You know how it is, Darling: recollection of my trailer trollop fun came to me, and I couldn't get into that outfit soon enough. Polyester leopard print skirt, a faded and torn orange blouse this time, the tacky wig, gold slippers, cheap hose with runs: no sooner did I put that stuff on again than I was itchy with slut juices, ready to gush fountains. Then I'm pouring myself a Scotch and putting a rolled up quarter sheet of paper in my mouth and drinking and pretend smoking while doing the same inept striptease Stevie commanded me to do, and—ha! the sensations I experienced with him return to me so stunningly I'm half believing I'm back at the Essex House. I get a pair of scissors and cut a hole in the hose where my troublesome lil' twinkle box is and, once my fingers have unlimited access, am seated with my back to the wall with legs spread and facing myself in the mirror, doing a gentle number on my love-bud, and—Jesus! how quickly I crest! It's not often I cry out with the force of flooding when all by myselfsie.

Was merely the warm-up, Angie. Moments after Miss Trailer Trollop compels me to cream, Miss Nun steps forward. You must understand that, by being the first in line, Miss Trailer Trollop had primed pinkling for further needs, imparted increasingly compelling itches: I couldn't get rid of her torn hose and put on Miss Nun's habit soon enough. Make no mistake: Miss Nun entered my bloodstream with authority, and I was truly a dazed girl possessed. First, lipstick: I was atremble like a sapling in high wind while smearing on the moist scarlet. While applying lipstick and proceeding to eyeliner and mascara I was made to fully understand what it is to be a lust-flayed kitty. I kid you not, there was a picture in my head of a female leopard clawing at a hot African savannah's long golden grass, snarling with impatience to be seized by the back of her neck by a fierce male and plowed 'til she yowled—my body was ashake with the image. Then I slipped on the fishnets I'd worn for Stevie on our nun-game Tuesdays, added the racy lacy red half-cups, then the nun costume—customized version of what nuns wear: the silk swishing crackling smoothness all over me—my legs flashing through slits up the sides—the black and white habit elevating my complexion's glow, making me look very inspired. I was regarding myself in the mirror and suddenly it was as if I was Stevie looking at me with hunger ablaze in his eyes. And *I* was ablaze with hunger, believe it! I could barely endure two minutes of it before I was on the floor, back to the wall again, and petting kittikins as if for the first time last night.

Damn if I didn't find myself hungering for that ridiculous novelty dildo! I'd never used it: when it comes to sending myself off, I'm really just a rub-a-dub-my-bud girl—a stroking-of-petals girl, rarely slipping my fingers within. For some reason self-pleasure's usually lessened if I seek to duplicate a full-fledged plowing. But last night, while draped in Miss Nun's get-up and with recollection of Stevie's skill seething in my blood, I couldn't help but crawl across the floor to the dresser. Dear, you would've laughed to see me, as I laughed when glancing back and spying myself in the mirror: on all fours, nun's outfit spilling all around me, with my exposed behind twitching something fierce.

I retrieve Sir Dildo from the dresser and return with him to my place against the wall, then—damn! the thing's plastic surface is dry and won't go in comfortably, wet though I am. So I'm licking it like crazy to goo it up and I drop it on the floor and maybe it gets dust on it and, clearly, I don't want dust in my vagina; so I must go to the bathroom to wash Sir Dildo and I'm blazing with so much impatience I'm about to scream. Finally, I get Sir Dildo cleaned and lubricate him, with that water-based gel, and return to my post. I ease Sir Dildo inside me while squirming against the wall and staring at Miss Nun in the mirror, and then I'm no longer Ella! Suddenly I'm Stevie staring at Miss Nun—her crimson lips, black and white habit, obligingly open legs—while plowing her, delving slow and hard. Right, I steadily work Sir Dildo deeper and Sir Dildo is Stevie's sword in my sheath and I'm Stevie watching me who's Miss Nun in the mirror! Get it? But there's one aspect of this trading-places-with-myself-in-the-mirror game, or illusion, that doesn't entirely work, and that's the way my sheath clenches Sir Dildo tightly and ripples—way my tummy shudders, the tremble-wave arriving! La deuxieme la petite morte assuredly belongs to me, obliterates the role-switch stuff in a second! I'm Ella again when I slip sideways onto the floor, rolled up in a ball, gasping with pleasure.

So such is how I partially spent last night, Angie, why I didn't manage to shut my eyes in slumber 'til way late. As for the other part of last night, it seems my double dose of being doubled over with procreative pyrotechnics placed me in an electric daze that further shoved sleep away. (With my blessing, as it was most delightful to be enveloped in the wonders of post-orgasmic gratification, lie on the floor shimmering serenely.) And there was also a bubble bath and some reading. But I ask you, in hope of mitigating your annoyance: am I to blame I'm frequently bedeviled by my imagination? Is it my fault recollections of my adventures often approach the intensity of the adventures themselves? Are you going to hate me for being at the mercy of an imagination-stung body? And there's been plenty going on lately to feed my imagination, mind you. It's been a fortnight's worth of Stevie festivities, two new costumes added to our ever-expanding collection. So it's hardly surprising I overflowed last night on account of being a good lil' law slave all weekend, failing to heed the lashings of lust. Then again, I am a bad girlfriend for missing our girls' room rendezvous—a *bad* girl! Here, I'm exposing my behind and whacking it for you, using a ruler! Bad girl! Red streaks appear where the ruler strikes! Bad girl! I'm keying with one hand, swatting myself with the other! Bad girl! The ruler stings, Honey! It smarts like hell! Are you happy?

Of course you're not happy! You're still hating me while burning up in your office! All I can say is I'll be at the firm for you tomorrow.

Bye for now, Sweetheart. I'm starving and need to devour a cantaloupe and an egg and slab of lox. Then another bubble bath, general lounging. I adore doing absolutely nothing sometimes, don't you?

Your,

FantasyFlayedFloozie

P.S. Surprise, Angie! I'm in my office and have been here since around 10:45. Sorry to play a lil' joke, but wished to account for myself via above narrative before revealing my presence. Now I'm going to call you from my cell and pretend I'm still at home (tee hee!) and tell you to read this email *toute suite*. That way, it shouldn't be too long before you know I'm here. We still have the afternoon for fun at the firm.

VI.3
Angie to Ella
Monday, July 14, 2003 5:07 PM

So annoying to be separated! After all your hard work over the weekend, the opposition had to cross comments with you and get you torn away from me. As much as I admire Sturmheld and am grateful to him for involving you in the most important deals, I could've raked my nails across his face when he grabbed you on the way to my office.

At least we got in a few lickies in the girls' room. First, our pretty-each-other-up session between the mirrors, multi-refracted angles in which to admire our radiant complexions and tumbling hair. Sure, you indulged in mirror star stuff aplenty last night, but can a girl get enough of adoring herself? of seeing to it others join in on the adoration, by keeping highlights and shadows fresh, making sure she's optimally presented? (There's competition out there, smugness is death.) Which reminds me: we're overdue for a trading-of-make-up-expertise session in my bathroom. What a sweet microcosm of a perfect universe it is when we're under the vanity lights and the steam's flowing, making us slippery and aglow. Impossible to underestimate the positive outlook sustaining benefits of giggle-communion during let's-get-seductive games. And you're such a whiz with the mascara wand, Honey, Michelangelo would be lost in admiration. And is my lipstick a soother, or what?—coconut oil additive makes a girl's lips permanently wet—enables a girl to go through the day feeling she's just been kissed.

You're such a sly minx, Sweetie: sneaking in that ass-grab when Bertha wandered in and was boring us again with interminable whining. (Wailing about receiving next to no eye contact at meetings—never suspecting people avoid looking at her because they don't want to risk becoming captive listeners, subjected to moroseness.) It was all I could do to prevent myself from laughing in Frumpy's face when you seized and squeezed me. Complainer Bertha doesn't understand what can be done under the flowing fabric of dresses in front of others because she only wears baggy pants. I've never seen a woman so poorly rigged! She doesn't appear to understand breasts ought to be supported, seems to want everything to sag. Have you ever seen a ship lisp so badly? Poor Bertha's assets always look like they're about to plunk on the floor.

Finally, Bertha exits—in a flash we're cozy in the center stall. How your azure eyeliner sets off the silver brimming in your baby blues—silver's in your babies, plus lots of lust. Such sweet lasers your babies are, when you're crouching to squirm inside me with slippery-slide tongue—when you pause to gaze up at me as you're poised to dive. I wish you could see yourself, Ella—you're a cat aprowl for birds in the garden and a child with a favorite toy rolled into one. What an insistent creature your tongue is—insistent like an eel traveling upstream to its spawning grounds and wriggling tickling the while. Such a tease is your touch, then it's swiftly incomparable gratification—you impart a trembly assertiveness—shoot sparkles into my bloodstream, engulf me in gasps, whirl my thoughts. I taste Paradise when rocking slow and gently pumping my tummy while burying my fingers in your feather soft hair as you beam your sensitivity—fine-tuned nerves and focused desire—into me. It's like an electric ghost is slipping under my skin, strumming my senses, saturating me with stimulating vibrations. Then I'm breathing deeply and erratically as the inner vibrations intensify—my oh my, I flood *so* fast! That's my complaint! Don't you know restraint?

Ha! If we wanted restraint, we'd attempt to enlist prissy prude Ellen—oh, I'm sorry: *Shmellen!*—in our escapades, wouldn't we? And, of course, soon as I'm set to reciprocate the said Shmellen bumbles into the stall on our right. To prevent her from glancing under the divider and spying two pairs of feet, you climb onto the seat and crouch on your ankles, and I need to stand so she doesn't see someone's crouching on the floor. And I don't care if our regaining of territorial rights would've been better served had I fluffed your muff on my feet while Miss Priss was next door—I was thirsty for you and didn't want my attention divided between administering pleasure and guarding against being found out, plus was too impatient to wait for Shmellen to exit, plus further interruptions could've occurred and sabotaged the flow all over. I was in a pleasure-purist frame of mind, you see! I wanted to sip your nectar—make my cheeks slippery—absolutely single-mindedly, no distractions diluting the experience—wanted the two of us to be the only girls on earth until I was done with you. I didn't want to have to worry about gasping too loud—or of kitty-meowing, hyperventilating.

Alas, no sooner do I drag you out of there to finish you off in my office with door locked (and blasted shades drawn) than Sturmheld waylays us in the hall, steals you from me! So I'm here alone and, yes, you've treated me to a fine swoosh in the bloodstream, but we were only getting started. Springing to a start then forced to stop before the finish line's approached, much less crossed, is worse than not starting. Better to have not set my blood to racing in the first place—now I've been robbed of a direction to flow in, destination. My flushed face yearns for a muff-bath—itching pores scream for a flowerpuss facial. Coconut oil lipstick notwithstanding, my lips are parched for lack of your moisture. Yeah, I'm a girl's dream—I may very well enjoy giving more than receiving. I adore having your muffy at my mercy! All of it: lip-nips, bud-rubs, tongue-tickles!—the seizing of your behind, encouraging of your thighs to clamp me. When you firmly embrace my face with your thighs, are holding my head in a vise of soft smooth creamy skin as my tongue darts deep! As you know, I've gushed while making you gush.

I don't care about territorial rights anymore—only want to content my raging blood by contenting you. What's the likelihood of it happening today? How long must I wait until my head's clasped by your thighs as I tongue-tickle you to gasping in sweet surrender?—until I'm overcome by communion-sighs? Please advise, Darling! I'll get loopy if we have to wait until after work! If those pests keep acting up and you need to stay afterhours, I shudder to think where my frame of mind will go.

Your,

DesperateDeprivedDarling

VI.4
Ella to Angie
Monday, July 14, 2003 5:31 PM

Dollface, I'm in conference room 44S—alone for now, so hasten over! Now, Dear! One way or another, we'll seize some fun on the run.

Your,

PrincessPantingForPollination

VI.5
Angie to Ella
Monday, July 14, 2003 5:33 PM

See you in seconds, Sweets! Kissing you already!

Your,

OutOfMySensesAngie

VI.6
Ella to Angie
Monday, July 14, 2003 10:14 PM

You wrote of how nuts you were getting due to being blocked from returning the favor after you'd fluttered: what of the instrument of your flutter, inflammable me? Orgasms, as we well know, are highly contagious and not to be toyed with, and that goes extra when one's just been the cause of one. You wrote of me beaming sensitivity inside you while conjuring forth a crest? What of the way your climb towards the crest—gulping-of-breath pauses, delicate shudders, inner ripples—registers upon my nerves, sweeps me under my skin, desire's waves surging? I tongue-tickled your cream-machine and made you flood and, by so doing, placed myself in dire need of the same! So you start in on me—tease with light tongue tickles, their hesitation winding me up—and then Shmellen (What is it Giovanna said she looks like? An albino chicken? So devilishly spot-on.) enters the adjacent stall, and—well, who cares? Why didn't you knuckle down, complete your mission? I was humming with so much excitement I could barely see right—the air was watery, blurry—and then you decide you're in a "pleasure-purist frame of mind" and break off! Extremely irresponsible and selfish!

Angie, don't flare up in your beautiful brown eyes—dart an angry glare at my words. Sorry, but couldn't resist needling you a bit for having the cheek to complain of your plight when, of the two of us, I was by far the most deprived and to be pitied. Besides, you made the right decision: a "pleasure-purist frame of mind" is the only right and proper frame of mind to be in whilst absorbed in sacred procreation-communion.

Can you discern I'm slightly skitter-scatter? I reassert that you—we, actually—made the correct choice. How could we know Sturmheld would find us in the hall and derail our pleasure? When he was telling me to go to 44S and review the comments the opposition (Intimidated hicks suffering from anti-NYC syndrome: not sticking to the schedule's their way of showing us "big city folk" they're not going to be pushed around and taken advantage of. They don't realize we readily see through such shoddiness, detect feelings of inferiority, and will use such against them—Sturmheld's going to permit himself the pleasure of taking it personally, really drag them through the grinder. Not to mention that I, as the person who's most suffered from their insufferable unwillingness to stick to protocol, will take special care to slip in carefully worded passages that seem to be saying things they aren't and that the hicks will need to be very attentive to catch.) sent over the weekend while we were still preparing ours, I was bouncing off the walls with impatience to be spreadeagled on the carpet of your office, nearly out of my mind with denied desire. Such was the disturbed state of my body, I was half-convinced it was obvious to others and Sturmheld might guess what we were up to. Remember when I heatedly and lengthily cursed those dolts, assured Sturmheld I'd apply an extra critical eye to their manipulations? Heartfelt as it was, that was mainly done to mask my hot and bothered state—was me doing a cause-of-heated-emotion switcheroo, getting him to assume my unsettledness was a consequence of outrage at their behavior. And it worked out well—he said, "I'm glad you're on my team instead of theirs," with an appreciative smile. Which just goes to show that firing ourselves up at the firm's also a bright career move—adds to the amount of fervor we bring to our responsibilities, ensures we're appreciated.

Commonplace occurrences have birthed revolutionary ideas—Newton and the apple falling from the tree, Franklin and lightning striking his kite—and humble me was permitted to experience a hint of that, simply by virtue of my physical placement in the conference room. I was standing at the far side of the long wide table, yards from the door, when the lightning struck. I pictured you on your knees, pleasuring me under the folds of my dress, shielded from view by the tabletop, and thought: "All we need do is scatter papers on the floor. The necessity of picking them up will explain why Angie's on her knees if someone enters as she's tongue-fluttering me." And the rest, Honey, is history.

So pretty you were—a preciously blithe princess—when you entered the room, a pearly claw-clip bunching your hair, flinging it down your back in tangles of curls. You shut the door and were about to lock it when I shook my head (As others were occasionally popping in to assist, locking was inappropriate and could've aroused suspicion.) and you weren't sure what to make of that, whether our date had been cancelled or not. All I needed do was cast my eyes at my feet and you understood instantly, scampered to me laughing. I'd resisted temptation to soothe myself in any way, the better to thrill to your loving touch once we were together at last, and the move paid off nicely when you crouched at my feet and slid your hands up my legs devilishly slow, swirled sparkles under my skin and up my spine; when you applied your tongue to the task of spreading my wetness around, making me soppy warm; when you licked your fingers and slipped them inside me and strummed my spasm-strings with flawless technique. I was obliged to brace myself against the table, palms flat on it, the second you started in on me—seconds later I was squirming and gasping like a fish on dry land.

Damn if the doorknob doesn't rattle! Am *I* rattled? Nay! I'm amused when morose Justin skulks in to suggest a thoroughly useless and inconsequential tweaking of some obscure passage—he's attempting to create the impression he's involved in the deal, instead of a tagalong wannabe who probably won't last another month. Our regaining of territorial rights mission flickers in my thoughts, suddenly seems silly. I mean, of course the firm's our playground and we can muff-fluff one another galore! Why worry about regaining what hasn't been lost? In the meantime, I'm aware you're frozen under the table, poised to seize handfuls of papers. Justin has no idea you're there or that I'm on the edge of flooding. I'm very politely, through clenched teeth, thanking him for his input and stressing I'd like to be alone to think clearly—shoving him towards the door with my eyes. I'm also mirth-tickled, marveling at the daring of you and I—rather, marveling at how it's not really daring, because there's no chance he could know what we've been up to should he spot you. Once Justin's gone we have ourselves a lil' giggle fest, and my laughter meshes with your tongue divinely once it's back to business. No disrespect to your second-to-none skills, Darling, but my mirth had a hand in sending me to swoonsville.

I'm right that we couldn't have been caught, right? A rattling doorknob sends you under the table on hands and knees and there are papers spilled around: you're gathering them or—even better—searching for one I need that shouldn't have been tossed there, and the shades are down. (*That* won't be forgotten again.) My God, we were *so* solemn last week regarding our right to frolic at the firm, ridiculously worried! Caught off guard by an informant, it's true, but how could we have permitted self-doubt to oppress and depress us? Idleness is absolutely the enemy—idleness breeds thinking and thinking breeds fear, and action's the high tide that washes rot from the shoreline. The moment we returned to action self-doubt, smothering mental oppression, vanished—action's the ticket to a healthy sated body and overjoyed mind.

Who can rob us of a right if they have no idea we're exercising it? What's with this reclamation rubbish, when no one took anything from us? Not being hubristic—just realistic. It's not like I'm going to tackle you in the hallway with the Blumklins of this world looking on.

Action had vanquished trepidation, so why restrict myself to incompletely savoring orgasm on my feet? In a flash I'm on my back, halfway under the table, atop the papers we've tossed there. You're always stunning, Angie, but in this instance how your eyes pulsate with love! Then our kiss—your ardent spirit humming in my mouth, trading places with my pulse, shivering throughout me—a lithe lust-mad lass, mirror image of myself, to pull close and squeeze for all I'm worth—tact, sultriness, and grace to reverberate in unison with—silk soft squirminess to kiss and caress whilst adrift on procreation's swell.

We're on the floor—I'm gazing into your bliss-brimming eyes, reaching up your dress for handfuls of succulent girl tush, hugging you close, and what happens? Sturmheld chooses that special moment to bring me his latest changes: both bad and good, right? Bad because it's another interruption. Good because we get to confirm how excellent our contingency plan is and how clever we are, plus hopefully to drive home the fact the firm will always be open season as far as frolic goes. The way we spring apart at rattling of the doorknob, fling our hemlines down, commence gathering those papers before Sturmheld has time to circle to our side of the table. Then he's bending down to see what we're doing and I say, "Picking up the mess I made." and he chuckles a bit, joke-asking if you'd like to work on [_____] too—the joke being Rikert would raise holy hell if anyone attempted to poach you. You leave nothing to chance—produce the Carnegie's menu, ask Sturmheld if he'd like to order with us. Well, it's news to me we're ordering—you catch me by surprise—but I'm instantly Miss PlayAlong. "I'm dying for a sturgeon omelet," I say. The menu's a brilliant touch, instantly confers legitimacy to your being in 44S. So the three of us place an order. Sturmheld actually is hungry, so you wind up doing a second good deed, the first being services rendered to yours truly, of course.

Angie, I estimate a couple more hours of perfecting the revisions (as if this email hasn't delayed us enough) before I'll be over so we can resume riding vitality's waves, transforming our persistently pesky itches into upwelling serenity. Speaking of which, don't you dare cheat me by dipping your fingers in your honey before I arrive. Not one dip—not one stroke—not one itsy bitsy fingertip flick. I want you as satiation-starved, raked across the raw wires of your nerves, as I am.

See you (hopefully) not too long after midnight, Angel.

Your,

MuffCravingMaenad

VI.7
Angie to Ella
Monday, July 14, 2003 10:49 PM

Not to worry, Ella Honey: I'm policing myself as much as you could wish. Muffy's itching for ministration aplenty, believe it, and Miss Hand's thirsting to dip below to stir her, but then Mr. Hand (the other one) immediately slaps Miss Hand away, thereby preventing her from cheating you. But do hurry! I can only last for so long before Miss Hand gets pent up enough to get fed up, give Mr. Hand a nasty scratch and send him packing and, should such happen, you know I won't be responsible for any fingerplay done without your participation.

But enough: you should be finishing the APM instead of reading this—please do wrap up your work and bring your nectar to me.

Your,

NectarCravingNubile

VII. Harlot Impersonation, a Cab Ride, & Pink Grapefruit Tarts

VII.1
Ella to Angie
Friday, July 18, 2003 11:01 PM

Hey Choosy Floozy: was today's one of our wildest lunch hours in history, or what? Three glorious hours instead of a paltry hour! Such a favorable confluence of coincidence. I'd been standing pat on the [_____] matter since morning due to standoffishness in negotiations. Assuming anyone noticed, no one cared I was gone so long, least of all Sturmheld. Then you're able to pawn off the due diligence on the *capable* first-year, Rikert to finally allowing you to do it. (Considering your starring role on [_____], you more than deserved a multi-hour lunch hour—in addition, that is, to your juicy bonus, nor to forget Intranet stardom, and the—ha ha!—commemorative statuette/trophy to add to the others.) Talk about being given the green light to put on our red lights. Talk about a golden opportunity to run amok like drunken sailors on shore leave.

When we hauled our svelte lil' selves to the Marriott, were milling about in the lobby, I had no idea what we'd wind up doing. I had in mind some random teasing—flashings of thigh, brief displays of stocking tops and lower reaches of ass cheeks, leanings-forward so's breasties half pop out of our bras. The usual exhibitionistic smorgasbord—nothing extraordinary, just girls being girls. But flashing games sometimes evolve as if with a will of their own, demand to become something more—drag us along, alter our moods, birth unexpected impulses. Suddenly being stared at wasn't enough and I needed additional interaction—more reverberation. I wanted irrefutable evidence a stranger was suffering due to lusting to grab me. When all's said and done, a stare's too vague and noncommittal: men who stare are often terrified of doing anything else. Staring's window-shopping, mental ogling of the goods, with no commitment to buy. Staring's too often a self-deluded clown endeavoring to persuade himself he's capable of bedding someone besides his significant other, assuming he has one. It's often self-flattery, as in a beaten-down domesticated dolt informing himself he'd happily nail me to the floor, if only he had the time—or freedom from responsibility—or any other excuse he can dream up. A drop-jawed gawk-eyed stare doesn't mean a man's interested in exchanging a word or even getting near enough to whiff my perfume (Note how quickly some glance away with reddening guilty faces soon as we turn to meet their eyes.) so, in a way, allowing such a man to merely stare is letting him off far easier than he deserves.

Sometimes I get to thinking: "So you guys want a free eye-meal, no questions asked? I'm a dizzy ditz of a doll with a delightful shape for you to sight-ogle and fantasize about, no strings attached? I'm here to provide you with masturbation-pictures and you won't be otherwise engaging with me, speaking to me? We'll see about that!" So I stare straight back at them, or strut straight up to them, or speak straight at them, and it's sad how often their expressions flail with panic.

OK, so sometimes the gawkers don't panic—sometimes I confront a man who's delighted I've done so when, of course, I have no interest in him. Has this lil' girl rashly backed herself into a corner, blundered into a maze she can't find her way out of? Hardly! The fake-tromped-on-foot routine works wonders. I abruptly step towards the guy, crowd him, compel him to shuffle his feet, then—ha ha!—abruptly bend down, seize an ankle, wail about being stepped on—dart him a glance of withering reproach. What can he do? Apologies avail him nothing. I gaze at him in fear, like he's a savage beast bent on harming me. "This is how you treat a woman? This is your idea of getting to know me? You crush my toes?" He can do nothing but stand paralyzed as I dart him a last look of terror, hastily scamper away. I'm never afraid of getting in over my head: it's easy to erase the seduction sequence, flip the emotional scenery from desire to dismay, exit in an ink-cloud of fabricated violation.

OK, I'm veering from our afternoon—call me a giddy girlie, on account of the fun we had masquerading and ass-parading. We were in the Marriot's lobby, a number of out-of-towners were there. I wanted an overt, apart from mere staring, declaration of hankering to grab me; wanted a dose of seduction-interaction-gone-awry; wanted to plunge a pompous asking-for-it dimwit into confusion and fear. (As civilization-pampered felines, we need to occasionally remind ourselves we possess claws, right? It's not emotionally healthy for us girls to be fluffy and conciliatory and submissive at *all* times. I'd wither and die inside if I didn't allow myself to be a devil now and then and I make no apologies, since I'd sooner die than convulse a *nice* man with confusion.)

Pretending to be hookers in the lobby—stopping short of collecting cash, thereby not overstepping legality, having the fun of toeing that line—so's to bring about the degree of interaction I craved was as otherworldly as educational. Seems I adore kicking "Ass Peddler Ella" fantasies into gear. Until today it's been innocent roleplay in my apartment, the man (usually Stevie) knowing I'm a gainfully employed oh-so-respectable girl: sidling up to strangers and aggressively date-chatting them lifts fantasy to dizzyingly transformative "I don't believe I'm doing this!" heights. And blocks from the firm! The instant I sprang my surprise on those two and they firmly believed I was a working girl the wildest of thrill-chills shot up my spine, engulfed me in giddy bliss, caused quimmy's flaps to flare. I'm starting to fear the harlot impersonation game could become addictive, and that I'll be hankering to play it regularly. Angie, you've got to stop me! A taste or two of harlot impersonation, well and good, but I'd rather not have to explain to a cop I'm a fake hooker—an attorney masquerading for kicks.

As long as no cash trades hands and we don't specifically mention what's for sale, have zilch intention of putting out, it's alright, right? No laws broken? But, God Angie! The fact sex-solicitation's illegal's the main attraction. The fact the firm wouldn't look kindly, to put it *very* mildly, upon two of its promising second-year's pretending to be rent-a-girls is added attraction. Ooooo! Fantasy dragging me towards danger, afraid I'll be undone by fondness for contrast! Like, one moment we're safe in our offices, the next were ass-flashing and fast-talking leering out-of-towners who believe we're for sale. And, oh no! I can envision myself becoming so infatuated with the pretend prostitute game that getting arrested will become something to strive for, instead of avoid. There's the potential of losing sensible perspective, which—unfortunately—is added temptation to travel the path, even if I don't want to. Again, Angie, I'm counting on you to stop me from going precariously far—tasting of being a fallen woman's one thing, turning into one's another. Sometimes my imagination devils and scares me.

Well, I'm so flingsy-aboutsy in my thoughts it's tough to settle myself enough to tell our adventure in order and, yeah, I *adore* the disorientation. Here's another stab at chronological presentation:

Chuck was loitering near the wall phones with his pal Troy and we didn't know we'd be debuting our hooker act: they were a couple of sillies to monkey with. Dearest, it was considerate of you to conceal yourself behind that pillar, allow me to fly solo at first. Supreme kicksville to start in on flustering them unassisted, knowing you were ready to jump in at my signal, add situational layering.

So Chucky and Troysie are behaving oafish by the phones. They have too much time on their hands and are revealing themselves to be petty, small-minded, meanspirited hicks. They're gazing out the window—screwing their faces into looks of contempt, puffing themselves up real stupid, ineffectually concealing feelings of inadequacy by spouting the usual intimidated out-of-towner trash: that New York men dress too fancy and are of questionable sexual orientation; that the women are snobbish uptight bitches who only like pretty boys; that the streets are filthy and smelly; that everyone's loud and rude; that they don't see what the big deal is, it's "overrated." Overrated is the favorite word of visitors baffled by our town's pulse—who find themselves unable to adapt, aflail instead of having fun; find themselves frustrated on the sidelines like this precious pair, staring out a window at the throngs on the sidewalk instead of plunging in. "Overrated" is their way of indicating they're unable to detect the profusion of personalities because they're possessed of a paltry one; way of announcing: "I'm

a one-dimensional dullard baffled and ill at ease because I'm surrounded by invitations to thrills requiring imagination and courage." That's
our pair of prank patsies! They're smugly delivering the pathetically
predictable verdict, "overrated,"—have no idea NYC, in the incarna-
tion of us, will be tossing them into the sort of strife and stress they
dread, so richly deserve. Are we agents of fate? Ha! Fun to pose the
question, but of course it's silly and I withdraw it, lest I be as smug as
our patsies.

Just think, Angie: when our targets are meanspirited venom-spew-
ing creeps pranking becomes a form of social justice—we're cast in
the role of vigilantes, meting out punishment to the deserving. Not
to suggest we need to feel socially sanctioned, though. Transforming
commonplace situations into playgrounds is our right simply because
it's thrillsville; the heady rush of joy resulting from masquerading is
the only justification we'll ever need. Pranking vitalizes our blood,
pure and simple healthy! Hail the emotional unity afforded by pranking!—no sickly second-guessing, self-dividedness, muddying resolve!

Damn! Why do I keep losing the thread, wandering from the
seduction-sequence? (At this rate, my telling will take 'til dawn.) You
duck behind the pillar, up I step to those two—an ass-peddling hussy
shamelessly advertising my wares. (That's when I knew I'd be acting
the part of rent-a-girl: the second I traipsed up to them it popped
into my head.) We had the gowns on, thanks to quick change in the
ladies'—very accommodating of the Marriot. Out of corporate wear,
into flowing formals. Do hotel lobby hookers often deck themselves
out in ball gowns? Is that the treat tricks expect? I tend to doubt it!
But, hey, always fulfilling to topsy-turvy conventions of fashion and
occupation, mix and mismatch. Besides, never underestimate the effect
of a swishing-at-the-ankles gown, especially if it has slits running up the
sides nearly to one's frilly scarlet skimpies. And if it's also sleeveless and
low-necked, with one's breasts peeping out a bit, and hugs skintight
above upper-thigh.

So I stomp up to our pair, say "Hello gentlemen!" with a wink
and a smile, wiggle of my tongue at my upper lip. Uh, oh! Seems
I've dropped my locket necklace—fancy that happening. Also seems
I turn my behind towards them while bending to pick up the necklace. My gown's so tight at my waist that when I bend forward it's

tummy-squeezing me, and we know what suchlike squeezies do to twatsie. Almost instantly dripping with wet I am when bending over, flashing those two with panty-lined behind. I feel them take hard swallows, get wrought up. I do a quick onceover of their expressions through the drapery of my dress: they have popping-from-the-sockets eyes. Amazing what a lil' cheeky-cheek shot (Ol' reliable!) will do to a man's frame of mind: suddenly they cease trashing our town—the sole occupant of their attention's your Ella. And my gown's slick silk's still gripping my tummy, caressing me electric, shooting tinglies into my tight warm place. I'm always off and sprinting dizzy fast when absorbed in exhibitionism: curious how lust gleaming in the eyes of others sparks me, regardless of my opinion of them. It's no doubt a toss-back to our primeval heritage, when the lustful eyes of males in the forest would cause females to freeze in their tracks, become squishy and compliant, receptive for propagation of our species. Interesting how the wilds live on within us; how in current surroundings the old signals persist and cause inner twitches, as of feathers tickling me deep. Very reassuring to remain in touch with our distant past.

So I'm bent over to pick up the accidentally-on-purpose-dropped necklace (Funny how the slippery lil' chain keeps eluding my grasp, thereby necessitating I continue tush-flashing.) and my gown's pressing tight to my tummy and I'm drawing deeper breaths and holding them, such that the air's a caress in my lungs; plus I'm being stared at intently, surging in response; plus I'm thrilling to the thought of how I'm leading these two on, inspiring desire I've no intention of sating: these elements combine to whip up steady heat in my passionflower. So who, it might be asked, is most being seduced? Yours truly or the tricks? Ha, I adore when roles blur and it's tough to tell who's most under the other's spell. I'd never wish to be the only one calling the shots—forgo unexpected flip-arounds, tastings of my own medicine. Chuck and Troy have a snowball's chance in hell of getting their hands on me and still I'm willing to concede I'm also being seduced, and why not? Male lust is male lust and, if a girl be as exhibitionistically inclined as I am, then male lust projected via steady staring is able to turn her oblivious of whatever shoddy personality a male may possess—that is, as long as we're only speaking of exhibitionism. At one and the same time I can be despising them and stimulated by the desire they're beaming forth. No wonder dolts commonly declare they "can't figure women out."

"Gotcha, tricky necklace chain!" I squeal, then spring up straight and roll my shoulders as if I'm in aerobics class, whip about to face them: renewed astonishment bursts from their gaze, palpable shock emanates from their bodies. I smile, do a slow clockwise of my tongue about my lips while thrusting out my chest, reaching behind my neck to put the necklace on. Once the clasp is secure, I step near them, blithely ask, "Would you like to see it?" as I pop open the locket. "See? That's me as a girl in Catholic school." (It's the picture Stevie took of me in April under the flowering trees behind the Met. I'm wearing a scarlet, black, and white plaid pleated skirt, white knee-high socks, and silver-buckle shoes—giggling as I lift the skirt halfway up my thighs.)

Seems our pair are embarrass-faced, speechless. Perhaps the fact I'm intentionally crowding them has something to do with it. I'm doing the girl-projecting-her-energy trick: pulling myself tight, tensing all muscles, surrounding myself with an aura of sizzling slut energy, drawing them into my magnetic field. Nor does it hurt that the locket's inches from my chest, such that Chuckso and Troyso have a front row seat at my breasts rhythmically swelling and subsiding.

"Do you like my Catholic school uniform?" I ask, fluttering my eyelids.

"Uh..." answers Chuck, apparently unable to articulate.

Troy does slightly better, managing, "It's a good dress...good colors...I..." before lapsing into confusion.

Despite their embarrassment, the tongue-hanging-out-look's still on their faces: discomfort combined with desire, each fighting for dominance, is what I'm looking for. I have my fish solidly on the line—time to reel them in, leave them gasping for air on the lake bank.

"So gentlemen, would you like to see me in this dress *(I jiggle the locket a bit.)*, upstairs in one of your rooms? It can be arranged...for a favor," I say in a bouncy-sugary voice. Blithe little girl pitter-patter is what truly disarms men: it goes against the male mentality to argue with little girls, even if the little girl possesses the physique and searching eyes of a mature woman. "I could wear that dress," I continue, "or be a nurse or chambermaid or librarian or nun or babysitter or secretary. I have lots of costumes, am willing to indulge any fantasy.

And this," I add with a giggling slap at my behind, "is part of the package, no extra charge."

Troy's cheeks twitch, hands fidgeting as if seeking to scamper away, hide. Chuck jerkily glances away, clears his throat to buy himself a few seconds of stall time. They exchange panicked glances, silently ask one another: "Maybe we ought to bolt?" But, ha! They can't bolt! Their eyes might dart towards the exit; their legs might get ready to walk fast; they might wonder if they're getting themselves into serious trouble; but, in the end, they're mesmerized by my svelte lil' number of an eager body and sweet voice and, especially, by the way I seize each of them by the wrist and passionately squeeze, thereby shooting sex-energy into their bloodstreams. Yes, the good ol' wrist-squeeze, another reliable girl weapon: pleasure suffuses their faces despite themselves, their bodies are informing their hesitation to get lost. Try as Chucko and Troyo might, they can no more fly away than a moth can from a flame.

"I'm sorry, but you're going to need to make up your minds for me," I say in the same honeyed tone. "I like both of you very much but if you can't decide I won't be able to talk to you anymore and must move on." I bring forth a pout, do the trembling eye thing, then gaze at the floor.

Again the eloquent Chuck enunciates: "Uh..." Troy's unable to make a sound.

"Are you going to be my saviors or not?" I ask with a sudden edge in my voice, adding: "It's not nice of you to burn up my time when I have so little of it. You're well off, I'm not. All I'm trying to do is show you a good time. Is that a crime? I'd hate to think you're leading me on."

Angie, that's when I begin experiencing unease in my own right, fear I'm drawing myself too far into the situation. I'm but vaguely aware of their reactions—am too distracted by inner warning-pulses, cautionary tightening. The moment I become confrontational's the moment the bottom falls out of my acting, nameless possible unpleasant consequences churning my thoughts. So I signal for you to rescue me and you don't waste time, arrive on the spot. From panic-flutters I whirl into finding it tough to hold in a laugh! The way you come stomping up (Your heels emphatically clackety-clacking, announcing your anger before your voice does.) and hiss: "Low-budget tramp, who gave you permission to come to my lobby? You're only fit for quickies in the back of delivery trucks in trash-strewn alleys!" You seize a handful of my hair. You kick at me and—thank you, Dearest—intentionally miss.

"Your lobby?" I scoff, but before I can continue am whipping my eyes away from those two to conceal my mirth, tilting my head to get my tresses to fall over my face. (Shameful lapse of playacting aptitude, unpardonably amateurish: something you should bring up when reacquainting me with Miss Whippie's kiss.) Ascertaining the state I'm in you glide between me and them—seize the back of my neck with one hand, grasp my upper arm with the other. I plainly perceive our pair's deer-paralyzed-by-headlights eyes, standoffish shock, through my hair, am seriously struggling to stop my laughter-pot from boiling over—must stoop to clamping a hand over my mouth. No matter! You're running interference to perfection—give my dress an up and down look of utter derision, say really poisonous: "So you're aping my look, are you? Can't come up with your own? Such a low rent wannabe, second-rate slattern!" Then you raise your hand to administer a slap.

"Gutter blowjob twat!" I yell, seizing your wrist to stop your slap from landing—you're frantically jerking your arm—I'm seizing a smidge of your hair—you get ahold of my tote (with my corporate suit inside) and fling it. Then what? (Though all an act, it's a blur: no better measure of how far we take it.) You say something like: "Get lost, trash!" and—ha!—full-out charge me! Then—after I scramble to retrieve my tote—we're making for the exit, trading scowls and hisses—sham pulling at each other's hair, and our kicks always miss their target.

We dash out the exit onto Broadway laughing ourselves silly, turquoise sky swirling high between the building-tops, and that cab's there: you yank open the door and we pile in, already half entangled, in shouts of hysterics. Meanwhile, the driver's inquiring with detached tolerance, "Can you give me a destination?" And that's when the challenging contest ensued: Prankster Princesses vs. New York Cabbie.

Your turn, Girlfriend! Let's see whether you're up to the *responsibility* of doing our cab escapade justice—gauntlet's flung.

Your,

PranksterPlayactressPrincess

VII.2
Angie to Ella
Saturday, July 19, 2003 12:57 AM

You know I love you, Darling—I love you true, I do, and ocean's blue will turn into pink and purple polka dots before I'll stop loving you. But we both know that doesn't mean I'm allowing your crack about "doing our cab escapade justice" to pass unpunished. Right, just keep baiting me—piling on subtle slights. Nothing's unnoticed! Tomorrow's Miss Whippie session's going to be a doozy; you'll be one woozy floozy, wailing for mercy, once I begin. But you'll get no mercy from me, bad lil' brat whore. I'll dispense justice and love like never before.

That said, Darling, I couldn't have given our next adventure a better label: Prankster Princesses vs. New York Cabbie. Here ya go:

We didn't plan on a cab ride, it wasn't anywhere in our heads, but the cab happened to be there—the way our faux harlot hijinks seamlessly dovetailed into the cab escapade, as if we were on escapade-autopilot, was perfection. We pile into the cab laughing, gesture for the driver to head forward and, as laughter's a powerful aphrodisiac for me, I'm mauling you straightaway—lifting your gown, thrusting my head underneath like a non-neutered dog snuffling for moisture. Ha! Where were we when the driver, losing patience, pulled the car to the curb and informed us, neither politely nor impolitely, that we'd either need to provide a destination or get out? At 8th Avenue? I had your panties off; my face was wet; your pinkling's lips were aglisten in soft purple, sunlight passing through your gown's lavender silk: what an otherworldly vision's your tense tummy, vaguely shivering thighs, moist flower! Mine, all mine! Then the driver interrupts!

I doubt you had The Four Seasons in mind before the driver delivered his ultimatum—priceless spontaneity, Dearest. What better place for a succulent lunch, with their pink grapefruit tarts? What better place for additional escapading? But I'm getting shamefully ahead! (Note to self: Bad girl! Bad! Rope giddiness in! Tell our afternoon in order!)

I'm before the gates of paradise when the driver demands a destination. My sweet Ella's honeypuss is dripping honey aplenty 'cause she's excited aplenty due to having hooker-baited out-of-towners, played at pushing for a rent-a-girl deal, and I'm not about to come out from under your gown. So you say, "The Four Seasons, please!" and, my oh my!—the urgent manner in which you enunciate, tremor that runs through you! A wave of electricity in your musculature leaps at me—shoots a jolt of euphoria to the pit of my stomach, tingles my breasts, surges up my throat, makes me seem to be disembodied mist! Disembodied? Ha, I'm very much a body, that's for sure—a hungry body under your beautiful volatile undulating body's spell. Not for me the ability to realize The Four Seasons isn't nearly far enough away to allow me to finish what I've started. I hear you say: "Sir, we'd like to circle around and shoot up Madison to 125th Street then cross to 2nd Avenue then come back down to The Four Seasons. Can you do that for us, please?"

"I'm not in business to take people for joyrides," is the driver's toneless response. "We don't make money that way."

"We'll give you forty dollars above the meter," you answer in a quavering, at once on edge and in bliss sounding, voice. Seeking to keep your intonation even keeled you are, and *not* succeeding.

"Deal," says our driver in the same flat tone.

The arrangements concluded, your attention's no longer divided and I note the difference immediately: you're mine again, body and soul—one hundred percent pleasure-aware, shut-eyed and savoring. (No need to see your face to know.) Your breathing's deeper, each breath held in longer, your body quivering with each breath—your quivering steadily more pronounced. Oh, once—twice—I'm sure I have you, and redouble with tongue flicks within your blossom, caressing of your tummy, thumb-rubs of your bud; but you escape me—escape into another interval of suspenseful climbing, hushed quivering, until—oh, you don't trouble to hide joy when you succumb. Gasping cry after gasping cry and your convulsive leaning forward over my back and hard grasping of my waist and closure of your thighs about my head. Ever louder you moan and cry while still clasping tighter, shaking and pitching. What a darling! The force of your release sends a wave of wet straight to my hot box, such that I nearly spill as well! When I emerge from under your gown, see your eyes smiling with love, I full throttle push you back on the seat and pin you under me and pounce for kisses, drink at your lips as if I'll die if I don't! Then I lick your cheeks and nip your neck, and I'm raising my head, glancing outside the window: we're on 2nd Avenue, almost at the Queensborough Bridge—the turn onto 53rd is looming and I'm far from ready for the ride to be done. So I tell the driver to go down to 14th and turn to fly up 6th Avenue.

"What?" he asks, betraying a trace of impatience.

"Sir, I've asked you to go to 14th Street then turn onto 6th Avenue and bring us up to The Four Seasons on 52nd. Don't worry, you'll get another twenty dollars. Sixty dollars total over the meter."

"Alright, then."

There's no chance our driver's failed to notice what we've been absorbed in, but does he reveal such by so much as a twitch of a cheek or glint in his eye? Nay! New York cabs are bedrooms on wheels, more convenient than hotels, and most drivers mind their own business, maintain professional faces of stone, suspend judgment. If I may allow my vanity to speak, sometimes it's mildly insulting when we're unable to affect them, get them to lose countenance, with our shenanigans.

Which brings us to what happened next, but I'll allow you to do the honors, Sweetheart. After all, you figured slightly more in the next sequence than I did, even if only by initiating it.

Mmmmm, boy! What a lunch hour we had!

Your,

BountifulBackseatBunnykins

VII.3
Ella to Angie
Saturday, July 19, 2003 3:08 AM

So here we're pulling an all-nighter at the firm again, mostly due to these email write-ups we need to get out of our system. You write an e while I pounce on the Credit Agreement, then I write an e whilst you exert yourself concerning the [____] post-closing items: a nice back and forth rhythm twixt work and play, means of staying entertained, fresh-minded, enthused about being at the firm—means of keeping our heads clear and staying clever and creative and focusing on our legal responsibilities. Certainly our adventures and joy of recollecting them make us better attorneys. Maybe we ought to run our reliving-of-escapades-via-email routine by HR, recommend it as a morale booster. Ha! Effective though our method be, why do I have the distinct impression HR would be somewhat less than pleased? HR's loss.

OK! After you tongue-flicked me to floodsville and kissed me fierce, I sat upright with erect spine, arched my back—ran my hands slowly up and down my sides from thighs to armpits to get the sparkles to flare further and linger longer (How wonderful that our bodies are interlaced with sensory fireworks easily conjured forth.), then ran my fingers through my hair, raised it high and let it fall (classic happily sated girl gesture), while seeking our driver's gaze in the rearview mirror.

Why seeking our driver's gaze? For the same reason I false-harloted at the Marriot. Because I'm a self-flaunting coquette ceaselessly seeking self-affirmation in the facial expressions of affected males. Because my will to emotional power never sleeps and I've an insatiable appetite for evidence of feeling I've inspired in others. Because I want this man to understand we've conferred an honor upon him by unabashedly frolicking in his cab, trusted him—want to see it in his eyes.

But, as you observed, there's zilch indication our driver's aware of what's transpired. Utter obliviousness is all I read upon his face as he continues to direct his gaze upon driving. I'm deliciously aglow and it's as if I don't exist! Am I miffed? Definitely! How dare this man fail to have a trace of a twinkle in his eye after having been treated to a ringside seat. He's minding his own business? Granted, that's always a class act, but to neglect to so much as crack a smile is borderline rude. I cease stretching and lean forward, ask: "Is it OK to change our clothes?"

"I don't care what you do as long as you do it back there."

His reply's so matter-of-fact I can't help but smile. And would you look at him? At first glance it seems he's barely begun to taste of manhood and is rather naïve—such a fresh choirboy face. But he's surely older and non-naïve than he looks, his amount of self-possession—ability to remain even-keeled, keep his intonation toneless—would indicate such. Admiration notwithstanding—or, actually, because of it—I test him further. Leaning forward again, I gesture at the traffic. "Can you do something about this?" I ask. "We'd rather be moving than sitting."

"If I was a magician I suppose I could make these Con Ed guys vanish and the lanes they've blocked open up," he responds nonchalantly.

The sarcastic brat! But he does it so well, absent an insulting tone—he could be describing furniture. He's correct, of course—Con Ed's tearing up the avenue, blocking lanes—but such is beside the point: I'm dead-set on obtaining an emphatic reaction, time to haul out heavy artillery. Sitting back and nudging you I ask: "How much did we milk those suckers for? Get the money out—let's see if we can quit for today."

Ever quick to latch onto a charade, you answer, "Lots, Sweetie! Let's see how much!" You open your purse, we rustle bills, lift some into view, appear very absorbed, giggle and squeal. Then you announce, "Crazy! One thousand four hundred thirty total! Pretending to be hookers sure pays well! Tourists fork it over like there's no tomorrow!"

"A bit o' flashing and fluttering of eyes, and men lose their judgment and misplace their trust!" I chime in. "We pleading need to visit the girls' room, and they buy it, allow us to traipse off with their cash minus services rendered! As if we'd ever be alone with them!"

"Bubbly girly voices go a long way towards hastening abandonment of sound judgment!" you declare. "As in (You switch to a *blithe bouncy* tone.): Oh, Sir, my heels are hurting my toesies something awful and I must please adjust them—my tights are bunched there. See you shortly, after I fix things in the ladies' room, OK? And wow! What a pretty tie—silk, right? I can't wait for you to swish it on my tummy! We'll be right back, too soon won't be soon enough, you handsome heads!"

"Oh yeah, Dollface!" I squeal. "Totally worked wonders in the disarmament department—they had no suspicions! The sillies didn't see us turn out the door after rounding the corner! They lacked the sense to follow us to the start of the corridor to check where we went! We played it so well they would've been ashamed to doubt us!"

"A con's facilitated by flipping matters such that a mark will feel ashamed, reproach himself, should distrustful thoughts suggest themselves, and this is best accomplished by being sugar-sweet!"

"Another way of suspending men's disbelief when we're stealing their money's by yanking open our dressy-tops, showing off our baby-sucklers!" Suiting the action to my words, I open the top of my gown and push down my brassiere, allowing my breasts to pop free. I sit up, smush my breasts together with my upper arms, jiggle. "They adore fresh air, don't they? Don't like being cooped up in bras!"

"Luscious loveliest twins!" you cry. "It's no wonder those losers became extra pliable soon as you gave them a glimpse, I'm affected too! Jesus! Come down here, girl!" you fairly yell, pulling me lengthwise across your lap, bending—out of our driver's view—to kiss me.

"Whoa, babykins!" I shout. "You're the craziest kitty sweetheart!"

We're making suckling sounds, hyperventilating loud, tossing off assorted sex-rapture sound effects—"Aahhh! Uuhmmmm! Ooooo!—and I need to hand-smother my mouth to arrest laugher. We're focused on doling out the noise, aren't actually doing much. I'm thinking along the lines of: "This'll smash through this driver's detachment, make his eyes brighten and face flush and voice tremble. This'll wake him up to the reality he's lucky we hopped in his cab. He'll have a fine tale to tell."

Then you announce: "Uh-oh! Time's flying away from us, we've lost track! We need to change back to corporate, and *now*!"

"Oh! Crazy dumb us! Too busy celebrating our harlot impersonation scam to be mindful of priorities! Yeah, we need to change fast!"

So we sit upright and, with grade-schoolish eagerness, I jockey for position to glimpse our driver's face in the rearview, and—ha ha!—he's unfazed, inscrutable, stoic. Give the man his due, I respectfully bow! Only an uncommonly balanced individual would be capable of concealing reactions after what we've been up to. And, whoa! We've escaped the Con Ed bottleneck, are already at 6th and 19th, might have just enough time to change. We do so, but with little fanfare, as quickly and efficiently as if at home—slip one dress off, the other on. Why bother to be theatrical, giggly, vociferous? If we haven't cracked our driver with noisy sexcapades, a simple changing isn't fazing him.

When we arrive at The Four Seasons paying the fare's my final opportunity to take a reading on our driver, ascertain if his armor's been pierced. "Here's for the meter," I say, awaiting the change. I do this intentionally so he'll—maybe—start to wonder if the promised extra sixty dollars will be forthcoming. Meanwhile, I'm subjecting every feature of his face to a probing stare—searching for telltale movement of emotion under his skin, flickers of his eyes—minute blushes, smiles, any indication he appreciates we've been far from average fares. His face remains impenetrable—neither friendly nor unfriendly: nothing.

Upon receiving the change, I say: "Don't worry—we're honoring our deal, thanks for the extra driving," and hand him sixty dollars.

"I wasn't worried," he answers, still dispassionately and professionally. "I can tell you're honest people. Thanks, and have a good day."

The outcome of "Teasing Tartlets vs. New York Cab Driver"? We certainly didn't win, and maybe that's more satisfying than winning, if only because we're unaccustomed to losing. I tip my cap—or, rather, lift my hem—to him. Truly a credit to the New York cab driver profession.

Dearest, handing the reins to you for the same reason you handed them to me: you initiated the fun that followed more than I did.

Your,

HumbledHarlot (Respect where respect's due: NY cab driver non-flustered by our antics, good on him. We *adore* strong men.)

VII.4
Angie to Ella
Saturday, July 19, 2003 6:00 AM

Please excuse the delay, Sweetheart! I finished with the post-closing surprise, then noticed sections were off-base concerning the four primary documents of the [_____] offering: no two alike format-wise, even though they're submitted simultaneously as a unified package to the client. Page numbering, margins, font sizes, headers, hyphenation (or lack thereof) of some defined terms, italicizing of "provided": all was non-conformed. Discrepancies make the firm look bad! (I'm super finicky, no apologies—never give clients shelling out millions reasons to complain, since they dream up enough reasons as it is.) And, sure, conforming formatting's paralegal territory and Jennifer's on it now, loving the OT. But I had to kickstart it, then find someone competent enough to see it through: another mess fixed. Also I discovered some of the MD&A language is inaccurate, so I'll be revising. But, first, since there's no timeline, more fun telling of our lunch hour gone wild.

You enter The Four Seasons ahead of me and what most strikes my eye (and that of the doorman) is the air of smiling satiation surrounding you—cheerful swishy aura of a sated wanton, jaunty post-orgasm prance. So uplifting to see my Ella uplifted! If you're elated, I'm elated, and lust-emanations are flying through the air, stabbing at my nerves—I'm itchy and burning up, blurred in the head, eager for my turn.

You were the primary in our harlot masquerade, got to ad lib the hands-on teasing—I was an observer, in charge of effecting our exit. Then who gets muff-fluffed in the cab? You do! Sure, pleasuring you's a pleasure—thrilling end in itself—but afterwards there's excitement-accumulation, a sense of drowning in my storming blood, temples throbbing. Ella, my skin's screaming when we arrive at The Four Seasons—your post-coitus radiance deliciously unnerving me, anticipation elevational! I'm entitled to kiss the stars too and know you'll deliver—we send one another starwards with our eyes alone.

Once we're seated at the side of the bar with the wall at our backs I phone Stevie, bid him join us. Meanwhile, I'm famished, and what better place to be so? Oysters to begin, highly appropriate food for Miss MuffDive me. I adore loosening oysters in their half-shells, squirting on lemon, lifting the shell to my lips, sweet slippery meat sliding onto my tongue: such puts me in mind of girl-flower meat, by far my favorite treat. (How soul-upending an oyster-slurping and muff-fluffing fest rolled into one is. We're overdue for a session, are we not?) Then some greens, sans dressing, for contrast, then another oyster and then more greens, then a few more, until their tuna burger with mango-papaya salsa—scrumptious-yumsters—arrives, accompanied by a flute of bubbly. (It's not for nothing Champagne's the only alcohol I'll imbibe; it's not regular drinking, it's tingling fuzziness, subtle joy.) Finally, for dessert it's the only pastry this tart will dream of eating: The Four's pink grapefruit tart, with a scoop of Champagne sorbet atop.

No sooner is a pink grapefruit tart placed before me than our Stevie, in heart-warming obedience to my summons, arrives grinning. What I do I suddenly want to do with the tart instead of eating it? There's another way to savor desserts—one can be the dessert. But I do spoon sorbet into my mouth—am not about to miss out on frozen Champagne titillatingly melting atop my tongue. (Ella, heaven on earth's when twatsie's sugarcoated with hungry tickles, randy slut juices electrifying my veins. Heaven on earth's when you and Stevie, two greatest aphrodisiacs of my life, are eager to make me feel like I'm the prettiest girl on earth. Hail the sextasy rollercoaster, life elevated towards ceaseless wonder.)

I lean in, chest pressed to the bar, and spread my thighs and yank my dress towards my waist, as safely out of the way as I can get it without being obvious. (Yup, guessy dressy's gonna get messy again, like last week and the one before.) You're standing at my left, forming a human shield, so no one can spy our action from the stairs, and you drape a shawl over your shoulders to make yourself bigger and arrange one on my lap (We steadfastly adhere to the Boy Scout Motto: Be Prepared.), and to Stevie's right is the wall. (This nook where the bar ends at this side, with a wall at our back and to our right, is fairly screaming to be put to floods-in-public use—the setup's a waking dream.)

Oh, my! So soothing when I smear the tart, cold gel of crushed grapefruit, on the insides of my thighs; and quick-study Stevie doesn't need but a smiling nod and glance at the mashed tart to know what to do. He knocks my purse to the floor, says, "Sorry about that—stay there, I'll get it." and slides off his stool, eases his head betwixt my spread legs—his tongue's licking the sticky chill off of me in long lingering swaths, sending shivers way up within wombsie, cleaning me up and steaming me up. Soon I'm rubbing my ticklish nips against the bar's edge whilst on the edge of procreation's sigh, electric swishies gathering inside me so forcefully they seem to swirl in my curls—gazing into the shivering folds of diaphanous drapery falling from the top of the ceiling-high windows to the floor on the other side of the room: the flitting of shadow and light on the drapery's mirroring my inner ebb and flow.

It's almost as if Stevie's oblivious we're in public. Once he's done lapping up the tart he, literally shaking with impatience, thrusts his head further up my dress, is tickle-licking my tummy, darting lip-dance reverberations further into wombsie's depths, stealing my breath from under me—I crest before I can think to guard against making noise! Ever Miss Vigilant, you're coughing like crazy to mask my flutter-cry—succeeding so well the bartender comes over concerned, asks if you're OK. "You're very kind—water, please, and thank you," you respond, me bursting into a giggle-fit as Stevie bangs my elbow with his head in his haste to finally fetch my purse. The bartender has a pretty good idea something naughty's afoot, but mum's the word, bless him.

Overcome by an urge to show appreciation of our bartender's discretion and class, I fiddle at and finally undo dressy's top two buttons, lean forward to breast-flash him (fortunately they're snug in half-cups, not spilling free) while gazing gratitude. I was surely ablur in the head, half gone from my mind! And, Honey, I'm getting sorta mindless—or, rather, single-minded—with hunger for some finger-flicking, pinkling-poking, right now—recollection's stirring me crazy such that I need to pause to please myself, purr like the pussycat I am. Otherwise, I'll go nuts and be a tantrum tossing tigress! I trust you'll take up the loose strands of our afternoon, wind them into a delightful wrap-up?

Your,

TightlyWoundTartlet

VII.5
Ella to Angie
Saturday, July 19, 2003 8:11 AM

Why, how kind of you, Dearest! You kiss off all sense of discretion in a public place—commit the *huge* No-No of crying out whilst flooding, seemingly lacking the wit to cover your mouth—and now expect me to clean up your mess, narratively speaking. Too much effort for you to tell it, you plead pinkling itches and leave it to me. You're a thoughtless, selfish, irresponsible, slackster girlfriend! (More fuel for Miss Whippie! Please do inform yourself when the time arrives: "The pampered priss dared insult me, as if I wouldn't make her pay!," and lash my rear with redoubled vigor. Always fun to bait you, do my best to deserve your lovingly administered alignment, Sweeeeetest! I'll never want you to go soft on me, fail to demonstrate how much you care, Sweeeeetest!)

On the other hand, I take the insults back—oh, not because I'm afraid of being called to account but because I'm glad of the opportunity to be your mirror, show you to yourself as you were after Stevie tummy tickled you into a daze. Honeysuckle, you were irresistible—truly a poster girl for public places pleasure, atumble in delirium, seemingly no ability to wonder or care where you were or what you were doing.

Let's back up a bit so's I can mirror you from commencement to consummation. First, you're grasping the bar as Stevie laps the tart off your legs—there's a slight clenching-of-teeth aspect to your expression, combined with complete relishment, and with a dab of astonished little girl tossed in—ineffable sweetness is in your eyes, they widening and silvering with wonder. Your slender frame's taut, rigid with sensation's acceleration, yet also supple, softly swaying like a sapling in light breeze. You're often giggling—such a babbling brook of a giggle.

Angie, watching you happily wrestle, frown and smile, with stimulation flings me into inner surging, my fingers itching to dance to my hot lil' butterpuss. As I'm on sentry duty I successfully resist, partially via emphatic clenching and unclenching of hands, and continue blocking the view from the stairs—I'll never fail to justify your trust. Then Stevie eases his head further up your dress and you might as well be in a bedroom, for all the caution you're caring to display—rubbing your titties against the bar very obviously, eyes half shut. Not content with visually giving the game away, you coo-cry-sigh too loud when your moment arrives, clearly in the throes. I'm coughing to drown you out and, at this point (it's with shame I confess it), I succumb to apprehension. You flash the bartender, all right, and I'm worrying because who knows how many people have seen you do it. I'm closing your dress at the top, tapping your waist with my knee, saying: "Stop behaving like a silly goose with no self-control. We're not in some out-of-the-way-no-name dive—the bloody mayor could be here."

The look you give me! Very fleeting, but still! And I deserve it! Such an inexcusable abandonment of will on my part! Disgraceful to reproach you for being My Angie! What it boils down to is I'm chiding you for doing what we're born to do, as in run wild in SexLand—CandyLand—like kids given fabulous toys—our toys being our ever-astir bodies, stimulation-addicted senses. Silly goose with no self-control? That's me, not you! I'm a silly goose for succumbing to fear while you're in heaven's realm, charmingly glazed. And classiest cutie alive that you are, you didn't bring that up, swat me for it, in your last e.

Angie, I'd hate to think my stupidity sabotaged your joy. I *did* immediately reproach myself, something like: "Why am I a pusillanimous wallflower? Why aren't I surrounded by the Holy light Angie is, savoring our game—a game we routinely play?" I snapped out of idiocy—your reproachful glance jolted me awake—but that doesn't excuse my having lost faith in the first place. Loss of faith, however fleeting, is high crime! I know better, am very ashamed! It's not like we don't know how to get our way, escape scrapes. Not only because of gorgeous-girl privilege, fluttering of eyes and faking vulnerability and fear if called for, but because we're streetwise, down to earth.

By way of atonement, I suggest we smuggle Stevie into the ladies' so's you can further your fun in a stall. How your eyes brighten, cutiepie mischief animating you head to toe. What benediction you pronounce upon unworthy me with that lil' squeal, as if you're a little girl who's won a toy! What forgiveness your generous soul pours forth!

To the ladies' room we tromp with Stevie in tow. I mope up to the towel girl, turn her away from the door and mirror by wailing that my boyfriend's dumped me. "I got naked for him," I say, displaying teary eyes, "and I don't get naked for just any man, I'm an honorable woman. Then what's he do? He falls for an overweight older woman and gives me the gate! Do you believe it? He trades this (Here I point at my rear, gyrate my hips.) for a fat woman old enough to be his mother."

The towel girl, give the minx her due, finds it tough to suppress a smile, but quickly erases it, lest she set me off further. Meanwhile, you and Stevie tippytoe behind her, vanish around the corner. (What a huge ladies' room.) When you rap twice on a stall door, signaling you're within, that's my cue to plop onto the plush velvet bench, bury my face in my hands, ask the towel girl: "Can I sit here, collect myself?" Towel girl wants as little to do with me as possible, nods assent, steps away.

I wait until you indicate with our cough signal (three rapid, two slow) that you and Stevie are done playing, whereupon I—staring sadly and blankly into the air until then—approach the towel girl again, say, "Sorry to bother you more, but would you do me the kindness...I mean, I'm embarrassed to ask, but... (All the while steering her to facing the wall away from the door and mirror, so you two can exit unseen.) ...could you slap my cheek, right here? It'll do me good, help clear my head and bring me to myself. I have an important meeting later and should be balanced for it. I only need to be brought down to earth."

The girl, unflappably professional, doesn't lose a beat. "Ma'am, I cannot do that," she responds in an even tone. Seeing I'm about to persist, she politely yet firmly adds, "I cannot and will not do it, Ma'am. Under no circumstances do we physically engage clients of the Four Seasons."

Silent as cats, you and Stevie reach the door, open it—ha! just as the stylish sixty-something woman enters. Luckily the woman's content to give Stevie a wryly bemused "Yeah, you'd better make tracks!" look and pays him no further mind. As for me, I've detected more of that subdued smile on the towel girl's face and admire her for it—a thought occurs to me: *Why not give her a better tale to tell her friends?*

Yeah, as I'm a conscientious girl who believes bright people should be rewarded, I say: "Since you won't slap me, I'll have to!" and slap each cheek hard enough for them to smart, turn reddish. Before the towel girl can remonstrate (because she's about to), I cease and step to the mirror, extract my clutch from my tote and mascara from my clutch, do a touch-up. Before exiting I thank her warmly, place ten dollars in the tip jar.

Dearest, hope I compensated for my negation of your fun at the bar by facilitating your ladies' room adventure. If I ever get stupidly uneasy again whilst you're enjoying thyself, do please slap me dizzy.

Your,

(HopefullyTemporarily)FallenFromFavorElla

VII.6
Angie to Ella
Saturday, July 19, 2003 9:04 AM

Ella, stop berating yourself! *Stop it now!* So what if you *temporarily* succumbed to trepidation? I only recall your hands flitting about my neckline, pulling it shut. I would've done likewise had you been dizzily—brainlessly, I might add—flashing the bartender in front of who knows who. You were being a conscientious girlfriend. And, Honey, if you think a tone of reproach will tumble me out of flutter-shudder for a second, lessen elevation, you seriously underestimate your Angie. You by no means sabotaged my fun, didn't mar my happiness, have a negative effect—you interjected necessary order into the disorder I was too blurred to identify as such. We enable each other's abandon with watchful eye, watch each other's backs so we feel safer being bolder.

I glanced at you reproachfully? I don't remember doing so—such wasn't on my mind at any time, could never be. Pardon me, Sweetie, but it's likely a case of you misreading the brightness of my eyes, projecting your misinformed guilt onto perception, allowing anger at yourself to attribute feelings to me I by no means had. You're Miss Positivity personified, Ella! And the way you flawlessly ran interference in the ladies' room, where Stevie and I had a high ol' stratospheric time—thank you for the priceless gift, but I'm too weary to describe.

I raise the shades: surprise! Sun's bright! The night just *flew*! All-nighter at the firm spent productively, officially and unofficially. "Take nothing for granted. Always over-anticipate." says you-know-who. I've accomplished a great deal between writing emails, feel good about preparation for what could be an extra frenetic Monday.

Dearest, I'm heading home, where it'll be all about sleep, winding down from our funfest day. Nighty-night, and get yourself some sleep too.

Your,

LawfirmLassieLustingForLassitude

VII.7
Ella to Angie
Saturday, July 19, 2003 11:24 AM

With you on that score, Angie: I've torn through the [____] financials, slammed the door on gamesmanship misinterpretation, so also get to head home. I definitely have the lull-before-a-storm feeling—tomorrow at the printer's likely to be Insanesville—and far be it from me to allow lunchtime fun to bedazzle me to the degree I forgo dedication to our profession. I'm thankful for today's gift of crazily extended lunchtime, but cannot and will not allow myself to be permanently swept into a world of recklessness. I anticipate tasting of recklessness many times on company time, laughing at the preposterousness of such, but realize it's only possible if I remain firmly grounded. To that end, I've focused on duty all night—am prepped to greet tomorrow's brawl.

Almost hope the other side's stupid enough to attempt resistance, comb for nonexistent loopholes—I'd enjoy a spat, waking the hicks up, swatting 'em down. Such is partially what I live for! I knew I wanted to be a corporate attorney in high school—didn't frolic a bit then, had no idea I'd wind up being a prankish pussycat slut, flip from wallflower to kicking down walls. Late bloomer me, for which I'm grateful, since it's motivation to make up for lost time, go to the "Life's brief so be a wildcat!" place. (Our bouncing between work and escapading's unforeseen heaven.) Oh, I channeled, Angie Darling, and channeled well! I channeled my hidden-from-myself sexual aptitude into becoming gainfully employed, and valued, by a prestigious law firm. So the tropics will turn Antarctic before I fail to knuckle down and do my job after having a lunch hour like the one we had, games stacked atop games.

Aside from the fact I adore my profession, it suits my free-dom-craving disposition. After all, there's the money—the outrageous salary. Money allows me to live in style, be a pampered pussycat aswim in sex kicks, while maintaining independence. I'm a trollop in At-torneyville, don't need to marry a rich man to live in a nice place or have nice things—don't need to kowtow to anyone, be treated like financially-dependent property, restricted in pursuit of pleasure. I'm a quick-witted, brainy, career-minded girl who also happens to adore being sex-stimulated, my imagination perpetually on overdrive—al-ways yearning, always seeking—never content to stand pat. Therefore, I'm a *corporate* attorney, where the money rains down like there's no tomorrow, and investment opportunities enable me to put nifty amounts to work. My life's unhindered kittycatting about town on the trickle-down from multi-million dollar deals without worrying about the bill.

Nighty-night, Angie!—trust you're fast asleep.

Your,

ConscientiousKittyCat

VIII. Friday's Fiasco (Angie Beds a Bore)

What, Angie? You were so desperate for frolic it clouded your reason? You, really and truly, brought home a clumsy incompetent clown who failed to do your sassy ass proud? You allowed a doltish bore to mistreat your lithe, wenchalacious, miracle-of-symmetry body? And here I thought only those who demonstrated, at the very least, ability to kiss you dizzy had a shot at drinking from your fountain, making you squeal. Here I thought a, shall we say, gentlemanly savagery—unrestraint tempered with good manners—was the only key that would unlock your treasure chest. Clearly, I don't know you as well as I thought.

You allowed yourself to get plastered? You, who prattles about only drinking Champagne and prides herself on *never* having a substance-addled brain, especially when it's a question of who you're bedding? And, further, you failed to take a reading on the clown before admitting him into your bedroom?—didn't trouble to apply your laser sharp intuition, note telltale giveaways such as eye-contact, tone of voice, aura of physical presence?—didn't determine if you vibrated in unison with his electrical field? You really were so inebriated you wound up mouthed by an oaf who thought kissing was a blundering thrusting of jaw and bruised your sacrosanct lips, slobbered all over your cheeks? And you *still* permitted him to continue, didn't give him the gate?

I never figured you for a masochist, Angie! You let him get far enough to pull his pants off, show off a whopping three-incher? You let him maul your breasts, wound with uncut nails? Uncut nails! OK, so you chased him off after that, but how could you be so utterly gone as to allow him to do such? Were you near to passing out?

It was traumatic for you? What of me? How do you think I feel when I'm informed my ideal woman's debased herself thus, blundered into a ridiculous fiasco? My Angie of steely resolve and deliciously ribald imagination, equally drenched in sophistication and perversion. My elegant, raunchy—level-headed, lust-flayed—classy, sassy, brassy—Angie! My modern day Marie Antoinette, who'd surely unflinchingly go to the guillotine—with aristocratic detachment—with serene resignation—just like the original Marie did. My brilliant Italian princess, no doubt directly descended from the Romans.

Thank you very much, Angie, for thrashing my world view—forcing me to realize my female idol's capable of getting mixed up and messed up with a clumsy, incompetent, uncouth, dickless bore. For sure, you'll be punished! After all, I respected you without having to fake it—I've never exaggerated when declaring everlasting admiration. But, now, what do you leave me with? Cruel disillusionment! So you'll be tied up—mercilessly stimulated, brought to the edge of a flood—and then abandoned, left to contemplate your shortcomings while in a state of high fever, searing scatteredness. The way to punish a slut's to heat her dizzy, melt all resistance, then refuse to follow through. I'll duct tape your wrists and ankles together, tongue you towards heaven on your feather soft bed, and then: *stop*! I'll carry you to your kitchen floor's cold hard tiling, deposit you thereupon in your aroused state, then ignore you for *hours*! I don't care how much you plead and wail, you'll stay there for half a day! No guilt on my part, you've got it coming.

For now, though, dearest fallen Angie, I'll content myself with a commemorative rhyme—it happened to pop into my head:

Angie bedded a bore:
Sex was a useless chore,
No better than a snore.

Apologies, Angie! Three lines doesn't come close to doing your earth-shattering downfall justice—please allow me to do better:

Friday's Fiasco (Angie Beds a Bore)

Angie, always fond of a rut—
The firm's friskiest nubile slut—
Found Friday night's love-fest a chore.
How so? Seems she bedded a bore.

Angie parted delicate lips,
Was sighing for scrumptious sip-sips
Of kiss-sensation; and then what?
Her mouth was mauled by a hard jut
Of teeth, an overeager jaw:
Quite possibly the worst *faux pas*
Any girl should have to endure.
(Shameful way to smother her purr.)

(refrain)

Silly Angie brought home a bore:
Her lips are bruised, a swollen sore!
Ditzy Angie bedded a bore:
Kissing was a clumsy jaw war!

Angie trustingly spread her legs,
Found herself facing a short peg
Of a useless, flaccid pecker.
(Nothing more able to wreck her
Equilibrium, send shivers
Of horror up her spine, numb thought,

Obliterate gladness to naught:
She stared, seized by chilly quivers.)

Silly Angie brought home a bore:
Her twat's unused, a barren shore!
Foolish Angie bedded a bore:
Size wasn't even inches four!

Angie bravely sought to postpone
Despair, manage at least a moan—
Slightest spark of stimulation—
Midst the limp-tooled situation:
She guided bore's hands to her breasts
In desire of being caressed.
Ha! Poor Angie's never misguessed
So! Uncut nails tore her soft skin—
Actual blood dribbled, raised a din
From her throat, caused her hands to slap.
(Bore ran out the door: what a sap.)

Silly Angie brought home a bore:
Her chest's abused, in state of roar!
Stupid Angie bedded a bore:
Her tits were clawed aft and fore!

Yes, Angie's one curvaceous lass—
She's got creation's finest ass;
But she got mixed up with a bore:
What waste of a posterior.

And Angie's a hot twatted wench
That ten tuppings will never quench;
But she opened twat to a bore:
Mr. Flaccid was no minotaur
In her labyrinth, not a chance:
What a waste of pink petal dance.

Yes, Angie vamped and tramped a bore:
Her judgment's gone, beyond deplore!
Angie wasted time with a bore:
Bye-bye to lust, hello grief's door!

Angie, have I captured the high drama of the grand event? And, as far as that goes, it appears dalliance in verse has revealed my sincere feelings regarding your fiasco. As in forget destroyed ideals, disillusionment on account of my proud princess wasting a Friday on a fool, making a fool of herself—I'm just plain dying of laughter, rolling on the floor!

Angie, it would've been priceless to see your look of dismay when you got maul-kissed—I would've paid a lot of money to see your look of disbelief when the dolt disrobed to reveal: *very little*! I'm picturing it now and, excuse me, must step away to roll on the floor some more.

OK, what I'm thinking is that instead of punishing you I ought to reward you for amusing me. So why don't you hightail it over? I'm very willing to pleasure your poor abused and unused body into a blissy daze, obliterate last night's traumatic outcome, vanquish bad reverberations.

What are you waiting for? You've got the key! Give me a call!
Love,
Steven

VIII.2
Angie to Steven
Saturday, July 26, 2003 12:22 PM

What? You dash off highly insulting lines, boldly declare you're laughing at me, and vaingloriously assume I'll melt as a consequence and hasten to fling myself into your arms? You invite me to "hightail it over" after having the nerve to unkindly commemorate my misguided judgment night? You take it for granted I'll be eager to see you after you've mocked me? How backwards you have things, arrogant male!

Stevie, you seriously need an etiquette education—allow Angie to provide a few pointers. Foremost: if you're writing verse to a girl, you must flatter her. You must present her to herself in her best light—make her feel that, in your eyes, she's the most radiant creature on earth. Above all, do not insult her by reminding her of an event she'd rather forget. Absolutely *never* inform her you're laughing at her! Do not toss off mocking rhymes and expect her to deem you worthy of a wild night of riot. Never assume (how I detest male assumption) you've won the girl over with your versing: wait until she indicates that you have.

Not to mention you haven't troubled to exert yourself. Newsflash: your offering's laughably awkward, belabored-rhyme infected, amateurish slop! "Her chest's abused, in state of roar!" In "state of roar"? Pathetic! No girl's going to think fondly of you and wish to favor you after reading an offering in which you make an ass of yourself.

So I'm *not* hightailing it over! Not yet, anyway! I know your skills as a verser and, not being a wilting wallflower, demand that you apply yourself on my behalf and treat me to the caliber of work you're capable of, and that's drenched with the degree of admiration I'm worthy of. For instance, a poem like the last one you sent: I want another to add to my collection. You recall it, don't you? And recall the reward you received for it? It was the afternoon we first ventured into 18th century French fashion (Of a sort: we hadn't discovered the costume shop yet.), after reading Laclos and de Sade aloud and looking at the Boucher and Fragonard and Watteau prints and the Versailles book. The afternoon which, unbeknownst to us, was a preliminary trail of what was later refined and perfected 'til it became the Marie Antoinette Game. So who knows what'll result if you send me another delightful lil' ditty?

So do it, Stevie! See if you can equal your last feat, this one:

A Summer Sunday's Shimmer (Angie Lessons on Love)

On a June afternoon overheated—
One hundred two degrees—I was treated
To rapture undivided, courtesy
Of my blithesome-eyed purr-kitten, Angie.
(Naked but for her nightie—transparent
Scarlet, no neckline, its wavy length rent
Up the sides: midriff-high slits in the silk
Allowed flashes of charms fluid as milk.)
I stretched out on the couch, invitingly
She smiled and dipped, wiggled excitingly—
Followed a rapid sequence of hip-thrusts
With eye-high kicks, back bends, shaking of bust.
I ventured to seize hold—she retreated,
Inquired, "Why would you wish to be cheated?
Patience feeds euphoria: let desire
Gather, crest, invade bloodstream, soar higher,
Intensify us, inwardly explode—
The aim's for our grasp of thought to erode."
How could I not heed lovingly dispensed
Advice, surrender, await recompense?
　　Angie fulfills her promise, sinks to floor,
Slinkily crawling near enough to pour
Heated breath onto my tummy—tresses
Swishing, tickling, causing minor stresses,
Arrestingly feather-dusting my thighs.
She breathes deeper, quiveringly applies
Lips to base of tummy—slow-advancing
Towards my gaze, intuitively dancing
Shimmers into my nerves—abruptly grasps
My restive wrists, soft-chides with a glance, gasps,
"No, Stevie! As stated, I'll orchestrate
The action, lead our dance—ensure we sate
Bothered flesh, emotional commotion."
Angie's applying saliva-lotion

To my shoulders and neck, pinning my chest,
Pressing closer, massaging with her breasts.
    Otherworldly when her slender
Body's against mine. How render
The electric transports of bliss
Dizzying me as she kisses
Lingeringly, time's march blurring?—
Unexplored sensations stirring?

I expect another tribute, Stevie! I demand proof I'm your muse—proof you're willing to set aside the time and summon the skill to honor me with another luscious love rhyme. Believe me, I absolutely really and truly want to come to you—am *dying* to come to you—but cannot permit myself to do so until you move me.
    Love,
    Angie

VIII.3
Steven to Angie
Saturday, July 26, 2003 6:47 PM

There's the proud Angie of highest standards I know and love—you're absolutely entitled to more than "amateurish slop." When taking a turn for the verse with a girl one must fling one's whole soul into it—nothing goes down better with a girl than a sentimental mush poem. So here's a sentimental mush poem, written in humble acquiescence to your request:

As Long as She's a Bitch!

I'm not over finicky, am easy to please—
Capable of falling for a wide range of tease.
Only one condition I count, one little hitch:
A girl's got to be a strife sowing bitch!

Don't care if a girl's a star at debutant balls;
Or if she works at greasy eateries in malls—
Don't care if she's skilled at social one-upsmanship;
Or prefers isolation, being outcast hip:
All social caste—from the gutter to filthy rich—
Is fine, as long as she's a scheming bitch!

Don't care if a girl's plundered a lingerie shop;
Or if she's a rosy-cheek fresh from a sock hop—
Don't care if she's into Catholic schoolgirl plaid;
Or a biker tough who likes to look dirty, bad:
All fashion's acceptable, any style of stitch,
As long as she's a tantrum-tossing bitch!

Don't care if a girl's a nymphomaniac slut;
Or if she needs to be courted, plead with to rut—
Don't care if she's bedded two dozen baseball teams;
Or if not one person's penetrated her seams:
I'll take maid or whore, any experience niche,
As long as she's a fight-fomenting bitch!

Don't care if a girl's into rubber bondage kink;
Or if she's fond of coupling on a skating rink—
Don't care if she must be wearing 'luminum foil;
Or if I've got to dress as Tiller of the Soil:
I'll embrace any fetish, all means to bewitch,
As long as she's an unrepentant bitch!

Don't care if a girl's mouth ceaselessly runs riot;
Or if she barely breathes a word, tends to quiet—
Don't care if she often quotes Christianity;
Or if her vocabulary's profanity:
Any subject matter, all forms of vocal pitch,
As long as she's a discontented bitch!

Call it magnetism or addiction—
Call it an emotional affliction;
Or separation from rational thought,
Willful disregard of all I've been taught:
I've never combusted with peaceful girls—
Have little use for the Sunny-As-Pearls,
Will always favor a wildcat or fitch:
Nothing captivates like bedding a bitch!

What's the reason? I'm not masochistic.
Apparently friction's alchemistic—
A means of involving inner unrest,
Resolving self-conflict, emerging blest.
Nice girls are unable to dredge my deeps,
Exorcize the things that give me the creeps;
But a disquieted bitch—my oh my!—
Engages those things, routs them, bids them fly!
I'm in heaven—emotionally rich—
During rejuvenation via a bitch!

Nice girls are intermissions of blindness,
Submission to slow killing with kindness.
That's right, nice girls are the gravedigger's ditch!
So I'll retain clarity with a bitch—
I'll remain alive and thrive with a bitch!
Any female, as long as she's a bitch!

Angie, is the sentimental mush element in the above offering suffi-
cient to move and melt you—incline you towards favoring me? Have
I paid due tribute to your sterling qualities, made you feel valued and
adored, paved the way for you to admire yourself? Please let me know
ASAP if I've pleased you! Mind you, I'm not assuming (I'd sooner die
than offend you with detestable male assumption.), but should you
find yourself aflutter with kind thoughts on my behalf—should you
feel I've truly bared my soul in your honor, revealed the full depth of
my undying affection, then I'd positively dearly love to see you tonight!

Again, I'm absolutely *not* presuming you'll find the poem appealing enough to grant me a visit—I'm awaiting your verdict with baited breath, on tenterhooks of suspense, agonizingly hovering between hope and despair—devoured with doubt, wondering: "Will Angie deign to speak to me after reading it?—wish to gaze into my eyes again, allow me to touch her? Will she hightail it over and spread her thighs and glaze her eyes and succumb to fluttering cries as she orgasms sky high, then coo, 'Stevie, I adore how you versify!'?" Rest assured, I'm as flayed by uncertainty on your behalf as you could wish a male to be.

Praying, Angie, that you'll ease my trepidation!

Love,

Steven

VIII.4
Angie to Steven
Saturday, July 26, 2003 7:16 PM

Stevie, I could quarrel with the fact your masterpiece (I *do* aver it's a masterpiece) isn't addressed to me in particular and could be sent to any feisty-dispositioned woman, but I'll let it slide. Far be it from me to climb onto my girl-vanity high-horse and dream up reasons to be miffed when you've made me giddy with the giggles. Besides, that my request has resulted in the creation of such a wisdom-dispensing masterwork is more than enough to flatter me. I can proudly declare: "Were it not for me, this titillate-me-silly ballad would've never been birthed."

As you've shown yourself worthy, Stevie, it's a pleated scarlet skirt tonight, and seamed black silk stockings, plus surprises. Rest assured I'll be a mixture of innocence and perversion, just like you like me.

Give me another hour to get pretty for you!

Love,

Angie

VIII.5
Angie to Ella
Sunday, July 27, 2003 10:41 PM

My dearest Ella! You know of my traumatic Friday night, and we know few things are as unkind to one's equilibrium as a sex fiasco. Soaring expectation's swatted down, thrust back on one—goodbye high hopes, hello gnawing frustration—one's stranded in a state of arousal that's blaming and punishing one for failing to follow through. Unsated desire knows no mercy; by default, one's at fault for neglecting to sate it. Friday night I brought home an incompetent clown and not one itch was scratched, and so by Saturday morning those itches, many times multiplied, were subjecting me to the torments of the damned, and turning nastier as the hours marched into afternoon and evening.

Thank God for Stevie! Saturday morning I was hellbent on seeing him, yet I had to put on something of an I'm-not-*that*-easy act and require him to treat me to a polished poetic work (what I forwarded) before I'd agree to see him. On one level requiring him to do that was a farce (The swords that they say gird Paradise wouldn't have kept me from him.) but, on another level, some inescapable male -vs.-female ritual burned into our psyches forced me to play vanity games—be-worthy-of-me games. I knew I'd be seeing him later and he knew he'd be seeing me, but we still had to do a courtship dance before we could get on with it. Like, I'm a princess in a tower demanding my knight jump through hoops, perform a specific deed, before he can entertain any hope of doing what I want him to do more than anything else.

So Stevie and I negotiate the twists and turns of the apparently necessary courtship ritual. (There must be some on-the-subconscious-level psychic turnover involved in the said ritual, right? Who knows how we operate in our depths? Maybe these between-the-sexes negotiations clear the emotional landscape, lay the foundations, for a successful encounter? Or maybe it's a bratty girl and a bratty boy gratuitously indulging in psychodrama foreplay, gleefully seeing how *nuts* they can make each other, all in good fun! Or maybe... Oh, who cares?)

Suffice to say I'm tapping on Stevie's door by 8:00 PM. He opens said door, and from that point it's a dizzying whirl. I'm instantly in his arms, being kissed—forceful-gentle, long and deep, hyperventilating as our lips undulate and tongues dance. Stevie's kisses make me feel safe! It's by means of kissing that one knows if one can trust a man. A kiss is, by far, the most intimate form of human communication—the vibrations, impartation of life force, merging of electrical fields. Then he seizes my rear and squeezes and massages like he'll never get enough of relishing the smooth skin and solid musculature of a trollop who stays in shape, and that's my signal to leap up and wrap my legs about his waist and arms about his neck. We're still kissing as he carries me to the bed, where he stretches me out on the mattress, gazes at me like I'm the spoils of battle. Then he's inside me. I'm licking his face and neck.

Ella, I'd dearly love to go into greater detail, but modesty has leapt forth to stop me! Who says a sexually aptitudinous girl can't occasionally find herself inclined to play the part of discretional lady? It's sometimes fun to be bashfully blushful, of too delicate and fastidious a disposition to indulge in indiscreet confidences. There's much to be said for retreating in horror at the thought of availing oneself of a crude expression. (OK, playacting an attack of the modesties in an email to my Best Girl's utterly silly, but to be a flustered fragile thing in front of the boys is a treat. The way they, so to speak, cast a net over their natural behavior and rein themselves in on one's behalf is as flattering as funny. Yes, to suddenly wince and shudder at intonation of, say, the word "bitch" as if it's cut me to the marrow of my bones, shown me the sour underbelly of experience, exposed me to extreme danger; to gaze in wide-eyed alarm at the speaker, add hints of hurt and reproach: the speaker gazes at me with surprise (Because there's little about this girl that suggests it's easy to fluster her.), swallows hard, exerts himself to salvage the situation, apologizes profusely. He's forced to do a rearrangement in his head as to the sort of approach to yours truly that's needed to place her at ease—he's fearing the situation might very well be unsalvageable.)

Truth is, Dearest, I'm too tuckered out to fling myself into a full-fledged description of the manner in which I was soothed after being criminally flayed for nearly a day. Suffice to say Stevie and I were skin wedded to one another, doing one uplifting thing or another, until well past sunup and that by frolic's end I was something of a prepubescent girl gaily dancing in a flower-bedecked arbor, fountains plashing nearby.

OK, Ella! I'm so drowsy this screen's turning into formless white haze, words blurring. This lil' lassie's been lengthily lingered upon and loved and is adrift in lusciously lassitudinous languor. Her fiasco of a Friday's thoroughly flushed from her blood and nerves! She's 100% cured!

Nighty-night, Sweets!

Your,

SatedSlumbrousSlut

IX. Isabel's Capture

Angie, have you seen the new girl, Isabel? Size four, about five feet five, wavy raven black hair, blue eyes? She's difficult to miss—blue eyeliner, blue pumps, blue hair ribbon, blue dress. Such a brat, teasing with hair flicks, chest thrusts, dress adjustments—tickled to death with her cuteness, delighting in being a petite dishling all want to drink from. Such a knowing air of "Do ya wanna do me? Sure ya do!" coyness. A sly little flirt, *faux* innocence coquette. Have you seen her yet?

An hour ago at the coffee stand: Isabel's fretting at the machine, pretending not to understand how it works—very well done, her little girl frown and show of confusion. Michael falls for it right off, is overeager concern, fumble fingers at the buttons—drops a full cup on the floor. Poor Michael! He's given Isabel a perfect excuse to put on a little-girl-scared act. "Oh!" she squeals, jumping back, wringing her hands, glancing at him as if he's seeking to wring her neck.

"Sor...ry... I... Uh..." Michael stammers, lapsing into shame-faced silence, staring at her with pleading eyes, hoping she doesn't subject him to the supreme horrors of a further scene, or a cutting remark.

"Coffee on my shoe?" Isabel exclaims in disbelief, slipping in a teensy trace of a tone of terror—a fine bit of subjected-to-a-major-tragedy exaggeration. Then she whips her leg up and places her foot on the counter, starts wiping the droplet or two of coffee off her shoe—her display of limberness allows her hem to slide towards her tummy, reveal the flawless symmetry, softness and fitness, of her thigh. Michael's as if jolted with a cattle prod—flinches violently, abandons all hope of reclaiming lost honor, darts into the stairwell like a scared schoolboy.

Isabel notices me awaiting my turn behind her. Before I can inform her there's a shred of paper in her hair and assist her in removing it she snaps her leg back to the floor, does a quick half-pirouette on those pumps, yanks her dress tight against her rump to show off its shapeliness, scampers off giggling. Then a sudden glance back at me, flash of her eyes—minx is blatantly advertising amusement. Does she really believe she can tease me without the tables being turned?

Isabel recognizes an oftentimes-plays-with-girls girl when she encounters one—I'll grant she's clever. But she's got naïveté to burn if she thinks she's going to have me salivating for something I'll fail to obtain. She's got naïveté to burn and she'll be burned by it if she tries much more of that giggling backwards glance run away stuff on me.

Well, Isabel's too much of a younger version of us for me not to feel kindly towards her. Plus she brings off the blue eyeliner thing: how many girls can do *that* at work without looking like clowns? And what a swishy stride to go with that swishing mane of jet black hair.

But have you seen her yet? If not, do what the new arrival announcements advise. Stop by her office (4212) and welcome her to the firm, size her up. See if you agree we ought to turn the tease back on her, have her pining before she can say, "I shouldn't presume to believe it possible to toy with Ella Jody Susanna Washington!" three times.

Eagerly awaiting your report.

Your,

PlayfulPussycatAprowling

IX.2
Angie to Ella
Tuesday, August 5, 2003 11:59 AM

A new plaything on the premises, younger version of ourselves?—likely inclined to dabble in girl-on-girl games, like all well-bred cuties? (In bygone times, convents and finishing schools were girl-on-girl friendly; in the present day and age, an elite law firm fills in. We man-loving girls who don't shy at broadening our experience with same sex fun: there's always been places for us to meet and mingle in respectable surroundings, and we read one another straightaway and don't hesitate to pounce.) I'd hasten to assess Isabel as you suggest, but can't at the moment. Rikert has me picking up the slack left by an inept first year—the idiot offspring of a filthy rich client the firm must give a job and babysit, lest said client get miffed and take his business elsewhere. I'd dearly love to redden said offspring's pasty cheeks with a flurry of slaps! But I digress: rest assured I'll do an appraisal of new playlet Isabel as soon as I can get down there. And blue-themed, you say? Be interesting if she had a fetish for the color blue—I've an ancient gown, deep turquoise, I could rip into strips to tie her up with. Then we'd see her tight little swishy body appealingly squirm to the tune of Miss Whippie, wouldn't we? She'd learn a thing or two about having the cheek to tease my Ethereal Ella! She'd learn tease encompasses many dimensions, for instance as in ignoring a pretty petite plaything's pleas for mercy. But I haven't so much as glimpsed Isabel yet. Let's wait until I meet her.

So hang tight, Ella. I'll do an eye-up of Isabel before day's end, after I tidy up the baby's mess. (You should hear Rikert rage about having to put up with the baby—says it's blackmail, worst part of his job.)

Your,

CuriousKitty

IX.3
Ella to Angie
Tuesday, August 5, 2003 12:44 PM

Sheila told me Rikert was yelling about having his hands tied, putting up with the "simpering puppy," yesterday morning. From there, he's bewailing the shoddy business of having to stroke clients, humor their useless offspring, assign them to important deals. As the son of a cab driver who's where he is because of unwavering determination, authentic savvy and brains, Rikert's especially offended by the babysitting business, has kicked a couple baby's out. (And gotten away with it due to our sterling service. But it's not always possible.)

As for the baby, seems his daddy bought his admission and degrees by making hefty contributions to the schools he attended. Taking no chances, daddy started contributing soon as baby was born. This is known because baby's revealed it. So no wonder baby's such a baby: his future's guaranteed. Another sorry example of absence of struggle yielding absence of personality, dearth of wit, braindeadness.

Hope you'll have time to get acquainted with BlueGirl today—I'm itching for your impressions, feel she'll make a fine recruit.

Your,

GossipDispensingDamsel

IX.4
Angie to Ella
Tuesday, August 6, 2003 1:53 AM

My Ethereal Ella certainly has an eye for a spirited bit of snatchling: what mischief crackles within blue-coiffed Isabel. I went to her office, as you suggested, to welcome her aboard. She was at her desk, arranging some small stuffed animals atop her monitor—looking very snug and pretty in her blue things, with those raven locks tumbling down, as luminous a girl as I've ever seen. (Excluding my Ella, of course.)

I introduce myself and circle the desk to hug Isabel; not deigning to stand from her chair, she obliges me to bend to do so, merely wrapping an arm about my back. "Oh," she coos in something of a dismissive tone, "you're nice." She abruptly and rudely exits my hug by bending to retrieve a teddy bear from a box on the floor; rather transparently, she caresses one of her thighs to get her hem to ride up to her stocking tops, plus is insultingly smiling to herself, starts rubbing her cheeks and chin atop Teddy's head while fluttering her eyelids and gazing at me in a condescending manner. Ha! To be behaving thus towards me, as if I'm a desperately grasping social reject of a slush girl! Me, supreme drop dead gorgeous cutiepie (If I say so myself and, heaven knows, I hardly need say it when oodles of others constantly say it for me.), deemed by this clueless upstart to be unworthy of anything besides perfunctory and insincere acknowledgments of my presence. It beggars belief, Ella, the way this Isabel appears to believe I'm going to be instantly rendered mystified and dumb by a hiked up hemline and fluttering eyes.

Boy, did Isabel's attempts to toy with me—her smugness, that smirk—annoy me. I immediately resolved to teach her a lesson. And I do allow being taught a lesson may have been what she had in mind, albeit subconsciously. On the conscious level, I'm sure she was very pleased with herself and convinced she was soon going to have me stammering and goo-goo eyed. But, instinct-wise, is it too far-fetched to suppose Isabel's subsurface impulses caused her to play with fire so's to be awakened—yanked from her safe little flirt-world by an experienced girl, plunged into scorching desire? We both know how sure-fire accurate Mommy Nature is when it comes to getting people of like sex-aptitude to come together. And Isabel has aptitude, hungers for happenings. As you said, a younger version of ourselves.

So I'm incensed by the presumption of the girl; by the way she's continuing to rub her cheeks against Teddy's head, intone, "Mmmmm"; way she's smiling in a self-satisfied manner, with a trace of mockery about her lips; way she's very preoccupied with her cuteness, as if no other girl possesses a like amount. She's vaguely doing a masturbation thing with Teddy: squirming against the chair and squishing her legs together so that her stockings rasp; thrusting out her breasts and subtly stroking them with forearms, gaze becoming blurry bright. She's maintaining a steady stream of burbling pitter-patter—"Everyone's so kind and welcoming...I love the firm so much, am excited about my job...crowds have come here to make me feel at home and it's sweet of them...people are so nice..." while smiling the condescending smile.

Adding insult to insult, Isabel says in a flirty singsong tone, "Would you come around here, please?" indicating the back of her chair with a nod. "Could you be a dear and tie this ribbon in my hair?" She accompanies the request with a very deliberate, shivery, arching-of-her-back stretch—almost like a sigh, the stretch is, of nearly flawless execution (Using the scoring system for figure skating, I'd rate it a 5.7 for technical merit and 5.9 for artistic impression); then she raises her arms in the air and quivers them, holding the ribbon taut between her two hands; plus she's vibrating her legs, as well as doing additional chest-heaves. I also note mockery's still hovering about her lips, quite barefacedly: she's congratulating herself on having brought me under her spell.

I play it compliant and awestruck for a bit, reverently take the ribbon from Isabel's hands, see to it my hand trembles as I do so—something that doesn't escape her notice, and causes her to smile more of a prideful smile. Yes, I take the ribbon and am very docile and submissive, like all good conquests—I'm docile for a full minute more so Isabel can drink it in and gloat. Then I—how you'll laugh, Dearest!—wrap that ribbon around her throat (Not too tight, but tight enough.), and hiss, "So you think I'm an inexperienced dolt who can't see through your novice games, do you? You tease my friend Ella at the coffee stand with displays of leg, glancing-over-your-shoulder gloating, yankings of your dress against your uneducated ass! You play kissy and cuddles with Teddy while your hem slides nearly up to your snatch, and you suppose I'm hungering to trade places with Teddy and will be a simpering gutless fool! Don't you understand you're trying to toy with two sluts who put the capital S in Slutdom and that, whatever flames you fan, they'll roar forth to burn you? Don't you know this, silly girl?"

Ella, I confess I'm astonished at my boldness, even slightly scared—I've known Isabel for maybe three minutes! But there are emanations!—the mood of her, readiness of her, asking-for-it cheek of her, the—as we've noted—aptitude of her, the what I'd term, "predisposition to interconnectedness with girls (like us) given to extremes." What seems borderline loony on paper (As in: "Will I wrap a ribbon about a girl's throat and taunt her within minutes of meeting her? Sure, just as soon as the sky rains pink purple-polka-dotted possums!") was suddenly the most plausible, and only right and proper, course of action.

Isabel can only manage a gasp—nearly a grunt—as alarm surges in her eyes and body sharply twists. Feeling the ribbon could be too tight, inhibiting speech, I loosen it to allow her to speak. But she says nothing while still apprehensively squirming—only gasps, increasingly quick and deep, emerge from her throat. I relish the alarm in her eyes, look that's asking, "What have I gotten myself into?"; relish the contrast between her panic at this moment and her self-satisfaction instants before. Highly gratifying are her heavings of bust, unaffected now, that are like as not to burst the buttons of her pretty blue dress.

Precautionary measures are called for. "This is how it's going to be," I snarl, circling to the front of Isabel's chair—still with a firm grip on the ribbon about her throat—and pulling her to her feet. "This is the deal. I'll lead you to the window and you'll pull the shade down, then I'll lead you to the door and you'll lock it. Your execution of these tasks will be your means of indicating you agree to participate in what will follow and, even though you have no idea what will follow *(I briefly pause, gaze at her with malice.)*, you need to surrender without question."

Oh, Ella! You should see how swiftly Isabel becomes compliant, downturns her eyes in humble submission. She's still uneasy—her glance wavering, wobbly—but can't prevent radiance, pleasure's glow, from leaping into her expression. Spirited girls thrive on surprise—can't help warming to opportunities to step towards the unknown. The shades are pulled and door locked without a twitch of resistance, me still holding the ribbon—readymade leash—about her throat. Once I lead her back to her chair and compel her to sit, I say, "OK, presumptuous ninny, I'm going to sit on your lap and squeeze you with my well-exercised thighs, kiss you long and hard—going to wipe that tease-girl smirk off your face for good. Then I'll help myself to your honey with this free hand—see it? (I flutter my fingers in her face.) I'm going to rudely probe your flowerpuss and tweak your love-bud, irritate you instead of soothing you, because the idea is for me to enjoy myself, and for you nothing. And if you so much as flinch in noncompliance," I raise my voice, "I'll tighten this ribbon, wring your little flirt-tramp's neck." How tingles race up my spine!—which, of course, is to Isabel's credit. No ordinary girl would be able to get under my skin so quickly and thoroughly, something of possess me, essentially force me to embark upon a rash course of spontaneous disciplinary action. I'm assuredly stepping towards the unknown, tasting of heady apprehension.

I crush my mouth against Isabel's, am greeted by skilled responsiveness, her lips undulating, tongue fluttering and rolling—she's as thirsty for kisses as if deprived for weeks, her breath strong and quick, warmth bathing my cheeks. I yank her dress to her waist, command her to raise her behind, then pull her panties forward, intentionally roughly plunge two fingers inside her and stroke. With each forceful stroke, my fingers savoring her slippery softness, her body winces—she's mashing her tits and tummy against me, arms wrapped increasingly tighter about my back. Before I'm aware she's near her threshold (Shame on me!), able to yank her away, Isabel gasp-cries in pleasure, pitches and shivers.

"Disobedient twat!" I glare. "You've obtained satisfaction without permission, committed the unpardonable crime of gushing before servicing me. Furthermore, you've smushed your legs together, are rubbing them to savor your flood, prolong the reverberations—yeah, I'm wise to that, don't look surprised, you're as transparent as glass, and it's over. (I squirm atop her, wedge my behind between her legs, thrust them apart.) Such is a grave insult, as good as nails raked across my face—only I'm allowed to rake nails, missy." So saying, I lightly scrape her with a nail in a highly sensitive spot. "Ah, that's a jolt, isn't it? You flood again while on assignment and I'll scrape your love canal raw. Now, to business! You're going to tongue-pet Angie's pinkling with great care and skill, and if you fail to ensure Angie tastes of heaven during the whole of her journey towards *her* flood you'll seriously regret you met her." I tighten the ribbon slightly, by way of reminding her.

I stand and command Isabel to: 1) rise so I can sit in her chair, and 2) sink to her knees before me. "OK, honeykins," I sneer, "your assignment is as follows. You're to remove my shoes and place them squarely in the center of your desk, after which you'll slowly and respectfully slip my panties off. You'll fold said panties and be careful not to wrinkle them because if you do, prissy-poo, you'll have trouble breathing normally for a week (I tighten the ribbon slightly, smile a poison-laced smile.), and place them alongside my shoes. Then you'll decorously roll my hem up to my waist, as if you're in etiquette class at a strict boarding school where canings for incompetence are a given. Then you'll pray to Venus and worship Venus by treating Angie to a stimulating tongue-bath. You'll caress my thighs with both hands at all times, not touching anything else, with as much care as if you're handling nitro—because, believe it missy, you are handling nitro."

This is stated in a bitchy sugary tone, as imbued with as much subdued malice as I'm able to summon, and I confess to needing to push Isabel's head down to prevent her from detecting mirth on my face. (Alas, the stimulating apprehension I first experienced with regard to this unexpected adventure has departed—at least with respect to Isabel, who's clearly loving every moment. I *do* need to remain wary—mindful we're at work.)

When Isabel does as instructed she's no longer trembling. Her gestures radiate contentment and trust and she's pleased we've met. (Nothing like flooding to bond girls who were strangers shortly before.) She commences worshipping Venus and, to no great surprise, proves she's no novice: such liquid silk tickles, wild wriggles, does her tongue dispense! She's still on the ribbon-leash but I'm neglecting to remind her—losing myself in the warm electric slippery-slide, thrusting at her for more—scrubbing her face. "Deeper, harlot!" I instruct, beside myself quicker than expected. "And what's this caressing of my thighs nonsense? Put those slacking fingers to work and stroke my petals, rub my bud! Earn your forgiveness!" Ooooo! Isabel's locks are streaming over my thighs, swishing most stimulatingly as her tongue rhythmically probes! Damn! I crest sooner than I want to, the brat has skills.

I'm staring at the ceiling as orgasm's ripples whirl me under my skin, sparkle and tingle. I just want to get stupid-giddy, unabashedly surrender, hug Isabel close, inform her how adorable she is, am near to doing so. But a voice in my head announces: "For shame, Angie! How dare you acquiesce to delight when administration of discipline's forefront! How dare you express gratitude—reveal vulnerability—to this Isabel who's sought to tear the prima donna tiara from your head! The enemy's at your gate, and you're leaving it unguarded, giving this upstart a reason to be pleased with herself? Wake up, Angie! Duty first!"

Stoic me, right? I swallow joy, erase evidence of delight—damned if I'm going to allow transient bliss to cost me lasting triumph. And I'm right to shut down pleasurable sensations: when I glance down I note Isabel's gazing at me pleased-as-punch, self-congratulation in her eyes—blatant "Surprised you, didn't I?" in her eyes—and such is poisonous to me.

Ella, if you'd muffed me as magnificently I would've expressed gratitude with a reversal of roles—spilled you onto the floor, brought all energy to bear upon making you squirm and squeal. But because it was upstart Isabel my greater impulse was to wipe all trace of self-congratulation from her face, fling her vanity in the mud, return her to uneasiness concerning what was possibly happening next.

"What are you so pleased about?" I snarl, tightening the ribbon. "You've done what you had to do solely out of necessity of self-preservation, nothing more and no awards: any ditzy doll with a tongue could've done the same. You exerted yourself because failing to do so would've resulted in severe penalties. Think I can't see straight through you, deluded tossy girl? Think you're not transparent as glass? Unable to simply do your duty and stand pat, you've succumbed to the weakness and idiocy of parading pride! Grave mistake, because now (I stand, push her onto her haunches on the floor.) you're going to place one of my shoes on my foot and, once it's there, you'll respectfully and extensively kiss it while repeating, 'Thank you, Angie.' in an awe-struck tone that plainly indicates you're amazed I've deigned to discipline an inferior creature like yourself. And you'd better place that shoe on my foot gently, so I can barely feel it going on—you'd better pray you don't cause my precious foot the least amount of discomfort."

Ha! Nice try on my part, but the interval for dramatizing annoyance, playing at discipline, has expired. Breaking Isabel down again, undermining her self-esteem, is suddenly silly. She's a treasure and I can't prevent myself from smiling when issuing the "Fetch my shoe!" command. Isabel senses it's silly as well—gazes at me dubiously, even while humoring me with a submissive expression. She's flooded me, I've flooded her: icy commands don't cut it anymore.

All the same, Isabel makes a show of reaching for my shoe—an "Oh, well, what the hell." tone surrounding her, no evidence of distress. I'm feeling not a little ridiculous. After all, exactly what did Isabel's offense consist of? Hardly anything: harmless flirtation, a charming girl being a charming girl. So what if she was a trifle too sure of herself, naïvely assuming she had the upper hand? It's not like I didn't make similar blunders when a youngster—not like she didn't knuckle down and behave admirably after I undeceived her. Soon as she's about to put the shoe on my foot, I'm unable to prolong the charade, laughingly let go of the ribbon about her neck. Sweet-thing starts at the sound of my laughter—glances at me quizzically, as if to confirm it's authentic laughter, then she's laughing too—her laughter feeds my laughter and my laughter feeds hers and we wind up invaded by the sillies something fierce. I stagger to the side, pitch myself against the desk, support myself with one hand while gripping my tummy with the other. Isabel's soon sprawled in her chair, doubled over, nearly tumbling to the floor.

After maybe four cycles of eyesight-blurring attacks of hysterics (As when one's tummy's so achurn the expression "Dying of laughter." starts to make sense.) that subside only to flare up again, our amusement finally passes, and I'm able to gaze about. And, hey, there's Isabel seated on the floor, giving me the most beautiful look of affection. I go to her and her head's soon on my lap—I'm caressing her temples—she slides sideways and raises her head—we're joyously kissing.

Would you believe it? No sooner are we engrossed in kissing than there's emphatic knocking at the door: alarm contorts the darling's face—her entire body's paralyzed with apprehension—she yanks her eyes at me, a mix of "What now?" and "Oh, God!" in them. I'm sure Isabel's professional life is flashing before her—she's afraid she could be dishonorably discharged from the firm before her first week's done.

I'm atwinge with a hint of panic on Isabel's behalf instead of mine. "Stand, honey," I say, assisting her to her feet. She's clinging to my arm like a cat about to be flung in water, trembling verging on shaking. And the knocking continues, seemingly louder. "Just a moment," I call out with the calm even voice that comes to me when possible danger's nigh. Ha, I've been there so many times and, hey, happen to love it! Danger looms and I fall into place inside, find myself joined to a core of equanimity that surprises as much as it delights me. I become inwardly removed from the danger—acquire an instant vantage point—and know what to do without having to think; time seems to slow down and allow me additional time to act even though, of course, time hasn't slowed down and there are only seconds in which to act. Which isn't to say I'm devoid of uneasiness—far from it; if anything, it's uneasiness that pulls me together and, so to speak, *forces* clear-headedness upon me.

I'm guiding Isabel to her chair and spreading a document before her—I'm dispensing a final caress of comfort, tidying her hair, before putting my shoes on and advancing to the door—I'm unlocking the door to reveal Herslow, a partner I hardly know—I'm smiling at Herslow, informing her Isabel's a bright prospect, quick study, person who's eager to learn. Just showing Isabel the structure of a 10-K I say—also covering the general filing of documents with the SEC. Well, like myself (ha ha!), Herslow was there to welcome Isabel to the firm: she pats her hand and lets her know she'll be working on the [_____] offering. Isabel, still very much flustered, gets quite gushy—a bit over-gushy (quite cute!)—and babbles "Thank you! Thank you!" several times, plus assures Herslow she's there to work and eager to work, call her extension and she'll come running. (Admirable that the minx has collected herself enough to get those words in, she's certainly got her priorities straight: another quality that endears her to me.) Herslow, probably assuming Isabel's off-pitch voice and forced manner and air of embarrassment is a consequence of her visit, smiles, reaffirms her welcome, says please don't be intimidated by anyone, and leaves.

"My God!" Isabel exclaims, becoming utterly limp in her chair and flinging her hair in the air, such that it flops rather becomingly over the front of her face—a feathery black veil, with her trepidant blue eyes shining through. Isabel's not smiling with relief, as we'd be doing—she's not giggling, as we'd be doing: she's limp as a rag doll, lacking the will to even shake her head to get her hair to fall back into place. So Mommy Angie—after locking the door again—comes to her aid, saying, "Darling Blue Eyes *(I brush her hair aside.)*, you've had your first taste of what's routine for my friend Ella and I. It's known as enlightening, stimulating, and refreshing workplace fun and fear contrast."

"Allow me to elaborate," I continue, kneeling beside her and stroking her cheeks. "It being your first experience of workplace fun and fear contrast, you're a trifle shaken—that's only to be expected. But pause, darling, and take stock of your sensations—wait for the joy to appear. Joy at having spent the past hour experiencing the sharp contrasts life has to offer; joy at the fact a great deal of the spectrum of possible feeling needn't be neglected simply because you happen to be in a respectable law firm. Isn't it wonderful that, even though we're at the office, we're in touch with our primeval aspect?—tasting of an enthralling mixture of pleasure, unpredictability, and danger?"

Sure, I babbled some stuff Isabel seemed in no frame of mind to care about exerting herself to comprehend: the darling seemed somewhat uncertain as to what she was feeling or whether she liked it. Then again, nature-given slut aptitude always triumphs, regardless of whether the girl who possesses it wants it to. Isabel's shortly responding to my face caresses and, like the feline she is, rubbing against me for petting in other places; then she wraps an arm around my waist; then she sighs a deep throaty "Uuuummmm..." as dreaminess suffuses her gaze.

I tell her: "Later on, when you climb into bed, you may experience a special excitement-inundated peace reserved for the lucky. You may lie awake for over an hour because you won't want to stop relishing the reverberations and, when you do sleep, will sleep as soundly and refreshingly as you ever have. At any rate, you'll thank your lucky stars for having been hired by the law firm of [_____], where Ella and I run wild every chance we get. Cream of the crop, that's who the firm hires and, honey, you're going to cream aplenty while you're here."

"A nice surprise, and I look forward to it," Isabel smiles.

"Isabel," I continue, "we've traveled light years since I stepped into your office. I've shown you the error of your ways and you've revealed yourself to be a very classy funloving young lady. However, I still feel you owe Ella an apology for having presumed to tease her at the coffee stand. She's my best friend and it would make me feel so much better if you'd pay her a visit and beg her pardon." I kiss her forehead.

"Of course I'll apologize to Ella," Isabel says, kissing my forehead in turn. "Immediately." She stands, smoothes her dress into place, opens the door, and disappears into the hall. I raise the window shade and am fluffing my hair into order while regarding my reflection in the glass when I hear "Psssst!" and turn towards the sound. And there's Isabel in the doorway: without stepping into the office—albeit preceded by a quick glance up and down the hall—she yanks her skirt to her waist with one hand while twirling her panties in the other, then scampers off giggling. I can still picture her, pleased as a cat with bird in mouth: such a priceless air of delight-in-mischief surrounds the girl.

Thank you so much, Ella, for sending me on this welcome wagon mission, allowing me to initiate Isabel. You spied her first, perceived her aptitude, so double thank you, as by all rights initiation honors were yours. You were the one Isabel offended and who had reason to go on a comeuppance prowl, yet you tossed the sweetheart to me. To step into the office of a freshly arrived FlingThing, cute as a crimson button (Or, in Isabel's case, a blue one.), who's naïve enough to set about teasing and baiting me with her pert lil' body she's rightfully proud of! Ha, my jumping of Isabel happened so fast there was zero advance anticipation of doing such. I was a cat surprised by prey in this garden of a firm, and sprang for thrills without a thought. Nice n' direct n' primeval. No one else will enjoy that initial shock of Isabel's. My successor—you—will find she's unlikely to be surprised by an office take-down, probably expecting one instead. No one else will experience a first helping of Isabel's amazement and confusion. So thanks once more, Ella, for permitting me to awaken Isabel to workplace play.

But what happened in your office? Did the dear apologize and soothe your ego, behave exemplarily? Did you have a good time conscientiously continuing her education?

Your,

IngenueInitiatingAngie

P.S. Considering the hour, why haven't I heard a peep out of you concerning Isabel's visit? What's going on with you?

IX.5
Angie to Ella
Tuesday, August 6, 2003 10:28 AM

Again, Ella, profuse thanks for permitting me to initiate Isabel. And please note I conscientiously detailed our doings, sent my assessment, soon as I was able—spent a lot of time on such. Plus I sent her your way and near as I could determine she was primed for more action, pretty much expecting such, so it would be nice if you'd deign to remember your best girlfriend and send me the news, even if you only have time for two lines. I know Isabel went home around five-thirty (As it's her first week, she doesn't have to stay late, although that will soon change and she'll be as slammed as any other first year.) because she stopped by to blow a kissy bye-bye and lift her skirt again and say, "I'm not afraid of you!" before gigglingly prancing off. So tell me *something*! I'm sorely in need of amusement on account having to undo more of the simpering puppy's mess. (Sturmheld's ready to kill the puppy.) I'm sure Isabel's delightfully minxish personality lent itself to further fun.

Your,

AnxiouslyAnticipatingAngie

IX.6
Ella to Angie
Tuesday, August 6, 2003 10:57 AM

Hey, Angie! Think you're the only attorney slaving away? Think I haven't responsibilities of my own? Think I'm an incompetent daughter of an influential client (another babysit case) who can remain employed, and get bonuses besides, simply by showing up? Even if I had a filthy rich well-connected daddy, think I'd make use of him to reap unearned benefits? Think I could be a parasite? Think I wasn't raised by an achievement-oriented family? Think I could be happy without having to make my own way with brains, street smarts, charm, out-and-out lust for success? Answer me: what sorta girlfriend do you think you have? Just because I occasionally permit you to tan my bratty behind with Miss Whippie hardly means I'm to be classified as a submissive who lacks will and expects everything to be handed to me. I permit you to discipline me and don't cha forget it! I PERMIT you!

Believe it or not, Miss Vanity, I'm in Amended & Restated hell—from which I'm taking brief breaks to key the e that tells of Isabel. But am I going to send what I have thus far? Nay! I take great pride in my email accounts and aren't about to split one into bits, especially when it's barely started. I enjoy having a self-contained recollection in progress before me: to send part of it prematurely would violate my dedication to order and completeness. So you're just going to have to cool your hot lil' heels and get back to the drudgery and wait until I'm done.

Your,

Insulted'N'MiffedMiss

IX.7
Angie to Ella
Tuesday, August 6, 2003 1:37 PM

Darling, you will NOT believe it. I was gazing out my window, losing myself in the glimmering noon light, when—whoosh!—a falcon alighted on my windowsill. Sleek and regal, with large amber eyes. What a magnificent predator! The falcon stayed on the sill for nearly five minutes, myself lost in admiration. My reflection was on the window—feline and falcon side by side. When the falcon took off he (was a male: brighter coloration, purplish-slate feathers.) soared straight up, vanished in clouds. Still lost in awe I am—what a treat. Out of the bazillions of windowsills in town, Sir Falcon chose mine. Is surely a favorable omen, portending of fabulous events to come. So excited-scintillant am I, I'm like as not to surf the tremble-wave without touching myself!

As for your Miss Whippie crack: think a fierce kitty wastes time punishing spiritless slush girls? Think I don't know you're my delicate flower girlfriend with an inner core of solid will? Would I stoop to treating anyone but the wildest of girls to a taste of Miss Whippie? You permit me to lash your behind with Miss Whippie and without such permission I wouldn't dare? Well, duh! But I'm telling you this: before I bring Miss Whippie out again and make a gift to you of the calmness she dispenses, you're going to *beg* me to do so. Permission? Ha! Permission's your side of the equation. My side is: if I'm going to exert myself to reunite you with Miss Whippie's healing hiss and kiss, you're going to need to plead for the privilege. Not kidding, ungrateful brat! How dare you presume your best girlfriend punishes you solely for her pleasure. I punish you from LOVE, because you hunger for and acquire balance following said punishment. You know damn well

I don't strut like a fool and look down on you—ever—simply because I'm the one tiring my arm with floggings of your proffered behind.

Yeah, you're going to need to drop to your knees and wail the next time you're aching for serenity; plus bring two dozen long stemmed white roses—plus an angora scarf—plus a pair of butter-soft lambskin gloves.

And hop to with the Isabel stuff!

Your,

LosingPatiencePrincess

IX.8
Ella to Angie
Tuesday, August 6, 2003 10:41 PM

Well, Miss PatienceLost, if you're going to get huffy over some silly teasing, then you're not the girlfriend I thought you were and you can find someone else's behind to bruise. Beg you? Ha! I'm no longer giving you permission! I'm done with Miss Whippie, and with you!

OK—enough! Why do we get in these fake-feud moods, anyway? Why do we sometimes tease via mock skirmishes, tongue-in-cheek cat-spatting? I know why: we playact contrariness so we can better understand and appreciate the unwavering steadiness and strength of our love and admiration. And certainly better to act out contrariness than have the real deal raise its killjoy head. That is, assuming it ever could.

Sweetest, I'll *plead* on my knees for a Miss Whippie lashing, should you desire, and smother you with lilies as you lie lithe in your bed, and gift you with scarves and shawls and sweaters—all angora. And when I'm done showering you with silly objects (which, after all, are easily had with mere money), I'll shower you with my limitless respect and undying devotion and infinite love and all else at my disposal.

An admission, Angie Angel: I fibbed (Note I use "fibbed" instead of "lied" because it softens, even frivolizes, the meaning.), and haven't written a word concerning Isabel. Sorry to disappoint and deprive of entertainment but hardly anything happened, because I was flung into Amended & Restated hell without warning. New developments dictate it be filed by Thursday morning, and there's catching up to do with the other side's comments, so yours truly's going to be a law slave for at least a day and a half—only leaving for a shower in the AM, and any sleep I get will be on my padded exercise mat on my office floor.

You didn't alert me that Isabel was on her way, you prankish pussy-cat. Not that it isn't instantly obvious something's happened between you two—no other reason for her to turn up like a stray at my door. On the one hand, she's infused with a post-sexploit aura of excitement, joyfully glazed in her gaze, in something of a sleepwalker's trance; on the other, she's crinkling her face guiltily, staring at her foot while nervously twisting it against the carpet, fidget-fiddling with her hem. Then she announces: "Angie sent me to apologize for my coffee stand stuff—I'm sorry I offended you," while hesitantly raising her eyes. But I was in the thick of this rising tide of revisions (I shouldn't be taking time to write this) and unable to enjoy the situation, even think of involving her in further dalliance. Considerate of you to send me a doll who was both aflush with post-floodsville and a bit uneasy, but your timing was off.

I tell Isabel an apology's unnecessary, it being dreamed up by your wicked capricious brain. Tell her something like: "Oh, that's just Angie being Angie. She's got a nasty Mother Superior streak in her, is always angling for excuses to assign acts of penance for perceived offenses—'perceived' being the key word, since what Angie perceives as an offense isn't necessarily so in the eyes of others. You teased me? So what? Besides, if you hadn't, we wouldn't be getting acquainted now. Teasing's a way of saying 'Hello!'" I give Isabel a Granny Smith, plead a huge workload, and escort her to the door: we only get to cheek peck.

OK! The Amended & Restated demands my undivided attention! I'll be busy-busy 'til 'round Thursday noon. Bye for now, my Love.

Your,

CaptiveCorporateCoquette

P.S. Almost forgot: Isabel asked, "Do you and Angie masturbate at work?" Hahaha! Do we masturbate at work? Do fishies breed in the sea?

IX.9
Angie to Isabel
cc: Ella
Wednesday, August 7, 2003 9:55 PM

Isabel, I wish to address a matter of major importance. When you asked Ella if she and I masturbate at the firm, were you joking? I read you as a girl too sexually charged to go a day without flooding, lest you turn uncomfortably nuts. You're a fellow law strumpet who studied hard for the LSAT and endured the outrageous study load of a highly demanding law school and negotiated the minefield of the bar, so you surely already know what it is to be too pressed for time for others to be the sole instruments of your pleasure. So how can you ask Ella such a ridiculous question, as to whether she and I finger-dip the honey—butter our digits, eliminate the fidgets with a bit o' tuft-the-fluff—on company time? Sorry, but your question's preposterously ridiculous! Not only do Ella and I tweak our twatsies at the firm every chance we get, it's absolutely essential for health of body and mind—no negotiation.

It behooves us experience-enriched elders (What am I, a whopping two years older than you?) to advise, enlighten, and assist youngsters we're fond of. So here you go, Isabel—an informal instructional manual:

Beauty Enhancement, Career Advancement, and Self-Renewal

Do I masturbate before hitting the town? Is there a tramp in town who doesn't? How else acquire that extra glow? I want to be immersed in an aura of lust hunger and have the males sniffing at me like dogs—want post-orgasm elation to light up my gaze. And if the other trollops are doing it and I'm not, where does that leave me? There's a great deal of competition! Sure, I'm a nicely proportioned size four and men reliably whip their heads about on the sidewalk to drink me up with their eyes but I'm hardly the only one, and I'd be an idiot to think I don't need to constantly work at upping my game. A facial steam bath at the sink, the hot water turned on high, for a few minutes after applying makeup does wonders: heated moisture adds beguiling depth and radiance to a girl's complexion. It's a good trick and I often make use of it, but it falls short of the inner steam bath of masturbation. A spread-legged session on the couch, my pinkling probed by my delicate, tapering, ladyish fingers (What tales my fingers could tell!), is the trick to truly bringing the sultry slut look into my eyes—truly endowing my body with an electric sex quality man can't quite put their finger on, and which attracts them like bright lights do moths. Yes, a self-send-off session on the couch and I'm instantly immersed in desire's subsurface currents, magnetic with lust. It's more effective than a sleeveless one-piece cut low enough to show half my tits, with a hemline at the lower boundary of my ass.

I'm persuaded masturbation's useful for attracting attention at departmental meetings. The partners are constantly sizing us associates up, deciding whether to involve us in the latest potential windfall (bonus and advancement) of a deal, and especially so at meetings. I take my job very seriously and no one's going to tell me I don't do the grunt work like any other ambitious attorney, but there's no harm in covering additional bases, influencing the partners on a subconscious level. So I attend those meetings fresh from a self-stimulation session in my office: inner stirrings likely turn me into more of an attention-magnet. Then, once I have the partners' attention I shine with observations supported by research done with LiveEdgar, West-Law, and Lexus, plus good old fashioned law library books and visits to the Prospectus Room. When advancement opportunities present themselves, one must pounce.

Besides, I'm an itchy lil' beast and my senses can never dance entranced enough. Always, pussy's petals are slippery with tickles, bidding my fingers administer salvational strokes—pussy's a miracle toy, most precious plaything a girl could want—floppy petals and pert bud and panting passageway all rolled into one thrilling pleasure machine. My little shock box—reliable locket rocket. Catch my drift here? Is my message clear? Must I spell matters out? OK then: apart from the practical applications, I thoroughly adore finger-dancing myself into a procreative trance. There's nothing quite like knowing one has Mommy Nature's currents of rapture and renewal at one's disposal—a simple flurry of finger-flicks, and—magic! I'm communing with life's wellsprings, a Maenad running wild in the Theban woods.

Say it's lunch hour in springtime and my best frolic-friend, Ella, is swamped with work and can't get outside. I'm seated on one of the green chairs on Bryant Park's lawn, legs propped up on a second chair. I've brought along a fluffy angora shawl, even though it's seventy something degrees. A man or two or three or more (Well, yes, certainly more!) does a double or triple or more take at the sight of my shapely legs; and, my, how my skirty slides down my upraised thighs, nearly to the tops of my black silk stockings (thanks to timely fidgeting), and gives them more girl symmetry to gawk at; and, my, how aroused I become as their eyes stab me. I've gotten myself into a pretty lil' pickle, haven't I? On the one hand, I'm doubly antsy on account of them staring; on the other, how am I to pleasure myself in secret when skirty's revealing that much? So I make a show of being annoyed at having become a show and stop being the show by emphatically covering myself with the shawl from shins to chest. And, now that I'm covered up, it's not like I have a choice! My hand's under the shawl and 'twixt thighs lickety-split, fingers slipping within my soaked flaps—how rapidly electric tingles shoot up my spine, radiate across my back, blur my thoughts into clarity. Is "blur into clarity" an oxymoron? Not if one's describing how finger-dipping the honey sweeps one off one's regular-world bearings. It's when thoughts of everyday things—work, shopping, social scheduling, where to eat, who to call—dissolve because one's inundated with vivid sensation; it's when the life-force swells so forcefully one's unable to think outside the moment.

So long as no pompous dolt pesters me... And it's always the reeking-of-smugness investment banker clowns, or advertising execs or—sad to say—fellow attorneys who clumsily barge in on a girl's privacy before having received an eye-contact or hair-flick or suggestive-stretch invitation. Babbling about wealth straight off, like I'm a mindless gold-digger easily roped in by materialistic trash, and flashing showy watches, worth a car, apparently made for dumbasses begging to be mugged. Or it's the nonstop chattering artsy—I'm-a-photographer, I'm-a-filmmaker, I'm-a-DJ (Ha! A DJ? Pathetic!)—wankers who think nothing of intruding on a girl's be-by-herself time. I'll be somewhere minding my own business—window shopping along 5th, looking over a shoe store's new arrivals, actually chatting on my phone—and some pest will come up and say some immensely clever and bright thing such as, "You look like a Monica! Is that your name?" or "I really like your dress! Who designed it?" or "I'm confused: what's a beautiful lady like you doing alone?" or "What shade of eyeliner are you wearing?" Always the same inane rubbish. Calling me "lady," like they think I'll find them respectful and sensitive because they use "lady." And the inquiries as to what eyeliner, lipstick, perfume I'm wearing—they think I'll consider them to be special guys who're privy to girl secrets because they're mentioning makeup. I vastly prefer the unapologetically crude "Hey hot stuff, I have a big dick!" guys to those simpering asking-about-makeup imbeciles—at least the former know who they are. The pretentious ones are all the same pathetic loser who thinks nothing of foisting an immensely tedious personality on a girl because he's too dense to know how to ask from a distance, without words—ask with his eyes, await a response. Don't you just hate it when some bore thrusts himself on you, yanks you from your private world? Then you're obliged to pay attention to him, take the trouble to make it clear you want him gone—I start seeing blood when some twit won't leave me alone! But enough of that—apologies for getting sidetracked. Where was I?

Back to lunch hour in Bryant Park. Under cover of the angora shawl on my lap I've slipped my fingers within pinkling, am doing soft thumb-circlings on clitskie—arousal's undercurrents, shivery waves, building. At first my fingers multiply the itchy tickling—the more I stroke the more I need to stroke—and immediate surroundings recede from awareness. Sky's blue rushes down to embrace me—lawn's green turns silver in the sun—facades of 42nd Street's buildings seem to melt, merge with the air. I haven't a care in the world, other than the urgency of keeping pace with my urgency—staying ahead of the shivery stabs in my tummy, maddening heat. I'm gasping inside—slow, drawn out gasps—each gasp carries the promise of surging over the crest. I bear down—stroke in earnest—firmly caress the slick fire of my vaginal walls—probe deeper—continue worrying clitskie—my world's swirling into the funnel of my insatiable womb. I gasp deeper, swallow my sighs—ooooo! luscious inner turnover arrives! I'm flooding in the park, in the wide open, in plain sight! I drop my head to allow my hair to fall in the way and conceal my expression (a dense mane of hair has practical applications), permit me to privately revel in release-from-tension sensations—uplifted-in-suspension sensations—inrush-of-shimmers sensations. I adore cresting in the midst of a crowd, no one having a clue—concealment's another game, enlightening multidimensionality—hidden pulsations, undulations. Or simply: *getting away with stuff!* Darling, masturbation's *extremely* healthy—perhaps I've done it enough already to add a couple years to my life.

##########

OK, Isabel, end of my official pet-the-pussycat essay!

And don't cha worry career-wise, darling: you've been assigned to [_____], one of our biggest clients, with annual billing high as the sky. There's always something major happening with them, and it's a triumph for you. You'll be working mighty hard to stay afloat in these, your precious first-year hazing days, in no time—you'll be living at the firm. And always remember it's a good thing. The partners don't heap loads of work on those they feel are likely to wilt under pressure, and they're generally accurate in their perceptions, because of the heaps of income at stake.

As Ella says: welcome to the money, honey—you've chosen the right profession. You'll not lack for co-conspirators in the stay-even-keeled-via-pleasure department—you'll get your lil' hotbox diddled aplenty whilst busy raking in investment income galore, paying off that pesky law school debt, dolling yourself up in the finest fashion has to offer.

Goodnight, Isabel!

Love,

Angie

X. Rant Fest, the Slings and Stings of Frustrated Frolic, & Declarations of Love

What a pain searching for a cab in the rain! And no use unbuttoning my coat to give drivers a glimpse of my hot lil' tramp's body, either: no emptys were anywhere. Even the car service guys who hustle for outrageous prices had fares. I was on the corner for nearly half an hour, the wind flinging the rain under my umbrella into my face, soaking my hair. (It's total frizzlesville.) Finally, I admitted defeat and hightailed it to the dreaded subway—sweaty, filthy, noisy, crammed. Born and raised on Central Park West I may be—attuned to my beloved Manhattan's pulse and pace I may be—uncomfortable in all other places on the face of the earth I may be—but nothing will ever reconcile me to the horrors of the subway during rush hour. Darling, please do get your shapely behind to my office pronto and pet and pacify your pretty pussycat! I need your delicate tapered fingers to caress away the *trauma*!

Your,

Public Transportation Traumatized Tramp

X.2
Angie to Ella
Friday, August 15, 2003 9:28 AM

Sweetie Pie, I can't even think about seeing you now: Rikert's requiring me to hang tight in my office. A half dozen conference calls
are probably going to happen, scatterbrained clients (in Nebraska)
haven't set a time—only said they'll call during office hours. Can't
join you for lunch either, because the calls could happen then—we're
ordering out. Nor should you drop by: Rikert's in a foul mood, cursing
the Nebraskans up and down, bothered by everything. He can taste
the money—taste victory, and a huge bonus, and these clowns are
frittering around and delaying his triumph. You definitely need to stay
away.

I'll keep you posted, Honey!
Your,
LawBitchInBondage

X.3
Ella to Angie
Friday, August 15, 2003 10:47 AM

I'm subway-ravaged and you're confined to quarters: peachy day! Suppose I could mosey over to Joseph's office and indicate I'd like to be
calmed, but then he'd exaggerate matters afterwards, become a pest.
Joseph's an unusual study in contrasts. He exercises discretion as far
as not blabbing about what we've done, but then flips about and
does violence to my privacy with surprise stop-bys at my building—or
cramming my voicemail to overflow, saying he'd like to treat me to a
Hamptons getaway. Why can't he accept the gift of no-strings-attached
sex? Why does he want to wind so many strings around me I can
barely breathe? Some idle stimulation at the office with a cutie who
won't pout and pine and whine for attention and trinkets later: plenty
of men appreciate such things, but he doesn't. Yes, Joseph the closet
sentimentalist who well knows how to cock and rock a wench, then

about-faces and comes calling at odd hours with flowers and baubles and babbles about getting serious. Why can't he get it straight?—accept I'm very willing to be an office mistress, a frolic or so a month, and that's it?—accept that this particular pussycat isn't going to be his steady girlfriend? But I'm wandering, honey—I'm an idiot this morning, blame it on the subway. Your deal's peaking, my primary's in a lull. I've been temporarily added to the [___] IPO so I can get more billable, but Sturmheld's too busy reprimanding Kirkland over the [___] fiasco to trouble with the latest comments, and of course I'm a busy ambitious proactive lil' bee, reviewing old player's lists, but can do such in my sleep so I've plenty of time to play in our email world.

Here's something worth telling: the reason silly Cindy's costume party was cancelled—such a disaster for the poor dear. No sooner does she send invitations to practically the entire corporate and litigation departments (Not because she's on good terms with, or even knows, all of us but because she wants to show off, wrongly assumes everyone will be thrilled to participate in idiocy because it's happening at a Tribeca penthouse.), than her investment banker boyfriend gets fed up with being bossed around, shows some backbone, refuses to loan his place. As Jasmine tells it, Cindy was on the phone all afternoon yesterday blubbering about the embarrassment, and how she and boyfriend aren't going to Bora Bora: her office door was open and she was broadcasting loud and clear. Jasmine, being next door, had a front row seat—for as long as she wanted one, that is. It didn't take long for her to get that consorting-with-stupidity feeling and shut her door to avoid hearing.

I'll never understand those who want others to overhear them spatting, whining, sobbing. Whether it's no-pride parasite Tommy endlessly wailing that his wife dumped him without warning (good on her), or simpering John who crybabys with his ex every other day, or Stacy who screamed at her boyfriend: "I don't like how you watch TV after you bang me!": these worthies blather this stuff at high decibel volume with their doors wide open, as if they feel nothing, no matter how demeaning, is worth experiencing unless others are privy to it. As if they're eager to demonstrate there's drama in their lives, even if it's humiliating. As if they're desperate for attention, don't care what's needed to get it.

Sure wish, Dearest, you were here to ease me with your wicked lil' tongue and keep me from randomly ranting, staring at my messed up mop of hair in the mirror. As if staring at my hair will make it fall into place—as if cringing at recollection of the horrid subway will restore equilibrium to my frazzled nerves. But *you'd* effortlessly calm me, if you weren't shamefully imprisoned by whimsical Nebraskans.

Well, I'm just one big bad hair day, getting hungrier for you by the second. Nuts to be separated when we're swimming in downtime.

Your,

FrazzledFlusteredFloozie

X.4
Angie to Ella
Friday, August 15, 2003 12:29 PM

Not one call's happened. Rikert's pacing up and down the hall outside his office, muttering obscenities, yelling about moody fools delaying a multi-million dollar deal. He's doubtful any calls will occur today, but I'm still on watch-duty, can't visit you—might as well rant too.

You know how Midge has a picture of her adorable toy collie, Rumples, on her desk? Earlier a couple bankruptcy dolts shuffled near my door. One of them—the fat bad dresser who smells of not washing (forget his name, doesn't matter)—said if Midge wasn't so hung up on her dog and maybe doing stuff with her dog he might have a shot at getting in her pants. Then, following an interval of burping laughter, the other chimed in with, "She named him Rumples because she likes to Rumba with him!" Yuck! Self-satisfied idiocy like that outright gives me the creeps! Nothing worse than losers spouting mean-spirited garbage because they can't get laid. And saying such things about Midge! Seems a truly nice girl can't have a dog without louts suggesting she sleeps with him.

Another item: yesterday afternoon Nigel and Ralph and another fresh-out-of-school poke their heads in my door and ask if I'd like to go outside for some air. OK, they've always seemed like good-natured guys, so why not? I'm a sociable gal and am stir-crazy, haven't been outside yet, feel it'll be an enjoyable break. I go outside with them in good faith, and what happens? Instead of socializing they gawk!—at first appear embarrassed and unsure what to do, as if they've been chased onto a stage and are fearful of being booed. It gets worse: they—these infant-men—adjust to the being on stage state of mind and start puffing themselves up and trading stupid looks of triumph, patronizingly glancing at other males, and I realize what stage they're on. It's the "We're with a hot girl and you're not!" stage—as if the fact I've come outside with them for a breath of air means I'll be spreading my legs. Such clowns are a menace!—they and their pathetic preening before an imaginary mirror. All they want to do is live in the mirror that appears when they're with a pretty girl, the girl herself be damned. Acting like we're an item of sorts simply because I agreed to feel breeze on my face in their company—turning smug and self-important when not a caress has been exchanged between us and the thought of such makes me ill. I spy George near the flowers and hightail it over—leave the infants high and dry. George the gentle giant—an affable unpretentious mature man, well able to knock out the three infants with three punches, with nothing to prove and incapable of acting weird because he's in a cutie's company. Plus he lets me in on an interesting development concerning the [_____] deal I'll tell you about later. The infants are wounded-puppy-dog-faced in the distance, I catch a glimpse of them when returning indoors with George. One has the gall to dart me a look of reproach—some "How could you abandon us?" weepy-eyed slop. What most annoys me is I didn't discern their small-mindedness in advance.

Sure wish I was free to come to you—would be a far more constructive use of my time than verbally mauling imbeciles. I'm imprisoned—can hardly endure sitting, keep leaping up, pacing like a tigress in a cage. God willing, Honeybun, I'll be liberated *sometime* today so we can make up for lost time: this tigress will lick you into a frenzy. Oh, a purrrrfect union of my wildcat's appetite with your panting pinkling, muffy action 'til we swoonzy dizzikins—much slurping, given and received.

It can't happen soon enough, Ella!

Your,

TigressCaged&Enraged

X.5
Ella to Angie
Friday, August 15, 2003 12:41 PM

Hope springs eternal, right my Love? I'm hoping for your speedy release from jail. Every moment's eternity of agony as I await elevating news.

A prayer: please, wishy-washy Nebraskans, have mercy on me and my Girlfriend and either make those calls or call them off so's we can cease being pent-up, peevish, petulant bitches and heal ourselves and play.

Praying my prayer bears fruit, Angie!

Your,

ImpatientPrayerfulPlaymate

X.6
Angie to Ella
Friday, August 15, 2003 1:12 PM

Prayer be praised—sort of. I'll soon be temporarily an uncaged kitty. An order's been placed at Sardi's and Rikert's turning me loose for long enough to fetch it, instead of having it delivered. He was hesitant to allow me to venture into the rain but I told him not to worry—if I get wet, I'll change into one of my spare suits; aside from that, he understands my wish to go outside. Seething between clenched teeth he was as he told me the Nebraskan's emailed to say they needed until at least evening to think it over. I could repeat a couple cracks he made but, being a clean-mouthed lady, won't. Although when he said: "A hippo will crawl up a rabbit's ass before those pussies will be capable of acting like men." I was giggling. Nor to forget: "Those lard-stuffed slobs would rather beat off while staring at donuts than make millions."

We're pent-up spat-cats, right?—getting riled over nothing-stuff, attacking people who aren't worth the trouble, starting to sound like nasty Laundromat bittys who haven't had their twats used for years.

Time to remedy that, recover our good humor. Meet me in the lobby in twenty minutes. I'll have half an hour—maybe it can be extended to forty-five minutes. Hardly long enough for us to transform ourselves into pleased-as-punch purr-cats, but beggars can't be choosers.

Your,

TastingFreedomFeline

X.7
Ella to Angie
Friday, August 15, 2003 1:17 PM

Resourceful girls exploit every sliver of opportunity, and pent-up prayerful girls thank God he's deigned to toss them a sliver. If eternity can be reflected in a raindrop, a taste of salvation can be crammed into forty-five minutes. I'm crazy to savor every second of our sliver.

See ya soon, Doll-ling!

Your,

ShiverishQuiverishCutie

X.8
Ella to Angie
Friday, August 15, 2003 4:27 PM

The sorry truth is we're worse off than before our futile fifty-seven minutes of seeking to escape the frustration flogging us—fifty-seven nasty minutes of stoking desire with every attempt to sate it, heaping fuel on the fire. Not that we didn't make a valiant effort to beat down the flames—we did as much as two hunger-hounded hussies can do, including using the rain for show-off-our-assets purposes, not to mention the ordinarily soothing caress of fresh rain. You'd best believe I plunged into the storm unprotected, kept my umbrella rolled up. For one thing, my hair was still frizzled chaos and getting it soaked couldn't make it worse. As for my cotton-linen blend of an off-white pleated dress, it became gloriously nearly transparent soon as 'twas doused. I could just as well have been wearing a flimsy nightie, as the smallest details of my panties and brassiere were discernable, down to the mesh ruffles—fun to confirm in window-reflections. Bless rainstorms for supplying viable excuses to be publicly inappropriate, free of blame.

Midtown sidewalks are sweet heaven for exhibitionistic sweet-meats like us. It's positively tickle-me luscious when the clouds open up on a warm day, pour cool droplets delectably down, cause our clingy things to cling tighter and show off our curvature to stunning effect—always tough to tell what's stimulating me more, the sensa-tion of rain trickling over me like dozens of quivering fingers or the sensation of surprised male stares stabbing at me with bare-naked lust. The world becomes thrillingly expansive—light and shadows dance, beguile.

Stimulation's high delight, so long as satiation follows. Where was satiation? Was there any chance of us being alone together for long enough to quench the flames in our veins? The whole point of being fired up is cooling off! The rain, usually caressful and calming, was starting to tap and slap in a manner that grated instead of pleased. I was increasingly impatient to tramp it up at Sardi's whilst picking up the take out—surely flashing in a fine restaurant would fizzy me dizzy.

Then we're at the maître d' stand: two poor bedraggled pussycats drenched to our skin, fur matted to our scalps and necks. Fastidious self-respecting appearance-conscious kitties must needs shake the rain from their precious pelts, right?—squirmalacious delight to do the wet hair fling thing, send droplets flying every which where, undermine Mr. Maître D's professional composure. And we're too practiced at playacting for him to get angry, aren't we? Yeah, shamming at being too upset to be aware of our actions—two uptown princesses who've been rudely subjected to a dousing, and therefore deprived of our usual poise—shuddering with horror at being soaked, oblivious of the spectacle we're making of ourselves, how revealed we are. I reach back to gather my waterlogged locks into a ponytail and tie them—an action which (*quelle surprise!*) involves thrusting out my chest, straining the buttons of my dress with my almost-a-C-cup breasts. And you, my Dear, are vigorously shaking the hem of your skirt in front, pulling it tight against your rear, enunciating "Eeeewww!" most convincingly.

We're in all our glory—sending ripples of astonishment and lust through a public place while coming off as innocent. Sardi's is won-derfully arranged. The dining area's before us—we're as good as on a stage. Still shivering and shaking—doing a wiggle-jiggle here, a fiddle-fuss there—we barely manage to articulate our purpose, mention we're picking up food. But, damn! Who's emerging from the corridor that leads to the ladies', nodding a greeting? I blink in disbelief: it's Lois Kinnay-Realer, Ms. Managing Partner! Boy, does she induce rapid backpedaling, bring a swift end to stimulation-via-exhibitionism! We're fishing out our pocket rain slickers in less time than it takes to tell, slipping them over our heads, smoothing them down—soon trading obligatory pleasantries. I'm saying, "What a nasty storm, totally caught us." while wondering if she's wondering why we didn't already have our slickers on.

Sorry situation! No sooner are we launched—the center of attention, stabbed at and titillated by a roomful of guy-eyes—than we're forced to shut ourselves down, close up shop. No more eye-magnet Ella. No more commencing to melt on account of being a masturbation image. The men at their business lunches, or out-of-town dads dining with the wife and kids—yeah, blushing dads and angry mommies! Stimulation would've accumulated quick, sent white lightning straight to twatsie—maybe I would've flooded while upright on quivering legs. Ms. Managing Partner (cursed be her choice of restaurants) derailed my inner bacchanalia-to-be, added bitchiness to my itchiness.

Angie, denied desire's raking at my nerves, taunting and torturing me—I half want to slap myself, scream—am unfit for focusing on this email, surrender the task to you. Maybe you're of a rational frame of mind.

Your,
DistractedElectrifiedElla

X.9
Angie to Ella
Friday, August 15, 2003 7:14 PM

You're implying I'm less nuts with lust than you?—more level-headed, better able to transcribe our fifty-seven minutes of futile searching for a flood? You insult me, Ella! However, I shall be a lady, refrain from insulting you in turn. But rest assured that, like yourself, I'm Miss

Tinderbox—Kitty Kindling—Lady Lightningrod. Then again, please do note I'm the eldest and sluttiest and nuts lustiest—don't forget it.

Bad, Ella! How dare you, after my interminable ordeal—restricted to quarters, awaiting calls that haven't come, dealing with false promises, getting stir crazy out of my mind. Think my pinkling isn't insistently moist? that my petals aren't tickling-tingling? We're being kept apart, can't send one another anywhere near SwoonsVille, I'm unhinged.

Oh, but earlier a ray of light, right? We're FINALLY turned loose, allowed to run an errand. What a false promise, playing of a nasty prank on us, *that* turned out to be—Sardi's was a cruel tease.

I was thirsting to play flasheroo at Sardi's: my hopes were high as the sky we couldn't see on account of the rain. What's not to love when one's basically as exposed in public as the law allows and in a renowned restaurant to boot, only separated from full-out nakedness by a thin see-through veneer of storm soaked linen and skimpy lace underthings? What's not to love about being eye-raped by a roomful of men, feeling their hunger build, churn? Damn, does the sense-daze seize me fast! I ripple into dizzy bliss as the men's faces blur and table-tops spin and light gets bright! I lose the ability to distinguish one pair of eyes from another—the room becomes a huge united eye thrusting yearning under my skin, swooshing me towards the threshold of a spill.

But that didn't happen, because Ms. Managing Partner braved the rain to come to Sardi's too. I'm stretching and preening at the maître d' stand, arching my back most deliciously, birthing waves of tingles in my spine—tensing to the touch of brightening eyes, gasps of man-surprise sliding up my thighs, radiating energy about my tummy and tits and neck, feeling as expansive as intense, approaching the pinnacle, then appalling interruption! Lois appears from the corridor—I'm scrambling to veil myself in a rain slicker, revert to accursed modesty. It's as if I've been bound and gagged and blindfolded and backed into a corner.

I'm likewise wondering if Lois is wondering why we've allowed ourselves to get storm-soaked—an impulse to broach the subject, account for why we've waited 'til then to put our slickers on, briefly stirs within me. (Ill-advised, right? "He who excuses himself accuses himself." Never be overeager to explain, lest the explanation put thoughts in peoples' heads they wouldn't otherwise entertain. Obliviousness of a questionable situation supports innocence.)

"You should change out of those wet things right away," Lois says.

"We'll be doing that for sure. We have extras in our offices," I reply.

"Smart girls," Lois says, already exiting, reuniting with her party under the awning outside, perhaps in the midst of negotiating deals/firming up connections. (Like, why flatter ourselves? We're barely on her radar. Why would she wonder why we've waited to put our slickers on?)

Lois gone, I seek to salvage at least a hint of shudder-flutter from the situation—scamper to the bar, sit half off a stool, rub twatsie on its edge, rain slicker facilitating concealment. I'm seeking to tap into the lingering atmospheric reverberations, residue of the state of botheredness we've caused amongst the males. You read my impulse straight off, hasten over—fan out your slicker in pretense of adjusting it, shield me so I can rub twatsie more audaciously. Naturally—in keeping with the cloud of frustration hanging over us today—the bartender interrupts, inquiring if we'd like complimentary cups of coffee. He's assuming we're chilly, being drenched and all—very thoughtful and considerate of him.

Not sure why I plead a tummy ache in hope of getting him to leave us alone. Nothing else was enabling *la petite morte*. Why would that?

"Would you like an antacid, Miss?" he asks.

"I'll be alright...it'll pass," I respond.

"Are you sure?"

"Y...yes... I'm fine... Appreciate your concern."

Meanwhile you're putting on a worried face, using my alleged unwellness as an excuse to lean in close. Taking advantage of the cover of our raincoats you slip your hand up my skirt, dance your fingers over my petals—a finger darts within, vibrates—an infuriatingly brief taste of what could've been. There's no tickling of twatsie into final flutter.

Our takeout appears, a small group surrounding us (Does Sardi's have good service, or what? Actually, in this case, too good.)—two from the kitchen, a waitress, the maître d'. The latter's asking if we'd like a delivery boy to carry our order for us; and now the bartender's here, antacid and glass of water in hand. It's quite funny, actually—never mind the laugh's at our expense. Needless to say, your hand's long gone from being anywhere near my pleasure-treasure.

Defeated on all fronts! The delivery boy, however, isn't a bad idea: we accept the maître d's offer and give the boy the extension of Rikert's secretary: he goes ahead of us with our order. There are too many well-meaning souls at Sardi's: no one's going to leave us alone. We've no choice but to toss in the towel, reenter the storm.

Your turn, Ella! I could say I'm too flayed to concentrate any longer, in a state of excitement that's scattering my thoughts, showing no mercy, but it's a given. I won't suggest you might be of a more balanced frame of mind than me, hint your blood runs colder—won't pay you the backhanded compliment of believing you better able to compose a comprehensible email—won't imply you're a young old maid.

Your,

FrustrationFlayedFloozy

X.10
Ella to Angie
Friday, August 15, 2003 9:57 PM

How sensitive we are! A statement made casually, all in fun, at termination of my last missive gets twisted into a full-fledged insult. Lo and behold, we're suddenly playing a pointless one-upsmanship game, engaged in an "I'm more dazed and dizzy on account of raging unsated desire than thou!" pissing contest. Who's the more unhinged? Who cares? We're both unhinged out of our senses. But feel free to claim the title if it makes you feel better—calms you down better.

Lois Kinnay-Realer coupled with the sterling service: we never had a chance in Sardi's. We removed our rain slickers the second we rounded the corner outside—exposed ourselves to the rain again, intent on finally finagling some flutter from our painfully wound tubes. I recall glimpsing a clock in a laundromat's window—a half hour had passed. It seemed loony our short-circuited storm-tousled-pussycat routine at Sardi's had gobbled up thirty minutes. Time's a deceitful beast—in love with toying with us, behaving contrary to what our needs require.

If we've a smidgen of time in which to bring a pressing matter to fruition, time spins into overdrive and whizzes by in a blur and deprives us; but if we're buried in tedium and wish for time to hurry and speed us to freedom, time crawls as if crippled and allows us to languish.

OK! A half hour—the "approved" amount of time for your errand—was gone. We were already burning up our self-awarded fifteen minute "grace period." Soon we'd need to return to the firm. I was determined to snatch a few moments of euphoria from the remaining minutes.

Delicious cloudburst! Silver sheets of rain so dense they were like curtains concealing us, or so it suited me to think. We were on 46th, Restaurant Row—appropriate, since I *needed* to be your snackling—I was going to treat you to my pink meat, or die. Sure, I yanked my dress to my neck, was standing there in my underwear for a few instants. The mere act of raising my hem towards the clouds sent a thrill racing through me ('Tis not for nothing we call flashing "ol' reliable."), not to mention the rain's tickle on my tummy. And 'twas to die for, the precious look (as of a predator pleasantly surprised by the sight of prey) that sprang onto your face, washed radiant intent over your features. 'Twas incandescent heaven to be hunted by you as I scampered to the north side of the street and darted into a doorway.

Honey, I was huddled with my back to the wall, quivering dizzy with anticipation—picturing your hands on my waist, gripping firmly—seeing you drop to your knees and lift my skirt and tongue-rape me like the skilled scrumptious ravenous whore you are. I could already feel your breath upon my petals—feel your tongue squirming deep in my heat. Yes, seeing and feeling it in seconds, before you caught up. When you opened the door, paused to look me up and down with a smiling promise of pleasure to come, my temples were throbbing, chest heaving, wall as if dissolving at my back. A floating in air buoyancy overcame me: I was bracing myself for a wench-mauling, inhaling deep. You seized my tush; your mouth was closing in for a kiss; your hungry slut essence—energetic aura of desire—was suspended in the steamy air, sliding over my wetness, dancing in my nerves, scattering thought.

All's bliss, right? All's roses and clover, right? Wrong! There's suddenly clattering and chattering on the landing. We spring apart just before the door opens, revealing at least a dozen tourists crowding the steps. One is saying: "Excuse us, we're lost. Could you please tell us how to get to the Javits Center? Is it far?" Clearly they discerned our silhouettes through the cursed translucent glass of the door.

How can so much atrocious luck afflict a pair of petite nymphets in one short day? I can't mouth a word, so stunned—slammed back on myself—am I. I'm sure they're nice people, but I just tear out of there as if mad dogs are nipping at my heels. Couldn't help it.

We're dashing down the sidewalk, pause in front of the Milford. Why did we head south? Trauma's to blame for lost directional sense! No fulfillment in that doorway, when we were sure it was seconds from happening. Is it any wonder we've run the wrong way?

Time's running out—no more searching for satiation. The stars are aligned—maligned—against us. We shake our fannies north.

It's at the parking garage on 49th that I snap. I seize your arm, squeeze, imploringly gaze into your eyes: you instantly understand. We dash past the boy in the booth into the garage, slip behind one of those wide round pillars, and... Oh, the boy's calling after us—we have seconds—the concrete's whirling all around me—I'm tugging at you, tapping my neck. Ah, yes! A sucker-bite kissy, rasp of teeth.

"Bite me, Honey!" I plead; and you deliver, yes you do—a tingle-shimmer nip-bite, sweet little sting.

"Mark me, Sweetie! Brand me! I'm your property! Bite!" (Said as I flutter my hand, beyond the pillar, to stay the boy's approach.)

"Just a moment please, Sir," I hear you call, your voice pinging with blitheness. "We need a few moments of privacy to adjust our clothes because of the rain. We will appreciate it greatly and be grateful. We tip understanding gentlemen." Such a smart girlfriend you are.

So you finish what you started, gift me with a *beautiful* sucker-bite kissy. I love your love-marks, and treasure them so. Affection's footprints—sweet surrender's tattoo. (So I key before pausing to touch my neck for a moment, feel you there again.) There's a curse on us today, but your love-bite's keeping me company. We're marooned in FrustrationCity, but I have a keepsake to make it halfway bearable.

Have I told you lately how much I love you? Sweetest Angie, I love you so deeply I'm going to roll on the floor weeping with gratitude! Tears of joy and wonder are, quite literally, beginning to blur my vision!

Nothing more to say! No more bewailing our lousy lot of unsated lust.

I LOVE YOU!

Your,

LoveNourishedNymphet

X.11
Angie to Ella
Friday, August 15, 2003 11:44 PM

Dearest Ella! I love you so deeply that sometimes the sweet agony of yearning for you when I'm alone erases all else and it's as if I'm suspended in a sensory swirl separate from earth, lifted towards infinity! I'll be lying in bed awake at night and remembering something so simple, such as the way you flick your hair and downturn your eyes and smile inside, and I'll dissolve for love of you—for delicate, delectable, delicious you! Or your profile of a morning in the kitchen when the sun's beaming through your nightie—energetic, poised, graceful while performing simple tasks, such as cracking eggs, pouring them into a pan. Ella, I love your vulnerability—your quivering hands as you bend to unlace your booties; and love your toughness—your indomitable spirit—your fearlessness—your pride! I love that your petite body can be animated with unflinching daring; that your sweet face can show intensity of purpose that won't back down for anyone or anything!

I LOVE YOU!

However, as the eldest (by a whopping two months—count 'em: two!), I feel I must demonstrate maturity by putting our sentiment fest on hold, documenting the tail end of our fifty-seven minutes, as follows:

Shortly after heading north from the Milford we fished our rain slickers from our watertight totes and put them on again—wouldn't do to enter the firm's hallowed halls looking like we'd entered a wet dress contest, minimal amount of ourselves left to the imagination. Instant transformation: one moment we're shameless exhibitionists, the next we're innocent girls fully covered in pink (*toi*) and aquamarine (*moi*).

When we were in the parking garage and I fastened my mouth to your neck, began bite-sucking, you were head to toe quiver-shivers, beaming your essence into my overwrought nerves—such a delicious interval of suspension from desire denied. Yet now it's occurring to me I might be better off without said interval, as it's cruel teasing, agonizingly unfinished business—reverberations linger and prod and stab! You touch your neck and feel me there? All I need do is arch my back, then tingles surge and I feel you a thousandfold—feel a ghostly version of you I can't touch and lick, which winds me up me more.

Such an infuriating turn of events! We return to the firm soaked to the skin, as good as in our birthday suits under our colorful rain slickers, and it's not a thrill. We stumble from the elevator into reception, do the delicate flower routine—act upset at the weather, warn Abigail not to go outside, and there isn't anyone who doesn't firmly believe we're thoroughly discombobulated on account of a rainy day. Usually it's ticklish delightsville to be thought of as dainties who can't deal with a cloudburst: not today, when we've returned from a chasing-bliss excursion with nothing but greater frustration, stinging exacerbation, to show for it. Snowing people with our lil'-girl-lost act's priceless when we've indulged in sex shenanigans, but we don't get to taste of that. The joke's on us, and I'm ready to knock this monitor to the floor and chop it to smithereens with the fire emergency ax in the hall.

There's zilch sense of triumph when I change into pristine clean and dry corporate wear in my office—I don't get to congratulate myself on my preparedness, keeping three changes of clothes on hand at all times. I'm immaculately coifed and made up now? safe and sound and above suspicion? So what? I've done nothing to invite suspicion.

But you're more sensible than I am, Dollface. You're right: no use bewailing the fact the cards are stacked in frustration's favor today. No use cursing the curse the fates have placed on us, wondering why we can't manage to make a single move without some meddler making a mess of it. Far better to accept our losses, content ourselves with knowing we'll be reversing our bad fortune in each other's arms at least by Sunday. Thank God the God-fearing Nebraskans have announced they do *not* work on Sundays. Like, Sunday seems centuries away, inner torturing ticklish prodding as if scampering me up the walls, but how often do clients let us know part of a weekend won't be ruined, guarantee we'll have Sunday free? Anticipation's swirling me dizzy.

Who knows how long I'll be stuck here tonight? The Nebraskans have finally called off the conference calls (during which they mostly air neurosis, constructive input out the window), but Rikert's taking advantage of the lull to comb through a couple key documents, make them as absolutely client-favorable as the other side will allow, and is counting on me to assist. So I need to clear my head.

Wish I had a better idea when this'll be wrapped up—can't wait to wrap my arms and legs and love around you.

Your,

AnticipationAgonizedAngie

X.12
Ella to Angie
Saturday, August 16, 2003 7:07 PM

Angie, I'm done with my legal responsibilities for the weekend: what's my fine reward? My conducting rod of a body's slaying me every second—all manner of itchy stingy electrical pulses are holding a convention in my nerves, airing grievances. As I await your liberation denied desire flays me alive—grips me in a paralyzing vise. I'll go mad if I don't soon see your eyes gazing upon me with blithe beatitude; if you don't soon make a giggly lil' girl of me again, restore me to the equanimity I've lost! (*J'ai besoin de ta langue magique ce soir, Angie! Je mourrai a moins que ton serpent glissant ne m'apaise!*)

Angie, I'm your slave tonight—your *property*—to do with as you please. You're to thrill yourself by means of me without mercy, no rules. I want you to pounce on me like I'm the last girl you'll spend a night with for the rest of your life, feed on me like I'm your last meal. I want to be tumbled from my thoughts into the undertows of your lust, whirled out of my senses on the roiling waves of your love, and then cast ashore—to be uncomprehendingly gazing at where the waves meet the beach and mist endlessly drifts. Yes, see to it dazed exhaustion overtakes me and I fall into a bottomless swoon. See to it I'm a limp rag doll of a plundered girl unseeingly gazing into the blank atmosphere.

Angie, you're the narcotic I live to be addicted to, and I'm in cruel withdrawal's throes—I need multidoses of feisty Angie.

I LOVE YOU!

Your,

DyingToBeAliveElla

X.13
Angie to Ella
Saturday, August 16, 2003 10:21 PM

Sweetness! *Finally*, it's my long-awaited freedom: Rikert's turned me loose 'til Monday and I get to be a Maenad all night and tomorrow.

In a twisted way, our delay's been an aphrodisiac. The deprivation we've endured—no outlet for our lust, hunger building to a boil about to blast the lids off our pots. I'm so itchy-oversensitive it's as if I can feel the atmosphere's molecules brushing against me. The air's pin-pricking my legs, tickling my unpantied pinkling something fierce. I need a lascivious lass—*you*—to quench me as surely as I need to breathe.

Ella, your hunger is my command: I'll seize you the second you open your door and spill you onto the carpet, embrace and kiss you so insistently the vibrations of my bothered body blast into your bloodstream, blend with your riptide, carry us out to sea. I'm going to drink of you 'til I'm stumbling blind drunk, My Love—gasp my life into your passionflower 'til you flutter and your honey flows.

Ella, I'll feast on you as if I'm due to hang in the morning and you're the last memory of rapture I'll have in this life, and trust you'll feast on me as intensely as well! I'm salivating to roll onto my back and splay my limbs in surrender, be your playground. And I trust you'll play hard, Dearest—blur the boundaries of our bodies, undulate in my depths, flood me with so much sensation I'm unable to cling to a snippet of thought, comprehend what logic is. For a spell, that is, 'til the Phoenix of lust rises anew and I treat you to further loving molestation.

My cheery office isn't cheery anymore! The bright white of the walls is hammering at my head, throbbing in my temples, infuriating every nerve. I'm cornered, hunted, hemmed in because my unrest is too extreme and stabbing for anyone but you to contain. (I realize I've delayed our delirium by keying this, but wished to document the *madness*, as well as further prime myself for the *pounce*.)

I LOVE YOU!

Your,

SoonToSlayAgonyAngie

XI. Ella's Goblin

XI.I
Ella to Angie
Sunday, August 24, 2003 11:43 PM

How did I pass my morning? Do I ever know what variety of compulsion's going to be inhabiting me (And "inhabiting" is the word for it: a compulsion's a separate being that takes up residence within one, bends one's thoughts and actions to its will, kicks up a storm until it's slavishly indulged.) when I awaken? Absolutely not.

Sometimes I awaken giddy out of my skin with energy, happy slumber's done (sometimes I feel slumber's an annoying duty, even though I'd be an idiot not to know slumber keeps me fresh)—always a gift to wildly anticipate a new day, from tingling fingertips to tingling toes. In such cases I'm not aware of wanting anything, because I'm in such a bouncy buoyant mood it's an end in itself and wanting something would only obstruct. I'm quite the easy girl on such days: anything'll do, as far as recreation—or the lack thereof, simply staring into space—goes.

Othertimes I awaken with a clearly formulated craving in the forefront of thought that I know I'll need to indulge before attaining peace, often quite ordinary: a glimpse of the 59th Street skyline from Cat Rock, or a stroll about Cleo's Needle and Turtle Pond and Belvedere Castle and Cedar Hill; or an omelet stuffed with peppers, onions, capers, and mushrooms, with a side of sockeye; or a jaunt to Saks or a Duane Reade or Bed, Bath & Beyond or maybe even a hardware store—and not necessarily to buy anything, simply to be in those surroundings; or a cab ride to a neighborhood I haven't been in for a year—the Lamp Distinct on Allen, Flower District on Sixth, K-Town at 32nd and Fifth.

OK! Ordinary things, aside from the fervor with which they're craved, are precisely that: ordinary! What of non-ordinary compulsions?

I've awakened thirsting to 1) don a formal gown and tiara and rent a rowboat and row to The Lake's northernmost cove, run my fingers through the thicket of high reeds and listen to redwing blackbirds, 2) eat abalone sushi (Served in their pearly shells, which I still have on the windowsill: they seize the sunlight, turn into mini rainbows.) with my Best Girl while admiring the East River's powerful currents at Carl Schurz Park, we decked out in pink pleated skirts, white blouses, silver-buckled shoes (Remember? I was insanely specific about what to wear.), 3) go to Elaine's with Stevie in a limo as Marie Antoinette (Sure, I stole Marie from you; but what are girlfriend's for, if not to provide fashion tips? And remember: I was the first to be Marie in public.) and then, midway through our meal, traipse off to the ladies' to change into tattered cutoffs and a men's denim shirt with my hair teased into a frightful mess, 4) go—again, with you—to Tony's di Napoli and order "Tony's Famous Twin N.Y. Cut Sirloins" and silently stare into space while sipping sparkling water and ignoring the steaks. The waiter would inquire if anything was amiss and we'd inform him we were vegetarians—that meat was sickening and unhealthy—in a matter-of-fact tone. The waiter's astonishment rapidly spread to other staff members and nearby diners; continuing to serenely sit in our lavender dresses and hair ribbons, we blankly stared at nothing for over an hour, then paid our bill and departed with the steaks untouched and much wonder surrounding us. It was precisely that sort of subdued astonishment I wanted to bring about: the particulars of how to accomplish such greeted me the second I opened my eyes. And once home we (of course!) broiled succulent NY strips and ate them with our hands, tearing them apart with our teeth, utensils disallowed.

Why do I awaken with such compulsions? It's not like I bed down even remotely suspecting I'll awaken with such compulsions in my bloodstream, clear pictures of how to go about indulging them. Are they the residue of dreams I've forgotten? have they been birthed in slumber by a mischievous—infuriatingly exacting—subconscious? Yes, often very infuriating! It's not like I always greet these out-of-the-blue obsessions with a joyful heart! Sometimes they're an obstacle in the path of a peaceful day—a hurdle I need to clear. As I said, it's like another creature's taken up residence in my body and is calling the shots. I'll be thinking: "Christ, all I need right now—here we go again!"

Why, Dearest, do I bring the matter up? Because this morning I sprang out of bed hungering to be plowed silly in the men's room of a greasy Chinese diner. And more: I had to be snug in a fur with nothing on underneath. So I called up Jacob. I mean, he owed me, right? I played abducted Roman wench to his Nero, so he can certainly rearrange his Saturday on my behalf. He had a date with a Waspy girl, rendezvous at the Princeton Club and then golf at the 23rd Street driving range. (Ha! It's not easy to picture Jacob playing golf; but, in a twisted sort of way, the not being able to picture it—considering it laughably improbable—makes me like him all the more: the unpredictability thing, right?) Anyway, preppy girl had to take a backseat to yours truly: I told Jacob what I needed, and he rescheduled her tout suite.

My Sunday unfolds as follows: in obedience to the particulars dictated by my exacting imagination, I do my hair up beehive style (I don't have enough of a mane to build a hive that spirals way up so add extensions.) and put on silver stilettos, my faux red fox coat, nothing else. Jacob fetches me in a cab and we continue to Chinatown, emerge at Canal and Mott. We're in another world: rambutan, breadfruit, coconuts (whacked open on the spot), dragon fruit, and roast duck are hawked by sidewalk vendors; eels, carp, and frogs are splashing in holding tanks; bushel baskets overflow with whelk and moon snails; ginseng and ginger root and countless dried mushrooms are in drug store windows; bamboo plants, palms, ivory, jade are everywhere—incense suffuses the air.

Chinatown instantly stirs me, seems teasingly familiar in a manner impossible to pinpoint, almost as if I'm revisiting stimuli from a former life—noticeably carried outside my customary self. The music and conversations in Chinese and trays of fruit I don't even know the names of, the dirtiness (Fish heads and torn-up chickens in the gutter, glory be!), the clutter, neon signs aglow in daylight: all delves under my skin and gets in my nerves, makes me rabbit jumpy! I've no choice but to require Jacob to yank me into a doorway, smush me to a wall, rough me up a tad. We scamper down Mott past Bayard, south of the park where old men play chess and old ladies sell bootleg CDs and wild volleyball games are held. More residential here, interruptions less likely.

"I'm crazy antsy!" I announce when a suitably isolated doorway—in a dead-end alley (Do dead-end alleys even exist anywhere else in town?)—is found. "Feeling whirled off my foundations into splintered thoughts, blurry stress, blazing nerves! How am I to fully savor my degradation in a diner if I'm too overwrought, jittery? So pull me in here and take me down a peg or two, out of this tension! Lift my foxy and whack me, make my ass cheeks red—make them sting!"

"So you're bored with the fluffy feel of fur?" Jacob asks.

"Never mind what I'm bored with, or if I'm bored," I say. "Hell, I'm *not* bored! I'm hopped up nutsy! Just flog me! With a hand, rolled up paper—whatever! Damn! What nonsense my Goblin gets me into!"

"So I'm a goblin? How can you call me a goblin when you're the one who wants to be swatted? Sorry to disappoint, but I have no pressing need to slap you around! You're asking me to do it and I'll do it but I can take it or leave it—don't accuse me of initiating it."

"Jacob honey, I'm not calling you a goblin! I'm talking about my Goblin, OK?—the creature that invades me when I'm sleeping and confronts me with crazy cravings when I wake up! Think I want to be banged in a filthy men's room? My Goblin wants it, not me! I'm Ella the enfevered tramp who's been flogged from bed to Chinatown, robbed of a peaceful Sunday, by an infuriating creature, and that creature is: my Goblin! Get it? (I lift my coat with one hand and spank myself with the other.) So will you please take over, before I go insane?"

"In honor of your Goblin, then," Jacob smiles, shrugging his shoulders as he presses me frontwards into the wall, lifts the back of my coat to my waist, smacks my behind with his hand.

"Your hand only?" I taunt. "Am I a wilting wallflower of a girl, terrified of sterner measures? Did I back down and cry when Nero lashed me to the post? Huh? Where's Nero now, gone into hiding?"

"Nero can return, if you wish."

"If I wish? For Christ's sake, Jacob! Do you need pinching awake? Why do you think you've been selected for this mission? My Goblin needs appeasing, and—Jesus! you know very well I'm not a wilting Princeton Club preppy priss! What the hell?" I'm feeling something resembling panic, Angie—what's with Jacob? Have I chosen the wrong man?

"What the hell what, princess?" Jacob asks sarcastically—at which I whip my head about, observe him with intermingled anguish and anger. But all's well! To my immense relief, he's removing his belt. "Ah, yes! You want the belt, don't cha princess? Nothing halfway for princess!"

"I deserve it!" I say, excited and quivering head to toe. "A taste of belt hiss and kiss, leather's savage slashes! I am a spoiled girl, Jacob! Spoiled girls are disconnected from conflict—it isn't healthy! So use your belt and yell stuff! Yell that I'm a prissy sissy and need to be taught life's rife with contrast; that, without sampling of pain, it's worthless feeling safe! Say I'm a corporate whore who needs to be yanked from my sheltered existence, immersed in enlightening turmoil!" (Right, that was me missing you and Miss Whippie, Angie! Absolutely adore what you say during our Miss Whippie sessions: the speeches you shout while making me squirm are soothing word-flow, your tone particularly comforting, leading me to upwell, seemingly embrace the sky.)

"No talking!" Jacob commands. "No, strike that—spout whatever you wish, if you dare and are able! Soon you won't be capable of speech!" And, with that, he lays on a flurry of well-placed wallops (precisely in the most fleshy areas of my cheeks, like when I was his Roman wench) that have me raking my nails on the wall as my knees grow weak.

"Spout some stuff, huh?" he continues, laughing. "Sure thing! Fair skin gets bruised and the spoiled idiot learns a thing or two about the precariousness of safety! The corporate slut who's criminally overpaid to slouch at a cushy job discovers dark forces lurk in Chinatown's doorways! She starts to appreciate how well-situated she is in society by means of belt thwacks! She learns not to take a sheltered life for granted, courtesy of my kindly belt that deigns to raise welts of salvation!"

Jacob's mocking me and I'm not one to tolerate such. "Is that all you've got, wimp wuss?" I ask with mock derision. "When I ask a man to flog me I expect him to be a man and make me regret my ask! I want to be cracked and whacked and smacked and thwacked until I forget my name, get delirious, howl like a wounded animal, go blind! I want an out-of-my-body experience induced by liberating agony! Are you man enough to rise to the occasion, or a cowering blowhard mouse?"

Without another word (I've found the amount of words spoken is usually inversely proportional to the probability a male will spring to action.) Jacob presses me to the wall firmly, flings my coat over my head: a flurry of blows, landing squarely on my behind as before, follows. Ooooo, baby! My right cheek's smushed against the wall—arms are twitching as if seeking to run away from my shoulders—legs are wobbling jelly and Jacob's hand at my back is keeping me upright. I'm yelp-gasping, moaning shrilly, seeming to kick at the floor that's as if whirling towards the ceiling—ability to formulate logical progressions of thought is gone. After maybe thirty seconds of what seems like minutes of salvational treatment, I motion for Jacob to tone it down.

"Of course, Ella," he says, switching to light brushings, taps.

Am I defeated? Nay! Hard thwacks have enabled shedding of a perceptual skin grown too small, attuned me—adjusted me—to intensified sensation: light taps allow me to savor sensory rebirth, sighingly frolic—seem to swim—in inflamed nerves.

Glory to my Goblin! She keeps life fresh and unpredictable—improbable, even. Sometimes I can barely believe I've done what she's made me do. Here I am, a well-educated girl of fairly strict upbringing gainfully employed by a top tier law firm: I've been kicked out of my structured life by craving on a Sunday, am tasting of disorder in this doorway. And this doorway, by the way, smells of dead fish and urine (Nostril stinging, acidic.); there's tattered newsprint on the floor that looks to be a decade old; ancient notices in Chinese are pasted on the walls. Freshly showered and perfumed and draped in fur as I am, I'm being belted in a squalid setting and, God, I love it! I am, indeed, being torn from my tension, made sultry and supple and squirmalacious in my emotions! How can I not help but surge stratospheric with joy?

Then I jump aside, swat my coat into place, say, "Enough, Jacob—I don't want to flood here, need to save it for a restroom." But then again, I'm beneficently reckless of mind—aflush with a fresh flogging, blood racing miles a minute. An unexpected whim pops into my head, it's the notices with Chinese characters that inspire it. "Here," I say, fishing my lipstick from my pocket and handing it to him. "Paint me! I mean, don't paint me! Write on me! Copy some stuff from these fliers! Write in Chinese on my chest!" I turn to face him and open my coat.

Angie, soon as Jacob traces characters on my belly and chest with lipstick... Well, we're unpredictable creatures and there's no telling what will seize our senses' undivided attention! Instants after Jacob writes on me I'm slipping to the floor, aquiver with procreative shivers! "Daaaamn!" I moan. That's a button I never knew I had! I'm pressing my legs together in orgasm-prolong-mode, deliciously gasping. (Although maybe the lipstick was simply an instance of stimulation adding up: my need to be ravaged somehow—somewhere—in Chinatown, plus the belting, plus Jacob's touch! If he had swished a dead fish over me maybe I would've gushed from that too.)

Before I've time to chastise myself (As I am annoyed at not having saved the whole of excitation for a dingy diner's men's room.), a dignified elderly woman enters the building and regards us (Jacob's crouching over me.) with a smile. I'm disarrayed in my fur (Thankfully fully covered.), staring at her probably really stupidly. Adding a soft chuckle to her smile (Healthy balanced people love lovers.), she turns to open the second door with her keys, and then—God! a transparent plastic bag of live frogs in her other hand swings within a foot of my face! Yeah, a bag of awful, slimy, hopping frogs! I scream, am joint-strainingly pressing my back to the wall: why won't the wall dissolve, allow me more space? I need to get away from these bug-eyed amphibians that are conjuring up terrors associated with creepy crawly things, triggering nasty pictures in my head—pictures of sticky poisonous goo, venomous bites, debilitating parasites, disease.

I'm infatuated with the unexpected? Said infatuation has its limits! From savoring an orgasm, reaching towards Jacob for cuddles (The grateful girl pulling her champion close.), I'm shocked into a shaking fit, panic inundating my stomach inside out. I'm perceiving surroundings through dark violet light; black swishes are overrunning peripheral vision, making it seem I'm in a collapsing tunnel. I'm aware of con-vulsively clawing at the door, jerking myself to my feet—shortly find myself outside in bright sun, staggering with the force of my fear.

(A bag of frogs and intensity of terror suggesting a seizure's un-leashed! The seemingly irrational terror of small, scampering, slith-ering, crawling creatures, more characteristic of women than men... Head back in human history and the terror's *very* rational: sur-vival of our species, in part, depended on mothers experiencing punch-in-the-gut reactions to a rodent venturing near their offspring, or a spider dangling from a web. Fleas leaping from rodents onto people and infecting them with plague; cramps and fever, inability to tend to offspring, as a consequence of spider bites: nothing was understood scientifically, consciously put down to cause and effect, and such is where subconscious perception came into play: innate fear of creepy crawlies was our way of guarding against the poison some inject and diseases some spread. These fears persist, particularly in women (potential mothers), because the danger still exists: venomous or infected spiders, rodents, reptiles, insects haven't stopped biting; parasites still spread debilitation and death. So to hell with idiots who make fun of women for springing away from small scampering things like our life's in danger: sometimes our life is in danger! Don't get me started on rabies, which killed a toddler in my pre-school class. A bat bite was the cause—discovered too late.)

Yes, I'm quite the shattered girl upon emerging from the door-way—blurred of vision, unsteady on my feet, shaking. I've been light-ning-bolted by primal fear! Jacob supports me, guides me towards the park.

Once I've recovered on a bench for a bit the air seems extraordinar-ily clear, as after a thunderstorm—or an orgasm. And, hey, I've had an orgasm and inner storm, in rapid succession. Ha! Suddenly I'm aware it's a 90-something degrees day: I'm baking in the fur, parched.

We return to Canal Street for fresh young coconuts, to my mind the most invigorating juice in existence and, once I've drained mine, my Goblin's craving-of-the-day reasserts itself. (Perhaps a less strict goblin would've relinquished her hold upon me in light of the ex-tremes of sensation to which I'd been subjected, but my Goblin will *never* be pacified by anything short of slavish acquiescence.)

So we stroll south on Mulberry, below Bayard again, and shortly encounter precisely the sort of filthy diner my Goblin requires. Wild! My blood jumps at sight of said diner as if it's a cozy home I'm returning to after years of journeying in precarious lands.

The diner's weatherbeaten sign announces, "Fung's Tasty Dumpling." Roasted duck with heads attached are dangling by their feet in the window and appear too withered to eat. Soggy rolls stuffed with meat—grease oozing out of them onto the counter—are stacked beside the cash register, flies alighting on them. A thousand stains are on the floor. Behind the counter, an old man in a dirty apron tends an overcooked heap of fried rice on an unclean stove. "Perfect!" whispers my capricious imagination as I quiver with anticipation.

We sit on rickety wooden chairs, their dark green paint flaking, at a battered Formica table in back and peruse menus that look like they've been used as placemats for dozens of messy meals. We couldn't be paid to play Russian Roulette with our digestive tracts by consuming the food, but order two "Chef Special Lemon Flavor Duck Vegetable Mushroom" plates." If the diner's going to enable me to appease my Goblin the least we can do is order the priciest dish.

Angie, I'm perilously close to flooding again solely due to being in the diner, poised to be plowed in the precise manner my Goblin's dictated—quiver-jitters vibrate me as I clench the table's edges. A second premature flood must *not* happen, so I seize Jacob's wrist and yank him upright, indicate we need to locate the men's room, get unleashed there.

Soon Jacob's guiding me down dusty creaking stairs, badly lit by a dingy bulb dangling from a frayed cord. Upon reaching the basement we stroll through a passageway that's wide enough for about one and a half average sized humans, its walls dark burgundy, the word, RESTROOMS, in huge faded white lettering at its end. (The diner's surpassing expectation, Angie—it's like I'm in a secret sex club.)

When Jacob drags me into the men's room, pins me to the unwashed tile wall I'm utterly befuddled, trembling. My coat's open and he's guiding his length inside me—I'm reaching under his shirt in back, clawing just below his shoulders, his muscles tightening. Awareness spins from cobweb cluttered ceiling to non-mopped floor to unflushed urinal reeking of pee to rusted soap dispenser to moldy corners to stained enamel sink to my blurred reflection in the spattered mirror. I undulate in rhythm with Jacob, shove at him with all my might, inhale deeper.

I'm hissing: "Jacob, I'm a petulant bitch, royal pain, so show no mercy! I'm a selfish inconsiderate brat who capriciously sabotaged your Sunday morning plans, so pummel me dizzy! Think of every girl who's been late for a date because she couldn't choose what to wear—every girl who's flashed her goodies, driven you nuts, then brushed you off—every girl who's bored you with lectures concerning commitment, whined and complained, become a clinging pest! Think of all that, blame me for all that, punish me for all that! I'm every conniving wheedling manipulating girl rolled into one, so give me what I deserve! I don't want to be able to walk straight for days!" Ooooo! So liberating to say that, Angie! Seconds later I'm gasping squealing seemingly half-screaming—the tremble-wave shakes me so hard the restroom's a mirage.

Sure, it can be annoying when my Goblin appears unannounced, usually of a morning, and bends me to her will, but I wouldn't have it any other way. I'm blessed to have my very own unpredictably demanding Goblin who forces me to yearn for novel situations and not rest until they become reality—she's responsible for innumerable memorable experiences, introduces greater variety into my life. Once I've fulfilled my Goblin's demands and she's released me, it's usually as if my personality's shed a skin grown too small, expanding to occupy a greater boundary. When heavenly disconnectedness from strife and care floods me it's identical to kneeling in prayer, wholly surrendering my ego. I'm a girl of religious sensibility, in the sense I live for arrival at intervals of wondering inner quietude, and I'm telling you I was as if adrift in a vital otherworld flooded with light, tingles, and joy in a filthy men's room after Jacob brought me to a crest—I love my Goblin infinitely.

Upon returning to our table and not wishing to insult our hosts we fake a forgotten obligation—request takeout containers and scoop our meals into them, pay with a generous tip. Jacob's pure sweetness when I plead my previous engagement for brunch with my best girlfriend at The Boathouse, we deep throat kissing for maybe five minutes before I'm in a cab. And why wouldn't he be sweet? A lissome lustful lassie calls him up for spontaneous fun, then traipses off to elsewhere shortly after? Such encounters are the stuff of male fantasies, right? An ideal post-sex situation from a male's point of view: no obligation to spend the rest of the day clung to by a girl, listening to babble, buying her stuff. I believe in men's liberation—liberation for everyone, across the board.

OK, I know I turned up at The Boathouse looking a bit indiscretional! Glory be to sex dazedness and bliss shining bright in one's eyes and indifference as to whether a fur coat's folded up—doubled up—over my shoulders, hiked high enough to attract notice, over-reveal.

Time to sign off, Girlfriend, since I'm draped in foxy again, getting squirma-crazy in the sparkly fluffiness, piercing down into my nerves, jumpstarting blood—seems a hand (I'm keying with one hand) has strayed pinklingwards. Angie Dear, I dedicate this dizzy-me-plenty session to *you*!—since I'll be picturing your crystalline eyes and thinking of today's rapture on The Lake when rushing to a gush.

Your,

GloriouslyGoblinInhabitedGirlie

XI.2
Angie to Ella
Monday, August 25, 2003 10:51 PM

Dearest Ella, highly doubtful I'll be able to do our Sunday afternoon justice but will attempt such and, besides, it'll be a fun ride:

So I'm awaiting you at The Boathouse, dressed Sunday best in a turquoise, wool crepe, hem-below-the-knees number with wide neck and three-quarter sleeves—curve accentuating, but concealing them; and matching wide-brimmed hat with small, not overly ostentatious, white feathers; and very little make up, hair ponytailed. Yes, all dolled up as Miss Finishing School, eager to be respectable—sip tea and eat my meal daintily, like a well-bred delicate damsel should. Nothing unusual in that, right? We've been behaving thus at The Boathouse for nearly a month, ever since our dousing revisited fiasco, playacted CatSpat gone awry. We've taken care to ape ladyishness to the hilt because The Boathouse is one of our essential places to go, and we don't need that strict stodgy manager (Who apparently *lives* there.) asking us never to return. So what do you do? You turn up Goblin-inhabited, give said manager good reason to recall our misbehavior and start to worry!

You say you arrived "looking a bit indiscretional"? That's rather understated, Ella! Of all the times for you to blatantly be a slut without being able to help it, too enrapt in post-sex blurring-of-mind wonder to be aware of or care what face you're putting on for the world! There's more lipstick on your chin and right cheek than on your lips! (Since when do you neglect to touch up your make up after it's been mussed up? What happened to your reach-for-your-compact-mirror reflex? How could you fail to suspect your face was a dozen make up "Don'ts" rolled into one big advertisement concerning your trampish doings?) Yeah! Lipstick on your chin, eyeliner smeared to your forehead, blush wiped—or should I say licked?—into smudges! Plus one of your heels is broken, you're walking lopsided, and you don't seem to have the slightest inkling! Nor are you adhering to anything remotely resembling modesty, as far as concealment of your curves goes! You haven't troubled to button the lower half of your coat and it's flung open with your every minus-one-heel step, showing off the major part of your thighs! To top it off, a fold of your coat gets caught on a chair as you're turning around glaze eyed to locate me, and you continue walking 'til it's yanked back far enough to reveal you're not wearing a thing underneath!

Our cursed mock catfight seems like centuries ago, but it's only a month ago that we allowed ourselves to lose our bearings, act in a manner that wasn't pretty: taking that bad behavior day into account, I don't mind admitting I was alarmed at your appearance. Uncharacteristic of me to be propriety's guardian, but I couldn't rush over to close your coat and guide you to our table quick enough. I remember saying something such as: "Ella, can you please realize where we are and dispense with the displays of ass? We've put a lot of effort into being well-behaved and proper here, atoning for our flinging of Champagne in each other's faces, persuading the manager we can be trusted to be good girls going forward. You do realize we cannot be banned from The Boathouse, don't you? You're aware of how devastating that would be?"

Ah, Ella! You weren't seeking to create a scene—there was no trace of thrill-to-the-shocking-of-others about you. I realized such soon enough. You were simply a girl lost in post-coital bliss, who needed to be watched—I turned maternal instead of alarmed tout suite.

I seated you with your back to the wall, placed a chair to one side of you to shield you further and sat on your other side. What a study in conspicuous contrast we were—you non-pantied Heedless Harlot in fur, me Miss Immaculate in Sunday attire. Me recently arrived from church, you with sexcapade written all over you. Reminiscent of a respectable mommy strolling through town with a daughter decked out as a total tramp—each happily accepting of the other, proudly non-judgmental.

We do live for playing display-our-*derrières* games and ordinarily I'd be hiking my hem to stocking tops, loath to be upstaged by you in the frolicsome floozy department, out to equal your happily mauled minx aura. But my accustomed inclinations were straight-jacketed by our Boathouse history, which the manager well recalled. (Always darting us apprehensive glances, monitoring us from afar, no matter how well dressed or behaved we are.) So I was one very divided against myself girl!—itching to slut it up, but too enamored of The Boathouse to dare it; too aware of the manager's dedication to duty to test him. (Sure, there's the dissolve into tears weapon: if requested to remove myself from the premises forever I could raise a sobbing maiden ruckus, doubtless be able get people to blame the manager, get him to give us another chance, but such is just plain icky! Playing the unjustly persecuted girl, projecting distress and misery... Act it might be, but I'd be an object of pity and the mere idea of being pitied makes me retch.)

So you started giggling like crazy, tossed your hair wildly and shim-mied your shoulders, they on the point of popping out of the fur, its collar extremely loose—crossed and uncrossed your legs, dramat-ically lifting them high—rebelliously drew attention to us, whispered, "Old maid Angie! The killjoy!" Pushing my buttons—twitting me for reaching to keep your coat closed, mocking my "Shush!" gestures, making "Na-na! Na-na-na!" faces, sticking out your tongue! Cruel girl!—flaunting your freedom while I was laboring under constraint! I closed your coat again: you responded by yanking up your knee, placing your foot on the chair, bringing your naked leg into view—nearly to your trimmed bush.

But it didn't take long for me to be affected by, swept into, your state of abandon, freefall towards recklessness from my respectable façade. (How stop our magnetism from flaring in unison? It's stronger than me, glory be.) I was struggling to continue to be cautious, aware of eyes on us, then grasped your leg to push it down and out of view and all prying eyes ceased to exist. Suddenly it was you and I alone in the restaurant and I was gazing into your bedazzled eyes—feeling left out in the cold, eager to be elevated to where you were. Yeah, I seized your leg to push it down and, hair-trigger wench that you be, your muscles tensed electric—shot the sacred fire up my arm, straight into my bloodswirl—I gasped when grasping your skin inundated with energy! Before I half knew what I was about was easing my hand up your leg under the table, fluttering my fingers near your fluff. You cried out, "Ahhh-Woooo!" Such a pretty peal of joy, paean to happy healthy abandon.

Honey, your divine "Ahhh-Woooo!" shot straight to my pinkling, pranced about my petals something fierce! Uh-oh! That's when the suffocatingly watchful manager thought The Boathouse was in imminent danger of another scene, approached with frowning mien. Good thing I'm seeing out of the sides of my head, registering hostile presences! I understood he was going to issue a warning, or worse. I tossed money on the table, yanked you to your feet, started strolling with you in tow.

Of all the occasions for directional sense to desert me! Instead of leading us out the front door, familiar to me since childhood, I stumbled onto the enclosed deck at water's edge in back—the scene of our crime! Mr. Manager, now alarmed in earnest (I sensed the emanations.), was shadowing us as the deck see-sawed, tilted fore and aft—sunlight danced on the water, rippled in my eyes—you clasped my hand tight—more sparks of your sexed up nerves darted into my depths, whirled me.

It was then, when I was lusciously affected, that Mr. Manager made his move, strode up to us, said, "Ladies, I'm sorry but considering your unacceptable behavior right here *(He indicates the deck with a gesture.)* on a previous occasion and official warning regarding that behavior and present signs of not caring, I must respectfully request you to leave."

How does ordinarily even-keeled-in-a-crisis me respond? I say in a stammer-splintered voice: "What...which present signs? My friend is indisposed, Sir! A stomach cramp...it's why she cried out...the disturbance was unintentional...it's regretted, we're sorry! She needs to lie down, I... Sir, please! We...mean no harm... Anything that happened before... We've berated ourselves for it a thousand times, have amended...we adore...we love The Boathouse, Sir!"

Not my finest moment! How could my usual ability to thwart a crisis, tactfully talk myself free, desert me? Chalk it up to being as vulnerable to human foible as the next girl! Or, rather, chalk it up to being distracted by the state of you, inundated by hunger ripping the ground from under me. I just wanted to be away from there, alone with you—was saying anything, barely paying attention. Speaking was a bother. Arousal was throbbing, heating my temples. 'Lil RutSlut me was, aside from swaying on a deck gone topsy-turvy, smothered in denied-desire claustrophobia. Like, we're outside in brightness under the sky, and I adore expansiveness and spreading out within myself, but Mr. Manager's intruding, shoving me back on myself, imposing gloom.

It was a mistake to reveal awareness of the trouble we'd caused previously, display guilt and fear. A damsel in distress? As often as not, distress emboldens people to pounce, instead of rescue. Mr. Manager stepped close to me, in a brusque manner I'm unaccustomed to—imposed oppressive shrinkage of space, his eyes hard, he puffed up with purpose: at long last, he was going to lower the boom on the two bad girls. He said: "Let's be straight with one another. The three of us know you were warned last month. You were an inconvenience to other customers and have chosen to be so again. I'm running a business, you understand, so must regretfully inform you that you will not be welcome at The Boathouse going forward. Please accompany me to the exit."

Not welcome at The Boathouse going forward? Accompany him to the exit, bid farewell to The Boathouse forever? Ella, I'd just as soon lie in a hole in the ground and have dirt heaped on! My nerves were grinding in my chest; I was gasping for breath; an emphatic "No!" resounded in my very blood. I scampered in front of Mr. Manager, faced him, blocked his way, stopped dead; I felt energy rise from my core, collect and project itself; I said: "I'm very surprised, Sir, that you would choose this moment—when my friend's afflicted, maybe near fainting—to inform us we're banished from your beautiful restaurant. Is it official policy of The Boathouse to badger people when they're unwell?"

Remember Mr. Manager's taken aback flinch? Curiously enough, there was also an involuntary flicker of pleasure in his gaze. He appeared to enjoy that I vehemently felt Boathouse privileges were worth fighting for, and doubtless appreciated I was taking him seriously, instead of tossing off ill-considered stammerings without meeting his gaze. I was quick to further press our case: "We've been customers since we were toddlers, even infants, Sir! The Boathouse has been a constant in our lives, beloved celebration place, including my parents' twenty-fifth wedding anniversary party four years ago. Always, The Boathouse is the first choice of our families and we can't speak highly enough of it. We will not, I can assure you, be avoiding The Boathouse!" This last phrase didn't sit well with Mr. Manager's pride, and who can blame him? I didn't regret saying it, though—it was a good reason for me to become extra conciliatory. I hastened to say: "Sir, I'm very sorry, I absolutely did not mean any disrespect to you. It's just that *(Here I pause, swallow.)*... OK, without exaggeration, I can tell you The Boathouse is fully woven into the fabric of our lives since earliest memories and we'll die without it. We will never do anything remotely stupid and disruptive again. We love The Boathouse and are New Yorkers to the core."

"So am I," he responded, smiling. He was enjoying our discussion now. I could tell we were no longer banned, but felt more needed to be said, to gratify Mr. Manager's vanity as well as entertain him. He was clearly a people person, as would be expected of the manager of The Boathouse, who thrived on animated conversation, and would go insane if confined to a desk: this was written all over him, and I began to like him.

"We're mortified at our behavior last month," I continued. "It hasn't happened again and will never happen again: you have our word on that. As for today, my friend's cry out was because she's not feeling well, her stomach's cramping. And also, to lay it out, my friend had a rough time of it last night with a man who was no gentleman and she..."

"Ma'am," Mr. Manager gently interrupted, lifting a hand in an I-don't-need-to-know-what's-none-of-my-business gesture, "I may, in my eagerness to perform my duty, have acted too harshly. I'm glad we've had this chat. I'm sorry your friend's unwell. God knows, I don't want to make a bad situation worse. But we understand one another? No further incidents?" He was close to laughing, bless him.

"Sir, if there is ever another incident we will personally banish ourselves from The Boathouse," I said with sincerity, clasping his hand.

"Get well soon," he concluded, addressing you. "We look forward to seeing you here again."

"I'm Angie and this is Ella, and we both thank you."

"And I'm Alan," he smiled.

We were so chummy by the time we turned to leave that I almost blew Alan a kiss.

Of course we'll be the goodliest of good girls at The Boathouse going forward—The Boathouse has official "No commotion!" status. It's nice to have a place where shenanigans are forbidden—refuge from disruptiveness inclinations. A place to indulge mischief's flip-side, be impeccably mannered, radiant in our reserve—dolled up in finery as we sip tea. And it's hardly as if we'll be setting our exhibitionistic tendencies aside. Turning up in church-acceptable dresses which hug our curves, with a wee bit of a plunging neckline, and semi-transparency can be used to maximum effect, panty lines are stare-magnets. We'll be sending out plenty of sex-emanations, only in a sly—understated—way. An under-the-radar means of administering the pretty poison.

But back to yesterday's action:

Ah, The Lake! Lakes, oceans, rivers, streams—all bodies of water—affect me, whether by lulling me into spaciness and reflection or setting my heart- and nerve-strings aflutter, surging streamlets of stimulation up my spine. I dragged you to the rowboats, placed you in one, cast off—took charge of rowing, heading straight for the bend out of The Boathouse's view—wasn't going to ravish you straightaway.

Ella, you were an Aphrodite beaming sex beatitude, enraptured and magnetic. (Unwell? Ha! The more I think about it the more I realize Alan likely realized that was a lie.) I was rowing for all I was worth, the sooner to reach the concealment of where branches overhang the water and reeds crowd shore. How tingling-in-my-blood you were as you sat facing me with fur narrowly flung open, you holding its sides out to shield yourself from sideways view—sunlight rippling over your tummy rapidly rising and falling, as were your breasts, in rhythm to your heated breath—new urging displacing your post-sex daze, You slipped to the boat's floor, gazed up at me with a delicious look of wanting wonder.

There I was, amped up with exertion of rowing and overcome by the sight of you spilled out on fur at my feet but with more rowing to do, as we were in open water—you nefariously teasing, licking my shin, waggling your tongue. I had to push your hands away when you started flinging my hemline up my thighs. Do you remember? I doubt it! You were the perfect picture of a bedazzled kid in a candy store—unapologetically reaching for sweets, oblivious of the adult world of having to pay for them. In this instance, the adults being people in other boats and on shore who were watching us with increasing interest: you didn't appear to be aware of them, understand why I was restraining you. A heart-melting pout—darling look of "Why?"—was on your face.

Ella, you were *so* like a kitten come in out of the rain, in need of petting, comforting. I let go of the oars, crouched to take you in my arms. When I kissed your cheek you were aflush with hot chills, your heart going pitter-pat a hundred times a second. I was chafing at the restraint imposed by the presence of others; it was with the greatest of difficulty I held off from tearing your coat off, revealing you in all your splendor, pouncing—I had to slap myself away from you, sting my cheeks! To further steel myself against temptation, I began rowing so hard my shoulders ached, throbbed. But the sight of you lost in lust-animated lassitude dulled discomfort, lent strength to my slender frame: amazing how sex-hunger reliably adds endurance to a petite's muscles.

The boat's seemingly barely advancing, borderline suspended, over sun silvered water, but perception plays tricks: we're shortly near shore where none of The Ramble's paths are, among overhanging branches and rustling reeds. I guide the boat in, tug the oars to counter the resistance of tall emerald blades—they're ribboning as the boat's prow shoves them aside. Once amidst the reeds and low-hanging limbs... Sure, I'm exhausted from rowing, muscles rebounding, but also desire-inundated, bursting in my skin. Your tongue's between my lips in seconds, as if you're dying of thirst and I'm your cool drink of water.

Onto boat's bottom we tumble below cloak of fur... Ha, funny when we yelp due to skin on sun-heated metal, spring upright! (Yeah, I had it easier than you, only my thighs and tush scorched after hiking up my dress—my poor Ella got scorched all over.) Who says a flowing fur's superfluous in summer? Foxy's the perfect blanket to spread over the metal—spares our delicate skin more scorching. I'm on my back and you're seated on my tummy, gripping the sides of my torso with your thighs, pressing on my sore shoulders with your hands, swishing your black-as-night tresses. Perception's mostly blurs of motion: your hair, breeze teased reeds and foliage, red-winged blackbirds (Somehow I'm aware of their crimson spots.) wheeling against aquamarine sky. Darling, your Goblin's a force to reckoned with! You're wild and carefree with the primeval, gazing at me with ineffable sweetness behind which a hard glint shines—a cute cuddly cat excited by prey.

(Ella, you're proof positive that it's the honey-voiced blithe giggly girls who're best at getting taut with sexual tension; that it's the cutiepie sweethearts who're best able to fearlessly summon surges of desire that slay resistance; that it's the pretty petites who readily become flushed with lust and won't settle for anything less than blurring stirring gratification. To put it another way: it's the girls who are afraid of mice who most strike fear into men! Of course these sage reflections are a reflection of my admiration for you—I realize they're biased.)

You ram your mouth against mine, kiss me deep and hard—squeeze my shoulders so tight your nails dig in. Ah, Ella! Your nails unleash shimmering waves when they pierce me, jolt the whole of my body into a taut gasp. An electric wand's touching me all over from the inside and, combined with your kiss—ooooo! I'm aflutter-shudder, unfurling into full flood, before you've touched muffy! The rowing I've done, excitement of the sight of you gazing upon me with excited, half absent, eyes—being too absorbed in arousal to speak; the sensation of your hunger vibrating against me; your clawing nails, pumping mouth... All unites to orgasm me equally as effectively as muff-fluffing!

Are you there, Ella? How much of you—if not all of you—has your Goblin displaced? You're still kissing me as if you'll die without my mouth to drink from and digging your nails in, apparently oblivious of me cresting. Where's the girl who's always sensitive to the flutter of my flood, conscientiously gifting me with a savoring-of-orgasm lull in action? Where's the girl who administers post coitus ease-down caresses—does the ghost-finger swirl thing, soft as feathers?

Far from easing the tempo, Ella—or, rather, Miss Goblin—you accelerate. Your thighs grip my midriff tighter, rhythmically squeeze—a rhythm as of orgasm itself, such that it approaches continuation of mine. Then you cease kissing me, sit upright, release my shoulders, claw my chest and cut my skin, seemingly unaware of so doing—soon rubbing against my tummy with something approaching fury, as if I'm inanimate. You're single-mindedly chasing excitation, as if I'm not here, but the force of your chase—sheer willfulness with which you, that Goblin of yours, goes about it—lifts me towards the sky, dissolves my fleshly encasement's boundaries. I'm personality-blurred among the clouds and rustle of the reeds and songs of the birds and your hunger's insistence, losing ability to distinguish myself from other living things.

Ella, you're still clawing my chest, mashing me into the boat's metal (I feel it through the fur.) with your behind's gyrations, and I'm ignited with joy. No discomfort's discernable, as I'm inundated with energy, electric anesthesia whipping through my veins. You squeal (The word "squeal" doesn't do your utterance justice: it's a celebratory howl, except not loud like a howl.) and bend forwards, suck my neck while stimulatingly lightly scraping with teeth: you're invested with a tone of thirsting to slip under my skin and live inside me—in something of a pre-history, lifted out of herself into the elemental, state. You draw a deep breath and shutter, collapse onto me, turn limp in every limb.

You're inert for a spell and I'm caressing your forehead and cheeks, cooing love. The boat's metal at my back, despite the fur, ought to be uncomfortable approaching painful by now, but isn't. I want to remain in this state for days and days, our shared orgasms softly winding down.

We aren't finished, are we? Another miracle's nigh:

After slow-motion spinning in dazed bliss for a spell we're giggling, rolling on the fur, shouting, not caring if heard—wind-shivered reeds are bent over the boat's sides, tickling us occasionally, leafy low-hanging limbs swaying just above. I'm mystified how you managed to wriggle yourself within my clothing, and my top's cast aside, blouse half-unbuttoned, and I've no recollection how such happened—unable to even recall precisely *what* I wore to The Boathouse! As if 'twas a dream invading awakeness, and how can an experience be more enthralling?

Then you're seated upright, gazing at me with eyes, awash with kindness, that belong to you again instead of your Goblin. I gasp, start—blood's on your tummy! *My* blood! You've anointed yourself with me!

So gentle you are when caressing the cuts your nails made—your eyes upwelling with love as you bend to kiss them—not once do your eyes leave mine or cease to beam beatitude while you lap my blood.

I'm stunned and enthralled to my core, Ella! You lap up my blood to the last drop while steadily gazing, with unwavering devotion, into my eyes.

Nothing more for me to say, LoveOfMyLife!
Your,
AwestruckAmazedAngie

XII. A Princess on the Pavement, The Displaced Damsels Escapade, & An Aside Concerning Bewitchment

XII.1
Ella to Angie
Sunday, August 31, 2003 10:14 AM

Hey there, sleepyhead! Why haven't you been prodded out of bed, as I have, by lingering frolic-reverberations? How come you're not electric with carry-over energy, eager to greet this new day and keep the randy adventures rollercoaster rolling? Are those two extra months you have on me (Such an ancient thing you are!) wearing you down?

Last night was wildest romp and rapture, indulgence that ignites rather than tires, and I'm baffled how you can remain abed, shamefully tuckered out girl! Sleep's an annoying creditor constantly pestering my mortality for payment and I had to fling it an installment of a few hours, and now that I've done so, restored clarity... Damn it, Angie! Hurry up and get up so's we can play again, get some more of what we had last night and Friday night! Need I remind you it's Labor Day weekend?

Ah, last night! The East Village lounge place with violet velvet couches, red lights, silver-gray diaphanousness undulating on the walls, ceiling fans stirring the air. Jacob and Martin, boys that they be, are slouched on a couch while you and I, girls that we be, are dancing our svelte lil' tails off at their knees—doing can-can stuff with our micro-minis (quite superfluous to lift our hems), advertising our flexibility! A miracle of gravitational law: it's only Jacob's and Martin's hands grasping ours (maybe an occasional touch of our waists), but it's just the amount of contact with balance-parameters need to remain upright in our way elevated heels! Later on... Damn, I'm too scamper-skittles in my head to tell it! But when 'twas over... Angie, I do not exaggerate when I declare I was like unto a mystic blissfully exhausted by a visitation from God!

Sweets, your Holy Light illuminated Ella's so crazy bouncy with energy she's like as not to race laughing up and down the halls of her building like a child—itching to tear up the town again, eclipse last night's frolic fest. Carried away by compulsion, subservient to her ardor, twatsie getting her into mischief with ceaseless demands... It's what your Ella lives for, Angie, and so do you! So how can you be a lazy slush girl on this, our final three-day weekend of the summer? C'est incroyable!

I'm energy-inundated to bursting but you don't care, are indifferently sleeping away the day! What to do? Guess I'll write a serious essay, for the edification of young ladies. I'll call it: Signals Via Clothing.

Here goes:

Girls! Do we want sex kicks tonight, or do we not? How to dress for each option? or, more challengingly, how to dress for both? What sort of signals do we send—via our clothes—to indicate preferences? What says "Don't bother to entertain the notion!"? What says "Plow me now!"? And, further, what of accessibility? do we wish to surrender immediately, be tickled in our tight warm place in public places? or hoard anticipation, save all for the bedroom? More broadly, do we wish to be easy or impossible to get at? Yes, cathouse wench abandonment or chastity-belt guardedness: our clothes not merely say these things, they create the circumstances for furtherance of each choice...

Oh, who cares? Essays are written by imbeciles who feel a need to explain the obvious to imbeciles who feel a need to have the obvious explained. If someone can't do, they teach; if someone's on the sidelines, they explain. Essays are for the adventure-deprived.

I'm too giddy to focus on anything! Might as well seek to soothe myself with a bubble bath and Charpentier: Te Deum, Assumpta Est Maria, and Magnificat. Calming choral music for an uncalm girl.

Let me know when you awaken, assuming you get around to it.

Your,

PostFrolicFrenzyAfflictedFloozy

XII.2
Angie to Ella
Sunday, August 31, 2003 11:11 AM

You're assuming I'm snug in snoozyland, mocking me for tuckered-outness? Tell you what: why don't we trade places? You can be the girl with Rikert (The firm's most untiring partner!) on her back, and I'll be the idler lounging in a tub! You wonder if I'm worn down? Ha! I slept four hours at the most following our East Village romperoo, was up early to pour over the no solicitation clauses of this blasted [____] employment agreement that the other side won't stop quibbling over, plus the MD&A and financials of the S-1. So what do ya say, Smoochkins? Want to trade places with lazy me?

Sorry to burst your bubble, bubbles girl, but I've been taken out of frolic-circulation! I mean, this is a first: Rikert sent photocopies of his markups over by car and instructed the driver to tell the doorman to buzz me awake. The upheaval's such that I'll be busy today and tomorrow. Labor Day? Ha! Labor Day, in my case, means just that: labor!

'Tis a cryin' shame I won't be able to trampsy with you, but no use dwelling on it. Unannounced hijackings of weekends are a risk we run in our beloved profession: nothing for it but to get back to work.

Your,

ShanghaiedSheCat

XII.3
Ella to Angie
Sunday, August 31, 2003 12:24 PM

Such distress after a refreshing bath! Thus am I reminded, yet again, how fast ficklish fate can reverse our emotions, transform anticipation of soaring to heaven into a hellwards plunge! A warm soothing bath I had: strains of the divine Charpentier inundated the air; scent of ginger and lilac swirled in cheery steam; recollections of our funsy-fun swirl of a Friday and Saturday flitted in my head; thoughts of charging over to jolt you awake made me laugh. And, now? A suffocating—punched-in-the-gut, standing-on-legs-of-jelly—about-to-die girl I am, Angie!

I could kill Rikert for conscripting you into service! Worst case scenario that you're enslaved when I'm about to claw the walls! I *need* more all-night dancing—more displaced damsel games—more up against the wall bang-bang (I'll never think of Stanton Street without a smile again!)—more of what we've been doing since Friday evening.

Of course the attorney in me can't help but congratulate you on all the high-profile deal action you've been seeing—you'll surefire make partner sooner than most. So your conscription's a good thing, not least because of the fat bonus you'll get—think of that. And, Angie, when you make partner and I'm still a lowly associate, will you remain true to me? Will we still go for strolls in the park? Will you still adore being muff-mauled by me in your office? Will you still treat my needy behind to Miss Whippie's salvational strokes? Will you still be a rut slut on my living room floor? Or will you cast me aside, exchange me for someone higher up the totem pole, move in more exclusive circles?

Your,

TossedFromHeavenToHellHarlot

XII.4
Angie to Ella
Sunday, August 31, 2003 1:04 PM

Ella, you're a bad girlfriend: you know I don't have time to write, yet force me to do so! What needs to be said is: there's serious punishment in store for you for casting aspersions on my undying devotion with the question: "Will you remain true to me?" Rich or poor—partner or not (And who's to say you won't beat me to it?)—how on earth would I ever find another girlfriend like you? Beautiful, bright, sassy, prankish, fluffy, elegant, ceaselessly afire for frolic; and, most miraculous of all, with the wildest imagination a strumpet could hope to have.

As long as I'm writing, though, here's an update: no sooner do I fax Rikert my employment agreement comments, than he informs me the other side's already made changes. So now he's reviewing the lot and then I'll have to comb through again, basically do it over. The other side's not going to get us to agree to many of their suggestions, but we can't flat out fling their suggestions back in their faces—tact's required, and the more tact I've got to come up with, the more I see I haven't a prayer of having a moment to spare for you. (I was daring to hope!)

Your,

OnATreadmillTramp

XII.5
Ella to Angie
Sunday, August 31, 2003 1:19 PM

How am I to get calm, Angie? Rikert's claimed you, Jacob's gone upstate, Martin's your boy, Stevie's incommunicado (Why?), and to frolic with anyone else when I'm totally full-tilt's impossible.

Must implement drastic measures—going to fill the tup with ice water, climb back in—going to squirt a couple droppers of valerian and lobelia tincture into mineral water, knock it down. Hopefully it'll take the edge off somewhat, enable me to indulge in reading and

recollecting, A weekend of reading, writing you a long email... God knows, I adore such, but not today—not now! Alas, I have no choice.
Your,
KinkyKicksStarvedStrumpet

XII.6
Ella to Angie
Sunday, August 31, 2003 10:57 PM

Honey, I went full-out Scandinavian, ice-watered myself to chattering-of-teeth, then thawed out by flipping on the shower, making it as hot as I could stand, then turned it down to freezing again, then hot—swift alteration of temperature, shock of extremes, settles the nerves. Plus the tincture, then valerian tea: finally I was able to sit still outside the tub, focus on a given thing for longer than a minute—able to read.

My reading was our favorite day of the Decameron—you know the one: "Under the rule of Lauretta, stories are told about the tricks which women always seem to be playing on men or men on women or men on other men." Now, by all rights, our favorite day ought to be the seventh—"tricks which...wives have played on their husbands"—but the seventh doesn't have stories featuring our heroes, Bruno and Buffalmacco, whereas our favorite has three. I never tire of their pranks at the expense of Calandrino and Master Simone. Bruno and Buffalmacco are inspirations, mentors I admire unreservedly.

Ah, but such reading's inflammatory: I was twisting on the couch, eager to be out pranking instead of reading about it. By the time I neared the end of the ninth story... Ha, Master Simone was flailing in manure—"having choked down several drams of the filthy liquid and lost his doctoral hoods"—and I was flailing in laughter, dizzy and blind! Then Bruno and Buffalmacco twist matters such that Master Simone feels *he's* done them wrong—ha ha! I was incapable of reading the tenth story.

As restless energy dovetails nicely into writing, I'm inclined to preoccupy myself by detailing our recent doings. Writing's a means of winding oneself up so's one can have a hope of winding down.

Friday we danced 'til past noon yesterday: far too charged afterwards to cease moving, we walked from Chelsea to the park. Walked? Ha, we drift-strolled—shimmer-sauntered. Our feet had wings and we flew to the top of 6th Avenue. Then on Cat Rock, admiring the 59th Street skyline, the breeze-tossed canopies of the trees seeming to dash against the buildings like waves. Only then did I allow myself to feel drowsy. As rocks are uncomfortable to snoozy on, we headed for our customary lawn-bed, Cedar Hill—a shivery collapse in the shade of maples—luscious to snow-angel on a cushion of grass with the sky sparkling through flapping foliage above. We slept for—what?—over five hours.

We awakened nearly at eight, less than an hour of daylight left. We'd barely eaten since traipsing off to dance, only stopping for apples during our stroll to the park, and I had nasty claws in my tummy, as did you. The salmon, salad, and yogurt in my kitchen beckoned.

In about two minutes we exit the park at 79th Street, and—wowsie! Returning to our city's streets, feeling my feet on solid pavement, after being amidst trees for so long's instant application of jumper cables to my senses. My petite body quiver-shivers at the sight of brick and steel and glass surging skywards as if my cream machine hasn't tasted of the fizzy-dizzies for a week. My post doze daze, as well as craving for vittles, is instantly gone. Not by any means to denigrate our fabulous park, without which I'm sure a sizeable portion of my personality would wilt, but I'm, first and foremost, a *city* girl! My first glimpse of the world outside the hospital after I was born was of concrete and steel, not hills and trees; my nerves are attuned to city noise, not rustling leaves; I'm nourished by urban electricity, not countryside calm.

What lust-proliferation our freewheeling Manhattan is! The pulse of our town's a lip-dissolving kiss—an upskirt caress—sparkly fingers dancing shimmers into my blood. No wonder I'm ceaselessly seeking to put out the desire-fire, and never succeeding for long: no sooner do I quench flames than they flare back to life, fanned by our city electric.

No other town can hold a candle to New York's flame. The charge in the air of places such as Philadelphia, Boston, Chicago, Montreal, San Francisco is a pathetic sputter, barely a hint of our home. When visiting those towns (purely business related) I'm a baby flung from my cradle, cold and lonely, thirsting for warmth—homesick for New York's cuddly vibrancy. There's nothing like Manhattan's all-forgiving hum—her comfort-dispensing strumming in the depths of my body electric.

Right, we exited the park at 79th Street, well, what multitudes of recollections the thought of 79th Street conjures forth as I sit here. 79th Street's the setting of much twittering of my heart and soul and twatsie strings, as when Stevie recently backed me up against the building between 3rd and Lex under the construction scaffolding. (Scaffolding pricelessly shields from street lamp light, breeds the shadows in which love games thrive.) He made me feel stark naked, even though I was wearing a full-sleeved dress that went to mid-calf (The scrumptious white polka-dotted violet number of swishy soft silk.), because of where his hands were going. He was reaching up said dress—seizing my behind, squeezing, savoring the texture of me; his fingers were dancing up my tummy, circling around my back, framing my face. Such inner squirminess imparting sensitivity; such a flinging-down-of-the-sex-gauntlet tone of challenge; such unapologetic willfulness, like he knew precisely what he wanted and was going to get it! I ask: what's better than being an ardent man's playground?—an exposed shoreline onto which the breakers of his elevated desire are crashing?

(Angie, so much for our doings of yesterday—I'm pulled in this recollection's direction—want to fully reexperience the escapade.)

Stevie's caresses are as within my skin as breathing, my increasingly deeper inhales and stronger exhales as if one with his finger-flutters, and his tongue's slippery sliding in my mouth, about my neck, he doing the lip-nip-rasp-of-teeth-hint-at-biting thing, tracing of tiny knives that never cut. Yes, seizings of me here—swattings of me there—combined with stirring kisses and variations thereof—oh, be still my heart!

Suddenly Stevie's on his knees, his lips at the entryway of my pink palace; my dress is already tangled in my arms (I don't recall yanking it up.); he's tongue-flicking my petals, twirling our surroundings upside down, shimmer-blasting my spine. What next? Ha! He pauses and, always hell-bent on framing an encounter in some sort of fantasy, says: "Such a well-groomed sweetmeat of august pedigree, you are! Such a pampered Park Avenue princess, fawned-upon Social Register sophisto! Your picture's seldom absent from the society pages of the Times! And, yet, none of your fancy-schmancy social trappings are able to shield you from the desire your body inspires in the low born; your social standing isn't able to protect you from hunger that oozes from the gutter! Your sophisticated airs and fashion plate clothes and 'social must' activities swirl away like feathers in wind when a capable man stares at you like he wants to eat you alive, regardless of whether he's backstreet trash! No escape for you, princess! You're always going to get grimy with street dust (He drags his fingers along the sidewalk, gets them dirty, wipes them on my legs.), no matter how hard you try via a privileged life to avoid it! Desire's the great equalizer and you're no more immune to sensual cravings than a scullery maid! You can't cheat the disquietude of your bloodbeat any more than you can cheat death! So roll in the dust, Miss Privilege! Make a mess of your ridiculously expensive dress!"

So saying, Stevie eases me to the sidewalk and stretches me out on my back. We're at the building's base, shielded from windows above by scaffolding, shielded from passersby by a stack of concrete blocks. "Feel pavement at your back," he sneers, "as the man you mistakenly thought you were too sophisticated to be susceptible to busies his grimy fingers with soiling your immaculate skin! Too good for me? Too good for twisting on concrete, tearing your dress, as your geyser gets primed for a gush? Ha! What a gutter-mongering strumpet you are!" He commences probing me with his fingers, quivering them to vivid effect.

"You're nothing but a trollop decked out in high class dreck!" he continues. "You can patronize hoity-toity Madison Avenue shops, wear nothing but the finest silk and cashmere ensembles, prance about in floral patterned lizard skin pumps; you can adorn yourself with platinum bracelets, ruby rings, diamond anklets, bind your hair with gold and opal claw-clips; you can daub on thousand-dollars-a-drop perfume and bathe in saffron oil and slather your complexion with whale oil based creams; but neither the clothes nor the jewelry nor the scents will avail you a thing when it comes to coming to terms with your clamoring body! Pricey trinkets have nothing to do with the fact your love blossom's itchy and doesn't care where or by whom it gets scratched!

"You live on the twenty-seventh floor of a posh building, high enough in the sky to never be bothered by traffic noise, or even jackhammers? I'll bet that goes a long way towards convincing you you're worlds away from needing to hobnob with commoners like me! Guess what, princess? It doesn't change the fact you need to be regularly plowed to be content; doesn't change the fact you'll go to any lengths—do violence to your vanity, violate your code of manners, cast fondness for highest social realms aside—to get plowed anytime, anyplace, anyhow by anyone! You think you've escaped the lust of guttersnipes like me, upper class twat? Not likely when you're being flayed alive by surging blood! You'll take love whenever and wherever and with whomever you can get it! You're not able to be choosy when it comes to finding a time and place and partner for love! Nothing, Park Avenue queenie, is going to curb your appetite but a sword thrusting deep in your sheath; and, if you've got to be sprawled on a filthy sidewalk to get it, then you'll pant and squeal just like any randy washerwoman would!"

So cute, right? I adore high class strumpet stuff! The time-honored tradition of the fabulously wealthy refined lady of ancient lineage who lives for tossing ladyishness aside, getting sweaty with the hired help. Yes, here's Miss FlawlesslyRefined: she has class conscious prudes over for tea and chats of charity balls, then about faces to grunt and groan on the pantry floor with a stable boy reeking of manure. Here's Miss RollsInGold: she haughtily orders a roof man to repair a dozen leaks and taunts him all day with accusations of incompetence, then invites him to retrieve his manhood by roughly banging her against the kitchen sink! The Arabian Nights is chock full of royal ladies who live for getting gloriously filthy with uncouth workmen! I can't get enough of such tales. However, fact is Stevie's talking too much and forgetting follow-through. His fingers are imparting licked-with-slippery-fire-under-my-skin nutsiness and I need something more substantial—I'm primed for a rough riding that's failing to materialize. My turn to speak: "Stevie, when are you going to shut up and be the low life animal you say you are? To hell with speeches concerning privilege—nonsense about me living on Park Avenue, spending thousands on a dress, seeking to escape gutter urges! That's the trouble with smart guys: you're too enamored with parading mental gyrations! Where do language-acrobatics get a girl, when she's panting to be pummeled silly? So get with it, Stevie! I want the animal, I'm calling you out! Turn off the word-flow—I don't care about turning this into some commoner's-lust-trumps-Miss-Privilege's-wealth game! Just do as you say, grind me and make me taste of street grime! Just use me 'til I'm plumb tuckered out, and can barely walk! That is, assuming you're street scum enough for it!"

"Oh, ho ho!" he taunts. "You think you're going to flip the situation, be the daring one? You think you're going to triumphantly sting me, defuse my discourse, call my bluff? Most impressive, your insistence that you want to get nailed nasty on the street! I've surely been taken down a peg or two by your declaration you've never sought to escape sex cravings and aren't ashamed of your needs! Alright, tough girl, try this on for size: let's see if you're tough enough to withstand extended teasing! You are a wealth-pampered, pedigree-inflated, vanity-mirror-addicted queenie who lives in a realm that manufactures delusion! You think your wish is my command! You think that, simply because your ladyship requests it, I'm to rush to sate you! Wake up, Miss Privilege! It doesn't work that way! I will pounce upon and pleasure you when and if it pleases me to do so, assuming it does, and not a moment before!"

Stevie, on hands and knees above me, sets about driving me insanely itchy nuts with his nefarious fingers. Before I opened my big mouth he was at least occasionally plunging his fingers inside me, forceful-soothingly stroking, but he halts with that. Light feathery flutters—barely the ghost of touch—follow; soft skimming over my panting-for-a-plowing petals, swollen love-bud, so it's as if I only feel the air briefly breezing by. Then distracting lip-nipping of my tummy, light dragging of his nails across my legs and the insides of my thighs, followed by maddeningly slow creeping towards my mound again, anticipation shudderingly gathering. Again he hardly strokes, his fingers arousing far more than they satisfy. Stevie can read a girl, all right, for better or worse and, in this case, definitely for the worse. He's using girl-expertise against me—quivers a finger at my point of entry, leads me to gasping in advance of insertion, then pulls away, sneers, "Oh no, Miss Snippety! No satisfaction for you, for the simple reason you want it too badly! For the simple reason you're accustomed to barking orders and having them obeyed! For the simple reason you've presumed I'd hop to like an obedient puppy, toil on your behalf! High class? Ha! You'd chuck whatever entitles you to the high life if I told you it would get you a grinding, but don't bother because it won't! Hahahahaha!"

Evil man! I'm squirming, dress wrinkled and possibly torn on concrete and my elbows scraped, but I don't care: I only want to escape Stevie's hold, pounce on him, force him to attend to me. My body's screaming hunger and I'm losing my skin's boundary—the very air's an itching tickle all over me, palpable frustration. The plowing I need, flood my relentlessly teased and unpleased pinkling craves, seems further away with each passing moment. I'm a starving girl chained just out of reach of a table heaped with succulence. Stevie isn't letting me touch myself either, and... God, the smirk on his face! I want to claw it off!

"Admit your life's a lie!" he demands, placing a hand over my mouth. "Admit your position of privilege is a joke because it fails to account for the fact every female needs to be brought to heel by a no-nonsense man, regardless of whether such a man calls the curbside his home!"

I'll admit to all that, and anything else, if he'd lift his hand off my mouth, allow me to speak! But he doesn't do so, mockingly says: "Why the silent treatment? Oh, I know: it's because you consider me unworthy of a reply! I'm too churlish and low born to warrant a response!" God, I want to kill him and he know it, is immensely amused.

Turns out the building's entrance is only a few yards away. The wall where we're located recedes inward, such that we can't be seen from the entrance, but Stevie—normally tactful amidst public-places frolic—laughs too loud. Suddenly a voice is saying, "You can't do that here." I arch my neck, gaze backwards towards the voice: it's the doorman's profile, visible just around the wall's curve: he's not looking directly at us, but the steadiness of his silhouette—aura of his presence—bespeaks determination. "You'll need to leave," he adds. There's no judgment in his tone; simply an "I'm doing my job." He couldn't care less if we resume our doings elsewhere, but we need to go elsewhere.

Stevie's off me in a jiff, assisting me to my feet. I fling my dress to my knees, am immediately Miss Modesty. By the time we step from the wall and turn towards the doorman's voice he's gone: that's what I call class and I mean it sincerely. Far from flustered on account of the doorman's interruption, I'm grateful to him for setting me free.

Stevie and I resume strolling east. Twice he seeks to yank me inside a doorway and resume his horrid teasing; twice I strenuously protest, insist he come home with me: he laughingly relents. The second we enter my apartment I'm pressing him against the wall, hissing something along the lines of: "You want me to be high class? OK, I'm high class! I'm a snooty-snoot rich bitch! I roll in C-notes on my fur-smothered bed while swilling bottles of Champagne with a price tag that exceeds the minimum wage biannual salary! I'm a pampered, proud, petulant twat who lives a life utterly devoid of social responsibility! I mistakenly believe there's nothing a guttersnipe like yourself can give me! What I most need is a thorough plowing, but I insist on denying it because it doesn't sit well with my inflated opinion of myself! OK? Will that suffice? Am I rich bitchy enough to warrant a rude awakening? Am I enough of a money-sheltered twat for you to want to roll me on the ground, smear dirt on me? I'd better be! Because, Stevie dear, you have no choice! I *require* that you plow me 'til I forget my name!"

Suffice to say Stevie—finally—gave me a fierce plowing.

Seems the valerian's finally making me drowsy—chances are I'll be able to sleep. Catch you in the morning, Angie.

Your,

GaspingForGuttersnipesGlamourpuss

XII.7
Angie to Ella
Monday, September 1, 2003 12:22 AM

You're certainly nodding off, Ella—it's obvious from your sign-off. Glamourpuss? Infatuation with glamour has nothing whatsoever to do with being high class. Glamourpussing's plebian: refined ladies are not glamourpusses. Glamourpussing's compensation for being commonplace. Glamour's garbage wrapped in pink cellophane to look pretty. Glamour's a myth perpetrated by ad agencies, calculated to con gullible girls of limited means into forking over for overpriced dreck.

Clearly you wished to convey something of the high-born lady who finds herself lusting after the stable boy—here are better choices:

WellBredBitchWhoBedsBoysBeneathHer

HighClassHoneyHankeringForHandymen

LadyLustingForLowClassLove

I believe you'll agree the above three are superior to yours. To reiterate: a glamourpuss is a shop assistant who dreams of being the film star who wears the perfume she's scrimping and saving to buy.

Must return to the bottomless pit of these revisions.

Sleep well, my Love!

Your,

CultivationOfAccurateCommunicationCutie

XII.8
Angie to Ella
Monday, September 1, 2003 6:56 PM

Saddest of days, Dearest! Labor Day's arrived, summer's died! Sure, summer isn't officially over for three weeks, but the official date overlooks that the summery atmosphere drastically alters, all but disappears, well before then. Labor Day marks the true end of summer: our town kicks into serious mode again. As the temperature goes down activity at the firm heats up, and suddenly we're working our tails off triple time and there's no time to spend an entire day together.

September! The only months I like less are dismal October and November, when autumn makes itself felt by changing lush green into orange, red, and brown decay! Ha! October, when idiots head north to "Ooooo!" and "Ahhhh!" at fall colors! I don't understand the staring at autumn's leaves, unless it's morbid fascination. The leaves are yellow, orange, red? Guess what? It means they're dead! What was once greenery nourished by steady sap-flow is decomposing corpses about to fall on the ground! What's uplifting and cheerful about it?

Autumn's rot and decomposition, the triumph of death! There isn't a chance I'll ever feel fall colors are pretty, gawk at decay of what was once green, healthy, thriving. I loathe seeing leaves turn, it depresses the hell out of me. I hate the crunch of fallen leaves—empty husks of once living things—underfoot. But enough. Onto more uplifting subjects.

(Yup, I'm taking a break from legal slavedom. What better way than by documenting our biker bar adventure Saturday night? Here goes:)

Love that it happened by accident: we were wondering over the phone what to do before rendezvousing with Martin and Jacob. I joked, "We could go downtown ahead of time and wait for them in a biker bar."

"Yeah, and wear preppy stuff!" you suggested.

So idle jesting became action. First off, I'll describe our costumes.

Angie As Preppy

I scampered to my vanity, did my face up innocent sweetheart: trace of silver-pink with the eyeliner pencil, not above a couple wand swishes of mascara, barely a dusting of lavender shadow; a few pad-pats of ivory powder, clear lip balm. My hair? Ponytailed with a white ribbon. Apparel? 1) White blouse under a pale olive herringbone jacket with wide lapels, large twin pockets at the waist. 2) Hem-at-mid-calf felt skirt, light gray. 3) Cream pantyhose and olive sling backs.

Ella As Preppy

Sure, I laughed at sight of you. Your gray and black tweed jacket with thick silver buckle made you look as near to frumpish as you'll ever be (and you had a white blouse underneath too), nor to forget the flesh toned tulip skirt. Your locks were imprisoned in a bun (a couple curling temple tendrils framing your face) held fast by a clear glass claw clip in shape of a dove. White pumps and bronze hose completed your picture.

Our ensembles were masterpieces of opposite-of-our-actual-personalities presentation: we couldn't wait to get out the door, chase silliness.

We hail a cab, shoot down 2nd Avenue to the Lower East, exit at the biker bar. Priceless the "What the hell are you doing here?" stares that greet us when we enter and seat ourselves at the bar—looks that say: "Uptight uptown twats, get back to where you belong."

Note the hostility of the women looking us up and down with undisguised scorn: such boring one-dimensional dolts, only capable of predictable reactions. Such a commonplace uniform, their leather jackets and jeans. None dare to dress differently and stand out from the others.

There are places in Manhattan where small-town mentality, nurturing of pockets of prejudice, thrives. Bars with established groups of regulars often loathe strangers. We patronize the biker bar in preppy clothes and it's the age-old drama of stranger in a small-town encountering nastiness. They suppose they're daring and extreme, on the fringes of society: what a load of tripe. They have their version of conformity, equally as stupid and smothering as any other. They're no different than those at the Princeton Club, when we tricked them into letting us in with beige raincoats, then took them off to reveal we were—oh, horror!—wearing leather halter tops and skirts, fishnets, thigh high boots.

But here's the bartender—burly, tattooed, denim-shirted. To his credit, he isn't rude; at the same time, he can't conceal a vague look of perplexity combined with a hint of condescension.

"I'd like a cup of green tea, please," I say in a sweet tone.

"We don't have tea...here," he answers with gape-jawed surprise, even though our appearance might have warned him.

"No tea?" I widen my eyes in amazement.

"What did he say?" snorts the fake blond (Ghastly dye-job: hordes of dingy brown splotches the bleach didn't reach.) seated to our right.

"Be nice," the bartender addresses her.

"Tea at a bar? Get real!" fake blonde sneers, before resuming with staring at the counter, eyes bleary.

"There isn't any tea," the bartender continues. "Maybe you want to go to a café." His way of hinting maybe we ought to skedaddle.

"Mineral water, then," you say. No chance will we be exiting minutes after entering, cease messing with these gracious souls.

"There's club soda," he says, shrugging his shoulders, giving the scornfully incredulous guy behind us (visible in the behind-the-bar mirror) a "Stay out of this!" look.

"Soda for mixing with scotch!" says Miss Atrocious Hair. "Scotch! Ever heard of it?"

"I told you to be nice," says the bartender.

"Whatever!" she hisses.

I'm tempted to turn on this inebriated sow, demonstrate my costume conceals a girl unafraid to claw her face, but the surprise we have in store prevents it. "Stay!" I command myself. "Our moment will arrive."

"Club soda is perfect," I say, ignoring Bad Bleach Job.

Two women at the end of the bar are announcing they dislike country club people, snobs, conservatives, proper people—any stupid label they can think to attach to us—while regarding us derisively: pathetically transparent attempts to make us uneasy. A conversation about getting drunk (apparently this most typical of activities is their idea of being extraordinarily wild) is a further attempt to unnerve us. We extract Glamour and Women's Wear Daily from our totes and commence reading; the more we ignore the women, the noisier they become.

"What you reading?" one asks sarcastically, annoyed that their attempts to unsettle us haven't succeeded.

Glancing up with my practiced expression of utter detachment towards their hostile faces, I wordlessly tilt my magazine so they can see the cover; then I tilt it back and resume reading as if they're not there.

"So, precious," I hear, "you too good to talk to us? Too much of a laydeee?" Ha, this prematurely aged hag of alcohol-wasted complexion and 70's hair (frizzy shag) is upset. What an emotional weakling.

I'm on the point of responding with, "Just minding my own business." (Ha, as opposed to: "So, ma'am, you too insecure to let other people mind their own business?") when the bartender (Man who realizes keeping the peace is in the best interest of running a business.) abruptly strolls to her, urgently half-whispers something she doesn't like.

"Right! Don't want any trouble! Have to leave the laydees be!" is her way of informing us she's been compelled to leave us alone.

As for the males, none make a run at us; we're considered, as one of them loudly and charitably and courageously announces from the vicinity of the pool table, "a waste of ass." I also hear: "Those uptight bitches are ashamed of having pussies." (Ha, and here I always thought a hot-blooded male could sniff out a slut no matter how hard she sought to conceal sluttishness. Well, maybe these biker bar males aren't so hot-blooded; maybe they're just a bunch of limp-libidoed drunks; maybe they're glad we're dolled up conservative, because it's an excuse not to chase us; maybe they bunch together around the pool table and discourage women from playing because they're terrified of sex.)

Ella, isn't it interesting how we've become the center of attention, inspired a great deal of resentment, without doing much of anything? All we've done is sit at the bar, order club sodas, and quietly read while being polite. It's our clothes that offend them; it's our herringbone and tweed jackets that have made us the main topic of discussion, turned the place against us; it's the fact we've neglected to deck ourselves out in leather and denim that's an unpardonable crime. I repeat: these worthies who fancy themselves courageous and unconventional members of a society-shunning subculture are no different than the easily offended residents of an isolated, God-fearing, inbred, stranger-distrusting town.

Alas, I find myself compelled to prematurely end the charade, spring our surprise on them sooner than planned—and, sure, it's shameful inability to subordinate my feelings to our agreed upon course of action; however, Ella, you and I have not been placed on this earth to be excuses for boys not to lust after us! And allowing other females, no matter how pathetic, to feel superior to us, taunt us... That's poison I refuse to swallow!

Is it fun to erect a smoke screen with conservative attire, come across as straight-laced sissy girls? You bet it is, but only as long as we're doing it to deflect suspicion from trampish doings. Why do it to puff cowards up with pride, allow them to feel they can intimidate us? I'm rapidly becoming one miffed minx! Then that runt (She isn't svelte, has no carriage or grace; therefore, she's a "runt" instead of "petite.") accidentally-on-purpose bumps against me, snidely says "Oh, excuuuuse me!" That's the last straw: I sit bolt upright, project energy, give the runt a glare of poison; her face goes ashen—she sees something in me she didn't expect to see and instantly backs down. I'm thinking, "How insane to give twits like this reasons to be bold at my expense."

I yank you to the downstairs restroom (Cramped with the two of us and our totes: good excuse for bumps-za-rumpsy. (As if we'd ever need an excuse.)): off come our jackets, blouses, skirts, on go bright micro-minis and short-sleeve plunging-neckline sweater-shirts; off come our hose, on go seamed fishnets; off come our properish shoes, on go open-toed shimmery silver platforms with clear heels; then crimson lipstick, and: it's when we're glossing it glassy that there's banging on the door.

"What duhd...yuh do...dahie...en...nere?" comes the drunken slur-rasp of a difficult-to-determine-if-it's-female voice.

"My friend's sick!" I scream, angry in earnest. "Have a heart!"

"Uh...scuse...nuh...arm...eant," is the retreating response. "Tauke ur tuhime...bu...urry." Did she say, "take your time, but hurry"? Ha-haha!

We take our sweet time completing our makeup, all right; then liberate our hair and allow it to swish about our shoulders, plus add perfume. When we emerge who is it awaiting her turn, slumped against the wall, about to fall? It's she of the babyshit-brown bleach-splotched hair.

"Remember us?" I hiss: her surprise is such it's like as not to expand her face until it bursts. "I lied," I continue in a bitchy sweet tone, "my friend isn't sick at all, she's very healthy. We were modifying our makeup and tousling our hair, hope you didn't pee your pants while waiting."

"Bye!" you add, cramming an impressive amount of venom into one syllable.

"Nuts!" is all the drunken sow can muster, wobbling towards the toilet.

Once we're upstairs the baffled double-takes—bare-faced stares—that greet our changed appearance is a sweet electric balm en-gulfing me head to toe, caressing and stimulating every muscle. I'm in my element again—serene of mind, fearless. Nothing's able to fluster me. There's a score to settle: I march up to the louts at the pool table, and—oh, Ella! I'm atingle with joy when I seize the eight ball, say, "So I'm a waste of ass, am I?" and stuff it into a side pocket! Consternation and embarrassment seizes the clowns—they can't look me in the eye.

"Just as I thought," I contemptuously intone, "your dirty little secret is you're terrified of women! You play your silly little boy's game to cover up that you don't know how to make a woman love you!" I stomp away with a "Kiss off!" flick of my hair.

"Goddamned witches!" one of them mutters.

(We're definitely witches! One moment straight-laced prissy girls, the next trampy vamps! Mostly, we're what strikes fear into one-dimensional dolts: unpredictable and unexplainable. In a word: different.)

If the women hated us before, they doubly hate us now. Our very existence reveals them to be the drabs they are; our skill at presentation demonstrates they have none; our embrace of glorious girlishness makes them look more like men than women. (This pathetic bar's an anti-girl place—an anti-femininity place—where women must dress and act like men to encourage the latter to approach them.) We have the looks and the verve and the smarts and the wiles to eclipse these dim-witted shabbys in any captivation-of-males situation, and they know it. We might make the biker bar boys uncomfortable (after all, we're "witches"), but they can't stop staring at us with tongues hanging out.

But there was no reason for us to linger. I didn't like the looks some of those drunken pseudo women were giving us! Sure, the barman and other staff were peace-orientated, eager to ward off trouble. Perhaps there had been trouble before. Perhaps they'd received warnings from law enforcement. Always important to read a place, determine what we can get away with, and even more important to know when to leave, lest even one patron completely lose it. We pranced out of there fairly soon after my eight-ball stunt. Actually, we spent less than three minutes in the place after emerging from the restroom in all our glory.

All told, an amusing way to prime ourselves for our night. Indulgence in contrast, the resulting emotional seesaw, is a form of foreplay, an aphrodisiacal kick. Not long thereafter we were in Avenue A Sushi, entertaining Martin and Jacob with our displaced damsels adventure.

Alas, Ella, I must return to legal duties—see you bright and early. Your,

QuickChangeWitchWench

P.S. I've been a bit bitchy in this email, haven't I? I've virtually ignored the giggles dimension of our switcheroo-in-the-biker-bar game. Chalk it up to being confined to quarters, instead of free to play with you. (Interesting how present moods can permeate recollections.)

XII.9
Ella to Angie
Monday, September 1, 2003 10:37 PM

It was kind of the dolt to refer to us as "witches." He gave us our recurring Saturday night joke, as in saying to Jacob and Martin, "It's a given you need to be our unquestioningly obedient playthings—pet and pamper us unceasingly, indulge our every whim; otherwise, we'll change you into fluffy poodles primped up in pink ribbons and place you in an especially strict schoolmarm's shopping basket."; or, "A pair of Circe's, accustomed to transmogrifying men into swine, we may be, but you wouldn't appeal to us as swine, so don't worry."; as in them saying, "Stroll in front, wicked witchy-poos, so we can keep an eye on you! Just try invoking the spirits and sowing discord with incantatory waving of your arms! We'll seize your arms, bind them behind your back, march you to a post, build a bonfire at your feet!"; or, "Should we strip-search them for talismans, charms? Yeah, we'll strip-search them for charms, all right! Get over here, witches: show us your charms!"

Aptly observed, Angie, that the biker bar people were the same as stranger-distrusting residents of a small town. We were witches who'd wandered into their small town, right? It's one of them that said it.

Which suggests an aside: had you and I been residents of the affluent harbor neighborhood of Salem in 1692, we might very well have been sentenced to hang because of aptitude in the captivation-of-males department. Maybe you're wondering: "Why did Ella say: 'affluent harbor neighborhood of Salem'?" Because, Angie, that's where those accused of witchcraft lived. If you want to understand Salem persecution, follow the money: the harbor people controlled the arrival and departure of goods, were engaged in the highly lucrative occupation of import/export. The inland people were engaged in the less lucrative occupation of farming, many of them poor, and resented the wealth of the harbor people, so they used accusations of witchcraft to bedevil and gain ascendancy over those with money, flip the sphere of influence. The actual offense the witches committed in the eyes of their persecutors was that they were financially secure—the witch trials were nothing but shoddy envy, an economic dispute. Sure, there was plenty of preaching against evil but such was the pretext for murder and incarceration, obscured the base motive. Sure, it was an instance of women punished by men for their elemental hold upon them—the inescapability of sexual attraction—but were it not for economic disparity such would've remained in subliminal realms. It's always murder for money, the French Revolution another disgusting example. Equalitie, fraternitie, libertie? Anyone who believes the French Revolution was based on those inflated sentiments will also believe I just saw a dove give birth to a fox. The leaders of the French Revolution were middle class attorneys who executed the aristocracy in order to confiscate their wealth, loot their homes. Nothing but grasping greedy people attaching imaginary virtue to acts of thievery and bloodshed, dreaming up window-dressing to cover up crimes. It's never about freedom or combating evil—it's *always* about self-enrichment, climbing the social ladder.

Angie, as I'm in a buoyant go-off-on-asides frame of mind, allow me to seize upon the delightful captivation-of-males topic:

At the club Friday we were decked out in bright eye-catching colors, flashing oodles of skin—nothing unusual in that: merely exhibitionism that's second nature to funloving girls, our instinct to unremittingly flirt, stir-up, tease. Just a pair of cuties out to hook males with our fishing lure bodies—reel them into dancing with us before cutting them loose with plausible readymade excuses. Catch-and-release exercises measure where we girls stand in nature's scheme, are a mirror in which we glimpse the extent of our skill at seduction and conquest. It's essential we regularly confirm, via real life instances of males lusting after us, how appealing we are: we wilt without such feedback. Assorted judgmental fools will suggest such an activity's a shameful excursion into deception; it's not nice, they'll stress, to take unfair advantage of the hankering males have for females, deliberately induce frustration and confusion. Well, boo-hoo-hoo: it's part of being a healthy girl.

Does Mother Nature not demand we girls constantly do trail runs of our seduction skills, keep them honed, ready for action? Should a cataclysm threaten annihilation of our species it'll be up to us girls to inspire male interest, get ourselves fertilized. Such cataclysms may seem removed from reality at this point in civilization but for most of human history it's been our reality, as in plague decimating a third of Europe's population. Who knows if we're living in false security, with a new plague lurking months away? Nature demands we be prepared; she's not kind, she's efficient. So we'll keep on indulging in catch-and-release captivation games, bedeviling males. If an event threatens extinction of humans and we happen to be among the survivors, we won't hesitate to get pumped full of the seeds of a new beginning. How's that for justifying our gleeful toying with the boys Friday night—all nights?

Ah, Angie! What's more elevating than hitting a club as two single, and available, girls?—inviting high hopes and approaches with hair flicks, thrustings out of breasts, caresses of thighs?—the down-turned-eyes blushing routine when we then raise our eyes, and brighten, as if unable to help ourselves, always a male ego booster? What's more a kick than dancing with men who firmly believe they have a shot at us and therefore go all out to treat us to gyrational rollercoaster rides? Then we (tee hee!) inform them, "But I'm spoken for! Sorry for the misunderstanding! I thought you knew! I just like to dance, and you're so good at it!" and prance off to dance with other guys. (Or with other girls—the women-recusing-women recourse we all understand.) Together we hit the clubs and together we depart, having been twirled by a blur of men: shame on them for forgetting we only agreed to dance for a bit. Sure, dancing's an aphrodisiac, subliminal sex; sure, dancing's a swirly-whirl in our nerve-nets, approximation of a quickie: it doesn't mean we're obliged to treat our entertainers to twatsie treats.

OK, Angie! I realize you've burned up your spare time to write your last email and may not have much time to read this, so will cease distracting you, aid in completion of your legal duties, by signing off.

Until bright and early at the firm, Sweetie!

Your,

ConnoisseurOfTheArtOfCaptivationCutie

XIII. Romance Novel Hell

S weetest, brilliant as it was, I could strangle you for your ro-
mance-novels-as-chaperones innovation. Sure, we had priceless fun with the romance novels—they were an integral part of
our ditzy-sentimental-dolls-unknowingly-decked-out-in-slut-clothes
act—perfect way to sham at being split-personalitied, put off the boys
with syrupy slop after attracting them with skimpy come-hither out-
fits—but now the act's backfired on me, and the romance novels have
become the scourge of my life. You purchased them for game-play-
ing—they were props for Wednesday night and for future revisitations
of the game. (Yeah, admit you adore that the split-personality game
brings out the wildest in you, and won't turn you loose until it's forced
you to go to the priceless place where you're not consciously responsible for your actions. You adore it regardless of fearing it: apprehension
at what the game brings out in you is a dizzying kick! Your declaration
that we won't fake being split-personalitied ever again rings false, as
in you're lying to yourself. You were a fired-up savage beast when we
landed at my place later and we both know you're hungering for more
scary recklessness.) But curse you for leaving the romance novels on my
coffee table! Sure, I meant to dump them in the closet until we next
play the game, but when I arrived home yesterday following a frenetic
day I flopped on the couch, casually grabbed one, started skimming
through it for a laugh; then I got caught up in a chapter in the middle

and suddenly wanted to know what had happened beforehand and turned back a few pages. Before I knew it I was ensnared, reading from page one! I'm (with red-faced shame I confess) at page 136 now! Your fault! I curse you for leaving the poison behind, flinging me into Romance Novel Hell.

It's all this nefariously addictive golden-curls-wisping-in-breeze stuff as the idealistic heroine—decked out in a diaphanous violet gown—pines for love on the balcony of her mansion overlooking the sea. She thinks she loves the malevolent conniving schemester of a villain, instead of the Good Man, when she really doesn't: her feelings have been poisoned by lies. The Good Man languishes in heartbreak and neglect. Will the Good Man prevail? God! Why do I care? And I have you to thank for this sickness, Ella! So you'd better get over here and tear this terrible book out of my hands, and dispose of it. You're responsible for this romance dreck that's infecting me with sentimental mush thoughts.

I demand you hop a cab here pronto and intervene! Take this book and the others away and hide them, shred them, burn them, whatever! You're the cause of my illness, so you need to be the cure!

Your,

RomanceRotAfflictedAngie

XIII.2
Ella to Angie
Friday, September 12, 2003 9:28 PM

Hahaha! You're the more experienced of us (As you're fond of rubbing in.), yet not immune to the ridiculous temptations of a romance novel, as I am! You accuse me of being responsible for your affliction, curse me for placing poison in your hands? How was I to know you'd be susceptible to that maudlin, emotionally messy, fluff stuff? How could I have dreamed my Miss Whippie wielding Angie would become ensnared by sentimental slush books, end up caring what happens to the heroine, melting and sighing and crying to the tune of sappy slop? How could I have remotely suspected you were a sucker for trash?

Are you sure you'll be cured if I tear the romance out of your hands before you read it through? You're showing distressing symptoms, as of a typical addict: indulging in self-harm despite yourself, unable to stop. Skimming the book for a laugh, then the book hooks you, reels you in, holds you prisoner? I really don't think you can be rescued from it, and don't feel you're being honest with yourself. If I were to take the romance away, I'm sure you'd wind up scampering to the bookstore for a replacement. Then how stupid you'd feel and truly be.

Fact is, Honey, Romance Novel Hell's a fever that needs to run its course. You've got to surrender to the romance imagery, get your fill of seaside mansions, courtship in bowers in manicured gardens, ribbon festooned swings under the gnarled branches of Spanish moss smothered oaks; fill of swoon-inducing glances, dizzying heart flutters, soul-draining sighs; fill of the villain who must be outmaneuvered by the loving man, the pure and true heart who must overcome the world's inherent wickedness; fill of moonlight after midnight assignations, picnics on rugged shorelines, dreamy walks in shaded woods along rose-strewn paths. Sorry, there's no other way! You've got to read that mess—embrace the romance nonsense without reserve—until you're fairly retching with revulsion, find yourself flung back towards the sassiness, sharpness, funlovingness of your authentic personality. As when I was a girl of seven and gorged on a box of pastries, until I was so ill with lard and sugar I could no longer endure so much as looking at frosting-smothered sweets, never ate them again. Same thing: you've got to gorge on the rose-tinted melt-eyed crap until the mere thought of it makes you scream, and there's no chance you'll go near it again.

So I'm not coming over. Taking the book away would only postpone the cure only you can bring about. I'd be addressing a symptom, not the cause. To paraphrase Gandhi (who lived by the words, would sleep between two beautiful women and refrain from touching them): "An absent temptation is not a temptation; removing the object of desire from one's reach is not tantamount to overcoming it." Taking the romance novels away from you before you've become legitimately disgusted with them would be a false way of dealing with your affliction, since you'd continue hungering for them. You must read them until you're authentically sickened, able to dispose of them on your own. You must *earn* your cure—it's not my fault you got yourself into this fix.

Besides, your predicament's hilarious and I don't want to help! I'm rolling on the floor at the thought of my Angie going ga-ga over the fate of a deceived damsel in a flowing formal pining for everlasting love on a steamy night in the deep South! I can picture you on your terrace, sipping a mint julep with a magnolia in your hair while dreaming of the South and midnight trysts on the swing seat on a plantation mansion's porch. Is that what's become of my formerly level-headed Angie? Have you descended to yearning to be a romance novel heroine?

Please let me know when you're the sassy strumpet who's near and dear to my heart again—at news of which I'll joyously come running. To reiterate: I can do nothing for you. Nothing except perhaps prod you to action by taunting and teasing!—infuriate you to action with: Na-na! Na-na-na! You're making a ninny of yourself, and I'm not! You're victimized by sentimental tripe, and I'm immune! You're ensnared in romance dreck, and I'm laughing! To wit: you need to summon the inner wherewithal to extricate yourself from Romance Novel Hell by yourself. Believe me, Darling, no one's looking forward to the moment when you emerge from this laughable obsession (and punish me for making fun of you) more than I am. Until that happens I'll be abandoned by the supremely willful tower-of-strength Angie I love, won't I?

Your,

MockingMirthfulMiss

XIII.3
Angie to Ella
Friday, September 12, 2003 9:56 PM

Whoa! That's the sort of girlfriend you are? Instead of hightailing it over to save me from an affliction second to none, you uncaringly laugh! Instead of doing your utmost to take this debilitating drug of a romance novel away, secure my liberation, you gloat! Well, the true test of a friend is whether said friend rushes to stand by one's side when adversity strikes and you've proven yourself deficient!

So I'm on my own? I'm to cure myself of sickness you've enabled? You don't care that your Angie's fallen by the wayside of stability due to hazardous reading material you've irresponsibly left behind? Sure, you offer advice, as in indulge in blather without lifting a finger to help. We've had plenty of disparaging words for those who equate words with action—spout platitudes and preach and do nothing—and you've revealed yourself to be one of them. That crap about absent temptations not being temptation, needing to confront one's unhealthy desires oneself if one would obtain authentic liberation from them. Hey! Am I a nun? Am I treading the path of self-denial so's to reach God? Nay! I'm simply a girl who's been undermined by bad reading. The thing for you, as my best friend (Or is that: former best friend?), to do is take the bad reading away and dispose of it! So what if I get more? Then you dispose of that too! I don't care about meeting exacting philosophical criteria when it comes to ridding myself of this vice, just so long as I'm rid of it! But you only preach and laugh! Boy, is Miss Whippie going to slash the mirth out of you when I'm well again! Start saying your prayers!

Meanwhile—for shame, you!—I've got to read more poison! I'm dying to find out if the letter that the Good Man's written to the heroine has been placed in her hands by his devoted valet. It seems the two-faced estate-thieving villain has surrounded her property with unprincipled rogues in his employ, and that they're waiting to intercept anything that might undeceive her regarding his character. God! Why am I on tenterhooks, hoping against hope the letter—dipped in the Good Man's cologne—is safely delivered in time to warn the heroine before she's irretrievably dishonored, deprived of her inheritance, falsely accused of evil, paraded through town? I hate you for putting me through this!

Your,

ByBestFriendAbandonedAngie

XIII.4
Ella to Angie
Friday, September 12, 2003 10:17 PM

To whom am I writing emails? Is my Angie reading them? I fear she may be lost in the hackneyed plot of a romance novel—fear her chosen reading material has annihilated her sanity. Note that I intentionally wrote: "her chosen reading material." To assume Angie is a victim of unfortunate circumstances is logically incorrect: if Angie has picked up a romance novel and commenced reading and continued to read, then she has done so of her own free will. Strong-willed minx Angie would never read romance trash against her will—such would be selling the strength of her will short. I firmly believe Angie is very willfully reading the romance slop with the aim of casting a shadow over her clarity of thought and becoming a crybaby prissy girl. Clearly, Angie has grown weary of quick wittedness, spirit, and intelligence, and elected to become a blithering idiot. It's easier to be stupid than smart.

Is that it, Angie? Have you chosen to become a low-energy person? Have you grown afraid of how brilliant and ambitious and electric you are, decided to spend the rest of your life wallowing in happily-ever-after goo? Have you just plain become lazy, opted to spend your remaining days perpetually in a sluggish daze?

Your,

WonderingWhereMyAngie'sGoneWench

XIII.5
Angie to Ella
Friday, September 12, 2003 11:47 PM

Ella, the only thing that matters is the precious letter has been delivered to our heroine by the Good Man's faithful valet, and that she's read it and been apprised of the black character of the lying scoundrel who's surreptitiously placed her under guard in her own home. But our heroine still faces untold dangers. Should the villain discover she's been informed of the shameless levels of deception he's resorted to—how unrepentantly evil he is—he will abandon the charade and carry her off by force to his chateau on the dreary island in the swamp. But our heroine is of such innocent, pure-hearted, character that she has no experience masking her emotions, is unsure how to do so. Will she be able to conceal her apprehension when in the presence of the evil man? Will she be able to appear to be happy when she's not? Most importantly, will her true love succeed in storming the gates with his small band of devoted followers and rescuing her before the villain has time to forcibly dishonor her in retaliation, out of sheer spite?

Ella, I may have wanted you to rip the romance away from me earlier, but no more! Romance novel immersion's a thrill I'm pleased to have discovered courtesy of you—thanks immensely for leaving them here. I'm sheer aquiver-shivers; realms of shudderingly vivid suspense are revealing themselves; it's euphorically fulfilling to become attached to fictional characters, hold them near and dear, tremble with horror or surge with joy according to how miserable or happy they are. Bad me for bad-mouthing romance novels. I'm not in Romance Novel Hell, I'm in Romance Novel Heaven! In the fictional world I'm a girl unto myself, neither need to leave my apartment nor depend upon flesh and blood people who, when it comes right down to it, really aren't very dependable. So thank you, Ella, for *not* being dependable! Thank for ignoring my unenlightened request to tear this romance away from me! I'm even neglecting my work, and guess what? It's rapturous—you can't imagine how rapturous it is—to ignore the commitment letter Riker's counting on me to revise by Monday, and be in a daze in RomanceWorld instead. And best of all is that, once I'm done with this romance novel, you've left me three others and I'll buy dozens more!

Your,

RomanceRaptureRenewedAngie

XIII.6
Angie to Ella
Saturday, September 13, 2003 9:24 PM

I sure know my Ella! I knew when I faked adoring romance novels, hinted such might displace all else from my awareness and affection, you'd come running to cure me. What a delightful cure it was.

I'm curled on the couch, dressed appropriately to read a romance: silver heels with white tufts of fur at the toes; ankle-length silver nightie with ermine trim at hem and sleeves and along the high slits up each side; my hair's a curling upwards stack; finishing touches are opal earrings, pearl barrette and necklace, bracelets set with moonstones. Plus sipping champagne from a Waterford glass, occasionally scooping mouthfuls of melon with a Tiffany spoon, nibbling strawberries. I'm feeling extremely silky and lissome and scrunchy and cuddles, sighing every other second! Translation: I know you're *finally* coming over to cure me.

The door's flung open—bang! It hits the wall hard and loud, makes me jump! Very clever, your silent turning of the key. I'm caught by surprise, flustered into a fright. I don't even see you at first, so anxiety-scrambled is my sight. It's your voice that first informs me it's you—you're saying: "Hey there, glaze-eyes, it's your Ella! Remember me? Or should I say: it's your Barber and Curate and Bachelor Sanson Carrasco rolled into one? I'm here to relieve you of the cursed romances that are infecting you with disgusting sentimentality, draining away your brain! And what's this? You've draped your couch in red velvet, are reading by candlelight? Very cutesy the way your nightie contrasts with the red and shimmers like mercury in the amber flames! You've totally put yourself in the mood, haven't you? Good thing I'm here! Otherwise, you'd be up 'til dawn reading trash, become unhealthily absorbed in mushy slush, and forget you're an attorney, and forget you have a girlfriend!"

Dearest, so regal you are in the purple single-shoulder ball gown, fanning below your waist into a pleated swirl, hugging you above your waist tight as a second skin. (Right, you've dressed as a romance heroine to upstage the one in the novel.) I'm instantly jealous of your gown, because it's clinging to you and I'm not! I rise to embrace you, but you repel me—unflappably stoic, a veritable Joan of Arc! You sternly intone: "Do you really think I'll allow you to distract me from my mission with a kiss? The novel, please, and now—hand it over. There's no escape route for you via frolic, with you believing you'll be rid of me by morning, at liberty to return to the gloppy gossamer realms. No more saturating your emotions with sappiness! Surrender the novel now!"

As I'm disinclined to comply, you lunge forward, attempt to seize the novel—in a flash I'm seated on it, pleading as follows: "But, Ella, the heroine's tapped into a reserve of courage she was previously un-aware of! While the Good Man gallantly fights for her honor in the foyer of the mansion and steadily works his way towards the stairs that lead to her bedroom, she's confronting her persecutor! She's thrown a vase at him, and delivered a spirited speech in praise of virtue! She's grabbed a decorative sword from the wall and is cutting at the air with it to keep the scoundrel back! I need to know the outcome so hands off!"

Your mission clearly lends you strength, because you gently but effectively shove me onto my back, tear the book from under me, toss it across the room. Then you deliver a speech in praise of common sense: "Listen up, girl fallen from grace! You and I were not placed on this earth to fritter away our lives in denying our flesh, getting weepy-eyed and goo-goo over maudlin romance dreamworlds! It's not for us to cloister ourselves, displace not-sure-what-will-happen-next lustfulness with happily-ever-after tripe! Not for us to lose touch with our surging blood, turn into nervous-non-plowed-nellies who're only at home in a fictional world! What's gotten into you? Why would you wish to become a fearful-of-the-world creature—a reject of life, useless in nature's eyes? Why would you wish to relegate yourself to a sterile thought-existence, spend your time longing to trade places with heroines that only exist in print? Pathetic! You're shut in at home, neglecting the work you love, avoiding the people you love, and for what? For muddled mawkish slop, trite clichéd trash, drippy bathetic banality!" Your speech over, you dash to pick up the romance from where you've tossed it, start ripping its pages out, yell: "Death to the parasitical world portrayed in these pages that's blinding you to your body's needs!"

I cross over to you, attempt to salvage the novel—we're tussling entangled while standing. But then I glance down: your shoes are works of art! Silk slingbacks, white as the driven snow, with coppery bordering. Seconds later you've shoved me, are kneeling, shredding the pages on the floor into smaller bits: your black-as-night tresses spilling over your shoulder from where they're gathered by the prettiest of barrettes—a row of three silver circles, inlaid with opals and pearls. (Are we in sync, or what?) I'm saying: "You win by a landslide, Ella! I'm finished pretending to adore the stupid romance—please make confetti out of it! Wait, strike that! I won't be reading it again so there's no need for you to trouble, especially when we can be romping! What I want most on earth, Honey, is to swish your hair in my face, rub my cheeks against the skin of your shins, advance skywards until reaching your fountain of joy! Rest assured your stunningness has eclipsed the heroine in the book forever! Flesh and blood trumps fiction, and I'm dying to embrace your flesh and sense the flood of your blood!"

You spring upright, become rigid, raise a hand to bid me remain where I am (Dearest, you're infused with the sort of energetic restraint that suggests its opposite: ice that can flare into fire in an instant.), say quite coldly: "There are three more poisonous romance novels on the coffee table: is that all of them? I absolutely need to confirm. I'll not be engaging in other activities until all the romances are destroyed."

"There are no others, Ella," I intone in hushed solemnity, suited to this grave occasion. "May God strike me senseless if there are."

"Clarify what's meant by "no others"? Be specific, so I know you're not maneuvering to subvert these proceedings via employment of vague terminology. Are there other romance novels on the premises?"

"There are no other romance novels on the premises," I half whisper.

"Fine, I'll accept that," you answer, not wavering from your coldly passionate tone. "But make no mistake: if you're lying to me, there will not be so much as a kiss between us tonight and I'll walk out the door. And I will discover if you're lying." You examine my face for signs of deceitfulness with clinical detachment, almost hostile eyes. (But do I detect a trace of a smile lurking behind your expression? I do! Careful, Ella, lest you burst into laughter and ruin the inquisitional mood.)

Apparently satisfied I've told the truth, you gather the romances, declaring: "To the flames with them! Unlike the curate and barber, I won't bother examining contents: I assume all romances are equally guilty of perpetrating sentimental delusions in their readers—that, instead of enriching experience they subtract from it—that they subvert blood-urges with flowery imagery, infect readers with fear of frolic! Yes, to the flames!" Good as your words, you stroll to the kitchen, fling the romance novels down the trash chute that leads to the incinerator.

Returning with a hint of a cat-that's-toyed-with-a-mouse grin on your face, you announce: "Because the cause of your sickness has been disposed of, we can proceed to the cure." Ah, there you go! You're suddenly laughing, nearly doubled over near the dining table! A shameful lapse of self-possession, failure to stay in character.

"Ahem!" you exclaim, collecting yourself. "To the cure! An abrupt shift from the fictional world you've been inhabiting into the immediacy of fleshly desire is required. Darling, this is a thigh! *(You raise a foot to the back of one of the dining table chairs, pull your gown to the top of your creamy silk stocking.)* See? A thigh! (You caress your thigh.) Unlike a fictional heroine who only requires that you interact with her cerebrally, this flesh and blood thigh belonging to a flesh and blood girl requires that you hot foot it over here and commence caressing it near where it meets the other thigh. Also unlike an airy fleshless female of fiction, I'm going to need you to unfasten my stockings from the clasps that attach them to the garter belt, then roll them down my legs and use them to bind my arms behind my back to this dining table's leg." A priceless smile graces your face. On the basis of your sultry, sly, mischievous smile alone I could flop on the couch, lather myself dazed as you watch.

Then you say: "I'm sitting with my back to this table-leg so you can pounce, bind and pleasure me proper. I trust you'll be capable? I'd hate to think your ill-informed excursion into RomanceWorld has robbed you of your verve. You do remember how to turn over a girl's engine? You haven't gone frigid on me, become an old maid prematurely? You're not going to shudder at every sound in the hall, complain about the smell of the neighbors' cooking, be a nuisance to all you come into contact with because there's no sex in your life? You're not going to acquire the scattering-off-to-all-sides look a woman gets in her eyes when she's not being plowed? The blithe music of your voice isn't going to become nervous, shrill, grating, scolding? You haven't turned into a...?"

"Thoroughly enjoying yourself, aren't you?" I interrupt. "It's clear you'll rub in my romance novel addiction forever, never mind it was faked, a game—you'll keep on coming back to it."

"Shut up and attend to business," you say matter-of-factly.

Soon as I'm crouching beside you, unfastening your garter belt's clasps... Dearest, why would I read of romance when I can live and breathe romance?—joyously accommodate my best girl's needs, make a meal of her curves, fortify myself with her nectar? Mmmmm! Ella, within seconds I was unable to recall what a romance novel is.

Upon reflection, though, I may need to revisit romance novel addiction—your cures are *truly* addictive.

Good-night, Dr. Ella!

Your,

FlingThingFreedFromFiction'sLies

XIV. Missy Mayhem & Autumn's Chill

XIV.1
Steven to Angie & Ella
Friday, September 19, 2003 11:19 PM

A pologies, Angie and Ella, for being out of touch for six weeks. You've guessed correctly: I've met someone. Specifically, stumbled into an addiction/affliction with a petite princess hellcat named Missy.

Is it love? Ha! It's said love places one in a state of emotion—reveals a world—unlike any one's experienced before, and I'd be a liar if I said my involvement with Missy didn't do that; but the whole business often strikes me as being despite myself, sometimes even an outright annoyance, a gauntlet that must be run. I'm not sure if that's love.

Sure, Missy's picture is always before my mind's eye—causes a swirl of rapture and uneasiness to steadily throb in my breast—but I don't foresee our relationship lasting, because of the frequency with which I contemplate escape. An addict often contemplates escape from the drug that binds him, brings about fireworks in his veins, right? Does an addict adore the drug he cannot help but crave or resent it?

Angie and Ella, we've always been friends first, and frolic-mates second—we've been very clear about this. At varying stages of our friendship it's felt like love—has to be a variety of love: aren't all deep and abiding friendships?—but Missy's intruded, plunged me into disequilibrium that fascinates as much as it repels me. I often descend to disliking—maybe even hating—her, just as I often experience wildest upwellings of joy solely because of her; and fist-pumping onrushes of triumph; and fate-cursing recriminations that much energy's being wasted. Simply put, I'm not sure if Missy's a blessing or a curse.

I met Missy through Robert, at a party in a club. He pointed her out on the dance floor, said, "There's a girl you have to meet." Since that first encounter, I've pretty much been in a state of seizure.

To explain the enclosed email: Missy lives next door to Robert and they water each other's plants when one of them's on a trip, often chat on their terraces. She sometimes speaks about me, knowing her words will be repeated. The email begins by referring to a situation that arose as a consequence of spending last Saturday night with Missy and, from there, evolves into a description of the ups and downs of a Missy night and the nature of our relationship. I'm enclosing it (1) to give you an idea of what's going on, and (2) because it's easier than writing a new one.

The three of us have always seen other people, but none of these people have kept us apart for long. Missy's not only kept me from you for over six weeks, I've neglected to mention her existence. I think I haven't told you about her because I keep expecting us to break up soon.

It will be over between Missy and I...eventually. After all, I've never entrusted Missy with emotional confidences, especially concerning the two of you, and that's the authentic indication to whom one's closest, right? Who are the people to whom one confides everything?

But I'll let the enclosed email speak for me. Angie and Ella, you know my affection and gratitude for you will always be unwavering.

Love,
Steven

##########

Steven to Robert
Monday, September 15, 2003 1:41 AM

So Missy's in another uproar? wishing me dead for failing to see she got home with her stockings, the precious "Pinky Reds"? As if it's my responsibility to gather all her accessories gone astray and see to it she leaves with them! But thanks for the forewarning that forearms me—I'm surprised I wasn't the first to know of Her Highness' displeasure. Then again, she's probably waiting until she's fully worked up. Yeah, she isn't infuriated enough yet—no use letting me off easy.

No surprise that another Missy storm's brewing. If it wasn't the stockings, it would be something else—such as I didn't have roses delivered on Sunday to demonstrate how much I appreciate her; or didn't notice she was wearing a new perfume and praise it to high heaven; or had a trace of stubble instead of being freshly shaved; or neglected to be appropriately sad when she left. She's reprimanded me for those things in the past, and plenty else—all equally outrageous, a case of her reaching for reasons to be annoyed. It's a ritual with her—a night cannot end on a sweet note. Something has to be amiss and, if nothing's amiss, she'll invent something that is. Her Highness demands that my every thought revolve around her, regardless of whether she's present; that she be the beginning and the end and all points in between of my attention span: throwing tantrums over nothing is a way of reminding me. Yeah, I must constantly be alert to prevent "disrespectful and rebellious behavior" from making her feel unwanted.

But I've got bad news for Missykins—her "Pinky Reds" are in shreds, kaput, deceased. I've flung them down the trash chute—they weren't fit to wear, were in tatters, not to mention rather crispy with dried saliva and other love juices. I don't believe BratCat doesn't remember—am fairly certain she does remember and is pretending to be frantic on their account, for the purpose of propelling me into panic. I'm supposed to be galvanized to action, race out the door and purchase a new pair to pacify her; supposed to present them to her as a peace offering, apologize profusely for the destruction of the original ones, plead for Her PrincessShip's forgiveness. Ha! As if I ever indulge her "two-year-old behavior" (her words), permit myself to be shoved about by her snit-fits. Which is part of the drama: although Missy would die before admitting it, she adores my insubordination—I'm *expected* to rebel.

Anyway, here's what happened—a quintessential Missy adventure:

This morning she calls at around two AM, says she's outside my building, and coming up. OK, I'm not doing much, simply reading Don Quixote for the trillionth time, so I agree. Right, I violated my "No Barge In!" policy: allow a female to barge in once, she soon makes a habit of it. Every girl's perfectly willing to become a possessive pest, if one's stupid enough to allow it to happen. Every girl's got just-happened-to-be-in-the-neighborhood mania in her psychological profile. An inch is given, a thousand yards are taken. Pretty soon the girl thinks of one's apartment as her second home, is clamoring for a set of keys; pretty soon she's dead set on redecorating the place, having furniture she doesn't like hauled away; and then she starts thinking of one's apartment as her *first* home, is insisting on moving in. Before one knows it, one's confronted with a lot of pining, whining, wheedling, complaining drama concerning the fact one's none too eager to share, refusing to grow up and be a responsible man. Before one knows it, one's in the midst of a nasty breakup, dealing with a wailing, rancorous, screaming manic—being called ungrateful, misleading, false-promising, withholding, cowardly. Before one knows it, one's got to listen to the "Why do you want to destroy love?" lecture; and the "You really need to see a therapist!" lecture; and the "You're going to end up being a lonely old man!" lecture; and the "Well, you might as well kill yourself if you're afraid of a woman who loves you!" lecture; and plenty of other lectures, all served up from the point of view of a female who feels she has a right to take complete control of one's life. So, yes, I do the girl and myself a favor by not allowing her to pop over unannounced, give that nasty feminine possessive streak something tangible to latch onto. But, sometimes... Hell, a cutie's bright voice on the phone saying she's in the lobby and wants to see me, and if I'm not doing much... It's impossible to enforce "No Barge

In!" all the time. Girl's are too euphoria-inducing delectable, and their voices lead me to picture their wild eyes. It's especially tough to resist a girl who wants to fun around.

OK, so following a brief pause, I tell Missy, "Fine, come on up." Missy, being the vainest hellcat alive, is immediately annoyed at the pause: how dare I need two seconds to reflect before agreeing, instead of instantaneously and enthusiastically saying there's nothing I'd like better on earth? Missy doesn't ever believe a man has a choice in the matter of being treated to a visit by her; to pause and reflect and then somewhat resignedly say "fine" implies I have a choice and could also say "no" and Her Highness doesn't comprehend how a "no" could originate from anyone but herself. She once said: "I'm a delectable nymphet who's lusted after dozens of times a day, which means I'm entitled to undivided attention on demand. If I want a man's attention he ought to thank his lucky stars, because hordes would kill to be in his place."

But to resume with this morning:

"Oh, it's fine, is it?" Missy says sarcastically. "You know, if you're not sure, I can always visit someone else."

So now Missy's expecting me to exert myself to pacify her. Thing is that, precisely because she's such a proud and willful princess, there's constant temptation to go contrary to her expectations and rile her. I respond, "Fine, if that's your wish, visit someone else."

"You're not making sense!" Missy hisses, stamping a foot loud enough for her phone to pick it up. She exhales with exasperation, continues, "Don't take it out on me if you haven't slept or eaten, and are cranky! I've gotten pretty for you and am here to see you and you're not going to turn me away! I'll stand in your lobby all night if I have to! What will the doorman think? I'll tell him you're a creep!" (Big threat, right? She'll tell the doorman I'm a creep! Ha ha!) Then suddenly, in ineffably sweet gentle tones: "Mommy will feed you if you're hungry, honey. She's here to be nice. Let Mommy come up. She won't bite."

"But I said you could come up," I point out.

"I'll be right there," she says quick and business like, and hangs up.

I not only violated my "No Barge In!" policy, I did so with just about the most prideful, pushy, not-taking-no-for-an-answer girl in town. I'm sure you're highly amused a girl's finally "gotten to" me.

But if I'm going to allow a girl to get to me, push me around, she's going to be jaw-droppingly gorgeous. If I'm going to put up with spoiled princess antics, said princess is going to be heads-whip-ping-about-to-gawk-at-her stunning. Missy's not merely cute—cute's easy to come by. Cuties prance about the sidewalks all day, dozens every hour. Missy's beautiful as how Poe describes beauty: "There's no beauty that doesn't contain something of strangeness in its as-pect." Missy's beauty is a gasp of awe, punch in the stomach, surge of yearning strong enough to turn me inside out. Her blue eyes and pitch-black hair—lily-white complexion, with soft shadows undulat-ing underneath. Her indescribably sweet face charged with will. Her at once slender and curvy body, perfectly rounded twitchy behind, fit silky musculature, flawless grace.

The doorman buzzes and I tell him to admit Missy; soon she's banging on my door and kicking it, multi-ringing the bell. Nothing unusual in that: it's her way of indicating she's a girl who doesn't like to be kept waiting. Also, according to her, a way of showing she's eager to see her man. Mostly, it's part of the Missy theatrical entrance package: God forbid she arrive quietly—tap on the door discreetly—like most girls. I'm unsure what to expect. I know my "insult" has been duly noted (How dare I call her bluff in the matter of her "visit someone else" suggestion, tell her to do so.), and will be used against me at some point.

When I open the door Missy's leg is primed to deliver another kick. The intent-on-raising-a-ruckus look on her face is priceless—more charming than alarming, even if she's given me plenty of occasions to be alarmed—she never looks more like a little girl than when doing something she knows I'd rather she didn't do. Then she (It's fun to finally seek to encompass the phenomenon of Missy with a narrative of one of our nights.) yanks her dress over her head in an unbroken swish, flings it on the carpet, tromps on it. "Ta da!" she announces with a giggle—such little-girlishness is in her giggle. Missy's a ceaseless either/or of sweetness and snarls, and it's often impossible to predict which will appear: either can succeed the other at any time in the blink of an eye. Like a contented cat, Missy can suddenly become annoyed and glare and claw; like an infuriated cat, she can suddenly turn affectionate and cuddle close and purr. The sight of Missy being

Missy is perpetually fresh—her hair swishing as she executes a quick twirl, framing her radiant face when she stops. Smiling sweetly, she raises a leg over her head, does the splits standing up; and her legs are snug in her "Pinky Reds," mid-thigh high; aside from her shoes, she's wearing nothing else—fearless at being naked in the hall, giggling louder.

No sooner do I step forward to embrace her and pull her inside my apartment, than Missy snaps her upraised leg down—whap!—and snarls, "Don't touch me, son of a bitch!" She jerks her hands up to keep me away, revulsion on her face. "Uh, huh! That's right! Wake up and take a look at what you were going to pass on! How do you like it when I tell you to get lost? Feels good, doesn't it? Yeah, it feels good, creep!"

"Oh, Christ," I mutter, flinging my arms up.

"Well, how do you think it makes me feel when you tell me I can go visit someone else? I'm a human too!" she says, bursting into tears.

Many girls depend on instant tears to make the man in their life feel like garbage when he's done something they dislike or is neglecting to do something they want him to do. Instant tears are one of the most effective manipulation tools a girl has at her disposal, and Missy's the master. Not that I'm buying it, viewing her tears as anything besides the said manipulation tool, but I'm becoming concerned my neighbors might peer outside their doors to see what the commotion's about. I say, "Missy, you know I didn't mean for you to go elsewhere. How could I want you to do that? You know I thank my lucky stars you're in my life. I could never want you to be anywhere but here. You're..."

"Playacting creep!" she interrupts with a yell. "You'll say anything to get some snatch! Of course you like that I'm here, and naked! Do you think I don't know men like to see me naked? I could turn up at the door of any stranger, and he'd say whatever he thought would get me to come inside and be nice! Aaahhh!" she shrieks (Missy never raises her voice thus when people are around but if no one's in sight it's fair game.), thrashing her head, grabbing at her cheeks. "I feel like a fool for dressing extra nice for you, deeming you worthy!" Then her voice becomes quiet, a rapidly whispered hiss—is laced with an amount of disdain alongside which mere yelling's a joke. "See them, honey? See my red stockings on my perfect legs that you're *not* going to have wrapped around you tonight? See my pretty dress that I'm putting back on to cover these tits (She thrusts her breasts at me.) and this ass? (She wiggles her behind, lightly slaps it.) Does it make you feel like a man, knowing I came here to take care of you, and that now you're not going to touch me because you're small-minded and selfish? Huh? Do you feel like a man?" She raises an arm to strike me; I grasp her wrist to prevent it; yanking free, she yells "Creep!" again, and stomps down the hall. "Bye-bye, big man!" she yells as she vanishes around the corner.

It's the familiar stomp-off-in-a-huff routine. I'm expected to chase after Missy, outdo myself in compliments, proffering of affection, profuse apologies. I'm expected to declare my utter worthlessness, beg for her to have mercy on pitiful me. What do I do? I say to myself, "Good, now I don't have to argue anymore," and go back inside, shut the door.

Within a minute Missy's kicking at my door in a frenzy, wailing, "Honey, I miss you—please let me in!"

I instantly open the door. Missy flings herself into my arms as if I'm the beginning and the end of her world, declares, "Honey, I've missed you insanely!" in the sweetest of tones, kisses me with eyes shut while hyperventilating through her nose, moaning. She's tickle-clawing me—light delectable scratches as she reaches under my shirt, circles her nails about my back. The apple blossom scent of her hair surrounds me; I'm tingling to her tongue's writhings, insistent pulsing and rubbing of her tummy. My apartment's suddenly a sunny summer day—I'm immersed in a realm of beautiful Maenads, graceful cats, sleek movement.

Pretty nice, right? An uninhibited beauty turning up unannounced in the wee hours—one moment I'm reading alone, the next a lovely lust tart's inundating me with sensory riches. So much for my "No Barge In!" policy! I think Missy can barge in on me any time! I think I'll give her a set of keys! (And if you believe that, you'll also believe the moon just flew off to orbit Venus. All kidding aside, though: when Missy grabs ahold of me fiercely, ignites my blood with her energy-swirl, it's elevating enough for me to think I might be capable of waving bye-bye to freedom, allowing her to move in and push me around. Of course that'll never happen—it's simply a thought that pops into my head: a gauge of my appreciation of the force of nature that's Missy.)

"The bitch is here!" Missy announces with a giggle at our first pause. She gracefully (She can't be anything but graceful.) twirls a couple times, stops with her back to me; then she raises her arms over her head, by way of indicating I should pull her dress off. So off it comes for the second time. Again, she's naked but for her "Pinky Reds" and heels. Then she's facing me again. "Let's take care of these," she says, unfastening my belt and removing my pants; then as if in afterthought, "Oh, we're going to need this." She kneels to slip my belt from my pants and wind it around her wrist. "I'm going to need you to be strong for me tonight," she continues, standing again. "You're going to need to belt me without flinching, make me wail to high heaven. And then you're going to need to love me like your life depends on it, make me dead with exhaustion, obliterate my thoughts." Missy says this in an even tone, with seriousness and intensity, while steadily gazing at me; from the look in her eyes, you'd swear we were plotting a murder.

"If that's what you want," I say, holding her gaze.

"Good," she nods, emphatically dipping her chin. "I knew you'd be the man I need you to be tonight. Something's bothering your Missy. She's very disturbed and needs to have it knocked out of her. You can do that, can't you?" The question carries the tone of a threat. It's clear that if I fail to "knock it out of her" there'll be storms to weather.

"I'll do my best," I respond.

"You'll do better than your best," she says, hardening her eyes. "Otherwise, we'll have a problem." She seizes my hands and squeezes, lightly scrapes with her nails by way of warning, as good as saying: "Be careful to say the right thing, or you'll get scratched."

"If you want something from me, you ought to be more respectful," I say, my pride getting the better of me. As I yank my hands from Missy's grasp rage leaps onto her face, so I—ha ha!—advance to kiss her.

"Son of a bitch, don't you dare smooch me!" she yells, crisscrossing her arms in the air between us, leaping back in disgust. "Don't you dare change the subject, pooh-pooh what's important to me! I want to know if you understand! Do you understand or not?" She kicks me.

"I told you to never do that!" I yell, seizing her by the shoulders and gently but firmly wrestling her to the floor.

"Eeeerrraaahhh!" she shrieks, writhing like an eel out of water, frantically seeking to seize my fingers and bend them backwards; and while also scratching, attempting to bite me somewhere—an arm, my chest, a leg, anything near. The entryway of my apartment's spinning; the overhead light's whirling into silver; Missy's a thrashing, flailing, kicking blur. I hear: "You want to do it the hard way; you want to be an asshole; you want to make me be bad, then goddamn you!"

Here we go again, Miss Strife-O-Matic and I. Miss Strife-O-Matic? It takes two to tango, so I know I share the blame. Why push Missy's buttons, bait her, enrage her? What's the appeal of bringing violence into my life? Because, Robert, make no mistake: when Missy's out to bend fingers backwards and crack the bones she isn't playing. She doesn't bare her fangs for show, only for action. If she wounds me it'll be my fault for offending her: that's her reasoning, and she won't spill tears.

Minutes ago my apartment was peace and balance and equanimity—I was absorbed in Don Quixote without a care—and now it's exploded into urgent struggle. Why does Missy's inflammable disposition appeal to me? always bring a smile to my face when I'm thinking about her, make me proud to be involved with her? Do I have taming-of-the-shrew syndrome? (If that isn't an official clinical condition, it ought to be.) Is it a match-wills-with-a-wildcat contest? Is matching my will against Missy's, making myself stronger, the primary source of addiction?

"Let's see what you're made of, creep!" Missy taunts, her voice white hot with venom. "Let's see you tame the kitten, bring la petite to heel!"

I hardly know what I'm doing. I've pinned her to the floor, straddled her, placed my knees on her arms. I'm winding her hair about her throat—I hear myself say: "Stop, or I'll choke you with your hair."

"Pah! Why don't you do it, pathetic coward, instead of seeking to impress and scare me with empty showboating? I'm not afraid—I'm not afraid to die! Here!" she shrieks. "If you're so brave, grab the letter opener on the dresser over there and stab me! That would suit you just fine, wouldn't it? If I was dead you'd be happy! Only (Here she pauses to derisively stare at me, eyes ablaze.), you lack the guts, are worthless blather! You have no idea what to do with a girl like me, like the other baby boys! And to think I thought there was a chance you might be a man! Boy oh boy (Here she spits.), do I feel like a fool!"

With Missy's spittle on my face and enraged taunting eyes before me, I wind her hair slightly tighter, but instantly loosen it. What am I going to do, stay on top of her all night? Or shove her into the hallway, toss her belongings after her, lock the door? Or...? Dozens of clashing out-of-focus pictures are whipping through my head; I continue pressing my knees to Missy's forearms, pinning her on the carpet.

"If you let me go, I claw your eyes," Missy hisses, "so you'd better keep firm hold of your slut, discipline her! You'd better figure out what to do with this discontented bitch! I said I need to be calmed—asked you to step up to the plate, be strong for me—and you play silly games, quarrel with me, be mean to me! Eeeerrra..." I smother her shriek with a hand—her teeth are scraping my palm, seeking to bite—I yank my hand free. "Creep! Asshole!" she screams. Uppermost in my mind is that we're in the entryway by the door and anyone in the hall's going to get an earful—no telling what they'll think. I rise and grab Missy's wrists, begin pulling her across the carpet to the bedroom—I do it quick, because she's kicking every which way again, writhing like a snake in hot oil. A kick at the coffee table crashes a lamp to the floor.

"You drag me? The bed, you creep? Think your sweet Missy (She intones "sweet Missy" with the utmost venom.) will spread for you? You going to rape her? Huh?" Missy being Missy, the "Huh?" is phrased—just like that—in kinder tones. Yes, Missy being Missy is Missy suddenly ceasing to struggle, because enacting a rape fantasy appeals to her. But where does fantasy begin and actuality end with Missy? She baits, taunts, insults—out-and-out attacks—to incite a wrestling match; she wants to be calmed with violence and uses violence to force me. It's all a game to Missy—another night of "tame the kitten." Sure, she'll allow herself to be "raped"; but is it rape then? Of course not.

So we're near the coffee table. Missy's still squirming, but playfully—even giggling. The magic word "rape" and she's aglow with mirth. With mood-swirl Missy a storm can subside as quickly as it erupts.

Right, she can flare back to anger in a flash at any time, so I waste no time in taking advantage of her lack of resistance to get her onto the bed. On previous occasions I've had to drag, yank, lift a furiously struggling—seeking to gouge, kick, bite—Missy atop the bed and bind her. (Need I remind you that, although fighting me at every step, Missy always very much wants to be bound atop the bed? that she'll set about throwing things, destroying my apartment, if I fail to do so?) Tonight, she's—to use one of her favorite phrases—"letting me off easy." In fact, I'm just now noticing that there's a tone of sadness about her—of having been shaken by something, disturbed. While positioning her on her back on the mattress I'm wondering if real misfortune's befallen her.

Missy suddenly sits upright, says, "Please love me, Steven—I've had a ghastly evening. I really need you to be nice, and to be ruthless, and to knock the bad things out of me. You'll show me how much you care, won't you, and not hold back? Please, Steven?" Her eyes are pleading, her lips are trembling at the corners of her mouth. She's the picture of a little girl baffled by the capriciousness of a cruel world. It's too easy to forget she was a thrashing and kicking and wailing hellcat under two minutes ago, seeking to hurt me any which way she could.

"But what happened, sweetheart?" I ask. "Please tell me—I'm not going anywhere. I'll help any way I can."

Training pained eyes upon me, Missy says with utter seriousness, as if Fate's truly dealt her a nasty hand, "A mouse is in my apartment."

Clearly this is an extremely delicate—disposition-of-the-night-hanging-in-the-balance—moment and I need to negotiate it with sensitivity and understanding. Alas, when Missy says "a mouse is in my apartment" I'm caught off guard and my fate's sealed. I not merely crack a smile, which would be more than enough to infuriate her, I laugh. The mildness of a mouse in her apartment, when held up to the potential troubles I'd imagined! I couldn't conceal mirth if my life depended on it.

"You laugh?" Missy asks with disbelief, her voice rising.

"It's laughter of relief, Missy—I could never laugh at you," I hasten to explain, still grinning. "I was imagining horrible things, and am..."

Missy springs to her knees and punches me squarely in the stomach (Although diminutive she's a very fit dancer: it's punch enough to leave me gasping for breath.), starts flailing at my chest. "I could kill you!" she yells. "If I was a man, I would kill you!" Then she jerks herself away, glares at me with arms wrapped about her knees, is literally vibrating with hate, seems to be gathering herself for a lunge at my face. "Horrible things imagining!" she resumes. "You—you're sick! A mouse in my apartment isn't tragic enough for you! You were hoping for injuries, my building burning to ashes, the loss of someone near and dear? Would disasters of that magnitude please you? Did you want real hell and psychological devastation to afflict your Missy, so you could puff yourself up, feel superior, pity her? Huh? Disgusting creep!"

"Complete rubbish and you know it!" I yell. "Yeah, be a capricious vicious fiend all you want, but don't go thinking I want bad things to happen to you! Don't resort to that as a means to bait me! And ever hear of the boy who cried wolf? How could you alarm me because of a little rodent that's much more afraid of you than you could be of it?"

"Do you know what it does to me when you get that smirk on your face?" Missy asks, tears welling in her eyes. "Do you have any idea how much it hurts when you laugh at me? It tears my heart out! And you enjoy that very much, don't you? It excites you, you filthy goddamned... Aaahhh!" She lunges at my right arm, seeks to inflict a bite.

Missy's continuing to curse, but I can't discern individual words: the whole of my attention's devoted to entangling her in a blanket, so I'll have enough time to yank open the nightstand drawer, grab a handful of scarves—which I do just before she squirms from under the blanket, rakes her nails across my chest. Then I'm flinging the blanket over her again (as zookeepers do with dangerous animals), and... Where's one of her wrists? Here's one! I tie one end of a scarf about it, tie the other end to the bed frame. Then her other wrist. Then her infuriated legs. But with what? Turns out I've only grabbed two scarves. Very stupidly, I divert my attention from Missy to the nightstand, in order to grab more scarves, a trifle too long: she's able to kick the blanket off, jerk her legs up, deliver a blow with the ball of her foot to the back of my head.

Robert, I ask again: why put up with Missy? Am I masochistic? Do I enjoy being kicked in the head, such that my temples are throbbing? Or is it—ha ha—the visual pyrotechnics that please me?—as in the bright white of the bed sheets blazing at my knees, swirling towards the ceiling, splintering into glares?—the ocean of jagged motion? Do I enjoy the stress? enjoy the (might as well admit it) fear? When Missy announces she's coming over, I know I'm in store for more than a few tense moments—know she'll come after me in a very physical way, shrieking insults the while: what's in it for me? Clearly a Missy night's a purge of sorts, via extremities of emotion I wouldn't otherwise experience. Clearly I've been spoiled, made soft, by reasonable girls! Reasonable girls allow weeds of stagnation to appear in my psyche's garden, whereas Missy roots them out. Missy's an absolute treasure—I've never had my depths dredged, and cleansed, so vividly.

OK: Missy's landed a triumphant blow and I'm stunned for a few moments, slowly twisting my head. "Call this restraining me, Mr. Inept?" she snarls. "Call this conquesting me? Think you can maybe possibly manage to be half a man sometime this year?"

I spring at her legs, climb atop them, my back to her eyes. She still has her stockings, precious Pinky Reds, on. I peel each off in turn, bind her ankles to the bedknobs with them. Although bound to the bed frame at her ankles and wrists spreadeagled-style, Missy's furiously bouncing up and down, yelling, "A pathetic half-assed job! Maybe it's time for me to find a new boyfriend!" I slip pillows under her back to eliminate the wiggle room between herself and the mattress, render her nearly immobile. "Seems the cat's been declawed," I smile, standing at the foot of the bed and waving at her, then folding my arms across my chest.

"You really think I'm done for?" she scoffs. "Just wait until I'm loose! You can't keep me here forever, and will pay! I'll douse your bookcases with wine, ruin your precious books!" Her eyes are saying: "I know no limits when I'm angry; I'm not hampered by silly concerns about violating acceptable behavior; all is justified in expenditure of rage." I could turn off the tap of Missy's taunts by wrapping a scarf around her head and between her teeth (Safety is paramount and I would never tape a girl's mouth shut: sinus congestion could prevent her from breathing, effectively suffocate her. *Never* should ability to breathe via the mouth be obstructed.), but why would I do that? Missy's word-flow is a mirror in which I glimpse myself, as are her eyes, and gagging or blindfolding her would be tantamount to starving myself. There's immeasurable elemental beauty in storming Missy's speech and glances.

"Big bold scary words!" I respond. "Especially as they're coming from a girl who's afraid of a mouse! A mouse in your apartment? Whoa! Major disaster! One would think a bear broke in and mauled you! You're essentially a silly drama queen, looking for any inconsequential molehill to turn into Mount Everest! Too much time on your hands, is that it? No authentic stress in your life, so you need to dream some up? Yes, that's you're dirty little secret! Spew threats all you like, gaze at me like you want me dead all you like: such antics are nothing but an attempt to cover up that you're a spoiled only child daddy's girl who's had everything handed to her, and knows nothing of actual struggle!"

Ah, now I've gone and pushed one of Missy's worst buttons. Being spoiled by daddy's a sore spot with her: she's persuaded it's stunted her emotional growth, and that she's had a great deal of catching up to do. (I won't speculate as to whether such is true.) As for struggle, Missy's known plenty: what successful Broadway dancer hasn't? She's extremely disciplined and fit, never spares herself. Besides, her disposition's never going to let her rest—her demons don't take vacations. Calling Missy spoiled is like pouring gasoline on a fire and, sure enough, her body jolts with rage, every sinew stressed, straining against the scarves and stockings that bind her. What do I do? Why, I climb onto the bed to caress her, of course. "Don't you dare touch me!" she screams. "I hate the touch of you! If you touch me, you're dead!"

"You'll just have to kill me," I laugh, positioning myself between her legs and leaning in, seeking to caress the cheeks of her infuriated face. My oh my! Cliché it may be, but Missy's never more stunning than when wishing me dead. She's too enraged to articulate words, is squealing and hissing and spitting, stabbing with blazing eyes.

Missy never loses articulation for long, though. "Rape me, or I'll tell the neighbors you hit me!" she commands, motioning with her eyes for me to lie atop her. "Make me sore, or I'll call my dad! Plow me senseless, or I'll make up an abuse history, drag you through litigation hell!" Soon as my lips are within reach she's kissing me hard, tongue writhing. I'm entering her, thrusting deep, heat and shimmers and shivers engulfing me. She's jerking her hips upwards in fury, coaxing me deeper. "I love you!" she hisses while bathing me in the pulsating light of her eyes.

We both appreciate that feminine moodiness and petulance reliably alchemizes into invigorating friction during frolic, accelerates vividness. If a girl's sulking, capricious, tossing tantrums: such stirs one to cajole her into compliance and, once one's succeeded, it's far more satisfying than if she's been well-behaved. In the moodiness department Missy's unmatched—the tantrum-tossing of other girls is namby-pamby child's play when held up to her ability to wreak havoc. Missy's able to communicate real danger, elemental instability. Is a tiger ever tamed? One hears of circus people mauled by tigers they've cared for and trained from birth; and, feel free to laugh at my expense, but Missy makes me think of a tiger, compliant for years, that suddenly savages the person who's raised it. As to why tigers would do such, it's because tigers are wild animals and don't belong in cages, and especially have no business doing tricks for the amusement of another species. A tiger's inextinguishable allegiance is to the jungle—to its God given right, as an apex predator second to none, to stalk and kill. Why shouldn't tigers attack those who've unconscionably robbed them of their birthright?

Accuse me of turning Missy into a wish fulfillment, projecting fantasies, but I often feel she's an untamable tigress; that rebelliousness and resentment simmers inside her due to emotional attachment to me; that freedom to be a wild creature unto herself which said attachment's robbed her of could surge forth at any time to punish me; that she's never wholly willingly been in favor of our relationship. Perhaps these thoughts are illusion but it's highly enjoyable to have them.

Ah, but there's Missy's sweet side—few girls can be as loving. Extreme in all things Missy is—incapable of doing anything halfway—and when she does an abrupt flip into tenderness after an interval of raging it's, pardon the hyperbole, truly as if heaven's on earth. It's surely Missy's sweet side that's the strongest source of my addiction: the sharp contrast between the affectionate little girl and raging she-cat is a drug like no other. Missy's paradox is she's a sweetheart at heart, wants nothing more than to be loving and kind. Like the road to Paradise, the journey to her tender outpourings is fraught with peril but, once one arrives, experience transforms into inner upwelling, equanimity, one's only previously dreamed of—caught agonizingly fleeting glimpses of. As when, following our first spell of lovemaking—after I've unbound her—Missy goes to the kitchen for a glass of water, returns in a topless pink negligee with white lace trim (Obtained from her tote: she always arrives prepared.) and her hair ponytailed with a pink ribbon: she's beaming delight, half-skipping, looking for all the world like a sixteen year old. She flings herself onto the bed, wraps herself around me, says in a bubbly blithe voice, "I fit on you like a little monkey!" Gazing at me with eyes awash with affection, she adds, "Let Missy take care of you." She's caressing me—well, just perfect: soft ghost caresses in circle motion about my shoulders and back, such that I'm atingle head to toe, my skin's boundaries seeming to extend into the air. "I'm here for you, my baby handsome head," she continues. "Yes, it's me, living in the blankets for you. When you've been working hard and need love, it's Missy for you—always for you—living in the blankets."

Then she's guiding me inside her, gently rippling, alternately gripping and releasing: time's suspended in the continued caresses of her hands—in her sucking of my neck—in the sound of, "Oh, Steven! My love!"—as she clasps me tighter, and... God, the way she's looking at me—adoringly, imploringly, bedazzledly! Certainly I taste of undiluted bliss, all indications of care gone, during such moments. The thought that this little girl—so delicate, showing her vulnerability now as if her life depends on me continuing to see her... And she's so strong, absolutely untamed—doesn't flinch from anything, knows no fear.

Missy gets grimace-faced a bit when I commence thrusting harder, bang the back end of her womb—her eyes soon joyous, bursting with luscious light—she happily purrs, "That's right, honey, get your stress out! I'm your blanket girl and you own me, and you can and should split me open whenever you wish! I'm the bad girl who loves you! Uhmmmmm..."

Following my second release, Missy's happily squirming, figure-eighting her head on the mattress, blithely saying, "This is what I wanted all along, sweetie—love! I love you, Steven!"

"I love you too, Missy," I respond, thereafter pinning her head to the mattress with a kiss, she tickle-caressing my ears and cheeks, lightly writhing, running her toes up and down my shins.

So, Robert, you get an idea of the contradictory nature—multidimensional degree—of my involvement: I refer to Missy as my addiction and affliction, as if I'm attached to her against my will and seeking to escape but that's a lesser aspect. My sweet moments with Missy are such that they frequently, for lack of a better word, haunt me afterwards: pictures of the brimming crystals of her eyes linger, and I'm humbled and gasp with awe and surge with joy at the extent of her regard and trust. And, yes, I've told Missy I love her: one way of looking at it is that declaring such is inescapable, as in the above instance, but I probably am in love with her (in a but-I-doubt-I'll-be-spending-my-life-with-you way) and therefore make such declarations sincerely, while at the same time wary of the sort of trouble they can lead to when the subject of lasting commitment's brought up.

To resume with last night: not long after our exchange of "I love you"s playtime begins. We put on dance music, bounce about the bed, have pillow fights, engage in tickle wars; indulge in vocabulary games, whereby an innately funny word—wench, for instance, or hobgoblin—is seized upon, used in silly sentences—relentlessly punned upon, rhymed upon, mutated upon. We play the ass-mauling game, whereby, (1) Missy lies on her stomach with posterior provocatively displayed, brings an unguarded expression to her face, (2) I crouch in the covers on the far side of the bed like a wildcat in a jungle's undergrowth, (3) I spring upon Missy's posterior with snarls and roars and freely claw, knead, nip, swat its twin globes, (4) Missy makes a show of being ambushed, utters cries of terror, thrashes. Crazy thing is the ass-mauling game may very well be an essential ingredient of our relationship! Given the stressful elements of our encounters, we need to giggle ourselves dizzy in places.

Has Missy's tumult-sowing side bedded down for the night? Might as well ask: do slender cutie's rejoice when they gain a pound, fail to cringe at the slightest mention of fat? Missy's mood-spin personified and Antarctica will turn tropical before she'll fail to visit strife several times a night. It's as if any given emotion automatically turns sour on her—disgusts and horrifies her—if it's sustained for an hour.

Case in point: Missy's flung herself into playtime wholeheart-edly—is a darling picture of exultant abandon—when she suddenly tenses in every muscle, twists her face into a scowl, seizes my wrists and squeezes, says stridently, "Stop! You're making me uncomfortable! I'm wondering how much you really care about me! That's right," she rais-es her voice a pitch, "and all you do is act surprised! Surprised I'm onto you, plainly see you don't take me seriously! As if I'm nothing but a toy, only here for fun and games, and respecting me isn't necessary! You really do think I'm an acquiescent bimbo of a yes-girl, don't you?—a good time divorced from responsibility! Well, let me open your eyes! I'm a mature woman and I'm going to want a few things from you if I'm going to stay with you! Are you in or are you out? I want a future—a family plan! I would like for you to sell this studio and pony up some money and find us a two bedroom so we can live together like people do when they're in love! You did say you love me, didn't you? I sure hope you weren't lying! I'd hate to think you're foolish enough to think I can be snow-jobbed forever with false declarations! Because if I find out you've been lying to me... (Here she digs her nails into my wrists.) If I find out you've been playing me... (Here her eyes get positively malicious.) If I find out you've been leading me on, you're going to get hurt!"

Missy's way of introducing the dreaded subject of commitment doesn't inspire me with eagerness to entangle myself further than I already am. So far it's been the enthralling surges of attraction/fear variety of entanglement. As for the material, unite finances and real estate, variety of entanglement I'll outright state I've never come close to entertaining the possibly—it's too preposterously final, suffocat-ingly restraining. Females really do have a lot of gall, don't they? It's as if they're always waiting for the right moment (i.e., before or after lovemaking) to propose a merger; as if they're constantly working out relationship equations in their heads, as in: "OK, we've been seeing each other steady for two months so now's the time to make my move for a move-in, start applying pressure, end the free-samples-carefree-sex stage."

I'm on emotional overdrive with Missy as with no one else—living in the present, experience dizzyingly accelerated, unable to think as far into the future as next week—and she's asking me to sell my place?

As for Missy's threats, I don't take them lightly: as she continues squeezing my wrists and glaring, I'm wondering how to best respond tactfully.

"Do you know how pathetic you look when you're trying to dream up ways to blow me off, avoid what I know you hate?" Missy hisses. "If you're going to resort to stall tactics, at least have the decency to spit them out, instead of sitting here in silence and giving me that deer-caught-in-headlights look! You look so scared I feel sorry for you!"

"Missy," I say, annoyance rising, "I'm tired of being unable to relax with you, drop my guard! We were having fun: is that a crime? Suddenly you freeze up and scold, when I've done nothing wrong! And what's with the leading you on rubbish? I love you and haven't lied one bit! I love you, but you test it every hour! How can I trust you? You want to live together? How do I know you won't turn my life into a living hell? You say I'm ridiculous? Well, let me tell you something, Miss Missy: I'm not so ridiculous that I'm going to allow my love for you to make me miserable! You want a future plan man? Then go find someone else! And, actually... Why don't you just go home?"; then, following a brief pause, "Now look who's surprised! I'm not bluffing, Missy—it's not empty bravado. I've had enough and want you gone."

"Have you had enough to eat, honey?" she asks softly, sympathetically gazing at me and tapping my shoulder, not a bit flustered, as if the notion of her leaving's too preposterous to be worthy of consideration. "Have you had enough sleep? Because you're just not making any sense." Just like that the topic of commitment is abandoned—until the next time Missy deems the moment right to bring it up or, as in this case, it bursts forth seemingly on its own. Constantly there's tug of war between becoming closer to beautiful elemental Missy while endeavoring to avoid economic, as in scarily binding, commitment.

Another round of tussling, Missy abandoning herself to fun, follows. We're rolling on the mattress, I'm grasping satin skin, nipping and play biting and kissing, seeking to fall into Missy's silvered eyes. Oh, Missy's a roller for sure! She'll roll about laughing, seize the nape of my neck and squeeze me close, vibrate with joyous upwelling, then roll into a rage-fit lickety-split, then roll back into being a perfect angel, then...

An hour or so thereafter, as we lie on our backs side by side and sunrise ripples red-orange wavelets on the ceiling, and I feel Missy's well of unrest may have been drained, she reveals me to be a fool by asking, "Is there something, perhaps, you've forgotten?" in an acidic tone. "Don't think too hard," she continues, "I wouldn't want you to strain your childish brain! But just maybe you can remember? Why don't you try?"

I'm dumbfounded: what have I forgotten? I've endured several Missy eruptions, plus we've made love three times, as well as been awake since yesterday morning. Doesn't Missy have physical limits, if not emotional ones? Any other girl would be drop dead exhausted.

"Steven!" she persists, breathing hoarsely. "I told you I needed you to get the bad things out of me! I pleaded for you to be ruthless, unbending, as befits a bitch like me! (She pauses to catch her breath, adopts the tone and demeanor of a school principal admonishing a student.) You're thirty-seven, in years a grown man, but in reality a child, lacking in the level of maturity I need. When I inform you (She raises her voice, glares at me as if I've looted her bank account or pushed her father down a flight of steps.) that I want you to flog me senseless, do you think I'm kidding? When I inform you I need discipline until my mind clears and body settles, is it to be interpreted as an option? Is it?"

Missy thrusts her face within inches of mine, is glaring with such fury it's as if heat's erupting under my skin: none too pleased with her haughty manner, I shrug my shoulders, mutter, "Probably not."

"Probably not!" she shrieks, beside herself with incredulity—distorted of face, bursting of eyes, hyperventilating, well on her way to the limits of the amount of rage I imagine a human body's able to sustain. "Probably not! You...! Disgrace, disgusting...! Atrocious treatment of me, sick!"

Too inflamed to speak, Missy kicks at me and leaps from the bed, dashes into the living room—quickly returns to fling the belt beside me. Reobtaining the gift of speech (Ha ha! Gift!), she screams, "Pick it up, son-of-a-bitch! Do your job, damn you! Would you just do it! Punish your Missy! Yes! Your Missy! Shouldn't have to remind...cruel creep!" She collapses face down on the mattress, racked with sobs.

Flog a sobbing girl? Impossible! But Missy remedies that. "Real proud of yourself, aren't you?" she scoffs, raising her head, contempt gleaming through her tears. "Made a girl cry—such a big man you are! Well, tell you what, big man! If you don't show me mercy, bring me to heel; if you don't flay my ass and take my mind off myself (Here she raises herself to her knees, thrusts her chest out, as if boldly facing an enemy intent on harming her.), I'll turn my bad things against you—smash your family portraits, shred your drapes! Aaahhh!" she shrieks, lunging at the nightstand, seizing the alarm clock, readying herself to throw it.

I'm alongside Missy in an instant, removing the clock from her hand, wrestling her onto her belly, pinning her with a hand at the center of her back—she's snarling into the mattress, clawing at my thighs, writhing to escape. Down I bring the belt on the globes of her behind, again and again. Yeah, I'm holding Missy to the mattress and belting her, but am I the master? Is anyone ever the master of a cornered cat? If I allow Missy to escape, I'll get scratched! Who's the dominant one? Missy's the one who won't sleep; Missy's the one who won't stop raging; Missy's the one who's dictating I remain alert, attentive to her needs. I'm a slave to Missy's storms, her obedient servant—a prisoner in my own home.

What Missy requires of me is absolute dedication to exorcism of her unrest—meaning I must steel myself against urges towards milder behavior; must not allow the violence I'm doing her, sight of the welts I'm raising, to affect me; must continue applying belt-strikes even if she begs me to stop. She *has* begged me to stop before and of course I instantly complied and my reward was nails raked across my chest, accusations of not caring. She'll signal when I'm to stop and I must trust her to do so. Meanwhile, I'm to continue whipping her hard.

Fortitude I never knew I had surges forth from seemingly every sinew and guides me when I'm flogging Missy; ruthlessness I never knew I had tingles my blood; a variety of joyous terror grips my breast as the usual limitations I place on my behavior vanish; greater emotional leeway stuns me with the revelation I've ceased to be my familiar self.

"Stop, goddamned you! Release me *now*!" Missy shrieks, but—as mentioned—experience has taught me to ignore such requests, as they're essentially a test of devotion. If I give in, waver in my duty, there'll be hell to pay—we might be awake until beyond the next sunset, not kidding. Not that it's easy to continue—I'd far rather be done.

There comes a point at which it's as if I'm a disembodied spirit hovering outside my body, watching my arm continue raining cuts down—thought shifts and blurs, kaleidoscope-wise, through pictures of disruption and violence and I dissolve and sparkle in my depths. I also glimpse pictures of serenity—sunlit openings in remote forests, crystalline streams flowing through flower-bright meadows, blue waves breaking on white-sand shorelines. The pictures alternate between havoc and harmony and I continue recoiling in horror and surging with joy.

Finally, Missy raises her feet to her behind—our signal to stop. Just like that it happens: one moment she's resisting with all her strength, furiously hissing, the next she folds her legs up, silently lies still. She doesn't wish to be touched. I lie alongside her, feel as if my skin's being spun into strands of warm liquid silk, uniting with the air. Minutes later, Missy rises and strolls to the bathroom and water's running in the bathtub—the music of the water's plash and churn flows through my nerves like mist through dewy grass at dawn. When Missy returns her hair's soaked and her face as fresh and delighted as that of a ten-year-old cupping a butterfly in her hands. She eases onto the mattress with such gentle grace you'd swear she's never experienced a strident moment in her life—snuggles close, softly clasps and unclasps me, dances her fingers up and down my arms and about my back.

Then Missy sleeps, her aspect inordinately serene. It's nigh a miracle—she resembles a Madonna in a Raphael painting—an identical inner radiance of spiritual purity, blessed unity with the Creator. For this wonder alone—Missy in peaceful slumber, emanating equanimity, after eruptions of strife and strain—a night with her's worth the ordeal.

I'm feeling so quiet inside it's as if I've attained to a state of grace, and why not? A Missy night involves my depths, engages my secret places, like nothing else. The degree of emotional participation and physical exertion—contrasts of adoration, panic, desire, revulsion, rapture, anger, playfulness, fear, protectiveness—blast me clean of distracting stray thoughts, the flotsam of day-to-day life, leave me at one with myself.

In early afternoon Missy awakens like a wild animal awakens: no lazy stretching, lingering drowsiness, groggy glancing about. She awakens bright eyed, glowingly greeting the new day—sits upright immediately, bounces off the bed, is all scamper and prancing and pitter-patter, saying, "That's the time? My God! Why didn't you wake me? I've got to get to rehearsal, you know! I can't be late for rehearsal!"

Following a few minutes in the bathroom, Missy emerges fully assembled in indigo pants and white sweater shirt, hair ponytailed. She's as pristine as if she's showered—no shower, no makeup, and she's prettier than a girl who's primped for hours. Very few girls hold onto their freshness as Missy does—she never looks the worse for wear, is always as immaculately groomed as a cat. "I'm going to need cab fare, you know!" she says, darting into the kitchen for a cup of tea.

Then Missy's at the door, tote in hand. There's an air of rush-rush about her, but she pauses. "I'll see you again...soon?" she asks with sudden concern. Her eyes are abrim with hesitant hope—they're saying: "I'm out on a limb here, won't you please pull me in?" Then she says very quietly, "All the boys are scared of me. What's a poor Missy to do?"

On that note of vulnerability and hinting at danger I'll leave off telling of my latest Missy night. But of course I made it very clear to her I want and need to see her again. The Missy-Go-Round continues.

Later Robert,

S

XIV.2
Angie to Steven
cc: Ella
Saturday, September 20, 2003 10:58 AM

Stevie, it's very uplifting to be informed by my very best male friend in history I'm not unstable enough to fully dredge and renew him! Just the sort of news I want to be greeted by on a Saturday morning! Hissy Missy's indeed a wonder and I congratulate you on your find.

I'm not irrational and dangerous enough? I don't toss tantrums without warning, for no discernable reason? I'm too sensible and kind to make you afraid I might destroy your apartment? Well, I'm so sorry!

Ella, it seems our Stevie's found a wilder romp-cat to rumpus with! Seems he's disinclined to play with us because we're the cuddlesome kind of kitty, have neglected to claw and bite. Forgive us, Stevie: it really is preposterous that we've never sought to bend your fingers backwards, crack the bones. It really is inexcusable that we've never thought of punching you, kicking you, vowing to hurt you.

And Missy's not merely cute, but beautiful? Hmmmm... Seems to me you've paid me that compliment. What say, Ella? Have you heard that one too? But, hey, Missy's not merely beautiful, she's a veritable icon of the marvelous and strange! Whoa! I'd sure like to meet this marvel of a Missy, see whether she's able to enthrall a girl—I do have a certain weakness for girls. Will you pretty please fix me up with Miss Missy Mayhem, Stevie? I want to see if her extraordinarily powerful personality translates to girl-world, spellbinds me as well.

Sorry, Stevie! Couldn't resist doing a silly jealousy routine. Of course we've always been friends first and lovers second. Yet it *does* sting. Ella and I have each other, but we're so accustomed to being spoiled, sharing top girl billing in your eyes (all in the family), and for that to be gone is unavoidably disconcerting and will take some getting used to.

But why live in denial, Stevie? Why not be honest with yourself and admit you're in love? It's obvious you are. Why else would you hide Missy from us for—what?—almost two months, all the while putting us off with not even excuses, but considerable reduction of communication? Such behavior bespeaks seriousness like nothing else.

That you make a big brouhaha about telling Missy you love her is also a dead giveaway. If you didn't love her you'd toss off I-love-yous as needed to place her at ease (Shame on us girls for falling for it all the time.) and wouldn't care if it lead to expectations of commitment. You'd fob her off with fibs for as long as you could, then give her the gate the moment she seriously tried to hold you to them. Why would you worry so much about commitment, dread those conversations, if you didn't foresee commitment as a possibility? The thought of surrendering independence (and there's no surrender quite like the merging of finances variety) frightens you because you haven't ruled it out.

The Stevie I know wouldn't put up with a SpatCat like Missy for weeks if he hadn't fallen for her. There's either more happening than you're revealing, or you're deluding yourself. If Missy was a fly-by-night you would've informed us about her from the get-go, not gone silent.

The three of us have had a wonderful run and I'll be forever thankful.

I'm here—Ella's here. We know you know that.

Love,

Angie

XIV.3
Ella to Steven
cc: Angie
Saturday, September 20, 2003 11:21 AM

Aw, honey, ya mean Angie and I aren't nuts enough? Ya mean we've got to threaten violence to unlock the deepest recesses of your soul? We've got to be impossible to be around for longer than a night—if that—to inspire strongest strumming on your heartstrings? Is that why you've been neglecting us in favor of the Missy-Go-Round?

No wonder my nun habit's dusty from disuse, and I haven't been confessed and absolved for weeks, and am becoming too antsy sinful! No appointments made by you—no new rosaries in my collection!

(Angie, your email just arrived. Note the similarities. I'm persuaded we could write each other's emails and few would know the difference. I probably tend to be slightly less hissy, but our approach to a given situation's as if we're telepathically connected twins.)

Angie's right, Stevie: the fact you haven't revealed Missy's existence until now indicates the seriousness of your relationship. Love keeps its mouth shut, especially in the early stages when still feeling its way, coming to an understanding with the loved one. Love guards its privacy, emotions evolve and are jumbled. Love is cautious and protective and often feels advertising will unduly complicate, or jinx, its progress.

Another thing: you honored Robert with your first Missy communiqué instead of us so I'm sure it's been influenced by its original intended audience. As in you wrote it to a fellow male, which might explain why denial of being in love runs through it, in contrast to the content.

I miss you, Stevie, but understand. As Angie said, we're here for you, ever your devoted family. Never hesitate to reach out for any reason.

Love,
Ella

XIV.4
Steven to Angie & Ella
Saturday, September 20, 2003 11:10 PM

My dearest Angie and Ella, I know you're there for me, as I'm here for you. I'd put Missy on hold in a second if either of you needed me and trust you know that. Missy will never replace my two best friends.

You're convinced I'm in love with Missy? If so, then it's love with an expiration date. Of this I'm positive and here's why:

It's yesterday morning: we've danced all night and have returned to my place, I'm taking the day off for her. Without prelude, Missy haughtily announces she wants a bouquet of lilies, demands I obtain them immediately. To her mind, refusal's unthinkable. I'm expected to leap to action, unquestioningly indulge her whim, simply because it's her whim. OK, 1) we walked past the corner flower shop minutes before and she didn't so much as glance in its direction; 2) she's waited for me to kick off my shoes, recline on the couch; 3) she understands I'm happy to be out of the sunlight, which—as you know—I loathe after being up all night. She's being capricious for the sake of being capricious: precisely because I'm relaxing and at peace, it's time to remind me I'm dating a princess, and that such requires sacrifice and tribulation on demand.

Frowning at my hesitation to hop to like a trained dog, Missy slips the straps of her dress from her shoulders, undoes the tie at its back, wiggles until it slides to her open-toed heels; standing naked before me (because she has nothing on underneath), she—resorting to a familiar theme/tactic—says with supreme confidence, "I'm a cutie who takes care of herself and has a tight package of a petite body so it's no miracle you've brought me home—all the boys want to bring me home! (She arches her back, two-handedly pulls her hair behind her head, thrusts her breasts and belly at me.) Wake up, sweets! Snap, snap! You have the hottest little bitch with you and she's gotten naked for you, and she's gotten naked for very few, so you owe her! Get the lilies now!"

"You're far more than cute, you lift ravishing to greater heights," I say, rising and stepping towards her, opening my arms for an embrace. (Given the circumstances I suspected such a response would annoy her, but when a beauty's advertising her attributes, isn't it right and proper to express enthusiastic approval, seek to match words with action?)

"You think you can flatter your way out of this?" she hisses, jumping back in revulsion. "You think I can be bought off with slick phrases, calculated to melt foolish girls? Do you think I'm foolish?" She's staring at me with such fury an uncomfortable chill seizes my spine.

"How can you possibly think I'd ever think you're foolish?" I answer, aware I might be accused of persisting with flattery.

"How dare you answer a question with a question!" she yells. "Oh, you're really a creep now! What's the issue with lilies? My God, who are you? Little man denies devoted girl a simple wish! I honestly don't recognize you in this denying and petty personality! For shame!"

"Wow!" I exclaim, annoyance rising. "We're dancing ourselves dizzy all night, carrying each other to blissful heights, and you say such a thing to me?—make up nasty rubbish, insult me for kicks? For shame, yourself! And since when do you care about flowers? You make fun of men who've sought to woo you with flowers and baubles, are doing this to needle me. It's part of the nonsense you tossed off the other day, while just *so* pleased with yourself, about men wanting to be leashed, brought to heel. You're acting out a gratuitous power role, for the purpose of preening before your ego's mirror—feeding your vanity. As I said then, I have no intention of being leashed. But that's just a case of me vainly seeking to escape your irresistible charm, right? I don't know my own mind, right? I want a mommy who'll take control, absolve me of the responsibility of making decisions, but refuse to admit it, right?

"May I ask you something, princess?" I continue. "What does mindlessly obeying capricious requests have to do with affection? Do you think pushing me out the door to obtain something you neither need nor care about has any point, other than permitting you to feel like a despot, congratulate yourself on collaring me? What the hell for? Why can't we relax, enjoy one another's company? Why unpleasantness for no reason other than to primp your self-esteem? Why equate love—because I do love you—with willingness to be shoved around?"

"Do you want me to go home?" Missy asks very softly, switching from glaring to putting on a hurt face, then to looking what I'd classify as defiant-delectable: she brings a smoldering look into half-lidded eyes, runs her tongue about the full circle of her lips, thrusts her chest at me more emphatically, does the tighten-muscles-and-radiate-desire thing girls do when they wish to pull a man into their magnetic field.

Before I can respond Missy switches back to outrage, yells, "Look how I dressed for you! Why not try to appreciate these shoes? (She bends to remove her shoes, then holds them by their straps, dangles and jiggles them.) I bought them special for you, and they aren't cheap! I dress with care for you, always look my best for you! I ask myself each time before coming over, 'What will please Steven the most?' Getting ready for you is a two hour labor of love, I kill myself to be pretty for you! And now you, in incomprehensible selfishness, won't do an eensy-weensy thing for me, get lilies! You question if I need them, when the fact I want them should be enough!" This last declaration is made in a tone of hurt and dismay—she's regarding me with a heartrending expression of appeal.

Whoa! Missy's reversed my perspective quick as a gust of wind—she's not feigning the wobbling look in her eyes, trembling of her lips. Her logic, from her point of view, is undeniable: she does carefully consider what to wear before we hook up, as if the fate of civilization's hanging in the balance. It's beside the point that she places far more importance on how she dresses than I do and she'll always be off the charts stunning: the fact she puts a great deal of thought and feeling into her appearance on my behalf leads me to wonder if I'm being selfish. And, hey, it is delightful that Missy's always decked out to perfection. I hinted it doesn't overly concern me? That's a lie! One of the most endearing things about Missy is that she's always flawlessly coifed, dolled up fluffy and elegant. It's enthralling when a girl delectably presents herself, especially since it's implied she wholeheartedly intends to follow through on the presentation, treat one to a memorable time. If Missy's dolled up in tantalizing clothing—a veritable representation of desire—she'll be a wild hungering nymphet, overwhelm me with fulfillment. If a capricious request here and there's the price I pay for such delight, what of it? Paltry of me to succumb to shortsighted pride!

Seconds transpire as I contemplate the situation, hesitate before speaking—the pause isn't to Missy's liking. Her imploring hurt face twists into a snarl—her eyes flare. "What's the matter, you don't like what you see?" she asks. "Not good enough for you? (She does a couple above-her-head kicks, first one leg, then the other.) You think girls like me fall from trees? I defy you to find another girl who loves you like I do! Another girl who thinks, always, about what she says to you before she says it for fear of upsetting you! (This inaccurate proclamation brings a smile to my face.) Oh, you doubt it? You laugh? You don't think it's true because I'm angry? Why are you so mean to me?"

Missy collapses to the floor in tears; her whole body's shaking. She wraps her arms around my shins, gazes up at me with pleading eyes. "I'm sorry—I... Oh, please get me the lilies! Please!"

Seeing Missy at my feet... God! Her distress appears from out of nowhere; she surges from frightening places as I've never seen. She's overwhelmed with very real despair, and shame on me for allowing matters to go this far and not indulging her request from the beginning. Her self-esteem's hanging in the balance; the lily-errand's been transformed into a measure of how strong our bond is. The bottom line is Missy's a mood-tossed innocent: irritating as her capriciousness may be, she never resorts to it out of malice; she succumbs to it, as the ocean succumbs to tsunamis. Being involved with Missy carries the responsibility of knowing when to shield her from herself, and it's inexcusable that I've failed to do so and brought her to this state.

"I'm sorry, Missy!" I say, not daring to touch her. "I'm tired and cranky, and I know that's no excuse, a bad excuse, I should be better for you. I'm getting the lilies right now. Please stop crying." She releases my legs, trembling; tears are flowing down her cheeks. I dress myself probably faster than I've done in my life, fly out the door.

I purchase bouquets of five varieties of lily, as well as a rosemary bush in bloom. What greets me when I reenter my apartment? Missy's sitting on the floor, her back against the living room couch, with tears streaming from her eyes and her hair in disarray. Close to her is a heap of shattered glass. At first I don't understand, then realize the heap of glass was once the top of my coffee table. She gives me a poisonous look, says in an unnerving flatness of tone, "I wanted to kill myself."

I was prepared for additional strife, as well as hoping Missy would be partially pacified by my fetching of the flowers, but I was far from prepared for shattered glass, announcements concerning self-harm, Missy appearing crazed: disbelief and fear erupts in my breast such that it's as if I'm momentarily cast out of my body, flung into the distance.

"This is what you want, isn't it?" Missy says very slowly, in the same flatness of tone, while picking up a triangle of broken glass and bringing it to her throat. "You'd like this, wouldn't you?" she continues, making a cutting movement with the glass. "You'd be off the hook if I was dead!"

I might as well be lost in an inhospitable wilderness: I'm certainly deriving no comfort from being at home. "Home" no longer exists; the walls of my apartment—barrier they represent against the outside world's unpredictability—have dissolved; the dangers inherent in living hand to mouth in the wilds of indifferent nature have taken up residence in my living room. What's real? What can be counted upon to dispense feelings of security and comfort? If not my apartment, then what? Missy's as good as torn me from the world I've known since birth—I no longer reside in civilization. As for my eyesight, it's clouding; as for my voice, it's as if originating from a throat other than mine—I'm saying, "Missy, stop it—put the glass down! Please, put the glass down! *(Her eyes flare; she presses her other hand to the air, by way of warning me not to approach.)* Alright—alright! I'm staying over here—I won't take one step towards you. I'm letting you put the glass down, OK? I love you, Missy. Don't you know that? I love you very much."

"Love me?" she hisses, tossing the triangle of glass back into the pile with a gesture of contempt. "You love me but you hurt me! You insult me! You do just the most beastly things to me, don't appreciate..." She breaks off sobbing, slumps to her side, curls up on the floor.

The room's swirling—I'm gazing at Missy and the heap of glass half-blindly; flickering in and out of focus is the empty metal frame of the coffee table and the objects, now scattered about, that once sat upon it—there's a great deal of fury evident in what Missy's done, I can almost hear her accompanying shrieks, see her smashing the glass. And now? She's curled up—shivering—crying; her cheeks are quivering, face is a picture of abject misery. We had a wonderful night of dancing. We'd returned here, I was in highest spirits, and now surrounded by hell.

"I said I was sorry," I hear myself saying. "I've brought you the lilies, and a rosemary plant." Only now do I realize I'm still holding the flowers: I gaze at the colorful petals in surprise, watch myself set them on the dining table; and that diversion of attention, slight though it be, is apparently enough to make me angrily aware of how unnecessary our present circumstances are. I suddenly hear myself exclaiming, "This is insane! How can I leave you alone, trust you? Who are you?"

At one point I'm saying, "Apparently my heinous crime was being at peace with us—flush with joy—following our night out. You just had to toss stones in our calm lake, stir up waves. You've arrived at the insane and destructive notion that I must constantly be on tenterhooks on your behalf, never daring to relax, always prepared to indulge child-ish senseless whims. You're a mixed up, spoiled, only child brat with no sense of reciprocation—no sense of responsibility for doing your part to make a relationship work. In fact, what you're after is an abusive relationship and I want nothing to do with such poison. Life's far too short, and it's just plain sick and I'm not going to be a part of it."

"I am not," Missy says, sitting bolt upright and looking me straight in the eye. "I am not interested in an abusive relationship." She's self-assured and collected when she makes this statement; her enun-ciation's clear, even, firm: what's real? Missy's still the picture of a wounded disturbed little girl, but is suddenly laser sharp where words and tone of voice and eye contact are concerned: a redoubled chill goes up my spine. Is she putting on an act? Are her trembling and tears an act?

My gaze whirls from Missy to the heap of sinisterly gleaming shards again as I ponder the contrast between her tearful trembling face and the self-possession with which she's enunciated, "I am not interested in an abusive relationship." What sort of cold-blooded calculating fiend am I involved with? flashes through my thoughts. Then I'm yelling again, "Will I ever know what trifling thing will set you off? Nuts over flowers! And I went and got them for you! Hell! Are you laughing at me behind that touching veneer of tears? Are you that evil?"

"No!" she shrieks, flailing her hands near her cheeks. "I am not laughing at you, Steven, never could! How can you think I could? I love you! God, how I love you!" She collapses against the couch, sobbing again.

How long will this nerve-wrenching—uselessly energy consuming—back-and-forth between us continue? A delicate petite girl in misery: how can I not find myself weakening again, hesitant to be annoyed? On the other hand Missy's a mature woman, for Christ's sake, thirty-two years old, five years younger than me. She's an oft employed dancer on Broadway who fills in as a hugely popular aerobics instructor between runs, has social tact and savvy and intelligence to burn. She's shrewd at business, is the highest paid aerobics instructor in town because she knows her worth and how to negotiate, could teach me a thing or two about finances. She's very far from being a child. So, on account of my reflections concerning Missy's maturity, my anger returns. "Very becoming, your distressed-little-girl act!" I say. "Is that how you finish guys off?—make them feel guilty when they resist your baby antics, flagrant misuse of their affection? I must say you're very skilled!"

"How dare you," Missy says acerbically, abruptly rising to her knees—gone is all trace of trembling. "Head's up," she continues, leaning to pick up the ceramic vase that once sat atop my smashed coffee table. She throws it at the wall, shattering it to bits. She's gazing at me with mockery and defiance. Instants later, she springs at me.

"Are you totally out of your mind?" I yell, extending my arms to keep her away. "There's glass bits all over the place already, for Christ's sake! Wasn't enough, needed more, had to do the vase! What's wrong with you? You're barefoot! Want to cut yourself? *Stop*, to you hear?"

She pauses mid-step, glances about as if awakened from a dream, says—I swear—with a trace of a smile, "Right, there is sort of a mess."

"Sort of a mess?" I scream. "Sort of a mess? There are shards of glass on the carpet, cushions of the couch! Do you understand they're razor sharp, will cut us? I don't dare take my shoes off, you should put yours on! Have you any sense at all?" I'm pacing, gesticulating at the glass. "How hard did you hit the tabletop, you deranged maniac? And you dare smash the vase in front of me, as if this is all a child's game? Jesus bloody Christ! You *are* going to go home, and now!"

"Sweetie," she coos, lightly darting forward, grasping my wrists, affectionately squeezing. "I know I've been bad—your Missy's not perfect. I'll clean up this mess and make it right, OK? Mommy's not going home—she's going to make it right." She scampers to her tote, reaches within for slippers and places them on her feet, is soon at the entryway closet, bringing out the vacuum with a smile.

The kindness that's softened Missy's visage, blithe prancing quality infusing her step and gestures—the innocent-little-girl aura surrounding her! I'm too awestruck at the transformation to persist with getting her out the door. It's incredible how adept Missy is at flipping from one emotional extreme to its opposite—I've never known such a mood-change chameleon. She's able to switch realms of feeling instantaneously, with little memory of moments ago. Sure, it's a knife that cuts both ways, but also an indication of how readily she forgives.

True to her word, Missy cleans up every trace of glass: tosses the large pieces in boxes, vacuums the carpet and furniture, disposes of the boxes and dust bag via the trash chute in the hall. She insists on doing everything herself, won't allow me to assist, says it's "girl work." In watching her cheerfully work, listening to her happy pitter-patter, giggling jests, I understand she's decided there will be no further conflict today. She knows I'm trusting her to be good and will be so.

So Missy's smashed my coffee table and a vase, rained glass in my living room, and gotten away with it on account of her fundamentally sweet and loving disposition, which is on glorious display and flowing through my blood and nerves—the most succulent psychic balm a man could hope to be treated to, sensation suspended in otherworldly waking dream equilibrium. Missy *always* eclipses conflict with the fruits of conflict, the destination's more than worth a road perilously traveled.

As for what transpires in the bedroom, I'll keep that to myself, only say that when I finally sleep it's a gripping sensual sleep, continuation of the state of bliss I'm in when slipping into it. I awaken entwined with Missy, feeling like a child surrounded by colorful toys in a lush garden.

Here's something worth mentioning: shortly after we're in the bedroom Missy's seated lotus-wise on the bed, gazing at me stirringly, and announces, "No one can say there's no passion in this relationship!" She doesn't need to elaborate because it's clear what she's thinking. She's informing herself she's in a beautiful, tumultuous, storm-tossed relationship, the likes of which only the fortunate few experience. She's inordinately pleased she's found a man who won't turn tail and run, when so many are afraid of her. We're in this together, will taste of high drama galore, stay fresh and young all our lives, never stagnate and be bored, always envied by other couples: we're *so* lucky! She once said: "Love is when two people sometimes want to kill each other because of what they put each other through, then there's the make-up sex that's so electric they're in a condition of wonderment and seeing stars."

At one point, as Missy's sound asleep beside me, I'm addressing myself along the lines of, "How long will I be tangling with this hellcat brat? Should I end it today? Is the stress worth it? Stress not only because of what I know she's capable of, but also—more so—because I'm wondering what further travails are in store? A rational man would pretend all's peachy and then, once Missy exits the building, instruct the doormen to never let her in again. A rational man would refuse to answer the phone and turn off the answering machine's volume, erase messages she leaves without listening to them—sever all contact until she gives up and finds someone else to bedevil. But I'm not a bit rational where Missy's concerned! And what's rationality, anyway? Rationality equals: playing it safe. And there's far more to experience than playing it safe—boredom, eventual stagnation, is what comes from playing it safe. Plus, when all's said and done, Missy's an absolutely honest girl—an utterly sincere girl. I swear there isn't anything about her life that she hasn't told me, nothing she's omitted from her past; even when she does a brattish conniving something or other, she openly confesses it afterwards, and with such sweetness brimming in her eyes.

"Hell! Breaking up with Missy would be emotional suicide, there's absolutely no hesitation in firmly believing that! Missy's a mirror in which I see myself stripped of the falsity with which society drapes and conceals a personality. When I gaze into Missy's eyes the cumbersome dreck of civilization—shallow show-and-tell, preoccupation with trifles—melts away. For brief moments I appear to glimpse a world before self-consciousness existed, when one was one and the same as one's thoughts—before perception splintered to bits and a personality became like unto the shards of a shattered mirror, each reflecting a different angle of orientation and contradicting the other, warring with the other. When I gaze into Missy's eyes the din of self-dividedness departs: I'm a free flowing spring welling from my depths, not questioning in which direction I'm headed, simply thrillingly alive.

"Ditch Missy? Yeah, right! There are few things as debilitating as girls who are always nice. No moodiness—no drama—no ups and downs—no challenge—no opportunities to mature. The always-nice girls are like a monotonous parking lot of pavement: no surprises, no siree; and no conflict from which authentic peace of mind is birthed."

A final observation: Missy inspires me to protect her as no girl's done before—the trust she's placed in me, and her fundamental isolation on account of her stunning beauty and untamed disposition, is capable of yes, bringing me to tears, sweeping me into vivid intimation of the vulnerability that stalks us humans every hour. Civilization's but a veneer and we humans are still wandering desolate steppes as indifferent majestic nature carries on as if we're not here, and in my humble opinion people in love are less blind to our vulnerability than those who are not. I'm likely *very* much in love with Missy and, just maybe, the expiration date's further in the future than I'm able to realize, and maybe there's *no* expiration date whatsoever. So there's an admission.

Time for levity:

Missy loves conflict and has the temper
To prove it—she knows how to pout, whimper,
Sulk, summon tears, put on a wounded face;
How to be cold, aloof, erase all trace
Of regard from her voice and glance alike;
How to show disgust in the way she strikes
A pose, fling rage with the tone of a strut
Across the room. But how Missy does rut
Between arguments: such sexual pearls
Aren't found in the arms of peace-loving girls.

Bye for now, dearest Angie and Ella!
Love,
Steven

XIV.5
Angie & Ella to Steven (from Ella's apartment)
cc: Angie
Sunday, September 21, 2003 2:06 AM

Me first, Stevie, your Angie:

Was about to beg you cease with the miraculous Missy Mayhem info, mention we're well aware you have Missyitis and there's no need for you to rub it in, but that's what Ella and I are here for, right? We're pleased to be your sounding board! You've admitted you're *likely* in love with Missy?—that there *may* not be an expiration date? Steps in the right direction, even if you're not allowing yourself to, for reasons I'm failing to comprehend, wholly wake up and own it, parade it.

Nothing strange about you and Missy spatting, it's added proof your love's authentic. Being in thrall to the loved one can breed intervals of resentment, particularly as people hardly ever plan on falling in love—impulses to regain independence barge in and the loved one's not likely to respond favorably. Is there an inescapable element of hostility associated with love? Some lovers definitely bring turmoil to one another. (Ha! Love a rose-strewn path, with birds blithely singing? Only in silly romance novels, of which I'm unfortunately overfamiliar.)

But I'm wondering about Missy's propensity to yell "Kill me!"—brandish shards of glass, speak of letter-opener stabbings. What of the kitchen knives? Have you hidden them? Better do so, before she starts waving one around. (I'm *mostly* kidding: Missy appears to have a fondness for melodramatic threats, minus serious follow-through.)

Sorry, Stevie, but I need to say I *really* miss the lover part of our friends first and lovers second relationship, our frolicsome fun. Who else is going to bring out the Marie Antoinette in me? Who else is the caring jokester who greatly contributed to brightening my days? Ella and I have each other, but we've always had you to provide engaging balls-out masculine counterpoint! You're irreplaceable, Stevie! Right, Ella? We're two girls in love who had the perfect highly inventive, anything-goes-and-the-further-it-goes-the-better, man in our lives. Never to subtract from you, Sweetest, but Stevie's been icing on the cake.

Stevie, I'm a bit depressed despite myself—not seeking to be selfish, no Sir! You know I wish you and Missy the best and love you! We always knew you'd be moving on—there isn't a woman alive who'd allow you to continue playing with us while she's in a relationship with you.

Love,

Angie

###########

Hi Stevie—it's your Ella:

Missy's thirty-two? I was thinking she was younger, and she winds up being six years older than me. She teaches aerobics between dancing gigs? Maybe Angie and I ought to take her class and see what the fussy's about? Maybe we ought to do a girl assessment (Completely objective and unbiased—ha ha!) of Missy? train our female radar upon her? I'm very curious about Missy, and know Angie is as well! We'd like to see who's enthralled you—the girl who knows how far she can push misbehavior, then get off scot-free with ready-to-wear sweetness, trotted out just in time to get you to bless and forgive her. (Surely,

Stevie, you'd be disappointed if my claws didn't show a bit, since I've been displaced in your primary affections. You'd think I was one of the freaks of nature known as a "nice" girl if I failed to needle a bit.)

Sincerely, Stevie, I'm very happy you've found someone who's caught ahold of you from the inside out. It's clear Missy does for you what Angie and I never have: propel you to a place where you must make use of all available emotional resources to survive, where you're immersed in rejuvenating disequilibrium. I'm strongly sensing there will *not* be a Missy expiration date. I've noticed that, oodles of strife notwithstanding, your Missy nights always end on an overwhelmingly positive note.

I love you dearly, Stevie!

Blessings and Love,

Ella

XIV.6
Steven to Angie & Ella
Sunday, September 21, 2003 2:22 AM

My dearest Angie and Ella,

It's not as if I expected my Missy revelation to be greeted with overwhelming joy, so why am I feeling unpleasantly shocked into reality? I'm depressed due to the farewell tone of your emails.

I seek to place myself in your shoes: would I wish to be treated to the details of either of you spending a night with a man you'd become seriously involved with? No! So I'll cease telling of Missy.

Angie and Ella, we've carried one another for a long time, grown together immeasurably. I love you! Sometimes I almost wish I hadn't met Missy so we could continue carrying on. But it's an "almost" wish.

We need to meet for dinner soon. Do you agree?

Love,

Steven

XIV.7
Angie & Ella to Steven (from Ella's apartment)
cc: Angie
Sunday, September 21, 2003 2:38 AM

Angie here, Loved One:

Of course we'll meet for dinner. I'll always look forward to having dinner with my best male friend ever. As you aptly stated, "we've carried one another for a long time, grown together immeasurably."

We've played together for over three years, spun our senses into swirlsville galore. Whatever follows, we've shared a great deal of priceless experiences, and I'll always count myself very fortunate.

Is Tuesday good for you?

Love,

Angie

#########

Ella now, Angel:

You're certainly immersed in MissyWorld—all else dissolving, previous emotional ties turning unreal. You're whisked away on love's sails and Angie and I are on the beach you've abandoned—we're fading from awareness because you're busy negotiating love's storming sea.

Why did I write the above? Because of the halting manner in which you proposed dinner, as if we don't know each other as well as we do.

Hope to see you Tuesday, or anytime soon.

Love,

Ella

XIV.8
Angie to Ella
Tuesday, September 23, 2003 9:49 PM

Sweetie, I won't hide I'm depressed, a supportive rug yanked from under me during our dinner with Stevie—all's different, an unpleasant wake up call. I feel shoddy asking, but am I able to be friends with a man if we're no longer playing around? Liking a man and wishing to know him implies sexual magnetism, and to deny such magnetism's existence, pretend it isn't there when it's setting my nerves atwitter, isn't only unhealthy but impossible. Face it: if a wonderful man doesn't wish to rut with me—if there isn't eye contact that leads to lip contact that leads to an embrace that leads to easing one another to the floor—I don't see the point, and it's also painful. I'll find a new man to be "friends" with—a man eager to seed my garden, burst my flower into bloom.

So much has passed between Stevie and us, and for him to be sitting next to us except also miles away, speaking with restraint, neither touching us nor wishing to do so; for him to be radiant with feelings neither you nor I have inspired, vividly under another girl's influence, as good as entranced with deep involvement... I almost feel like I won't be able to see him again. Friends we are and always will be, but I don't feel I could endure another dinner with Stevie like tonight's. He's one of the two people who know me as well as I know myself—you, of course, being the other—and, to be blunt, it's just gone down the drain.

All things pass. Nothing's permanent. The only constant is perpetual change. And today's the first day of fall, how nastily appropriate! All's falling around me for sure! The one man I have virtually no secrets from has jumped ship, found fulfillment in another's arms. The foliage will be wearing its corpse colors soon—the oranges and reds idiots think is beautiful. Fans of fall colors are a milder version of the parasites who screech to a halt to stare at highway accidents—going around gloating at the death parade in the trees! Soon every last leaf will fall and rot to brown and the trees will be skeletons rattling in the wind! How dismal!

Autumn will hit me doubly hard this year, without our Stevie to keep me absorbed in frolic, constantly laughing. I'm not looking forward to the next few weeks at all. But enough—I hate being a whiner.

Your,

AutumnAngishedAngie

XIV.9
Ella to Angie
Tuesday, September 23, 2003 11:21 PM

Yes, sadness was hovering about our dinner with Stevie, but why mope? What's the good of that? I'm surprised, Angie! As you're fond of mentioning, you're the most mature of us. Or are you? Maybe it's a lie. Seems to me if you really were, you'd be more adaptable to change.

To see Stevie for dinner, and for him not to kick-start any-thing—for us not to be with him now—mostly strikes me as just plain strange. The sky's on the ground, world's topsy-turvy! Stevie's blood surges at the thought of his mayhemish Missy instead of us! What was once a sure path to frolic no longer is. Well, what are we going to do about it, if not be thankful we still have each other, and get on with frolic-flings?

Summer's departed, autumn's arrived? So it's melodrama time? Ridiculous, Darling! And some people swoon at the sight of fall col-ors? Let them swoon! And let us set about swooning over something far more substantial and thrilling, such as reaching up each other's winter coats on 5th Avenue during lunch hour as swarms of pedestri-ans swirl by.

What's so bad about autumn when summer's dragged on for so long? Don't you get tired of too much of a good thing? Or, rather, doesn't too much of a good thing result in surfeit and tedium? I, for one, am sick of heat and humidity and welcome autumn's chill! When the temperature plummets and first frost arrives I get plenty hot on the inside, by way of compensation. You're selling yourself short, Angie:

warm weather's hardly essential to keep our blood surging—we're fit healthy beasts who can't help but run down rapture in all seasons. Besides, without autumn and winter to cast a chill on summer, what would become of springtime's rush-gush of insanely delirious energy?

Have you forgotten what titillation it is to stroll about in winter draped in furs or down with only silk slips and thigh highs on underneath?—how delightful it is when cold slides up our legs and goose-bumps them, our body's bottom half shivering while its top half's crispy warm? The contrast between warm and cold goes straight to my fertile crescent, veins shimmering—thighs are freezing and quimmykins is soaked and flowing, sweetly bothered. You've said: "Isn't it funny how I seldom need a finger pleasing flowerpuss as much as when part of me's feeling frostbitten?" Wake up, Angie! We're delight-in-contrast wenches!

Why the blubbering concerning onset of autumn? I know why! Autumn's an excuse to drama-queen, an annual ritual. Every autumn I need to remind you onset of cold ignites our inner blaze, inspires rebellion along the lines of: "So summer's over, everything's dying, dreariness setting in? So what? Just try keeping two hot-blooded strumpets down! It can't be done! As with a bonfire on a breezy night, the sting of cold's only going to whip us into a stronger blaze."

Although there's certainly nothing drama-queen about losing Stevie. I attempted to gloss it over but am also engulfed in gloom. At dinner he was the picture of a man in love: he's never looked like that on our behalf. Stevie is, indeed, irreplaceable and I'm scrambled! But why waste time bewailing unalterable reality? And the more we do so, the more we come off as self-centered weaklings. We're happy for Stevie—anything less would be disgraceful. So let it go, Angie. There are adventures galore awaiting and we shall rush into their embrace.

Your,

WildestWintertimeWench

XIV.10
Angie to Ella
Wednesday, September 24, 2003 11:07 PM

Gratitude, Sweetie, for lifting the spirits of your distressed Angie, who lowered herself to whining! But the squeaky wheel does get greased, right? How lusciously you greased and rebalanced my wheel.

Letting yourself in before dawn and sneaking up to my bed, pouncing on me in your faux lynx while looking scrumptiously like a lynx, wildcat eyes ablaze! Was I dreaming? You were shaking my shoulders, admonishing me thus: "I'm fed up with your blubbering! So what if autumn's here, leaves turn brown? What's that have to do with the fact your pussycat's willing to come over anytime to rutalaciously romp 'til she's a frazzled feline seeing double, dizzied clean out of her fur? Leaves fall off trees? Boo hoo hoo! Poor lil' Angie, sniveling on account of alteration of the scenery! Silly lil' Angie, dreaming up an inane reason to be upset—desperate for something to get melodramatic about—as if she doesn't have a girlfriend who loves her! Goofy lil' Angie, who needs an ass swatting!" Still rubbing my groggy eyes I was when you flipped me onto my tummy, spanked my behind: I was so surprised I whipped my head around to confirm it was you.

"Astonished, are you?" I hear you say. "That makes both of us! I don't believe the way you're wailing about unalterable things, insulting yourself by feeling sorry for yourself! Dead leaves are inevitable, as is Stevie's separation from us. He was waiting all along for a wild willful beauty to smash through his jocular exterior, propel him into unfamiliar territory, where he sometimes doesn't know where his foundations are. We were Stevie's emotional holding pattern. He's now in a soul-altering relationship. What could be more natural, and necessary, for him? So stop being stunned Stevie's finally met his match! Get the bloody hell up!" And here you yank me to my knees, you wild lynx cat you! "Am I dogmeat?" you continue, nearly shouting. "Am I a drab? a wilting wallflower? a frigid prude, my veins drained of blood? Answer me!"

"You're sunlight blasting through dismal clouds, putting gloom and depression to flight—you're light, joy, and revelation!" I gush.

"Then why did you write these highly insulting words? (You read from a print-out of my last email.)—'Autumn will hit me doubly hard this year, without our Stevie to keep me absorbed in frolic, constantly laughing.'? Do you feel I'm unequal to the task of making you mirthful? Do you?"

"Darling..."

"Damn right I'm your darling," you interrupt yelling, "and don't you forget it! I'm your loving lynxish darling, and I'll keep you in laughter—keep you in lust!" You yank open your coat, are ultra-sizzlesville in a topless negligee—see-through black, frilly white trim. "Meeyowwwwl!" you cry, knocking me onto my back and flinging yourself onto me, grinding my tummy with yours, swatting my arms down.

No sooner am I subdued, sigh-shivering and surrenderish with delight, than you abruptly exit me, sit upright, back away. "Not here!" you say. "You don't taste of this she-cat in your safe apartment! You must accompany her into the wilds! She only kitty-licks you in doorways!"

I seek to pull you onto me, but you scamper from the bed. "Up and out of bed with lazy Angie—get up!" you say, pulling me to the floor. "Get a fur, it's chilly out! Nothing but the fur and shoes! See? I'm taking off my flimsy! (You squiggle from your nightie, half tripping in your haste when it becomes tangled on an ankle.) A mid-shin-length fur like mine, mind you, because you'll be broadsided by arctic winds! Chill will do crybaby Angie worlds of good, knock her out of simper-slop mode!"

"Yesterday was Autumn's first day, today it's making itself felt," you observe once we're on the sidewalk strolling east. "Unseasonably cold, in the mid-thirties, special for you! Because you were bewailing summer's end so badly! Since when has blubbering changed anything and since when have you, of all people, been unaware of the fact? Bellyacher Angie! Aren't you ashamed of yourself? Huh?"

What you're saying's imminently sensible, but will I admit it? Nay! It's far more fun to resist so's to prod you further into wildcat-mode. I'm our designated disciplinarian; I wield Miss Whippie, lash you 'til you quiver and thrash and cry, but I'm not averse to relinquishing the reins—it's nice to be on vacation from Take Charge Bitch. So I say: "Sweetie, it's frightfully frigid, ridiculous to be here! Please let's return to my cozy bed before I catch cold!" I tug at your arm, seek to turn us about.

"Looking for this cat to claw you?" you hiss, seizing my fur's collar in front, shoving me backwards against a building, spreading scarlet nails near my face. "It's beyond belief what I've got to put up with! You're unable to appreciate the beauty of this pristine morning? streetlamp amber extra vivid, like a liquid, in crisp clear air? You're stubbornly a dreary complainer? I dare you to tell me you're failing to appreciate what a gift it is to be outside in bracing breeze before sunrise!"

"Are you loony? It's icy and dismal, death's on the wing! Cold's killing everything, freezing my blood!" I respond. Ooooo, baby! How wonderfully your kitty eyes spark, fasten on me, turn predatory.

"I'll show you icy, ridiculous girl! (You fumble at my coat's front, scowl at its buttons.) You buttoned? Add bad manners to naïveté, why don't you! One miserable faux pas after another! Open your coat, do it now! Pah! (You grab the front of my coat, yank it rough enough to rip buttons off, they clattering at our feet.) See? A scrumptious shock! Chilly wind clasping your nakedness, give thanks! Far from killing anything, cold's the wakeup medicine you need, unleashing rejuvenating lifeforces!"

"Frightful stabbing horror!" I complain, vigorously shaking. "And my buttons! Very mean of you, Ella, to tear my buttons off, they're not cheap, are carved opals I think!" I bend to retrieve the buttons.

"Shamefully misplace-prioritied girl!" you yell, preventing me from kneeling. "Materialistic trash is what you care about when an inflamed kitty's intent on loving you to thrillsville? Here, into this doorway! Now!" Oh, Ella! The door to Paradise has swung open.

"This lynx cat's a gonna rape and bother you delirious, lucky girl," you coo once we're within the doorway, immediately inserting two fingers in my wet warm place, wriggling them fierce, such that I tumble into gasping undulation. Where are we? Near East End? Silver-amber streetlamp light's spilling through the outer door's glass, lapping against our skin—oscillating colors meshing with your oscillating touch.

"Just perfect!" I gasp, inhaling deeply, greedy for more air.

"Ah, you like it, do you? You're a prize rut-slut—my prize this magnificent morning!" Nefarious minx, you full-palm seize my right breast with the hand you've chilled on the tile wall! How I jump and shake! I can barely feel the wall at my back, or even my fur on me. "Much more in store!" you grin, baring kitty fangs. "Time to truly electroshock my strangely not-herself Angie! My out-of-character whining Angie!" Tickled pink you may be, but it doesn't blunt the edge of mischief, sugarcoat action. You spin me around so I'm facing the wall, yank both flaps of my coat behind my back, press my nakedness firmly against ice cold tiles, hold me there. It's not easy to describe the stun of the chill—an inner clawing burn so forceful I nearly flood.

Where are your salvational fingers? My pink pansy's in painful bloom, slippery hot and swelling, craving your skills, inner slithers! I'm a battleground of heat and ice rushing towards twatsie for resolution, and need you there! "How dare you abandon me!" I hiss. Your teeth appear at the nape of my neck—soft play-bite scraping. Throb-throbs are whipping up my spine—I'm arching my back, leaning backwards onto you, wide open in front with legs spread. "Shape up and get with it and rescue me, mean girl! No more pussyfooting with flowerpuss!"

"So Angie feels a dictatorial attitude's wise? She's wrong! Maybe I'll leave!" you giggle. But then I'm spinning towards the floor as you pull me by my ponytail and, once I'm on my knees, mercy me! You reinsert your fingers in quimmy, and not a minute's needed to fling me half-fainting into a flood. Oh, my lynxish lass! My face is buried in your coat, I'm biting fur, shaking, moaning—seizing handfuls of fur to steady myself. "Please," I manage to say, "get on me and lick my tits!"

"Nay, my Sweet—upsy-daisy. *(You stand, assist me to my feet.)* This building's huge. Sun isn't rising yet but some people will probably be emerging to greet the new day, a miracle no one's interrupted us. No more messing about on the floor. Bothered nipples? Fine, stand here."

You fasten your mouth on a nipple, semi-clamping with teeth, sucking hard—ouch! Send me through the ceiling, why don't you! Irritation exceeds relief! "Only licking, please," I say. "Make my chest wet."

A shadow appears behind the inner door's opaque glass and the doorknob's rattling, turning. Ol' faithful strikes again: soon as a negative thing's mentioned aloud we're jinked! Your mention of people emerging has conjured forth an interruption. My arms slap my coat shut almost before your head jerks clear, then we're out the outer door on the sidewalk—two sweet innocent girls out for a pre-dawn stroll.

"I, for one, adore today's winter preview," you smile. "The frosty wind's a swizzle stick stirring me nutsy—raises goose bumps, grimaces my face and grits my teeth. Then blood rushes to where the cold's attacking and heats me from within, flips me inside out, seems to spread me across the sky. Admit it, trollop! You're glad lynx-cat Ella's dragged you outside."

"Am I ever, Lynxish Miss, and please finish what you've started," I say, we crossing East End Avenue to Carl Schurz Park. "I'm heated despite cold nipping at my ankles, whisking up my thighs, or probably because of it—shuddersville head to toe, sailboated out of my senses."

Whoa! A few people are walking their dogs, even if sunrise is still a no-show. I'm jerking at your wrist, guiding us to the circular flowerbed down the stairs on the off-path where less people go—semi-isolated in the depression, obscured by tall shrubs. Once there I'm seated on the flowerbed's rim—open my fur, thrust my chest skywards, gaze into your giggling eyes. I'm cradling your head, gently rocking, thrilling to your talented tongue and lips at my nips as your hair swishes on my chest, spills down my tummy, runs in rivulets over my upraised thighs. I'm half-unseeingly gazing at greenery and flowers: so incongruous, a summery scene (leaves blessedly not turning yet) in frigid air. Nor to forget the titillating aura of surprise—unexpectedness of our excursion. Tough to believe I was fast asleep an hour ago, glory be! Now outside in wintry wind in a garden pre-sunrise, licked by a laughing lynx-girl.

Ah, Ella! The tickled-to-death light in your eyes when you raise them to mine after making me gush—your luminous visage framed by your black curls glistened by wavery gold lamplight—the spiral-patterned cobblestones seeming to whirl, late blooming flowers brushing us, shrubs and trees walling us in: all combine to tear me from the present, carry me back in time. As when, in reading the Decameron, one's flooded with the peacefulness of a bygone age, glimpse of life as it was previous to technological ravages, modern clatter and clutter. I'm in NYC, surrounded by little that isn't artificial, but tasting of a pre-industrial, comparatively unsullied, world. A priceless gift, Sweetheart.

Then our escapade's abrupt ending: you flash your watch in my face, tear me from sex-daze reverie. Although I *do* greet the unrelenting march of the minutes laughing—you've made me such a happy nymphet, I giggle in your watch's face for a spell. We've been playing in a doorway and the park so heedless of time nearly an hour and a half's swirled by, plus onset of sunrise is turning the sky deep blue. Like, there's a firm to be at by 9:30, we don't take unannounced days off.

Tempting to take a nappy once we're at my place, but we've learned not to—would only counter excitation, sap energy, make us groggy. Nappies are effective after work, when a night out beckons, but not before. Far better to whip up a fortifying breakfast—eating healthy, drinking minimally, keeps feisty brats feisty, our energy high. Then we're mirthful-manic in the bathroom—shower's steam fogging the mirrors, a blur of splashing water, make up application, perfume. We arrive at work on time, as always after pre-dawn-on-worknights playtime.

Thank you for the intervention and cure, Dr. Ella! First you liberate me from Romance Novel Hell, now from Post Stevie Distress Syndrome. What heals quickest is allowing an engaging escapade to work wonders: by placing frolic between myself and yesterday's depressing Stevie dinner you've resurrected me. Idleness is the nastiest enemy—idleness leads to thoughts piling up, turning to sludge, choking emotion, killing spontaneity, dragging one towards gloom. But my lynx-cat girlfriend won't allow me to remain severed from life-sustaining spontaneity and daring—thank you again, Sweetie, for defeat of depression.

Wild how our pre-dawn adventure, and its sequel at the firm, has blurred yesterday's dismal dinner, made it seem like an inconsequential something that happened months ago. As for autumn's chill, maybe I welcome it—Stevie belongs to summertime and summer's out the door. Hail autumnal winds knocking dead leaves down, winter's freeze!

You stated: "Wake up, Angie! We're delight-in-contrast wench-es!" Oh, I'm wide awake once more, Honey! I'm Miss Scar-let-Dress-in-a-Sea-of-Beige! Miss Sassiness-as-Others-Wallow-in-Sap-piness! Miss Hyperactive-when-Amidst-Lazy-Slobs! So let's have some savagely wintry weather! I'll sizzle aplenty to naysay it, autumn's chill's a thrill.

And there's the other reason I'm joy-flooded, right Ella? It's be-cause we'll be informing RS (Our so-called creator: ha!) our corre-spondence will be reverting to private. What a pest he's been! It'll be a blessed relief to be rid of him—no more spatting with him to keep our emails as they are, tampering forbidden—no more informing him we'll claw his face if he suggests we fabricate friends, populate our emails with people we don't know, again! OK, so he has assembled us into a novel—I'd be a liar if I said I wasn't pleased (What prankish prima donna pussycat wouldn't be?), but enough of making our per-sonal lives public. However, I do have a few things to say to RS—and know you do too—which will be done in the Afterword. See you there, Dollface!

Your,

LynxCatLovingAngie

XIV.11
Ella to Angie
Thursday, September 25, 2003 11:33 AM

Begging your pardon, Angie, I'm not ready to hightail it to the Af-terword. You're forgetting a sequel was mentioned—you wrote: "our pre-dawn adventure, and its sequel at the firm." So, as the girl who conscientiously righted the wrongful state of self-pity and depression you'd fallen into, directing you towards unhindered life-affirmation's embrace, I insist upon detailing a last escapade, carrying our novel (Yes, our novel: RS isn't even our editor, although I'm sure he'd like to think so.) forward to finale. I'm pleased and honored to be posi-tioned to wind up our summer escapading (simply a matter of how events fell into place) but primarily I insist because I'm an immensely moved—deeply in love—girl who wishes to pay tribute to her Dearest One.

Naturally our outdoors-in-the-wee-hours frolic necessitated follow-up, especially as your Ella had twice finger-flicked you to fountain-burst, licked you wet—giving's delight unto itself but ignites a girl, brings on itchiness, scatteredness, dizziness. Too pressed for time this morning before work to calm me down, we succeeded in bothering me more than sating me. Even our kissy session amidst shower-steam gets cut short—your lipstick's dropped, I accidentally mash it on the tiling—we hardly had time to mop it up. (My footsie's still scarlet.) Yeah, this feline's needs were fiercely fanned and she was roaring to soar at the firm—nonstop pacing in her office, doing yoga-writhings on the floor.

Rhymes were swarming my head, as in: "Your twixt-thighs kit-'n'-kaboodle's itchy? You're fiendish outa senses bitchy? Atwitch to shed every stitch? Insane as if to the wrong man hitched? Surely bewitched? You need finger-fiddles, minx-cat! Are craving tittles, lynx-cat!" It's excess sex-energy that enables the rhyming—wild how there's an association. If I'm rhyming Ella, it's because I'm on the lust-too-long-ignored rack, inwardly flayed. Sometimes being an inflammable feline seems like the torments of the damned; sometimes sex-hunger stings so sharply it's as if venom's streaming through my veins; sometimes I think: "What an insane treadmill I'm on, ceaselessly racing from one orgasm to another to keep from kissing sanity bye-bye!" Sometimes I wish my internal combustion engine would leave me alone.

Totally kidding! I'd never want my internal combustion engine to leave me alone—adore being ceaselessly flung towards rashness, an adventure-rich life, as in the supply room at noon! So spun into swirly blurs was I that... But I'm leaping ahead—will tell it in order:

Lunch hour arrives and I'm at your office door, motioning for you to come out to play so frantically a twinge jolts my wrist. You're perusing a document, understand the state I'm in soon as you raise your eyes. The way you tense taut, leap to your feet, lifts alacrity to new heights.

Funny how we'd never played in that supply room, as it's ideal: can be locked from within, is in an obscure inner corridor hallway, plus confined spaces excite me. (Doorways, right?) Soon as we happen upon it we dream up a plausible reason for us to be there if interrupted (Looking for spray-wash, to disinfect our desks.) and step inside. Once the door's locked you're on your knees, two-handedly holding my hemline to my tits, pressing your shoulders against my thighs, backing me to the wall. Your mouth's tantalizingly near pinkling, avoiding touch—your breath's maddening rhythmic warmth. Swish! Swish! Your breathing's pulsations curly-cue up within my womb, tense me into what I'll term fiery paralysis. All you need do, following a couple agonizing minutes that seem like hours, is lightly graze my tummy with your tongue, and—bang! I sink to the floor gasping, back to the wall.

It's a foreplay-orgasm, tease of a taste, too hair-trigger to be the full deal. It hasn't changed me into a blithe burbling brook, I'm not a limpid stream in the sun! Agitation's multiplied! Am I swiftly on my back, thighs wrapped about your head? Ooooo! Finally, I'm twitching to your tongue feeling me far up inside my shock-box—probing, wriggling, undulating, twisting. Electricity's bursting up and down my spine, I'm picturing asterisk patterns—breathing's so forceful I'm seemingly swooning while almost unbearably wide awake. Am I bouncing my behind up and down on the floor? I recall spasmodically reaching over my head, grasping something solid, shaking: bomp-clatter-clack!

"Damn!" you yelp. Something's fallen.

"You OK in there?" a voice, middle-aged female, asks from outside the door.

"Uh-oh!" echoes in my head, along with the thought: "Of course something had to crash to the floor right when someone happened by!" Aside from that thought, I'm helpless to respond.

"We're fine, ma'am—we dropped something—nothing serious," you call out.

"That's a facilities room," the woman responds. "If you need anything, you ought to let us know. I'll help you find what you need." The door knob jiggles.

"Uh...just a moment...we need to unlock...unfasten the door!" I very stupidly, in a stammery (self-accusatory!) voice, call out—a miscue you're not hesitant to express displeasure with: the cute way your eyes widen in a "Shush! I'll handle this!" glance of reproach.

"Ma'am, you'll have to wait a moment," you state with the self-possession-during-crises aplomb I can't admire enough.

"Okaaaaay," the woman responds. Amazing how much suspicion can be communicated with a drawn-out "OK."

You pull me to my knees, then to my feet. Then there's rapid placing of our dresses in place, smoothing of wrinkles, and you open the door.

Delightful! It's Lottey Staul, head of the Facilities Department, gazing down at us from the height of her blond Amazon physique. "Are you ladies...alright?" she asks, her eyes piercing, predatory. We've aroused her "I'm sure there's something fishy going on here and I'm going to find out what." instinct. Make no mistake: Lottey Staul would dearly love to catch anyone in compromising circumstances, and if two well-put-together girls of the petite (non-Amazon) variety are the culprits, and if they're in high-standing with influential partners, so much the better—be her opportunity to demonstrate few are above her law. Her demeanor states: "Facilities is the backbone of the firm. Without us to perform janitorial duties, orchestrate repairs and deliveries, keep supplies stocked and distributed business would not be possible. Anything that threatens to undermine efficiency of the facilities department is my business."

"We're fine," you answer, unflinchingly holding her gaze. "We..."

"Yes?" she interrupts. What a pounce is in that "yes."

But you're too fast for her, aren't cha Sweetheart? "OK, I'll be honest," you say with well-feigned resignation. "She's having her period and was cramping badly, so we ducked in here. I was worried and the ladies' room's too far. I know this isn't the place for such things, but... *(You pause, put on a flawless you're-forcing-me-to-tell-you face.)* OK, here's the deal: we were afraid she might dribble blood in the hall on the way to the ladies' so we prevented that from happening." Ha! Power-drunk Amazon though she be, Lottey Staul's yanked up by her roots and flung out to dry! She's briefly dumbstruck, gaze wavering.

"I...I think you probably did the right thing," she says after a couple seconds, embarrassment overspreading her face despite herself. "Are you good for the ladies' room now?" she inquires, addressing me.

"I can get there," I reply, not having to trouble to appear worked-up and shattered, as sex-hunger symptoms, post-flood quivers, dovetail nicely into playing at botheredness by menstrual cramps. "I'll (I draw a deep breath, look at the floor, tremble.) go there now...finish tidying."

"Sorry for the alarm," you say, glancing at me with concern, then back at Lottey Staul with a glint of annoyance, as good as saying: "Ma'am, I resent your suspicions. The implication that we were up to no good when my friend's well-being was at stake does not sit well with me."

"I must look out for matters—areas, if you will—that concern my department, you understand," Ms. Amazon says by way of apology, not doubting for one moment the veracity of my emergency.

"We appreciate that, and appreciate your understanding and will-ingness to help," you answer without apparent irony, lending me your arm for support. When we commence walking, I'm strained and slow.

"If you need the first aid kit in HR..." she ventures.

"That won't be necessary," you respond, pausing to glance at her in a manner that states: "This is a delicate matter, ma'am, and we'd like to get through it with minimal fuss." Again, flawless execution—an-other deflation of Lottey Staul's exaggerated sense of importance. The implication is: "You're an insensitive plodding beast, aren't you?"

"I understand," she says with a trace of sheepishness. She knows she's a clumsy plodding beast, regardless of whether she wants to or not (It's why she doesn't like svelte graceful girls.), and she's also bringing to mind her own menstrual discomfort experiences, count on it.

So the "woman problem" excuse, long a standing joke between us, has been put to good use at last. We petite pretty nymphets, with bad experiences of jealous ungainly big girls in grade school play-grounds, have the better of them now. Imposing physiques avail them nothing in the adult world, where emotional dexterity and aptitude for playacting reign supreme. They can puff themselves up, glance at us haughtily, but can't follow through with a shove or punch. We ignore their hostility, deflate them with plausible fiction, leave them twisting in the wind. Yeah, and Lottey Staul may rule the roost with regard to portions of the firm—storage rooms, service elevators, coffee stands—assigned to her precious Facilities Department, but she's not entitled to so much as suspect what we do in our offices. Far from permitted to enter unbidden, she must discreetly knock and await a response and, should we inform her we're busy, she must leave: I'll bet that gnaws at her craw.

After visiting the ladies' to cover the lie we hightail it to my office, where I'm immediately on my back on the carpet. "Here's to Lottey Staul," I laugh, hiking hemline to tits, splaying thighs. "Bless her for intruding on our supply room venture, ineptly attempting to intimidate and dominate us! Extra excitement and *very* gratifying confirmation of our get-away-with-wildest-amounts-of-play-on-firm-premises skills! Soon as you threw menstrual cramps in Lottey Staul's face, her face caved, stare faded, manner became uncertain! Don't need an aphrodisiac but recalling the way you swatted her down's heating me!"

"Bamboozling pompous twats, who're hankering to back us into corners to feed their shoddy envy, adds to escapading immensely," you grin. "Profuse thanks to Lottey 'Loser' Staul, who can't dream of intruding on us here! And just think: flipping situations, getting an arrogant woman to believe the opposite of what's occurring, ties in with being attorneys, dueling with the other side, ensuring they can't slip anything past us."

"Right," I giggle, squirming in anticipation of your touch, "familiarity with boundaries, knowing how far they can safely be pushed, serves us well outside of frolic—we're better able to read strategy, anticipate countermoves. The firm ought to *sponsor* our escapades."

"In a way the firm does, even if unknowingly," you wink, working your soft/hard massage magic—feather-caresses alternating with firm kneading of tenderest areas of my inner thighs.

I'm hugging your head with my thighs when I gush and, ever attuned to my nuances, you're vibrating your head, breathing ticklish heat, grasping and ungrasping my tummy and midriff, hints of teeth lightly scraping. As always, Sparkle Princess, your ministrations extend shimmer-wave's duration, add to multidimensionality and depth—lift me towards the miracle of barely sensing my body's boundaries.

Angie Angel, today's stimulation ride from your bed to the doorway to Carl Schurz to the supply room to my office floor's a favorable omen—bodes well for autumn, and the long haul of winter. Our immediate plunge into pleasure in my office following Lottey Staul's interruption: how could the auspices better smile upon us? Yeah, we'll be tasting of orgasm's ripple-rustle very reliably, whenever we wish and with no one able to rein us in, throughout autumn and winter! Springtime's sap-surge, seemingly eons away, will be upon us again in a flash.

So time to wind up this collection of our missives. As you mentioned, we're giving RS the gate: too long we've wrestled with the knowledge our correspondence will be published, with varying consequences: we've occasionally played to the audience, othertimes restrained ourselves for—ha ha!—modesty's sake. But I'm jumping the gun: such reflections are for the Afterword, where we'll take RS to task for some of the nonsense he's put us through. See you there, Sparkle Angel.

Your,

LovingLynxishLassie

Afterword: Angie & Ella Address the Author

ANGIE: So how's the composition-of-this-novel ride been, RS? Have you been sufficiently entertained? Have Ella and I taught you a thing or two about trust, better enabled you to appreciate the fruits of faith? Have you learned it's advisable to allow your characters to determine what direction they're going to go in, instead of meddling with it?

RS: How have I meddled with your direction? I never wanted you to be anything but your sassy bratty selves. I never toned you down.

ELLA: Granted, you've never sought to whitewash us, mitigate our mischievousness, make us out to be mindless doormats. You've encouraged us to revel in our intelligence and independence, use it to add meaning and quality to our lives. But what of your unnecessary plot concerns? What of your suggestions we dream up circumstances that have nothing to do with us, for the purpose of providing readers with a steadily unfolding ongoing situation to follow? What of your attempts to get us to dream up fictional people to interact with—enemies, foils, allies? I recall one instance specifically: you said, regarding the Circumstances of Spying chapter, that it would be more "gripping" if we inserted a nemesis character—someone determined to hound Angie, see to it she was severely punished, demoted and humiliated. Rather pointless, RS, considering no such person existed.

ANGIE: Yeah, RS! What of when you said we ought to invent a pestering male, a stalker? You said if there was a tangible threat running through our emails it would spice things up; that readers would have an ongoing storyline to follow; that a constantly looming external reference point would help hold our emails together. You trotted out academic trash—as distasteful to us as foreign to our purpose—pertaining to the introduction of conflict, creation of oppositional tension. Aside from annoying us, you were implying our lives aren't exciting enough. You were telling us to falsify our emails, lie. Why insult us, RS?

RS: No insult was intended. I simply meant...

ELLA (*interrupting*): Hang on and pay attention, RS! You were suggesting we waste time writing of things that have no bearing upon our doings. Then, to further try our patience, you reverse direction and start raising concerns about the plausibility of some of our escapades. You do this after advising us to invent fake happenings, pretend to be entangled with fictional people. Needless and unproductive meddling, RS! Angie and I are who we are: readers can take us or leave us, believe us or doubt us, comprehend us or misconstrue us. One thing will always hold true: Angie and I can proudly declare we haven't falsified a single sentence of our emails, written of anything we haven't done.

ANGIE: Right! First, RS, you proposed implausible plots and then you about-faced, had the temerity to question the plausibility of our actual activities. How many bright hardworking attorneys have a stalker in their lives? Do perceptive escapading girls blunder into relationships with possessive pests, project vulnerability that attracts grasping losers? Nay! The perspective escapading bestows upon us—vantage point that's its priceless gift—is the most accurate radar a girl could have, warning us away from predatory involvements. A plausible plot? Listen: how many flesh and blood people have steadily unfolding events in their lives that are interesting to others? Next to none. Even people with jobs that reliably involve them in memorable adventures—police officers, firemen, cab drivers—rarely have a gripping ongoing situation unfolding in their lives; they experience isolated events that bear no relation to one another. The plots of many novels are blatantly unrealistic, the alterations of personality their characters undergo laughably beggaring belief. Ella and I (regrettably lacking a stalker or any other constant conflict-instilling situation in our lives—ha!) are real girls and have presented ourselves as such. As Ella stated, we haven't falsified one sentence and are very happy about that. So to hell with anyone who feels we should've been threatened by hostile forces—stalked, kidnapped, roofied, abused, swindled, forced to search for ancestral secrets, blackmailed into spying for enemy governments. We're two girls who adore our town and know how to achieve fulfillment via frolic. We've been faithful to our worldview and can hold our heads high.

RS: Fine, I raised concerns. Influenced by misguided notions as to what a faithful portrait of two bright escapading girls might consist of, I voiced the possibility of introducing a hostile presence into your lives. But was it anything other than me thinking aloud? Did I seriously set about changing your approach? Nay! You countered and I paid attention, agreed you should do it your way. Will you browbeat me forever for raising such concerns when I readily conceded you were correct?

ELLA: True, we brought you around to our way of thinking, but why did we need to trouble to do so in the first place? A waste of time.

ANGIE: Plus we girls need to occasionally needle the men in our lives—dramatize dismay at their shortcomings, exaggerate their mistakes, so's to better keep them in line, or initiate dialogue.

RS: You think we men don't do likewise? Think we don't know timely pricking of a girl's vanity often gets her to behave better? Maybe I suggested you introduce fictional items into your emails for the purpose of getting you to rebel, more willfully be yourselves? Maybe my intention was to inspire you to oppose me, relate your escapades with greater gusto? Has that occurred to you? There's nothing like a spirited girl for getting riled at intrusions on her way of doing things, rushing to the defense of her independence with plenty of entertaining moxie. A proud girl's disposition can be put to good use. If one wants gossip or rumors spread one tells them to a feisty girl and swears her to secrecy; the swearing of her to secrecy, implication of distrust, offends her self-respect such that she immediately dissimulates the info as if her life depends upon it and, in a flash, entire crowds know.

ELLA: My, how clever! Bravo! As if men aren't equally as gossipy as any girl, if not more so, and don't need to be prodded to spread stuff on one's behalf—simply telling it to them suffices just fine.

ANGIE: Can we please dispense with the nonsensical notion one of the sexes has an innate advantage over the other? One's sex has zilch to do with having an advantage: courage and intelligence have the advantage.

RS: Need I point out you started the sex-war stuff with your uncalled for crack about needling men?

ANGIE: So flog me! Who cares?

RS: Typical female: acts impatient, gets miffed, when she's the one who carried matters into a pointless pissing-contest direction, and is called out on it—no acceptance of responsibility. No apology ever.

ANGIE (*crossing her arms across her chest, eyes flashing with warning*): Do you really want to start something, RS?

RS: I apologize. The comment was uncalled for.

ANGIE: It certainly was! (*She lightly kicks RS.*)

ELLA (*playfully swatting the shoulders of each*): That'll be enough, you two! Always baiting each other—always spatting! You behave like grade school children when we're together and make me feel like a mommy and I'm the youngest! Stop making me feel like a mommy!

RS (*brushing Ella's hair with his hands, petting her like a cat*): Aw, you know you like it. Youngsters always want to feel they're adults, it tickles you to death that you're the best-behaved when the three of us get together. As for you, Angie, you owe me an apology for that kick.

ANGIE: Why would I apologize when you deserved it?

RS: You've lost me there: I admitted I was wrong to make the crack I did and apologized. So why kick me? Makes no sense.

ANGIE: Maybe you got kicked because of something else. Time to search your brain and see if you can tell me what that is.

RS: I haven't the foggiest.

ANGIE: Sadly, I'm not surprised! Last week you said something extremely insensitive and were oblivious of my feelings.

RS: Count on a female to hold a man to every teensy thing he says, dredge it up later to justify her own bad behavior. I say "teensy" because if my words were truly awful you would've rightfully told me so on the spot. But I give up: what did I say that's your excuse for kicking me?

ANGIE: Why did you inform Ella and I that you created us when the opposite's the case? Unbelievably preposterous and pompous, RS!

RS: You're characters in a novel I dreamed up, but you think you created me? Hahaha! Sorry, but you're preposterously deluded!

ANGIE: Laugh, will you? (*She makes as if to kick him again.*)

RS (*stepping back, regarding Angie incredulously*): How can you possibly believe the two of you created me?

ANGIE: Because we *have* created you, made you who you are at this point in time, revamped your personality for the better. We've been scamping about in your head, adding spice to your life, for nearly a year! Regardless of what you were doing or where you were or who you were with we were suggesting new episodes and means of presenting them. Think it's for nothing your girlfriend was jealous of us? She had every right, since we had claim to the greater part of your attention. You couldn't climb into bed without mulling over further escapade possibilities. Nor could you escape us in your sleep, where you'd write emails with us in your dreams, and it was priceless fun to awaken you, compel you to jot notes. We also vastly improved your vocabulary.

RS: Whoa! Sorry to burst your bubble, Angie, but Ella and yourself are inventions—I dreamed you up to serve *my* needs. You're a means of projecting myself into experiences I wouldn't otherwise have, cloaking myself in other personalities, amusing myself by playing parts; means of routinely staying up over a day and a half straight living in a dreamworld while thrillingly awake. You're a means of accelerating experience, extending my emotional boundaries, becoming a world-unto-myself. I'd rather spend my time electrifyingly awake in your company, composing your emails with you, than doing anything else under the sun.

ANGIE: What's this nonsense about emotional boundary expansion, living in waking dreams, calling the shots like God? I'll tell you what it is! It's your male-ego-burdened personality lying to itself—concealing the fact Ella and I took possession of you and you had no choice but to knuckle under. If we clamored for an episode to be written, you had to write it or would know no peace. Sorry to burst *your* bubble, RS, but you're a male brought to heel—a pet on a leash. Two girls, Angie and Ella by name, have been dictating the terms of your life for nearly a year and naturally you're embarrassed: you attach acceleration-of-experience mythology to our domination of you to avoid admitting you're our doormat! Deny all you wish but we tromp all over you at will!

ELLA (*with mirthful eyes*): Remember how he'd be looking forward to a hot date, and we'd say: "Not so fast, buster! You're staying home to finish the *Ella's Goblin* chapter; and, if you fail to stay home to finish the *Ella's Goblin* chapter, we'll raise such a ruckus in your nerves—turn your physiology so topsy-turvy—you won't be able to think clearly or sleep. You'll be sitting around blankly staring, tension rising. So kissy that date bye-bye and attend to *our* needs! Finish the *Ella's Goblin* chapter now!" And he'd kissy that date bye-bye! Wasn't that fun?

ANGIE: RS thinks he created us to serve his needs? Pah! We're airy inhabitants of the spiritual realms and needed a body to inhabit so's to get our emails transcribed: we made use of RS's corporeality to step into the light of day. We chose RS because he's healthy and able to put in long hours on our behalf. We used him but our use of him considerably enriched his life. So how's about some gratitude, RS? How's about admitting we're the best thing that could've happened to you?

RS: As if I haven't already made it crystal clear you've been an unforgettable rollercoaster ride for me and I'm eternally in your debt. How many times do I need to spell out how grateful I am?

ELLA: He's right, Angie.

ANGIE (*playfully swatting Ella's behind*): Traitor! How dare you take his side when he's... (*She dissolves into laughter.*)

RS: Why spat about who created who? Maybe I dreamed you up to serve my needs, maybe you invaded my dreams to compel me to serve yours. Who cares, when we three have been handsomely rewarded every step of the way? I'm deeply grateful and will miss you immensely.

ANGIE: You're not turning sappy on us, are you?

RS: Alas, I fear I'll become chronically depressed, indifferent to things that formerly pleased me, unable to muster enthusiasm concerning much of anything: the usual abrupt-end-of-a-dynamic-relationship fallout.

ELLA: Yeah, like there's a chance we'll believe *that*, RS! With your facility for attracting characters who wish to make use of you for transcription purposes, we know you have other irons in the fire. We don't know what they are, though. Would you mind telling?

ANGIE: In other words, RS, we're willing to set the stage for you to indulge in some self-promotion, alert our readers to coming attractions. But be quick, before we change our minds.

RS: Many thanks! Another novel, *Self-Murder*, is finished. I wrote most of it before making your acquaintance and it's opposite in tone from *Tease and Dare*. It's a dark tale, in which obsession...

ELLA (*interrupting*): Hey! Why not read an excerpt, instead of indulging in lame and insufficient summarization crap.

ANGIE: Ever heard of, "Don't tell, *show!*"?

RS: As it happens, there's a copy here. Let's see...

ELLA: The first paragraph or two will do, RS!

RS: Excellent suggestion. (*He reads.*)

"Dearest reader, I'm not facing this blank page willingly; not addressing you willingly; not commencing this recollection willingly. I'd vastly prefer to have succeeded in returning to the relatively balanced life I was blessed with previous to when the experience I intend to recount shattered that life; vastly prefer to have succeeded in reassembling the pieces of that life, assimilating the experience that unsettles me; vastly prefer to pass my days in obscurity, be dead silent.

"Although the events I'll be describing transpired over three years ago, the unanswered questions connected with those events continue to distract and disquiet me, swathe my thoughts and dreams in oppressive shadows, transform efforts to sleep into cold-sweat-anointed ordeals. *Time heals all wounds*, is a cruel, false-hope-propagating, lie. Time has not healed this wound, only further opened and infected it; time has not induced merciful forgetfulness, only prodded and stung me with unceasing speculations as to what actually occurred during those tumultuous months; time has not restored me to a manageable frame of mind, only brought about a degree of mental distress which is tougher to force into the background—lose in any amount of mindless diversion or conscientious effort to resurrect a professional life—than the searing pain of a knife's cut. I need to wrestle with the memory which haunts and flays me, transfer an unnerving experience onto these pages, because I feel it's my only chance of purging myself of my past."

RS *(after finishing reading)*: As you can see, it's opposite in tone from *Tease & Dare*. I like that I'm following a frolicsome novel with a dark one, even if I'm not wholly sure why, possibly it's due to fondness for contrast or aversion to predictability or...

ELLA *(interrupting)*: Do yourself a favor, RS, and let the sample speak for itself. It's not necessary to point out your next offering's dark in tone. Suffice to say my appetite's whetted.

ANGIE: As is mine. Appreciate the sample, RS.

RS: Appreciate you giving me the opportunity to read it. Again, I'm strangely pleased that your escapades will be contrasted with...

ANGIE *(interrupting)*: Have we not made it clear, RS, we can do without blather concerning darkness contrasted with light? The sample spells such out just fine! In fact, enough of you for now—out!

ELLA: Yeah, out! *(Ella and Angie shove RS from the room.)*

ANGIE: Good, now we can attend to what's of greatest importance, without distraction: well-wishing our readers.

ELLA: Absolutely, Dollface.

ANGIE *(with a curtsy followed by playful ruffling of her dress, flashing of thigh)*: Dearest readers, thank you for allowing us to entertain you—we couldn't be more honored, tickled pink. Ella and I are off to Central Park for a celebratory picnic among Cedar Hill's evergreens and invite you to join us. We'll be there 'til dawn, chasing delirium on the lawn, rolling in the shadows. Can't make it? Then throw your own frolic-picnics! We owe it to ourselves to fearlessly romp, shake our bodies with joy and mirth, invite euphoria to dizzy us—giddy elevation's waiting to rejuvenate us! May your lives be otherworldly—may you taste Elysium every day!

ELLA *(with a curtsy followed by two rapid twirls, two-handed fluffing of her hair)*: Kind readers, so many thrills and secrets we've shared it's nearly traumatic you'll no longer be in our lives. As Angie said, we're off to Central Park for 'til sunrise playtime and you're invited—please come and spare us the distress of farewell. Alas, most of you are in other towns. OK, then: do Dionysus proud, appreciate your loved ones every day as if it's your last day on earth—drink of rapture with a serene heart and clear conscience, laugh killjoys out of your lives. Be delirious with elation always! May fortune fall over itself in eagerness to favor you!

ANGIE & ELLA (*after bowing together, while blowing kisses*): We love you millions!

About the author

Robert Scott Leyse was born in San Francisco, grew up in various locales about America, lived in Paris for a spell, and presently resides in Manhattan, Sun Valley, Idaho, and Puerto Rico. Upon arrival in Manhattan he lived in East Village dumps and worked as a New York cab driver on the night shift, with the aim of atoning for a sheltered upbringing and having adventures the likes of which he'd never had before and expectation was vastly surpassed. Subsequently he worked in the legal field, where he was pleasantly surprised to find adventures of the office shenanigans variety were to be had and sought them out at every turn. Thereafter he switched to the more tech-friendly advertising industry, where he favored working remotely (well before COVID), and amazed himself by getting away with an insane amount of escapades on company time. He eats insects and drinks blood, but can't be paid to eat potato chips or cake.

www.ingramcontent.com/pod-product-compliance
Lightning Source LLC
Chambersburg PA
CBHW050133120726
47903CB00002B/336